THE BAD MOTHER

Amanda Brooke is a single mum who lives in Liverpool with her daughter, Jessica, a cat called Spider, a dog called Mouse, and a laptop within easy reach. Her debut novel, *Yesterday's Sun*, was a Richard and Judy Book Club pick. *The Bad Mother* is her eighth novel.

www.amanda-brooke.com
@AmandaBrookeAB
www.facebook.com/AmandaBrookeAuthor

Also by Amanda Brooke

Yesterday's Sun
Another Way to Fall
Where I Found You
The Missing Husband
The Child's Secret
The Goodbye Gift
The Affair
The Bad Mother

Ebook-only short stories
The Keeper of Secrets
If I Should Go

AMANDA BROOKE

The Bad Mother

HarperCollins*Publishers*

This novel is entirely a work of fiction.
The names, characters and incidents portrayed in it are the work of the author's imagination. Any resemblance to actual persons, living or dead, events or localities is entirely coincidental.

HarperCollins*Publishers*
1 London Bridge Street
London SE1 9FG

www.harpercollins.co.uk

A Paperback Original 2018
1

A catalogue record for this book is available from the British Library

ISBN: 978-0-00-821915-4

Set in Sabon LT Std by Palimpsest Book Production Ltd, Falkirk, Stirlingshire

Printed and bound in Great Britain by CPI Group (UK) Ltd,
Croydon CR0 4YY

This book is produced from independently certified FSC™ paper to ensure responsible forest management.

For more information visit: www.harpercollins.co.uk/green

For Jessica and Nathan

Prologue

Coils of copper hair fly across her face, and when she pulls them from her damp cheeks, it feels like ice-cold fingers stroking her skin. She takes a step into the darkness and her foot snags on a tree root threaded through the craggy ledge – or is it another skeletal hand impatient for her fall?

Far below, the night is punctured by a thousand lights that splutter and die where land touches the sea. She's too far away to detect the salty air washing in from Liverpool Bay, or the urban mix of exhaust fumes and takeaways that remind her of home, but that's where her thoughts lead her. She follows the dark path of the Mersey and her gaze settles on the sprawling city. She doesn't dare imagine the pain she is about to inflict on her family.

You can do this, she tells herself.

You have to do this, comes a stronger voice from within. It's a voice she had all but forgotten since carving her name next to Adam's on this desolate sandstone ledge. Life had been so full of promise back then. There were a few frayed edges perhaps, but nothing that couldn't be mended with the love of a good and patient man, or so she had thought.

She had realized too late that she had been unravelling and now she was completely undone.

Buffeted by another gust of wind, her summer dress billows out like a parachute and if she dared lean over the precipice, she might see the heavy boughs reaching up, promising to catch her when she falls. They won't have long to wait.

In the light of a torch, her wedding ring shimmers and unwelcome doubts assail her. If there was another way, she would find it, but even as she tries, her mind spins. The queasy sensation is a familiar one and she knows if she's not careful, she will lose sight of the path she must take.

'Lucy.'

Adam's voice rises above the howling wind as if he has the power to still the night. She knows he will blame himself for this, but there will be enough people to support him after the loss of his beloved wife. She blocks out his voice as she prepares to make the leap, but there's another voice that cannot be ignored. What mother could fail to respond to the sound of her baby's cries?

She feels the softness of her daughter's skin on her lips.

'Hush,' she whispers. 'Mummy's here.'

1

Six Months Earlier

'This is a bad idea,' Christine said as she stood by the garage door watching her daughter battle her way through what amounted to three decades of detritus. 'Please, come out of there.'

'I'm fine,' Lucy said, stepping over the last fingers of light on the concrete floor to immerse herself in the shadows.

Her hip brushed against a sun lounger that hadn't seen a summer since the noughties when she and her school friends had lazed about in the garden while her mum was at work. They had knocked back blackcurrant alcopops as if they were Ribena, hence the dark vomit stain in the middle of the sagging canvas and the reason it hadn't been used since.

'It's probably not even in there, love.'

'Judging by how much other junk you've kept hold of, I don't see why not,' Lucy countered. 'And I'm sure I remember it being at the back somewhere.'

'Will you tell her?' Christine said, turning to the man standing next to her.

Adam stood with his arms folded and his tall, lean frame silhouetted against the cold light of a crisp winter's morning. When he spoke, the warmth of his words appeared as vaporous swirls above the halo of his dirty blond hair. 'Your mum has a point. I should be the one in there.'

'Firstly,' Lucy said, 'I know what I'm looking for, and secondly, you're terrified of spiders.' She had stopped forcing her way through the junk to face her husband. Sweeping back a coil of copper hair, her emerald-green eyes flashed in defiance and she told herself she would stand her ground even if Adam insisted. To her relief, he didn't.

'I tried,' he said to Christine with a shrug.

Wrapping her Afghan shawl tightly around her shoulders, Christine muttered something under her breath that was unrepeatable. She appeared tiny next to Adam's six-foot frame, but Lucy's mum was stronger than she looked. She had brought up her daughter single-handedly since Lucy was eight years old and although the last twenty years hadn't been easy, what should have broken them had made them stronger and they made a good partnership. They were best friends when they wanted to be, and mother and daughter when it was needed. At that precise moment, Christine's maternal instincts had kicked in and she wanted to protect her only child.

'I'll be careful,' Lucy called out.

Taking another step into the past, she sized up the gap between an old bedstead and a dressing table. Where once she might have slipped her slender figure through with ease, now she paused to stroke a hand over the slight but firm rise of her belly; her mum wasn't alone in having a child to protect. Raising herself on to tiptoes, Lucy stretched her long legs so that her bump skimmed the surface of the dresser as she passed.

'Don't go wedging yourself in or we'll never get you out,' Christine called, before adding, 'Tell her, Adam.'

'Don't forget you're fat,' he said, laughing all the more when Lucy scowled.

Christine swiped at her son-in-law. 'You can't call a pregnant woman fat, not ever,' she said, her smile softening the hard stare she was giving him over the rim of her spectacles.

Her mum's glasses were her only nod to older age. Her spikey dark locks showed no sign of the grey her hairdresser artfully disguised, and her skin glowed from a strict beauty regime. Lucy hoped she would look as good in her fifties, but she had inherited her pale complexion and ginger genes from her dad, so there was no knowing how she would age.

Wiping the dust from her white shirt, Lucy attempted to work out her next move while fearing it was time to admit defeat. Even if she did manage to find what she was looking for, there was no way she would be able to reclaim it without emptying the entire garage. Her mum and dad had moved into their semi-detached house in Liverpool when they had married some thirty years ago, and that was probably the last time anyone had seen the back wall.

Wilfully ignoring her doubts and doubters, Lucy continued on her quest. As she squeezed past a pink metallic bicycle with torn and tattered tassels hanging from its handlebars, it began to move and she put out her hand to stop it from rolling. From the shadows, the orange reflector on the rear wheel shone out like a beacon, drawing her back in time.

She could see her dad kneeling in front of the upturned bike repairing a puncture. He had turned the pedal with his hand so fast that the wheel had become a blur and the reflector transformed into a glowing orange circle. Lucy recalled how her stomach had lurched when the spokes had turned so fast that it looked as if the wheel had magically changed direction. The memory alone made her queasy and threatened to resurrect the morning sickness she hadn't quite left behind in her first trimester.

'Can you see anything?' Adam called.

Lucy had gone as far back as she could reach without taking unnecessary risks. 'Not yet,' she said as she peered into the gloom, searching for the faintest suggestion of white painted spindles. It was there somewhere and she wouldn't leave until she had settled her mind.

'Seriously, Lucy,' Adam said. 'Your mum's right. It probably isn't there and if you go any deeper, you don't know what's going to fall on top of you. Come out. You're scaring us.'

'I'll be careful,' she said, not daring to look back. 'Please, give me one more minute.'

As Lucy swiped at ancient cobwebs covered in dust, a particularly heavy clump clung to her fingers. Shaking it free, she glimpsed the carcass of a giant spider caught by its own web and let out a yelp.

'Fetch her out, Adam,' Christine ordered, panic rising in her voice.

There was the creak of furniture being moved and when Lucy turned, she found Adam standing on the other side of the dresser. He had buttoned up his checked shirt to protect his T-shirt and could probably squeeze through the gap at a push but the sight of the dead spider dangling from Lucy's index finger stopped him in his tracks.

'Not funny,' he said.

At thirty-six, Adam was eight years older, but in that moment, he could so easily have been a sulky younger brother. She could still win this argument.

'Don't come any nearer,' she warned.

'I know why you're doing this,' he said, without returning the smile she offered. 'If you say it's there, I believe you. And truthfully, do we really want a battered old cot that would probably fail every modern-day health and safety test?'

'It's not any old cot, it's my cot and I'm twenty-eight not fifty-eight. They had health and safety in the nineties too.'

Shaking the dead spider free, Lucy took one last look at the remaining junk. There were boxes piled on top of each other in a leaning tower of decayed cardboard. If Adam were to challenge her, she could describe the contents of each one. They contained her dad's life, from the manila files kept from the advertising business he ran with his brother, to his sketchpads, his worn-out slippers, and his second-best suit. His best suit had been burnt along with his remains and the picture an eight-year-old Lucy had drawn of him teaching the angels to paint as he had once taught her.

'It doesn't matter,' Adam said. 'None of this matters.'

Lucy pulled her gaze from the boxes and was about to retrace her steps when something caught her eye. 'There it is, look!'

The cot had been dismantled and she could see only the two side sections. The wooden spindles were spaced a couple of inches apart and, as Adam had predicted, the wood was splintered and the paint chipped. It wasn't much of a family heirloom and although her dad had been a gifted artist, the rabbits and squirrels she recalled on the headboard were factory transfers. Her mum was pretty sure they had bought it from Argos.

When Lucy turned, Adam had his lips pursed tightly. She knew what he was thinking and although she wanted to feel vindicated, what she actually felt was foolish. 'OK, you're right. I don't want our baby in some out-of-date deathtrap, and I certainly don't want to get buried beneath an avalanche of boxes.'

When Adam continued to offer his silent judgement, it was her mum who broke the tension. 'I don't know about you two, but I'm freezing out here. Are you leaving it there, or what?'

Lucy reached out for Adam to take her hand but to her horror, he leant backwards. 'Sorry,' she gasped, but then followed his gaze and realized how stupid she had been to think, even for a moment, that he was rejecting her. She wiped her hand on her shirt to leave a trail of sticky cobwebs before waggling her fingers. 'Look, no spiders.'

Adam held her hand as they slipped past the trinkets from her childhood, travelling through her teenage years and towards the most recent additions. There were the stacks of polythene-wrapped canvases she had accumulated at art college, not to mention the camping equipment that had survived several music festivals. A thick layer of dried mud covered the tent she had brought home from Leeds and, with hindsight, it would have been simpler to abandon it, but eighteen months ago she had been unaware that her free and single festival-going days were about to come to an end.

'Well, that was a waste of time,' Christine said after returning to the house.

They were huddled in the small galley kitchen that felt cosy rather than cramped, or at least it did to Lucy. Adam had his shoulders hunched, unable to relax in the space that had been exclusive to Lucy and her mum until he had stolen her away.

'Not a complete waste,' he said, giving Lucy a wry smile that was warm enough to chase away the chill that had crept into her bones during her ill-conceived search.

With cheekbones a little too sharp and a chin not sharp enough, Adam wasn't classically handsome, but it had been his pale blue eyes that had captivated Lucy when she had first spied him over the smouldering embers of a barbecue two summers ago. He had looked at her as if he could read her thoughts and then, as now, whatever he saw amused him.

'Go on, say it,' he told her.

Lucy pouted. 'I *knew* it was there.'

'And I believed you,' replied Adam.

'I could have sworn I'd given it away,' Christine muttered as she opened the oven door. A cloud of steam rose up to greet her and the smell of rosemary and roasted lamb filled the kitchen. 'But what was so important about finding it anyway? You obviously didn't want it.'

'She was trying to prove a point.'

'Ah, that's our Lucy for you,' Christine said, wiping the steam from her glasses as she crouched down to baste the roast potatoes. 'I thought you would have worked that out by now, Adam. She likes to be right.'

'Except when I'm wrong,' Lucy said, dropping her gaze.

'But you weren't wrong,' Christine said. The light from the oven underlined the confusion on her face as she turned to her daughter. 'Is there something I'm missing?'

'I've had a few . . . lapses lately, that's all.'

Her mum closed the oven door and straightened up. 'What do you mean, lapses?'

Lucy wasn't sure how to describe them. They were silly mistakes that might pass unremarked if it were anyone else, but not Lucy. Her brain stored information like a computer and when information went in, it was locked away until it was needed, and she could retrieve it in an instant. She had known precisely where the cot was and she had been proven right. 'They're memory lapses, I suppose. I get confused for no reason at all,' she offered.

Adam cleared his throat. 'We were late this morning because she couldn't find her car keys and her car was parked in front of mine so I was blocked in. I found the spare set, but you know what she's like . . .'

'I *always* leave them on the shelf in the kitchen, or sometimes in my coat pocket, but they weren't in any of the obvious places,' Lucy explained. She scrunched up her freckled nose when she added, 'They were in the fridge beneath a bag of lettuce. I must have kept hold of them when I unloaded the shopping yesterday.'

A bemused smile had formed on Christine's lips. 'Welcome to my world,' she said. 'I almost put a loaf in the washing machine the other week.'

In no mood to be appeased, Lucy felt the first stirrings

of annoyance, not liking that her mum should take the matter so lightly. 'And do you find things in the wrong place when you have no recollection of moving them?'

Christine took a step nearer until she was close enough to lift Lucy's chin. 'No, but I live on my own.'

'And I work from home, *alone*. I'm talking about when Adam's at work.'

'Have you mentioned it to the midwife?' Christine asked, looking to Adam.

'I wanted to raise it at our hospital appointment last week,' he said, shifting from one foot to the other. 'But I was overruled.'

Confusion clouded Lucy's expression and she was grateful that no one was looking at her. She would like to think that she had laid down the law, but Adam was mistaken if he imagined she had been the one to decide against voicing her concerns. It was true that she had been reluctant, but it was Adam who had convinced her that her blunders would be laughed off. So far, he alone knew how unsettling the episodes had become.

'You still should have mentioned it, Adam,' Christine said, her smile persisting.

'I'm glad I didn't now,' Lucy grumbled. 'It was my twenty-week scan and we got to see all her little fingers and toes and I didn't want to spoil the moment. This memory thing is separate anyway.'

'Oh, honey, I'm sorry – it's anything but. They even have a name for it,' Christine said as she cupped her daughter's face in the palm of her hand as if she were still her little girl. Her thumb brushed against Lucy's cheek to encourage a smile that wouldn't come. 'It was called baby brain in my day. Though I can't say I mislaid things, I definitely became a tad scattier. It's your hormones, that's all, and I'm afraid it's only going to get worse. Just wait until you add childbirth and sleepless nights to the mix.'

Lucy's lip trembled. 'Baby brain? Really?'

'Why didn't you mention it before?'

'I was scared it was something else,' Lucy said, holding her mum's gaze long enough for her to realize at last how frightened she had been. Tears brimmed in her mum's eyes as she too caught a glimpse of the lingering shadows of the past that had been haunting her daughter.

With a sniff, Christine kissed her daughter's forehead. 'You've had such a lot of change in the last year or so, it's no wonder your mind's playing catch-up. You shouldn't keep your worries to yourself.'

'I don't,' said Lucy as she pulled away from her mum to look at Adam, who had been waiting patiently to be noticed. Her husband had a habit of tapping his fingers in turn against his thumb whenever he felt out of his comfort zone, and he was doing it now. It was a reminder that beneath that blunt exterior was a man who had his own moments of vulnerability.

Christine wrinkled her nose. 'I know you have each other but, no offence to Adam, he's a man.'

'None taken,' Adam said. The finger tapping continued.

With her gaze fixed on her daughter, Christine said, 'I was telling Hannah's mum the other day how you two girls should make more time for each other now that you're pregnant. She's been through it enough times and it would be a shame to let your friendship drift.'

'I saw her not that long ago,' Lucy said as she attempted

to gauge exactly how long it had been. It was after she had moved in with Adam but before they had scurried off to Greece to get married last summer. 'It wasn't long after she had the baby.'

'He'll be turning one soon,' Christine said. 'I know you both have busy lives, but it would do you good to have someone else to talk to. Don't you think so, Adam?'

Before Adam could answer, Lucy said, 'I do love Hannah, but don't you think she's a bit chaotic?' An image of screaming kids and barking dogs came to mind when she added, 'The boys were all over Adam last time we were there and he ended up spilling coffee all down his shirt.'

'Lucy was convinced it was deliberate,' Adam offered.

'And you weren't?' asked Lucy, astonished that Adam should be smiling as if the memory had been a pleasant one. He had tried not to show his annoyance at the time but the atmosphere had turned thick, and Hannah hadn't helped by making a joke of it, clearly used to such disasters. 'You couldn't wait to get out of there, and it was a wonder you didn't get a speeding ticket on the way home.'

'I don't see how I could when it was you driving.'

'No, it was def—' she said, stopping herself when she saw the frown forming on Adam's brow. She could have sworn he had taken the keys from her, but it was so long ago now, maybe she was thinking of a different time. 'Was it me?'

Adam winced as he looked to Christine. 'Can you have baby brain *before* you're pregnant?'

'That's why I think she should talk to Hannah, and New Brighton isn't that far from you,' Christine persisted. 'Apparently she's another one who thinks you need a visa to get back across the Mersey when you move to the Wirral.'

Lucy didn't need reminding that she hadn't seen nearly enough of her family and friends of late, but she had been busy building a new life with Adam. He had to come first and, while she would willingly make the extra effort for her mum, she wasn't sure if keeping in touch with Hannah was the right thing to do. Feeling slightly wrong-footed, she turned to Adam. 'I don't know, what do you think? I could always try to meet up with her without the kids around, and you wouldn't have to come.'

'It's entirely up to you. If you're sure it will help, of course you should.'

'I'll think about it,' she said after some hesitation, to which Adam wrapped an arm around her and she relaxed into his shoulder. She heard him blow on her unruly locks, but if he had spotted a trailing cobweb he didn't complain.

'At the very least, speak to the midwife,' Christine said. 'I don't mind taking the day off and tagging along with you for your next appointment.'

'You don't have to do that,' Lucy said, knowing that her mum had used up most of her leave on the wedding and a couple of other holidays abroad. 'And I promise, I will mention it.'

'Make sure you do,' Christine said. 'Honestly, Lucy, it's nothing to worry about, it's just a temporary blip.'

'That'll last the next eighteen years,' joked Adam. In response to the look his mother-in-law shot him, he added, 'Am I bad if I like the new Lucy Martin – version 2.1. with all its idiosyncrasies? It keeps me on my toes.'

'So my daughter's one of your computer programs now, is she?' Christine asked. Her voice was soft but firm when she turned to her daughter and added, 'It won't be forever, love.'

Lucy was more inclined to agree with Adam's prognosis, but she held her tongue and smiled, willing her mum to do the same. Adam didn't always say the right thing, but there was no doubting his love and, more recently, his perseverance.

'Why don't you two go and relax while I crack on with lunch?' Christine suggested. She had returned to the cooker to poke a fork into a bubbling pot of broccoli. 'It won't be long and afterwards you can show me the scan photos again. I think I'd like another look at *her* fingers and toes.'

Lucy heard a noise escape Adam's throat that was a half laugh. 'Is that what I said?' she asked, already knowing that she had. Her shoulders sagged. 'You won't tell anyone, will you? We were hoping to keep it to ourselves for a while longer.'

'In that case, I think I might be about to have a memory lapse of my own,' her mum said, her expression fixed with an innocent smile. Lucy wasn't convinced and justifiably so because as she turned to leave, Christine squeaked, 'A granddaughter!'

2

Lucy listened to the wind howling through the eaves and was extremely grateful that she had avoided an uncomfortable commute to work through torrential rain, unlike poor Adam. Converting the loft into an art studio had been her husband's idea and had been undertaken shortly after Lucy had moved into the house in West Kirby a year ago. She could have continued to rent studio space in Liverpool but Adam knew how she hated driving through the Kingsway tunnel and it was a journey she was happy to surrender. She liked that she could set to work whenever inspiration struck, although her artistic flare seemed to be misfiring of late.

Wrapping her hands around a mug of peppermint tea that was too hot to drink, Lucy inhaled the scented steam to ease her mind. It was late morning and she had yet to pick up a paintbrush, while Adam had probably fixed whatever system bug had caused him to rise at five thirty.

He had left for work hours before Lucy had crawled out of bed, and she had lounged in her PJs, eating porridge and watching morning TV for far longer than she intended.

When she had dressed, she had forgone her usual uniform of paint-splattered crop pants and T-shirt for an oversized shirt to make room for the swell of her belly that grew by the day.

Setting down her drink on the workbench, Lucy tied back her hair with an old bandana and lifted the dust sheet covering her current work in progress. Her easel had been set up close to the Juliet balcony window to catch the natural light, but the storm had stolen the day and she wasted the next few minutes repositioning her work beneath one of the spotlights.

Taking a step back, she took time to consider her latest commission. It was a portrait of a dog called Ralph, or at least that was the plan. Since leaving college, Lucy had made a decent living painting portraits and most of her work came from either personal recommendation or online requests. She painted people as well as pets, but preferred animal fur to flesh because it suited her style. The last time she had painted a cocker spaniel, it had been one of her best ever portraits and she had been excited by the prospect of doing another.

What Lucy hadn't realized from the initial enquiry was that Ralph was completely black except for the flash of white on his chest. The first photo her client had sent was impossible to work from, and even though Lucy now had a series of images pinned to the top of her easel, there was a chance that the end product would be no more than a silhouette set off by the spaniel's sparkling – and admittedly adorable – eyes. The only aspect of the composition she was confident about tackling was the background. Her trademark was the inclusion of symbolic references, which in Ralph's case was the window where he awaited his master's return. There would also be a slipper caught beneath his paw with the toe torn to shreds.

Having sketched an outline and blocked out the basic contours of the dog's head and body the day before, Lucy's task for today was to add some much-needed texture. She picked up her palette and began adding her oil colours. She squeezed out a generous amount of titanium white, a dab of Prussian blue and, as an afterthought, some French ultramarine. There would be no black on the canvas until she was happy with the curve of the dog's snout and the ripples of fur on his silken ears.

Picking up an unlabelled glass bottle, Lucy twisted the cap and squeezed the dropper to draw up the clear liquid that would thin the paints. She dribbled a few drops across her palette before selecting a wide flat brush and, as she mixed her colours, she couldn't help but notice the smell of her paints had changed. She wondered if it might be the steam rising from her tea, or perhaps the metallic scent of the storm in the air – or was it simply that her perceptions were changing along with her body?

Adam had a point about her becoming a newer version of herself but, in the software industry, that implied an improvement to the old. In some ways, Lucy *was* changing for the better. She had clung on to her student days a little too long and it was time to accept that she was a proper grown-up with a husband and a baby on the way.

Taking a deep breath, Lucy began to add paint to the stretched canvas. She used curved brushstrokes to add texture, but the oils worked against her and after half an hour of trying and failing to add some depth to her painting, she put down her palette. With her brow furrowed, she picked up the bottle she had used to thin the paint and raised it to eye level. She made up her own thinner mixture from equal parts of linseed oil and turpentine but one sniff confirmed her suspicions. If there was any oil present at all, it was the remnants from a previous mix.

The rain was beating down on the roof hard enough to make the tiles quake and as the noise intensified, so did Lucy's frustration. She poured the contents of the bottle on to a rag and used it to wipe clean her palette. She could have rescued the paints she had been using, but she would feel better starting over. She was almost tempted to cast aside the canvas too, but it was salvageable, assuming she did everything right next time.

Lucy took extra care as she half-filled the offending bottle with turpentine before adding the linseed oil. Such a simple task would normally be undertaken while she was planning her work, or thinking about what to have for lunch. It shouldn't need her undivided attention and Lucy's ineptitude annoyed her. And then it worried her. What if she made similar mistakes when the baby was born? Mixing incorrect ratios of thinner and oil was one thing, but what if she were making up formula milk? What if something went terribly wrong because of her carelessness?

The thought of being a mother terrified Lucy more than she had ever anticipated. She hoped her daughter would be blessed with health and happiness – nothing short of a perfect life – but for that, she would need the perfect mother. How could life be so perverse that part of preparing a woman's body for motherhood should involve giving her an overdose of hormones to screw up her mind?

Shaking the bottle, Lucy attempted to release some of her tension. She was being overdramatic. It was a simple slip-up.

'Bloody hormones,' Lucy muttered.

Picking up her peppermint tea, Lucy studied the canvas. It wasn't that bad and she wondered if she had been too quick to jump to conclusions about the thinner mix. With renewed determination, she picked up her paintbrush and this time used gentle strokes to transform her previous dabs of paint into a smooth wash that gave some sense of light and shadow to Ralph's features. She felt calmer, and Adam chose the perfect time to call.

'Hello,' she said with a soft smile.

'I can hardly hear you,' Adam shouted. 'Are you in your studio? Am I disturbing you?'

Lucy took another look at the canvas. 'No, I'll go downstairs,' she yelled back as she dropped her brush in a jar of thinner so it wouldn't dry out.

With her phone cradled against her shoulder, Lucy held her mug in one hand and used the other to grasp the handrail as she made her way down the staircase to the door on the first-floor landing. The entrance to her studio fitted seamlessly in with the rest of the house and Lucy reminded herself that she had reason to be proud of her accomplishments.

It had been hard graft, project-managing the building work and the wedding at the same time, but she had done it without so much as a mishap. Of the two, the wedding had been the simplest because she and Adam had chosen to marry on a beach in Santorini with only their mums in attendance. Adam's boss had insisted on hosting a party for them on their return but it had been deliberately low-key because their budget had been tight. Adam had already invested all his money in the house, and most of Lucy's savings – or at least the money her mum had saved up through the years on her behalf – had been earmarked for the loft conversion. They hadn't wanted a big fuss anyway. They had each other and that was what marriage was all about as far as they were concerned.

Reaching the ground floor where the staircase split the house in two, Lucy said, 'Can you hear me now?'

'Perfect,' he said. 'Do you need to make a drink?'

'No, I've got one, but I might grab a biscuit unless you're going to tell me I'm fat again,' she said, turning right. Her bare feet slapped against the ice-cold porcelain tiles as she crossed the kitchen diner in search of sustenance. If she had been around when Adam had refitted the kitchen, she would have insisted on installing underfloor heating but at least the room itself was warm. In fact, it grew distinctly toasty as she passed the gas hob.

'I would never call you fat and you know it,' Adam said. 'A bit bumpy around the middle maybe . . .' He was expecting a retort but was met with silence. 'Lucy?'

She was staring at a flickering blue circle. One of the burners had been left on its lowest setting. 'Sorry, what?' she asked as she quickly extinguished the flame.

'Are you OK?'

Lucy considered whether or not to tell Adam. She certainly wasn't going to mention the mix-up with the thinner because, the more she thought about it, the more likely it was that she had simply been doubting herself. Leaving the gas on, however, was irrefutably her fault. She had made breakfast hours ago and although she had eaten her porridge slouched in front of the TV, she had returned to the kitchen to wash up, and once more to make her peppermint tea. She had been distracted by the storm and her reluctance to set to work, but it was no excuse. Taking a sip of her tepid tea, she said. 'I left a burner on.'

'On the hob?'

'It must have been when I made breakfast. Unless . . .' she added as a thought occurred. 'You didn't use the hob this morning, did you?'

'Did you see the gas lit when you made your porridge?'

'There's no need to snap. I only left it on for ten minutes.'

In the silence that followed, Lucy sensed Adam judging her and her anger began to build. She knew it wasn't his fault but if he dared suggest she could have burnt the house down, or that the flame could have flickered out and sparked an explosion, there was a good chance she was going to scream.

'Lucy,' he said at last. 'You have to be more careful.'

'Do you think I don't know that?'

'OK, sorry, forget about it,' he said as kindly as he could, but Lucy took offence anyway.

'Oh, don't worry,' she scoffed. 'Forgetting is the one thing you *can* count on with me.'

No longer feeling hungry, Lucy left her mug on the counter and headed to the far end of the kitchen. The large patio doors looked out on to a simple courtyard with a scattering of pots and planters. Her eyes settled on the winter-bare fruit shrubs she had failed to nurture during the summer, which were now being bullied by gale-force winds.

West Kirby was on the exposed western tip of the Wirral,

a peninsula pinched between the fingers of the Dee and Mersey estuaries, and there was little to stop the storm sweeping in from the Irish Sea. Lucy felt its force as a sheet of rain hit the patio doors, causing her to slump down on to a chair at the dining table.

'I take it you slept in this morning?' Adam asked with a yawn. He was taking Lucy's snappishness in his stride and his patience was irritating.

'Only 'til about eight,' she said. It had been nearer nine, which still wasn't bad for someone who had refused to rise before midday in her misspent youth.

'I wish I could have stayed there with you, but then again, your fidgeting is getting worse. I hardly slept a wink last night.'

'Is that why you got up so early?' she asked as she trailed a finger across the surface of the table, leaving a faint mark in a layer of fine dust that had no right to be there.

Lucy hated the monotony of housework. She and Adam shared their duties but he was a little more particular and she felt guilty whenever he came home after a long day and picked up the chores she never seemed able to finish. She didn't remember housework being this hard when she lived with her mum, but that was probably because her mum had done most of it.

Adam groaned and she imagined him stretching his spine. 'I needed to make an early start anyway. I thought I'd cracked it with this new user interface but unless there's some miracle breakthrough in the next few hours, I'll have to go to Manchester tomorrow to work on site,' he said, his tone giving away his disappointment and his lethargy. He worked for a software company thirty miles away in

Daresbury and while he loved his job when it was going right, dealing with clients and their ever-changing needs was the bane of his life.

'I suppose I shouldn't keep you then,' she said with a distinct lack of enthusiasm. She wasn't ready to make another attack on her painting and she sensed Adam was in no rush to get back to his modules and macros either.

'Are you going to have another stab at Ralph?'

That's what I was doing when you phoned,' Lucy said as she pulled out a second chair to rest her feet. Arching her back, she unbuttoned her shirt to reveal her white lace briefs and the gentle rise of her stomach punctuated by a belly button that had recently popped out. 'I've spent an hour getting nowhere when I would have been better off catching up on housework.'

'But I thought you'd just had breakfast?'

Lucy went to open her mouth to correct him but she knew why he was confused. She had lied about how long she had left the gas on. 'What is this, Adam? Since when did I need to report all my movements to you?' she asked, knowing the answer was an obvious one.

'How long did you leave the gas burning, Lucy?' Adam asked, his gentle tone fuelling her anger.

As she hauled her legs off the chair to straighten up, Lucy's feet thumped hard enough against the porcelain tiles to sting her heels. 'I don't know, an hour or two. Does it matter? Nothing happened.'

'Thank goodness it didn't, but why bother lying about it? If you could stop getting so wound up over these things, you'd relax more and maybe then you'd make fewer mistakes.'

'I am relaxed!' Lucy said as her finger drew sharp lines through the dust on the table to form two words in capital letters. There were a lot of 'F's.

When Adam didn't respond, it was as if he could read what his wife had written. She hung her head in her hands and as she leant over the table, she felt a strange fluttering in her stomach – except it wasn't in her stomach, but a spot lower down. It was the first time she had felt her baby move and for all Lucy knew, her daughter's movements were signs of distress caused by her mother's roiling emotions.

She wanted desperately to say something to Adam. Only the night before, he had splayed his hand across her stomach, impatient to feel a part of what had been exclusively her experiences of pregnancy so far. They needed to share this special moment together, but now was not the right time.

Taking a deep breath, Lucy reminded herself that none of this was Adam's fault. 'I'm sorry,' she said.

'It's OK. Maybe I'm the one who needs to up my game. I could juggle my schedule and try to work from home more often.'

'Except when you have to go to Manchester,' she reminded him, proof that her short-term memory didn't always misfire.

'Isn't it time you started to take things easy?' he tried. 'You could always stop taking commissions for a while. It's not like you haven't been slowing down already and I'm sure we could manage without your income.'

'Painting isn't simply a job, it's my passion. I can't not paint.'

'Then paint for pleasure,' Adam persisted as if he could

solve her like one of his programs. 'Let me worry about the bills. Please think about it, Lucy. Why don't you go for a walk along the beach and clear your head?'

Glancing towards the tall beech tree in their neighbour's garden swaying from side to side, she said, 'Have you seen the weather?'

'Then go somewhere indoors, go shopping.'

'Maybe,' she said as a means to halt Adam's attempts to fix her. He meant well but if he threw one more suggestion at her, she was going to explode.

'And when you do go out,' Adam said, his voice rising as he sensed he was getting through to her, 'make sure you turn everything off and lock up.'

Lucy's lips cut a thin line across her face as she stared at the words written in the dust. She could feel them forming on her tongue and cut the call dead before they spilled out.

3

Lucy huddled against the corner of the large L-shaped sofa that took up most of the space in the living room. The black leather upholstery complemented the monotone colour scheme, as did the sixty-inch TV screen dominating one wall. With the exception of a couple of paintings Lucy had hung up to soften the sharp edges of Adam's choice of décor, the entire house bore the hallmarks of a bachelor pad, although Lucy was grateful that no previous love had stamped her mark on the place before her.

There had been only one significant other in Adam's life prior to Lucy, but Rosie had never moved in, which had been a lucky escape by all accounts. She had been a work colleague and had used Adam to rise up the career ladder by taking credit for his work and apportioning blame to everyone else when she messed up. Something had gone disastrously wrong and Adam had been forced to move jobs, but he had put his past mistakes behind him and Lucy was determined not to be the next.

Adam was different from the other men she had dated, and there had been quite a few. She had flitted from one casual affair to the next, avoiding commitment and responsibility as best she could. When Adam came along, the eight-year age difference had felt pronounced and she had been embarrassed by her immaturity. She had been a wild thing and he had tamed her, or so Adam told her. He was probably right, although Lucy was beginning to wonder if she had accepted the role of Adam's wife under false pretences. She couldn't be trusted to take care of herself or the house, and she didn't know how she was going to look after a baby.

The transition might have been easier if she lived closer to her mum, but Lucy was getting used to life on the Wirral. She loved that it was a five-minute stroll to the beach, although that proposition had not been a tempting one today despite Adam's helpful suggestion.

When she heard the front door opening, Lucy lifted her book higher to obscure her face. She hadn't spoken to Adam since hanging up on him, nor had she replied to his text messages. He had apologized and she wished he hadn't. She was the one acting like a child.

When the house fell silent, Lucy realized Adam had gone straight into the kitchen, confirmed a moment later when she heard the oven door slam. Adam had offered to pick up some food from Marks and Spencer on his way home and had asked her what she fancied. She wondered if he had responded to her radio silence by choosing his favourite cuisine, which was Chinese, or opting for hers. Her mouth watered at the thought of garlic dough balls; one of her many cravings in recent months.

Adam was head chef and they didn't often resort to ready meals but she presumed he had thought his time would be better spent shoring up his wife's fragile ego while keeping a safe distance from the offending gas hob. As the seconds ticked by, however, Lucy began to fear that he didn't want to speak to her at all. She put down her book and tucked her knees as close to her chin as her bump would allow.

Rather than return to her studio after the argument, Lucy had spent the afternoon soaking in the bath and feeling sorry for herself. She had taken time on her make-up, which was perfectly understated, and had teased her damp mane into copper coils. She wore leggings and a sloppy jumper to give the illusion of vulnerability, but that feeling became unpleasantly real as she waited for Adam to appear.

Lucy chewed her lip and stared at the door as she listened to Adam coming out of the kitchen. Her pulse quickened when his footsteps paused and for a moment she feared he had retreated upstairs, but then the door swung open. A breakfast tray appeared with a single red rose in a vase, two glasses of what looked like pink champagne but would be sparkling cordial, and a bowl of cheese puffs; another of her cravings.

When Adam stepped through the door, his expression was one of caution, as if he were approaching a wild animal. 'I know Valentine's Day is a week off but I feel like I should make an effort,' he said. 'The lasagne's going to be a while so these are to tide you over.'

Lucy went to speak but it came out as a sob. 'I'm such an evil cow,' she cried. 'I'm so sorry. I don't know what's wrong with me. I'm being so horrible to you and I don't deserve any of this!'

Hiding her face in shame, Lucy couldn't see Adam's

reaction but she heard him place the tray on the coffee table. The sofa sagged and a moment later, he was pulling her into his arms. She heard him take a breath to speak but she got there first.

'Don't you dare say nice things to me,' she warned. 'Tell me I'm a bitch.'

He kissed the top of her head.

When she looked up into his face, she hoped their daughter would inherit Adam's kind eyes. They melted her heart. 'I know you're only trying to take care of me.'

'And failing miserably,' he said.

'No, you're not,' she replied as she relaxed into him. 'I shouldn't need taking care of.'

Adam had taken off his suit jacket and tie but, despite a day in the office, Lucy could still smell the fabric conditioner on his shirt. Adam could choose to go to work in T-shirt and jeans if he wasn't meeting clients but he liked to dress smartly. He had been wearing a formal jacket when she had first met him that fateful summer's evening, albeit matched with chinos.

Adam's boss, Ranjit, had organized an impromptu mid-week barbecue to celebrate a big contract and make the most of the glorious weather. Lucy had simply been dropping off the painting his wife had commissioned and she had been in a rush, needing to get home to pick up her backpack and tent before catching a coach to Leeds. She was dressed in her festival gear complete with cut-off jeans and flowers in her hair and was champing at the bit to get moving, but Ranjit had insisted on introducing her to his friends and showing off the portrait of his two kids. Adam had shown a keen interest, despite having no children or pets for her to paint, and she had given him her number. She had moved in with him six months later, had married him the following summer and this summer they would be parents. It had all happened so fast.

'This forgetfulness is really getting to you, isn't it?'

'I felt better after speaking to Mum but knowing it's my hormones doesn't make it any less frustrating.'

He gave her a quick squeeze. 'Could it be that you're not completely convinced it is this baby brain thing?'

'It does make sense,' she tried.

'But . . . ?' he asked, and when she didn't answer he added, 'You're thinking about your dad, aren't you?'

Despite her best efforts, Lucy could feel her frustrations rise up again, twisting her insides. She was trying *not* to think about her dad, and while her little mishaps were getting to her, she could accept that they were the benign symptoms of life as a new wife and mother, or at least she would if Adam's prodding didn't unsettle her so much. Did he see her unravelling in ways that she could not?

'I know you mean well but this has nothing to do with what happened with Dad. I'm not the first person who's survived a troubled childhood.'

She shot him a pointed look but Adam didn't flinch. He had told her only the salient facts about his early life, but it was enough for Lucy to realize that there was more than one way to rend apart a family. Adam had chosen to block out the pain of his past, which was fine, that was how some people survived. It had worked for her mum, and Lucy was eager to follow their example.

'I'll be fine,' she continued. 'I'm annoyed by my own carelessness, that's all.'

'Why won't you talk about this, Lucy?' he asked. 'Is it too scary to admit that what happened with your dad might have left its mark?'

Adam scrutinized her features but before he could find what he was looking for, she dropped her head back down on his shoulder. Squeezing her eyes shut, Lucy let her mind fill with memories of her dad reading to her, playing with her, laughing and joking. There were darker memories too, sounds of raised voices, doors slamming, and silence. It was the silence that had scared her most, but she had been too young to understand why.

'I'm not denying it left its mark. I was eight years old and I was confused, especially when no one would give me proper answers. I was scared that what happened to Dad would happen to Mum.'

'Or to you?'

'Maybe,' she confessed, holding herself so taut that her body trembled.

With his chin resting on her head, Adam's voice was muffled by her curls. 'I'm sorry. I didn't mean to upset you, but I'm not sure this is something we should ignore. You're about to give birth and it's natural for you to worry about what one generation might have passed on to the next.'

'I know, but worrying won't make it go away and talking about it isn't helping,' Lucy said as she forced herself up and reached for the glass of cordial. Taking a generous sip, she swallowed her fear.

Adam tugged at her jumper to bring her back to him. 'How about we start this again?' he said. 'Let's forget about lost keys and gas hobs.'

'Tell me about your day,' she said as brightly as she could

manage. 'Did you sort out that interface thing, or will you have to go to Manchester tomorrow?'

'It couldn't be fixed,' he said, 'and I'm going to be on site for the rest of the week, so expect some early starts and late nights.'

'I'll try not to fidget so much in bed,' said Lucy, recalling his earlier complaint. 'I don't want you driving all that way with no sleep.'

'Don't worry, it's not like I haven't got used to all your thrashing about.'

She dug her elbow into his side. 'I do not thrash about.'

'It's worse when you stop. Then you snore.'

When Lucy giggled, she was surprised how quickly she could switch from tears to laughter. Her husband had a special gift. 'Now I know you're lying.'

They were quiet for a moment, comfortable in each other's arms. She felt safe enough to picture a scene four months from now when there would be chaos all about them. She imagined their panic as they threaded tiny limbs into complicated baby clothes, tripped over boxes of nappies or waged silent arguments over who had lost the TV remote as their baby slept. It was going to be amazing.

'So what do you think?' asked Adam.

'Hmm?' she said, coming back from her daydream.

'The Sandstone Trail.'

'What about the Sandstone Trail?' she asked, confused by his non sequitur.

She knew the trail well because it was where Adam had taken her on one of their first dates. His firm had organized the gruelling two-day trek and one of their first stopping points had been a craggy outcrop on the sandstone ridge that ran from Frodsham to Whitchurch. Adam had lured her to the edge to take in the stunning view across the Cheshire plains and towards Liverpool, not realizing how she had trembled in fear. It was there, on the spot they now referred to as Heart's Leap, that she had told him about her father and, if she wasn't mistaken, it pinpointed the exact moment they had fallen in love.

'Did you hear a word I was saying?'

Lucy straightened up, certain that her husband was teasing her and she would catch a sneaky smile on his face; instead his expression was one of concern. 'But you didn't say anything.'

Adam took a breath but whatever he was about to say was released with a sigh. 'Never mind. I was saying that Ranjit's organizing another charity walk this year.'

Lucy's heart rattled against her ribcage. 'You never spoke a word, Adam. Are you sure you weren't simply thinking it in your head?'

Adam's raised eyebrow spoke volumes, and while she didn't understand how she could have remained oblivious to what was going on around her, she couldn't face another debate that would only serve to highlight her shortcomings.

'I must have been miles away,' she said with a casual shrug that sent a cold shiver skittering down her spine. 'I was thinking about the baby and how manic it's going to be when she arrives.' Draining her glass, she returned it to the tray with shaking hands. 'So go on, tell me about the walk.'

'Lucy . . .' Adam began, less eager to gloss over what had just happened.

'When is it?'

'At the beginning of August,' he said with a note of resignation. 'I told Ranjit you probably wouldn't want to do it.'

'Too right. The baby will be less than two months old and I'd rather not risk it,' she said. Although her lips were moving and words came out, her mind was elsewhere. She forced the panic to the corners of her mind where she wished it would stay. She needed to concentrate if she were to avoid another mistake. 'Do you still want to do it?'

'It depends on how you and the baby are doing. I wouldn't leave you to cope on your own for the weekend if there were any problems.'

'There won't be,' she said. 'And I could always come and meet you at the refreshment stops.'

'OK, I'll put my name down,' Adam said with no enthusiasm whatsoever.

Lifting her head slightly, Lucy said, 'I can't smell garlic. Are you sure you switched the oven on?'

Peeling himself away from his wife, Adam stood up. 'Of course I switched it on,' he said with an air of confidence that wasn't meant to annoy, but it did. 'I need to put the dough balls in for the last ten minutes though, and I might give the kitchen a quick wipe down while I'm waiting. There's some interesting marks on the dining room table I think I should clean.'

Lucy winced. 'That wasn't a message for you.'

'No?'

Adam remained looming over her until she gave in. 'I told you I was an evil cow,' she said.

Lucy's sweet smile faded after Adam left the room. She swung her legs up and slumped back on the sofa so she could stare at the ceiling, but despite her brain's apparent ability to disengage without notice, unwelcome thoughts turned inside her head. Like the orange reflector on the wheel of her pink bicycle, her mind spun faster and faster. She was ready for that horrible lurch of her stomach, but what she felt was a different kind of quickening.

'Adam!' she cried.

Having pulled up her jumper, Lucy's hand was pressed over a spot a few inches above her groin when Adam burst into the room with a knife in his hand and his eyes open wide. It looked like a scene from a horror movie but Lucy was laughing.

'I can feel her,' she said.

Placing the knife on the coffee table, Adam dropped to his knees. 'Are you sure?'

Leaving him to assume that this was the first time, Lucy took Adam's hand and placed it where hers had been. 'Can you feel anything?'

Since that first flutter, Lucy had been conscious of every gurgle in her stomach but she hadn't felt anything as distinct as she had just now. Come meet your daddy, she told her daughter as she and Adam held their breath.

When her lungs started to burn, Lucy prepared to give up. 'There!' she said, pressing Adam's fingers over the exact spot. 'Did you feel that?'

Lucy wanted him to say yes. She needed the bond between them to be stronger than ever, but she could tell by Adam's face that he hadn't picked up the gentle flutter of butterfly wings inside her belly. She wouldn't have minded a lie.

'No,' he said, tugging his hand away when she tried to keep it in place. Seeing the look of disappointment on his wife's face, he added, 'She needs to build up those footballer's legs first. It won't be long, and I can wait.'

When Adam returned to the kitchen, Lucy stayed where she was. She wished she had her husband's patience but she was desperate to get past the last months of her pregnancy and, if she were honest, those first months after the birth. She wanted to be free of her raging hormones so that she could be reassured that they were the cause of her problems and nothing else. She was holding on by her fingernails to the hope that by the time Adam set off on the Sandstone Trail, normal service would be resumed.

4

'How are you feeling, love?' Viv asked as she passed the bread basket across the table. 'No more morning sickness?'

'I'm much better, thanks,' Lucy said, tearing a piece of the bread over her soup bowl and letting the warm butter ooze between her fingers. She wished Adam's mum would allow her guests to butter their own bread, or have it dry as Lucy preferred, but Viv liked to pre-empt her son's needs and it didn't seem to occur to her that his wife's tastes might differ. Licking her fingers, she added, 'But you should have seen my ankles last night. I've spent the last couple of days on my feet in my studio and I couldn't have put on a pair of shoes if I'd tried.'

'I told her they reminded me of elephant legs,' Adam offered.

'No, you didn't!' Lucy said before she had the chance to wonder if this was another conversation she had missed. A smile crept across Adam's face and she relaxed. 'You might have thought it, but you're too much of a gentleman to say such a thing.'

Adam's smile disappeared behind a soup spoon. He took

a sniff of the gloopy liquid and his brow furrowed. 'Did you put something different in this, Mum?'

Viv's head snapped up. 'No, it's the same as always. Except, well, I did add a bit of leftover sweetcorn, but that's all.'

Adam gave Lucy a knowing look. When they had first met, he had warned her about his mum's cooking, and although they had fallen into a routine of visiting each of their mums on alternate Sundays, the difference was marked. Lucy's mum made the perfect Sunday roast with enough trimmings to feed an army whilst Viv provided simpler fare, which was almost always soup. Adam told Lucy they were getting off lightly, but it didn't stop her worrying about what might be in the muddy green liquid that had been blended beyond recognition. She preferred to wait until Adam had tasted it first.

'At least you've passed the halfway mark,' Viv said to Lucy. 'It's surprising how much a baby takes it out of you though.' Lucy looked up in time to catch a glance between Adam and his mother. 'You can't expect to feel like you did before. Being a mum is a big adjustment and your body often races ahead before your head has a chance to catch up. It's all perfectly natural.'

Lucy's smile was tight as she realized Adam had snitched on her. How was she meant to feel less anxious when he was worrying twice as much on her behalf, and inviting others to join him? In the last few days, she had checked and double-checked everything she did and, so far, her efforts had been rewarded.

'I've been a bit scatter-brained lately but nothing worth mentioning,' she said, aiming her last comment at Adam.

'How's work going, son?' Viv asked to ease over the awkwardness.

'Couldn't be better. There are problems as always but Ranjit trusts me to fix them. I don't think it'll be long before I'm leading my own projects, which will put a few noses out of joint.'

Viv's eyebrows raised. 'Naomi's, by any chance?'

'Naomi?' Lucy asked as she scanned her memory for the name. She had met many of Adam's colleagues at the various social gatherings Ranjit organized to keep his team tight. Adam wasn't keen on such events but he put on a good show and it was paying off. She knew that. So why didn't she know about someone called Naomi?

'The new software developer?' Adam offered. With a surreptitious roll of the eyes, he returned his attention to his mum. 'She thought she could wow Ranjit with her new ideas that were obviously meant to show how archaic the rest of us are. It's taken a while for her to realize that the boss is more impressed with people who pull together than trip each other up. He wants staff who offer stability, at home as well as at work, and that's what he thinks I can offer, thanks to you two.'

'And the baby when she comes along,' Viv said, her eyes dancing.

'She?' Lucy asked. She was developing a crick in her neck from the looks she kept shooting at Adam. He had called in to see his mum earlier in the week to drop off her birthday present. She lived five miles away in Moreton and the detour was a minor one in comparison to the trek to visit Lucy's mum. He hadn't stayed long, but apparently long enough to fill Viv in on all the intimate details of their lives.

'I couldn't not tell her,' Adam said. 'Your mum knows and it seemed only fair.'

'Oh dear, it wasn't a secret, was it?' Viv asked.

'Why? Who else have you told?' asked Adam, his sudden change of tone undeservingly harsh, given that he had been the one to spread the news further afield.

'It's OK,' said Lucy when she saw the alarm on Viv's face. 'We might as well let everyone know. I call the baby *her* all the time and if anyone's going to slip up, it's going to be me.' She watched Adam tap his fingers against his thumb, and when his agitation didn't ease, she pushed the conversation on. 'How was your birthday, Viv? Did you like our present?'

Lucy had bought her mother-in-law a long, woollen cardigan in a beautiful Tahitian blue that would brighten up some of the dark dresses and tunics Viv tended to wear. It was easy to forget that her mother-in-law wasn't much older than her own mum. Her dour appearance disguised the fact that she was a good-looking woman, with a stunning shade of silver hair that Lucy envied. She wished she knew Viv well enough to tell her so and hoped the baby would bring them closer.

'It's lovely,' Viv said. 'I'll save it for best.'

'You've got a lot of flowers,' remarked Adam.

Lucy had counted four vases dotted around the open-plan living space in Viv's small bungalow. The blooms were mostly lilies and roses in complementary colours that suggested they were from the same bouquet. On the far side of the room, she had also noticed a line of birthday cards on the bookshelf. She could see the one Adam had picked out for his mum, dwarfed by its neighbour with a similar dedication to a loving mother. Although Lucy was unlikely to ever meet Adam's brother, the signs were everywhere that he was rebuilding his relationship with his mother, and the look of apology Viv gave her eldest son was one Lucy had seen many times before. Whatever mistakes Viv had made in the past, she remained painfully aware of the damage she had caused.

'Did you do anything nice on the day?' Lucy asked to break the silence. She spoke louder than normal, as she often did with Viv. It was too easy to think she was addressing an elderly relative.

'I was in work but I went for a pub lunch with the girls and the boss paid for it all. For an accountant, he can be quite generous.'

Adam dropped his spoon into the soup bowl with a loud plop and pushed it away. He had a playful expression on his face when he said, 'Can he now?'

'He's half my age and happily married, Adam.'

'Yeah, well, stranger things have happened,' her son warned as the colour rose in Viv's cheeks. 'It's great that you have people around you that care, Mum, but I'd hate to see someone taking advantage of you.'

Lucy sipped her soup quietly. Personally, she thought it would do Viv no harm to live a little but she understood why Adam was being protective. His mum had been divorced twice and the break up with Adam's stepfather, Keith, had been particularly nasty, but that didn't mean all men were bad, or that Viv's choices would always be poor ones.

'As long as I have my family looking out for me, I'm sure I'll be fine,' Viv said as she pulled at a loose thread on her cardigan. Unaware that the cuff had begun to pucker, she glanced briefly at Lucy, who had a spoonful of soup halfway to her mouth. 'Are you ready for pudding? I picked up an Arctic roll the other day. Remember how much you used to love them, Adam?'

'That wasn't me,' he said.

Viv's features twisted again and Lucy couldn't tell if she were angry at herself for the slip or was preparing to say something else. It turned out to be the latter. 'I've decided to treat myself to a little break for my birthday,' she announced. 'All I need to do is sort out my passport.'

'Ooh, that's good!' Lucy said, already impressed. Viv had a sister with an apartment on the Costa del Sol and Lucy was about to ask if she had finally agreed to go away with her when Adam voiced another theory.

'You need a visa too if you're going to the States.'

From the way Viv's eyes brightened, she had been expecting a different response from her son. 'Yes, I know. Scott's given me all the instructions.'

Adam stopped fidgeting with his fingers and placed both hands palm down on the table. 'Yeah, I bet he has.'

'When are you going, Viv?' asked Lucy, desperate to keep the conversation on track.

'Next month, in time for Mother's Day if I can get everything sorted. I've never been to New York before and there's so much I want to see.'

'So the son who's spent half his life forgetting he has a mother wants to see you on *Mother's* Day?' Adam asked quietly. It had taken a moment or two for the news his mum had imparted to sink in, but the reaction Viv had feared was beginning to emerge. 'Why then? They don't even celebrate Mother's Day in the States until later in the year.'

'I didn't want to go away too close to Lucy's due date.'

'You've told him about the baby?' hissed Adam.

The spidery thread Viv had been pulling from her sleeve came away with a snap and she rolled it into a small ball between her finger and thumb. 'You didn't say I had to keep it a secret, love. And Lucy said before it was OK.'

'I'm not talking about the sex of the baby,' Adam said. 'I didn't want *him* to know we were having one at all and I'm surprised that needed saying. Since when did you get so pally?'

'I'm there whenever he needs me, as I am with you,' Viv said. 'And Scott's changed a lot in the year since Keith's heart attack. I think the scare made him realize how important all his family is to him. That includes you, Adam.'

'No, it doesn't. And if you had any sense, you'd keep away. What hurts you, hurts me, Mum. Remember that.'

'We have to give him a chance, Adam.'

'I don't have to do anything,' Adam said, standing abruptly.

He left the two women staring after him and then at each other. There were tears in Viv's eyes when she asked, 'Will you speak to him? Will you tell him I'm sorry?'

Lucy wanted to ask Viv what she had to be sorry about when it was Adam who was behaving unreasonably, but she knew she would be asking the wrong person.

5

Sitting behind the wheel of his Lexus, Adam's gaze was fixed on something ahead that no one else could see. He didn't flinch as Lucy climbed into the car and slammed the door shut, or when she huffed and puffed while fastening her seatbelt.

The pressure around Lucy's chest tightened as she recalled the anguish on Viv's face. She would never talk to her mum like that, and she hadn't expected it of Adam. Now that he had had time to cool down, she was sure he would go back inside to apologize before driving off.

The engine roared into life.

'No, Adam,' she said as he put the car in gear. 'Don't leave like this.'

Releasing the handbrake, Adam pulled out on to the road. 'Why? What did she say to you?'

'Just that she was sorry. Is it so wrong that she wants to spend more time with Scott? She said he'd changed.'

'And you're the expert on my brother all of a sudden, are you? Exactly how has he changed, Lucy?'

'I don't know. I don't know what he was like before,' she stammered.

'Exactly. Don't get involved.'

'How can I not get involved? You're my husband and Viv's my mother-in-law, and in case you need reminding, we're about to have a baby.'

'*Me* need reminding?'

'I know you're upset but can't you see how unreasonable you're being?' she said. 'We need our family around us rather than at each other's throats.'

'Some things can't be fixed.'

'Look, forget about Scott. What about you and your mum?' Lucy asked as they pulled up at a set of traffic lights. 'Please, Adam. Family feuds seem like such a wasted effort. It happened with my dad and his brother. One minute they were running a business together and the next, whatever went on between them couldn't be undone. Uncle Phil didn't even show up to the funeral and maybe he doesn't give Dad a passing thought, but what if he has to live with that bitterness and regret for the rest of his life? I'm thinking of you as much as I am your mum.'

The lights changed and they were on the move.

Quickly losing patience, Lucy said, 'You can't treat your mum like this!'

Snapping his head towards her, Adam said, 'So you're taking her side?'

'No, I simply think—'

'That I'm in the wrong,' Adam finished for her. 'Not all of us have to agree with what our mums tell us, Luce. Some of us quite like having an opinion of our own.'

'What's that supposed to mean?'

Adam sniffed and returned his attention to the road, his jaw clenched. Lucy didn't like this side of Adam. He reminded her of a gerbil she once had. Most of the time he had been the most gentle of creatures, but if he didn't want to go back into his cage and she had to corner him, he wasn't averse to the odd nip.

'Are you suggesting I don't have a mind of my own?' she asked.

'Have you *ever* gone against your mum?'

'It's not about going against her. We talk things through and we reach a decision together.'

Adam continued to stare straight ahead but after a minute of tense silence, his shoulders sagged and he released his anger with a sigh. 'Is it too much for you to recognize how controlling she can be sometimes? She even picks your friends for you.'

'She didn't pick you,' Lucy said, attempting to make light of the comment now that their argument was on the wane. 'If this is about Hannah, it was only a suggestion.'

'Yeah, for you to get parental advice from someone who's had more kids than she can cope with. You do remember saying that, don't you?'

Lucy pressed her hands to her burning cheeks. She could hear someone saying the words as they drove home after their last trip, but since she couldn't even remember who had been driving, why did she think she could remember who said what? 'I suppose,' she said, ready to accept that Adam's memory of that particular event was more reliable than her own.

'And you can't deny you told your mum how chaotic Hannah is.'

'Because I thought that was how you felt. She didn't mean to laugh when you spilt your drink, that's just Hannah. I'm used to how she is. She's one of my oldest friends.'

'Are you saying it's because of me that you stopped seeing her?' Adam asked with more hurt than annoyance.

'I don't know, I suppose,' Lucy admitted, falling short of suggesting how he had used the spilt drink as an excuse to leave. 'You never exactly enjoyed her company.'

Adam slumped back in his seat. 'I honestly don't know where this idea came from that I don't like her. I'll admit I'm worried that you might not be able to cope with all that extra *stimulus* when you're around her, but if you want to see her, go right ahead. I'd hate people to think that I'm the one keeping you from your friends.'

'I choose who I see. No one's blaming you.'

'Give them time,' he muttered. 'I'll tell you what I think's going on. You're feeling guilty because it's you who's been distancing yourself from Hannah, and you're using me as the excuse to make you feel better. Am I right?'

'Can we stop talking about Hannah?' Lucy asked, not liking the way she was losing her train of thought as she tried to unravel the reasons why she had lost touch with her friend. 'I'll go and see her if it makes you feel better, but right now I'm more concerned about you and your mum. I don't want to see you falling out with her, Adam, and I don't think you want that either.'

'I know how this must look but you have to trust me on this,' he said softly.

'I do.'

'Even though you said I was the one in the wrong?'

'If I said that, I'm sorry.'

'If?'

The question hung in the air and when Adam stopped at another set of lights, he dug out a tissue from the glove compartment and handed it to Lucy as if he expected her to burst into tears at any moment.

'You don't know what Scott's like,' Adam told her gently. 'He couldn't have planned this better, and if there's one thing I know about my brother, it's that he did plan this. He wants to drive a wedge between me and Mum.'

'So prove him wrong.'

'Mum knows I won't stay mad at her for long.'

Sensing that she was winning him over, the pressure against Lucy's chest began to ease. 'That might be true, but does she have to work it out for herself? Please, let's sort this.'

'Fine,' he said, releasing a sigh. 'If it makes you happy.'

As they drove along a country lane some five minutes from home, Lucy looked for somewhere to turn the car around, but when she spotted a lay-by, Adam drove past. 'Aren't you going back?' she asked.

'I will,' he said, 'but it would be better if I went on my own. You've been upset enough for one day. It's not good for you.'

'I'm stronger than you think.'

Adam glanced down at the crumpled tissue in Lucy's hand. 'It's not what I think that worries me.'

6

It had been a while since Lucy had been left to her own devices on a Saturday afternoon. She and Adam spent their weekends as a couple and rarely deviated from their routine of pleasing themselves on Saturday and their mothers on Sunday. Living life to a timetable was something Lucy was still getting used to but she had to admit it provided a sense of stability that she needed more than ever, hence her reasons for pushing Adam out the door after lunch. It had been a week since the argument with his mum and Adam had avoided her for long enough.

Lucy was happy to sacrifice a Saturday with her husband for the sake of family unity, but once Adam had gone, she was left to ponder what she should do with herself. The subject of her friendship with Hannah had been put on hold, but it seemed the perfect opportunity to resolve the matter once and for all. When Lucy had picked up the phone, she had told herself that if Hannah were too busy to meet up, at least she could say she had tried. There had been the sound a child's tantrum playing out in the background and Hannah had jumped at the chance to escape.

Lucy left the house wrapped in extra layers that made her look twice as big as she felt. She hoped the concealed hood in her padded jacket wouldn't be needed but as the wind tugged a loose curl from her hairband, she regretted not wearing a beanie hat. There wasn't time to go back but she retraced her steps anyway. Yes, she had locked the front door.

'Sorry, I'm late,' Lucy said as she rushed along the promenade to give Hannah a hug. No sooner had they embraced than her friend's chocolate-brown Labrador yanked them apart. He had sniffed out the scent of another dog a hundred yards away and was eager for introductions.

'That's all right,' Hannah said as she was dragged off in what was thankfully the direction they intended.

In front of them was Marine Lake, a manmade coastal lake edged by the River Dee on three sides. Around its perimeter was a walkway wide enough for two friends and a dog.

'I'm just glad you rang,' Hannah continued. 'It's been too long, Lucy. You used to be our social secretary and I miss our nights out.'

'Don't get too excited. This bottle of water does actually contain water,' Lucy said, recalling how they had smuggled vodka into bars and proceeded to chat up the barmen so they didn't question why they were getting drunk on diet Cokes.

Hannah looked Lucy up and down as only close friends might. 'That's not all that's changed. Where's all the make-up gone?'

'I'm wearing some,' Lucy said, not surprised that it would be the first thing to be noticed. There had been a time when

Lucy would spend more money on mascaras and eyeliners than she would ever admit to her mum, but it had been liberating to discover that Adam preferred a more natural look.

Hannah hadn't changed at all and was as stunning as ever. Her dark silken hair was pulled back into a ponytail and her complexion had a natural glow that emphasized the vitality sparkling in her dark brown eyes. The thick eyeliner flicks might be bordering on what Adam would call gaudy, but it was a look that her friend had owned since their teenage years.

'It really is good to see you, and such perfect timing,' said Hannah. 'It's chaos back at home.'

'I can imagine,' Lucy said, smiling that Hannah would use the same term that sprung to mind whenever she pictured her friend's house bursting at the seams.

'You don't fancy running off somewhere, do you, Luce? We never did manage to backpack around Europe.'

Yes, please, Lucy thought and was surprised how close she came to uttering the words aloud. She had been telling herself that her only reason for seeing Hannah was to prove how they had grown apart. She hadn't expected to feel such a strong pull back to the life she had left behind. Or perhaps she had.

'Things are different now,' Lucy said, stroking a hand over her bump, although Hannah was too busy wrestling the dog to notice. 'You have three kids to look after, in case you've forgotten. *And* a dog.'

'And the cat's had kittens.'

'You have a cat too?' gasped Lucy, taking a closer look at her friend and wondering how she managed to look so serene.

'It sort of adopted us, though goodness knows why. I blame Samson,' she said in a tone that made her dog's ears prick. 'I thought dogs and cats were meant to be sworn enemies, but I'm telling you, they're in love. I wouldn't have been surprised if the kittens had come out chocolate brown.'

As they veered off the promenade to begin their circuit of the lake, the tide was high and water lapped against the shale and rock marking the edges of the path. They faced the misty Welsh mountains on the opposite side of the river but Lucy's gaze was drawn seawards. The leaden sky had sunk low enough to make grey ghosts of the wind turbines, while Hilbre Island and its smaller companions of Little Eye and Middle Eye remained dark outlines at the mouth of the river.

'They are bloody cute kittens though,' Hannah continued as Samson lost interest in the dog he had been stalking and began splashing in the puddles that pockmarked the path. 'You don't want one, do you?'

'We did talk about getting a pet when I first moved in with Adam. I fancied a dog but I know they're a big responsibility,' she said as Samson shook his coat and sprayed the two women with salty seawater. 'Adam liked the idea of a cat but I think we're going to have our hands full with a baby.'

The subtle refusal was lost on Hannah who didn't know the meaning of restraint – she had been the one responsible for the vomit stain on the sun lounger festering in Lucy's mum's garage. Pulling out her phone, she began flicking through reams of photos of fluffy kittens. 'I thought you might like this ginger one,' she said with a devilish smile.

Lucy peered at the screen being thrust under her nose. 'Oh, it is adorable.'

'They won't be ready for another month, but it's yours if you want it.'

'Is it a girl or a boy?' Lucy asked as if she were interested, which of course she wasn't.

'Haven't the foggiest, but someone did tell me that ginger cats are usually boys.'

'Don't they spray everywhere though?' Lucy said. Her previous experience of pets was limited to one nervous gerbil and a rabbit that had escaped after six months.

'My advice is that you get him, or her, neutered as soon as you can,' Hannah said. Seeing the sidelong glance Lucy gave her, she added, 'Yeah, I know. I should take my own advice, but in my defence, Nutella was a fully grown cat when she rocked up. I was sort of hoping she'd already been done.'

'Nutella?'

'The kids named her, probably because I kept saying we'd be nuts to keep her.'

By Lucy's calculation, Hannah's three boys were aged one, four and six and from the brief glimpses of them in the background of the kitten photos, they were all thriving. 'How do you cope with three kids?' she asked.

'Who said I was coping?'

'You're managing it better than I could. I don't ever want to be pregnant again.'

'Never say never,' Hannah said. 'Who would have guessed two years ago that you'd be married with a baby on the way? Your head must still be spinning.'

'Actually, that's not a bad description.'

'You're not having regrets, are you? I did worry that you might have rushed into things. It seemed like you were single one minute and the next thing I knew, you were married,' Hannah said, her tone edging the last comment towards an accusation.

'I'm sorry we didn't invite you. We didn't want anyone feeling obliged to pay for an expensive trip abroad, and neither of us were up for a big party when we got back,' she added, hoping that Hannah hadn't heard about the wedding reception Ranjit had thrown on their return – which had been attended mostly by Adam's work colleagues anyway.

Resisting the pull of Samson's leash, Hannah paused to give her friend a closer look. 'You really have changed, haven't you?'

Lucy chewed her lip. 'I suppose I have, but for the record, I couldn't be happier.'

'You don't have *any* regrets?' asked Hannah, her tone suggesting she had something in mind.

'Such as?' Lucy dared to ask.

'Such as marrying someone who doesn't care too much for your friends.'

'That's not true.'

'Oh, so it's just me he doesn't like then. You can't tell me he didn't deliberately spill his drink over himself that last time you were at ours.'

'Is that what you think?' Lucy asked, glossing over the fact that it had crossed her mind at the time. 'For the record, Adam does like you, in fact he said as much the other day.'

Hannah pulled a face that was a half-hearted plea for forgiveness. 'Maybe I don't know him well enough. All I can say is he must have hidden depths to have you so besotted.'

'He does,' Lucy said, thinking back to how Adam had sneaked into her heart simply by asking the questions that no one else had ever seemed interested in finding out the answers to, mostly about her past, but also how it had shaped who she was. He knew her like no one else, faults and all, and that was what worried her now. 'And if anyone should be regretting getting married, it's Adam.' Her hand swept across her bump again, wiping off splatters of seawater from Samson's boisterous attacks on the puddles. 'He's had a lot to put up with lately. I may not be as tired as I was when I first fell pregnant, but I'm getting more hopeless.'

'I don't believe that, and even if it's time, it's only to be expected.'

'Is it? I never seem to get anything finished. We both do our fair share of the housework but all I seem to do is make extra work for Adam. He had to wash a whole load of washing again the other day after I'd accidentally left it in the machine. I couldn't even remember putting it in, but it must have been there a while to come out all wet and stinking. And that's only one of a long list of stupid things I've done lately. Mum says it's baby brain.'

Hannah's laugh was whipped away by the sea breeze and caught by a gull's cry. 'I still use that excuse.'

'But it's not an excuse,' Lucy said. 'Not with me.'

'You're actually serious, aren't you?' Hannah asked, catching sight of Lucy's stricken face and slowing her pace to give her friend her full attention. 'You're due mid-June, aren't you?'

Lucy nodded solemnly. 'And I'm counting down the days.'

'My emotions were all over the place with Isaac too,' Hannah reassured her. 'But that goes with the territory when it's your first. With Josh, I felt sick from the minute I conceived until the day I delivered, while my little Sammy was a walk in the park and I couldn't have asked for a better pregnancy. The one thing they all had in common was that it was worth it in the end. If I'd known you were going to hate it so much, I'd have offered to rent out my womb.'

Lucy looked out across the choppy waters of the estuary. At low tide, the exposed riverbed could be crossed on foot to reach Hilbre, but you had to aim first for Little Eye or else risk becoming trapped by sinking sand. Despite her boots clicking against solid ground, Lucy had the distinct feeling that she had taken the wrong path somewhere.

'I don't hate being pregnant,' she said. 'But it's not exactly how I imagined it would be. It annoys me how slow-witted I've become. I've got this habit of zoning out, as if my mind can't cope with growing a baby and listening to Adam at the same time.'

Hannah caught her next laugh at the back of her throat before it could escape. 'It's perfectly normal not to listen to your husband, Lucy.'

'Is it?' she asked. 'I was late today because I couldn't find my boots, or to be precise, I couldn't find one of my boots. Who in their right mind loses one under the sofa and puts the other away in the closet?'

'If we were meant to be in our right minds, no woman would willingly grow something inside her that was way too big for the opening God gave her.'

Lucy groaned. 'Don't remind me. I made the mistake of mentioning how worried I was to the midwife and she's signed me up for an introductory antenatal class next month for nervous first-timers. Part of me would rather not know what's coming,' she said, taking the final corner and turning her back on the receding tide that would gradually expose the hidden dangers beneath.

'If you're anything like me, everything they tell you in those classes will go straight out of your head when the time comes, but if you need someone to talk to, I'm always at the end of the phone,' Hannah promised. She tipped her head forward and lowered her voice when she added, 'Now that you've remembered my number.'

'I know, I'm sorry! We left it way too long. It's finding the time that's the problem,' Lucy said, which felt like a poor excuse when Hannah had managed to hold on to her social life after she married. It was different for Lucy. She and Adam had their routines and it wasn't that he didn't like her having friends – not at all. They simply liked each other's company more, and when Adam had given up his rock-climbing club so they could spend their weekends together, it felt right that she should make sacrifices too. She missed her friends, but of all Lucy's relationships, Adam was the most important.

'I get it, you only have eyes for Adam,' Hannah said, 'but I'm here if you need me.'

'It will get better, won't it?' Lucy asked as they left the path and stepped back on to the promenade.

'I promise. You'll have this baby and wonder what all the fuss was about. Give it a year and you'll be planning the next,' Hannah said. She checked her watch. 'Look, I'm really sorry, I know I said I'm here for you, but I should head home. There's a limit to how long I can trust Jamie to look after the kids without putting his sanity or theirs at risk.'

'I'm so glad you came. I've been cooped up in my studio all week and it's been nice getting out of the house.'

'Speaking of which, I might need a favour from you. Do you remember my nan and grandad?'

Lucy had a vague recollection of gate-crashing a family party. 'The ones who celebrated their diamond wedding?'

'And some,' Hannah said. She paused to look up and scowl at the gull screeching above her head. 'My nan died on Christmas Eve and, as awful as it was for us, it's been devastating for Grandad. He's eighty-two and he says he's managing on his own but he misses Nan. He talks to her photos all the time and I was just thinking, it might be nice if the family clubbed together and had a portrait painted of her, and I know you'd do a bloody good job. Would you?'

Lucy's heart clenched. She was putting the final touches to Ralph's portrait and hadn't yet decided what to do next. Adam's idea of painting simply for pleasure was a tempting one and her walk around Marine Lake had already given her some ideas. 'The way I am at the moment, Hannah, I'm not sure I'd do a painting like that justice.'

'Still the perfectionist?'

'I guess so,' Lucy said with a sigh.

As they retraced their steps along the promenade, Lucy thought about the sure-footed woman Hannah assumed her still to be. The old Lucy got things right first time and never thought to double-check her work. Lucy missed her. Her new life was more of an illusion made up of smoke and mirrors, but if she could somehow carry on pretending to be the person everyone expected her to be, she might stand a chance of believing in herself again.

'I tell you what, why don't you send me some photos of your nan and even if I can't do it now, I promise it'll be my first job once I've had the baby and I'm free of all these stupid hormones.' When Hannah screwed up her face, she added, 'I know, I know, it's not going to be easy with a new baby in tow, but Adam's promised to work from home more and Mum's cutting back on her hours so she can help too. I really do want to do it, Hannah. I wouldn't even charge you.'

'Firstly, of course we'll pay for it, and waiting isn't a problem,' Hannah said. 'The reason I'm hesitating is because I think Grandad needs to pick out the right photo. Maybe I could bring him along next time we meet and you can help him choose?'

Lucy's face broke into a smile, liking the idea of another excuse to meet up. 'That sounds perfect.'

'Then the job's yours,' Hannah said as they reached the spot where they had met. After making their goodbyes, Hannah gave Lucy a fierce hug and as Samson dragged her away, she called back, 'Don't forget about the kitten!'

Lucy kept her smile all the way home. Adam had been wrong to worry that Hannah would make her feel worse. After simply one breezy walk along the promenade, Lucy felt so much better. And if meeting her friend was to prove a point, the point was she missed her. As was the norm with Hannah, she had put temptation in Lucy's path, and not only the kitten, but the commission too. Lucy often painted portraits that came with stories that could break her heart, but the tears were worth it when she saw the expressions on her clients' faces, especially when she added those little extra details that would mean something to the family; like Ralph's slipper.

When Lucy reached home and found herself testing the lock on the front door yet again before going inside, she resented the relief that washed over her. She peeled off her layers and wandered into the kitchen where her eyes were immediately drawn to the gas hob. There was no blue flame because she had checked it at least three times before leaving the house. Why did she doubt herself at every turn?

Lucy switched on the kettle and dropped a teabag into a mug and as she waited for the water to boil, she played with a sprinkling of crumbs lurking on the countertop behind her jar of herbal teas. She crushed a particularly large clump into dust before sweeping the debris in her hand. The trails left behind were a level of messiness she could live with, and she doubted Hannah would consider it a mess at all, but Adam would notice and she would finish the job properly before he came home.

With her tea brewing, Lucy sat at the table to pull off her boots – which she would purposefully and consciously put away under the stairs before getting the rest of the house in order. Her feet were swollen and as she tugged at the first boot, her knee knocked against the table and a shower of petals rained down on to its surface.

The bouquet Adam had given her for Valentine's Day took up most of the table top. Lucy hadn't wanted to disturb the stunning arrangement so had left it in its pink box with its own water reservoir. She had added the sachet of food to prolong the life of the blooms but to her dismay, they were shrivelling up before her eyes. Many of the roses were denuded of petals and their stems drooped over the edge of the Cellophane cuff.

After pulling off her other boot, Lucy lifted the bouquet only for more petals to fall to their death. The box was lighter than she expected and as she tilted it from side to side, she felt no movement of water. She had topped it up the night before and it seemed impossible that the flowers would use up that much water so quickly, which left her wondering if it had been the night before. Cursing under her breath, she rushed to fetch a jug, knowing it was already too late.

This was why she doubted herself. Adam had wanted to spoil her by giving her a bouquet that rivalled the one his mum had received from Scott, but if they were meant to be a symbol of their relationship, Lucy was in trouble.

7

Hearing Adam's car pull up outside, Lucy rested an elbow on the banister and settled into what she hoped was a casual pose. 'How did it go with your mum?' she asked as he stepped through the door.

Adam blinked in surprise. 'Erm, good thanks.'

'I've made a beef stew,' she said. 'And don't look so worried. I checked with mum and she talked me through it. It tastes really good even if I do say so myself. Are you hungry yet?'

Adam slipped off his jacket and unfurled the scarf from around his neck. As he moved to the opposite side of the staircase to put his things away in the closet, Lucy repositioned herself in front of the kitchen door. The knot in her stomach tightened.

'I had something to eat at Mum's,' he said, raking his fingers through his hair and scratching his head. 'I thought you were going to suit yourself.'

'But you never eat at your mum's.'

'I told you . . .' His words trailed off. 'Never mind, it doesn't matter. Why don't you have something else and we'll save the stew for tomorrow?'

'But we're at Mum's tomorrow.' She swallowed hard. 'What doesn't matter, Adam?'

'What?'

Her heart palpitations made for an unpleasant mix with her churning stomach. 'You started to say something and then you said it doesn't matter. Tell me.'

Adam looked suddenly tired, or had Lucy simply not noticed how the worry lines criss-crossing his brow had deepened over the last few months? His cheeks were ruddy from being out in the cold but that didn't explain his watery eyes.

'I said this morning that I'd risk Mum's cooking.'

'No you didn't!' she said, not meaning to snap but unable to contain herself.

She could recall the conversation in question quite clearly. They had been lying in bed, Lucy pressing Adam's hand firmly on her belly as they waited in vain for him to feel her baby's kicks. She would swear that she hadn't lost track.

More calmly, she added, 'You didn't say anything about eating at your mum's. We talked about what might be lurking in the freezer, that's why I wanted to use up the braising steak.'

Adam raised his arm but couldn't quite reach her, or he didn't want to. 'You're right we did, and then I said how I might need to eat some humble pie, figuratively and literally.'

'No, that's not possible.'

'So I didn't say it?'

'I'm not doubting you, but I don't see how I could have forgotten something like that.'

Passing a hand across his face, Adam said, 'But Lucy,

you *are* doubting me.' He released a sigh with a hiss. 'Fine! I'm the one having conversations with myself. I'm the one who leaves the gas rings on.'

Adam made a move to go into the kitchen but Lucy stood her ground. 'No, I'm not saying that.'

'Yes, that's exactly what you're saying,' he said, pushing past her. 'I know you like to be little miss perfect and this stuff is driving you crazy, but have you ever stopped to think about what effect it's having on me? You're not the only . . .'

Adam had walked past the gleaming kitchen cupboards and the bubbling stew to stop a few feet away from the dining table. The sun was going down and the spotlights Lucy had selectively switched on in the kitchen had left the dining area in shadow, but not the complete darkness she had hoped for.

'Adam,' she began.

'What have you done to the flowers?' he asked, his voice full of the hurt Lucy had wanted to spare him.

She had thinned out the casualties and revived the remaining flowers as best she could using tricks she had searched for online, including snipping stems, adding sugar to the water and even something called the hat-pin trick. She had managed to prop up some of the weaker stems using the evergreen foliage but the end result was a haphazard arrangement of twigs and brown-edged blooms.

'The water ran out and I hadn't noticed.'

Adam sank down on to a chair and pulled at a rose with mottled edges. 'You let them die.'

Lucy came behind him and folded her arms around his chest, resting her chin on his shoulder. 'I didn't mean to.

No one's ever given me such a massive bunch of flowers before and I didn't realize how much water they'd need. I've saved what I could.'

Adam covered his face in his hands and whether it was deliberate or not, he pulled away from her as he bent forward. Lucy went with him, making her posture unnatural and uncomfortable, but she refused to let go.

Adam exhaled. 'I don't seem to be able to get anything right.'

Lucy squeezed her eyes shut. They were words she had flailed herself with so often and it seemed wrong, hearing them uttered by her forbearing husband. 'Don't say that.'

'I can't help thinking it's because I'm not looking after you. I wanted to wow you with the flowers but they were too much. I can see that now.'

Despite an overwhelming sense of guilt, Lucy felt a bite of anger too. If she were in a better frame of mind, if she wasn't pregnant, if she wasn't making so many stupid mistakes, she would tell Adam it was only a bunch of flowers. It wasn't as if she had let a living creature die.

But Lucy wasn't in a better frame of mind so she said nothing. Yes, they were only flowers, but they were also a symptom of something far more unsettling.

'And it's not just you I've failed,' Adam continued, sighing deeply. 'I've messed things up with Mum too.'

'But you said it went OK.' She held back from framing the remark as a question. She couldn't assume that was what Adam had actually said. She had been too busy worrying about the dead bouquet to pay much heed to what he had told her. 'You are speaking again, aren't you?'

Adam straightened up and, taking Lucy's hand, guided

her on to his knee. He kissed her neck before pressing his cheek against her chest. 'Yes, Mum never stopped,' he said. 'I was the one behaving unreasonably, as you so rightly pointed out. I went there determined to make it up to her but she didn't give me the chance. She's refusing to go to New York now. I did try to get her to change her mind back but she says it's her decision. Not that it matters. It'll still be my fault.'

'If it's Viv's decision, you can't be held responsible.'

'You don't know my brother.'

And that was the thing; Lucy knew very little of Adam's half-brother, other than it pained Adam to talk about him. Scott had been twelve when Viv's second marriage collapsed and it had been his choice to live with his dad. Fifteen-year-old Adam had been left with their mum and, already estranged from his own father, the fractures in the family had deteriorated. Long before Lucy had arrived on the scene, Scott had moved to the States and Adam had cut him out of his life completely. Viv's relationship with Scott was only marginally better, although it was hard to tell because she rarely mentioned his name in front of Adam.

'I did try to make her change her mind.'

'I believe you,' Lucy said, rocking him gently in her arms.

'It seems like she spends her whole life saying sorry, but she can't go back and change a single thing, so why try?'

When Adam fell silent, Lucy chose not to ask the many questions filling her mind. She wanted Adam to open up voluntarily about whatever childhood traumas made his relationship with his mum so fraught and the one with his brother untenable. She was desperate to hear his fears. Anything was better than considering her own.

'How was your day?' he asked. 'Did you do anything else except decimate my bouquet?'

Lucy let the comment pass. 'I went for a walk around Marine Lake with Hannah.'

'You met her?' asked Adam, pulling away from Lucy so he could see her face.

'I said I would.'

'No, you didn't. I was under the impression that you thought seeing Hannah would be too much stimulus for you at the moment. That was what you said.'

'Adam . . .' Lucy began but suddenly her mouth was as parched as the shrivelled flowers she had thrown away.

'When we were lying in bed and you were ignoring what I told you about eating at Mum's, were you having a nice conversation with yourself about meeting Hannah, by any chance?'

'No.'

'So you didn't tell me?'

'Not then, but we'd talked about it.'

'But you didn't think to mention it this morning? Why sneak behind my back, Lucy?' he asked and before she could answer, he added, 'I suppose she's as mad as ever. She hasn't had any more kids, has she?'

'No, she was fine. I liked catching up with her. Look, I called her on the off-chance she was free, it was a last-minute thing. You said I could.'

'I – said – you – could?'

'I didn't mean it like that!'

'Repeat after me,' he said slowly. 'Adam is not my lord and master.'

Lucy felt foolish but Adam held her gaze expectantly.

'You're not my lord and master,' she mumbled quickly. 'I know that. What I meant was, we both said I should see Hannah after Mum set me up.'

'Luce . . .' Adam wiped his hands over his face. 'OK, fine, we said you should see her. Even though we said no such thing. So how was it?'

Lucy felt herself shrink inside but carried on bravely. 'It was OK. She didn't bring the kids with her and, for the record, even Hannah admits her life's in chaos.'

'Just like you said.'

'Yes, just like I said,' Lucy agreed, rather than open up that particular debate again. 'And she doesn't have more kids, but her cat's had kittens.'

'Poor mites. God help them in that house.'

Lucy bit her lip and, wanting to remind him of the people they once were, she said, 'Which is why she's looking for good homes. Remember when we were thinking about getting a kitten?'

'Yeah, I wish we had now. I'd feel better letting you loose with a cat than I would a baby – at least it could look after itself,' he said and, oblivious to how his barbed words had made his wife wince, he added, 'So, aside from adding a cat to our household, what else have you two been conspiring about? Are you going to see her again?'

'Only for business. She wants me to do a portrait of her nan. She died at Christmas and I said I'd meet her grandad to discuss what he wants.'

Adam's body jerked. 'Lucy, you said you'd stop painting.'

Lucy knew she had promised no such thing but she didn't have the stomach for another argument. She could feel Adam tensing as he prepared to slide her off his knee. She stroked the side of his cheek. 'I told her I'd do it after I've had the baby. I'll keep putting her off,' she promised.

'Because it's what you want or because you think it's what I want?' asked Adam, his stare intensifying as he waited for the right answer.

'It's what I want, Adam,' she whispered softly.

Adam lifted the folds of her brushed-cotton shirt and began exploring her body with his hand. He pulled at her vest top until he found a route to her warm flesh. His fingertips were ice cold and she felt a shiver as he worked his way up to cup her breast. As his lips brushed against hers, he whispered, 'That's my girl. Now how about we go to bed and put all of this behind us?'

With a rush of relief, Lucy was eager to agree. Unlike the flowers, she had survived to fight another day.

8

Christine glanced anxiously at her daughter. 'I'd feel better if you came in for a quick cuppa,' she said. 'It's a long drive home.'

'I don't know, Mum. Adam should be back by now.'

Lucy took her hands off the steering wheel and dug her phone out of her pocket. The last text from her husband had been the apology for missing their introductory antenatal class.

Christine peered over her shoulder. 'No message?'

'Nothing,' Lucy said through gritted teeth. 'He can't still be caught up in traffic.'

'It must have been pretty serious to close off part of the motorway. We should be grateful Adam wasn't the one involved in the accident.'

'I know,' Lucy said, 'but I'd told the midwife how supportive he's been and I felt really stupid turning up without him. He knew how important it was to me. He should have left earlier.'

'And Adam will be thinking the exact same thing. Now come inside and relax before you race home to give him an earful.'

Lucy was forced to agree, and not simply because she didn't think she would last the next forty minutes with the baby pressing on her bladder. The delay would give her time to build up the courage to drive back through the tunnel, a journey she would never have chanced if she hadn't needed to pick up her mum as a stand-in. She expected Adam to be mortified when he found out.

There had been a time when Lucy joked with Adam that she was the better driver, but the one-and-a-half-mile drive beneath the Mersey had become a passage of fear. It stemmed from one particular incident when she had been driving through the tunnel with Adam, not long after she moved in with him and before she could use her baby brain as an excuse. Adam had been forced to yank the steering wheel to keep the car from drifting across the narrow lanes before Lucy even knew what was happening. Tonight, it was her anger alone that had kept her focused on driving between the white lines.

'He'll be as disappointed as you,' Christine said after handing Lucy a cup of chamomile tea and taking a seat next to her on the sofa.

Lucy watched the rising steam curl and twist as she sighed. 'He knows how much I want him to feel more involved. So far, all he's been able to do is listen to my complaints about how sick I feel, or how tired I am,' she said, stopping short of adding the more serious complaints about her ineptitude.

Since the disaster with the flowers a month ago, Lucy's life had been peppered with similar mishaps, if not on such a grand scale. She wasn't sure how she had managed to finish her painting of Ralph without calamity, but the end result had been surprisingly good. Lucy had been used to juggling three or four paintings in a month to earn a steady income, but it had been worth the time spent focused on just the one. When she handed over her latest piece to her overjoyed client, she had briefly regretted the call she had made to Hannah to put off her next commission. Her one consolation was that she was now painting for pleasure.

Freed from that sense of trepidation whenever she accepted a new commission, Lucy had made her latest work deliberately abstract. Capturing the ideas she had felt tugging at her imagination the day she had met Hannah, Lucy had produced three canvases that were experimental, to say the least. She had been so pleased with the end result that she had posted photos of them on her website a couple of days ago and although she was apprehensive about how well they would be received, her change in direction had taken the pressure off, as Adam had predicted. The baby was their main priority now.

'I've been trying to get Adam to feel the baby's kicks,' she continued. 'And he said he did the other day but I think he was only saying it to appease me. I want him to get excited about the baby instead of wondering why the hell we ever thought I was ready to be a mother.'

'But you are ready! And do you seriously think he isn't excited?' said Christine with disbelief heavy in her voice. 'He wants this baby as much as you do, Lucy. When you talk about her and your eyes light up, so do his. Trust me, I've been watching.'

'But when I worry, so does he,' Lucy said, lifting her cup to her lips and willing the chamomile to work its magic.

She knew Adam hadn't deliberately missed the class and

he had been full of remorse when he phoned to explain how he was sandwiched between two stationary cars on the M60, but she had refused to make him feel better. The last text he had sent had been a follow-up apology to the one he had tried to make during their call when Lucy had been yelling too much to hear it. She also knew that, however bad Adam felt, at some point she would feel worse and there was a good chance she would be the one apologizing by the end of the night. Even so, she couldn't let go of her anger.

'At the very least he owes *you* an apology. I didn't mean to wreck your night out.'

'Don't be silly. I'm just sorry you had to drive over to Liverpool to pick me up. If I'd known I'd be needed, I wouldn't have had a drink. You don't think anyone noticed I was a bit squiffy, do you?'

'You were there for me, that's the main thing.'

'Perhaps this should serve as a warning. I should be ready for any eventuality.'

'I've still got three more months to go,' countered Lucy. 'And you should be able to go out and celebrate whatever spurious excuse for a celebration you happen to have. What was it this time?'

'Nothing more than surviving another day at the tax office with double the workload and half the staff.'

'You should retire if it's getting too stressful,' said Lucy, almost believing that the suggestion was purely for her mum's benefit.

'I couldn't afford to, not yet,' replied Christine. She looked into the depths of her cup and refused to meet Lucy's gaze when she added, 'And I hate to say this, but I might not be able to reduce my hours either. I haven't put in a request yet because I'm not sure it would get approved.'

Lucy took a gulp of scalding tea that burnt her tongue. 'But you'd be saving them money, surely?'

'Our department is already cut back to the bone and the savings wouldn't be enough to offset the disruption. My best chance would be to wait for a fresh round of budget cuts, or yet another reorganization.' Christine took hold of her daughter's hand when she added, 'I want to help you more than anything but I think we both have to be prepared if it doesn't happen as quickly as we'd like.'

Lucy kept her head down so her mum wouldn't see the tears brimming.

'I'm sorry, this is really bad timing,' Christine said. 'A more sober me would have picked a better day to bring it up.'

'It's not like I was expecting you to be on call twenty-four seven, Mum, and it's fine. It means Adam will have to work from home a bit more than we were planning, that's all. His boss doesn't exactly chain him to the desk. As long as the work's done, I'm sure no one would mind.'

'And Adam will look after you, won't he?'

'Of course,' Lucy said, her instinct to defend him overriding her present annoyance. 'I know he has his moments, like tonight, and he can be . . .'

'Awkward?'

Lucy found herself smiling. 'Something like that,' she said. 'But he's so loving, and incredibly patient.'

'And I'm sure he'll make a really good dad.'

Hoping to take advantage of her mum's loose tongue, Lucy asked, 'What about my dad? Was he a *good* father?

Up until he died, I would have said he was the best, but what did I know? What was he really like, Mum?'

When the sofa creaked as Christine shifted position, Lucy gave her mum's hand a tight squeeze. She wasn't going to make it easy for her to evade the questions she had been dodging for two decades.

'He loved you more than anyone,' Christine said. There was a catch in her throat when she added, 'He idolized you.'

'If that's true, then why did he do what he did?'

'It's—'

With her heart racing, Lucy shook her head. 'Don't say complicated.'

Lucy had never been given much information about the events surrounding her father's death and as a result, she had spent most of her life making up her own theories. Her greatest fear of late was that whatever had been wrong with her dad had been passed on to his daughter, lying in wait until she was at her most vulnerable.

'But it *was* complicated, love,' Christine said.

'Complicated how? What was so bad that he felt he couldn't bear to spend another day with the daughter he idolized?'

'He wasn't thinking straight.'

'I know that,' Lucy said, her words strangled by twenty years of pain. 'No one in their right mind jumps off a bridge for no apparent reason. Why did he do it, Mum? Were there any warning signs? Why wasn't he thinking straight? Was he ill?'

Christine had never spoken of the possibility that Lucy's dad had suffered from a mental illness, but Lucy was beginning to understand how something like that could creep up on a person. He could have been hiding it from everyone, even himself.

Closing her eyes briefly, Christine bowed her head and refused to meet her daughter's gaze. 'It was because of me,' she said at last. 'Your dad and I had a strong relationship when we first married and we told each other everything. But as time went on, we got in the habit of saying nothing rather than worrying or hurting each other. Eventually, we fell out of practice of talking at all except through you. You were the glue that kept us together.'

A shudder ran down Lucy's spine. If she had been the glue that had kept her family together, why wasn't she sitting there with both her parents? What had been wrong with her dad? What was wrong with her? Lucy could feel herself shutting down in panic – did she really want to know how bad things could get?

'My biggest regret is that the last time we talked, we argued and I never got the chance to put things right,' Christine confessed in a whisper.

Her quivering voice gave Lucy the excuse she needed to retreat from the past. 'Oh, Mum, I'm sorry, I didn't mean to upset you,' she said. 'I shouldn't have brought it up, but it's been playing so much on my mind lately.'

'You're about to become a parent yourself and it's natural to want to look back, but you need to concentrate on what lies ahead.'

'I am,' Lucy said, her half-empty cup trembling in her hand as she set it down. 'And if you don't mind, I'd better make a move.'

Lucy worked her way to the edge of the sofa and arched

her back as she stood. She was about to put her phone in her handbag when it beeped.

'Another apology?' asked Christine.

Lucy grimaced as she read the message. 'Actually, it's from Hannah. She wants to know if I still want the kitten. They're ready to leave their mum.' Her friend was practically begging her to take one.

'You're not seriously considering it, are you?'

An image of wilting roses flashed through Lucy's mind but she pushed it away. Adam had said she'd be fine looking after a cat and she had read somewhere that animals had a positive effect on mental health. A kitten would brighten her day and, more importantly, build her confidence in time for the birth of her daughter. Those poor kittens needed homes and even Adam had felt sorry for them.

'It would be nice to have some company through the week, and Adam quite likes the idea,' she said. She was stretching the truth a little, but he had talked about the addition of a cat to their household as if it were a *fait accompli*.

'But you're going to have your hands full as it is when the baby arrives.'

Lucy turned her phone to show her mum the photo Hannah had sent of a fluffy ginger kitten with a handwritten sign in front of it that read, 'I love Lucy.'

Christine pushed her glasses up the bridge of her nose and smiled at the image. 'Aww, he is cute.'

'You could get one too. I don't think she has homes for all of them yet.'

'At least one of us has to keep hold of our senses,' Christine warned.

If the comment was meant to dissuade her daughter from making a rash decision, it had the opposite effect.

'He's been de-flead and wormed but I'll get him health checked anyway and neutered when he's old enough. By the time the baby comes, he'll be all settled in. I might even pick him up on my way home,' Lucy said, liking the idea of snuggling up with a purring kitten that very night.

'Shouldn't you run it past Adam first?'

'After tonight, I really don't think he's in any position to object. Do you?'

'But you're not prepared! You'll need food and a litter tray.'

'And cat litter, and food bowls, toys, a collar, and a bed,' Lucy said as her musings turned into a firm decision. 'And possibly a hot-water bottle to keep him warm until he gets used to not having his brothers and sisters around. There's at least one twenty-four-hour supermarket on my way home. I can work fast.'

With a plan forming in her mind, Lucy messaged Hannah to let her know she was on her way. Her next message was to Adam, warning him that there was a surprise coming and as she pressed send, Christine picked up the coat Lucy had flung across the back of the sofa.

'Are you sure this is a good idea, love?'

'Honestly, it's fine,' she said as she slipped on her coat. 'I'm glad I came in for that cuppa now.'

Lucy was grinning as she dug her hands into her pockets for her car keys, but her smile quickly faded.

'I can't find my keys. What have I done with them?' she said as she searched her handbag. When her fingers failed to connect with anything vaguely key-shaped, she shook it close to her ear in case her sense of touch had deceived her.

Christine disappeared into the hall, and returned a moment later. 'You didn't leave them by the door.'

'You don't think they're still in the ignition, do you?'

'No, I'm sure I remember you locking up.'

Seeing the furrows deepen on her mum's brow, Lucy knew she wasn't certain. She had parked her little Fiat 500 on the road, and for all she knew, someone could have driven off while she sat contemplating whether or not she was responsible enough to take ownership of a kitten. She rushed past her mum and out of the house. The car was where she had left it and when she pulled the handle on the passenger door, she found it locked, confirming she couldn't have left the keys inside. Nevertheless, Lucy cupped her hands around her face and pressed her nose against the window. The keys weren't there.

'Lucy!' shouted her mum from the doorway, her arm raised. 'I found them!'

Walking up the path, Lucy wondered where she had left them this time. She wouldn't be surprised if they were dripping wet because she had tried to flush them down the toilet. 'Where were they?'

'At the back of the sofa. They must have fallen out of your pocket.'

'Thanks, Mum,' Lucy said, taking the keys and keeping tight hold of them. She kissed her mum on the cheek. 'I'd better be off.'

'Are you *sure* about the kitten?' Christine tried one last time.

No, Lucy thought. She was no longer certain about

anything, but she hoped her stubborn streak meant she would never stop trying. She gave her mum one final hug and tried not to notice the spot where her dad might have stood, asking Lucy if she had the right change for the tunnel toll, or recognizing her anxiety and suggesting an alternative route through Widnes and across the bridge.

It was only when Lucy slipped behind the wheel of her car and spotted the flash of coins her mum had left in the cup holder that she was reminded it was a mistake to underestimate a mother.

9

Lucy was sprawled on the sofa with her laptop resting on a cushion and a ginger ball of fur balanced on the generous swell of her stomach. The kitten, who had been in her care for less than a day, paddy-pawed her gently as she sifted through emails and politely declined a couple of requests for portraits. The one message she couldn't dismiss was from someone who wasn't looking for a commission at all, but expressed an interest in her most recent work. What little savings Lucy had wouldn't last for ever and an extra boost to her income would delay the day she had to ask Adam for pin money.

Her potential buyer was interested in all three paintings and Lucy was in the process of arranging a viewing. She knew better than to invite someone she didn't know into her home, especially a man. Adam had given her a lecture the first time she had suggested it, and although she had accused him of being more jealous than concerned, he did have a point.

She had been about to send an email suggesting they meet at a local coffee shop when she heard Adam's car pull up on to the drive. Setting her laptop to one side, she lifted the kitten and tried not to wake him as she placed him on the warmed cushion. He opened his milky blue eyes and gave her a curious look before settling back to sleep.

Adam's keys rattled as he opened the front door and Lucy's smile tightened as she waited patiently. When he didn't appear, she heaved herself up, tugging up her leggings and smoothing out the olive-green smock before padding barefoot to the door. Wrapping her fingers around the handle, she thought she heard the rustle of shopping bags, followed by silence.

The door creaked as she opened it slowly, making her flinch. She had assumed Adam was in the kitchen but he peeked his head around the other side of the staircase. He had put his coat away in the closet but his scarf remained snug round his neck. 'I thought I heard you creeping about.'

There was no telling from Adam's expression how he was feeling and, if anything, it confirmed he shared her sense of confusion. 'Hello,' she said.

Lucy had spent the day going over what had happened after driving back from her mum's the night before. She wasn't sure if she was more scared that she couldn't remember parts of their argument, or that she didn't want to. Her strongest memory was of Adam's first words.

'What the hell's that?' he had asked when she had stumbled into the house laden with pet supplies and a kitten making woeful cries for his mum and litter mates.

'We said we wanted a kitten and here he is! Isn't he sweet?'

Although she'd had a smug look on her face, Lucy's heart

had been hammering against her chest. Adam's glower had been the first warning that she had made another terrible mistake.

'You actually think you can look after a kitten?'

'Why not? You didn't think it was a problem the other day when I mentioned it. You said they practically looked after themselves.'

'Was this before or after you killed off the flowers I gave you? Oh, and let's not forget the plants in the garden last year. Every single living thing you've ever taken responsibility for, you've killed. Why on earth would I think you could look after *that*?' he had said, glaring at the poor mite trembling in Lucy's arms. Or had it been she who had been trembling?

'But you felt sorry for the kittens staying with Hannah,' Lucy had tried. 'You wanted to save one.'

'By bringing it here? Are you *mad*?' he had hissed.

And that was all it had taken to light the touch paper to an anger that Lucy had been unable to control. Those three words. That one accusation.

A quarrel had ensued during which she had become more and more agitated. She had been in the right – Adam had definitely said she could look after one – and besides, he was the one who was meant to be repentant. He should have agreed to anything she wanted, but he had refuted her arguments with ones of his own, and unfortunately, Adam had so much more ammunition. They had thrown insults and accusations at each other from across the kitchen.

'Do you even see the mess you make?' he had yelled, pointing out the greasy smears on cupboard doors. 'I dread to think what state my house is going to be in when you've got a cat *and* a baby to look after.'

'Your house?' she had shouted back. 'I'm not your housekeeper, Adam! I can do what I like in my own home. I can kick off my shoes and leave them where I want! I can wear the same clothes for more than one day if I want! I can leave dirty dishes until the next day – if – I – want. And I can open a packet of biscuits without reaching for the fucking Hoover!'

Lucy couldn't quite remember what else had been on her list, only that she had screeched it from the top of her lungs with her hands balled into fists. Determined to prove a point, she had flung open a cupboard and taken out a container full of porridge oats. She had grabbed a handful and, in a shower of oats, had turned to face her husband again, but to her horror, Adam had been backing away with his arms held out as if to fend off an attack.

'No more,' he had begged. 'Please don't hit me. Please, Lucy.'

Except it had already been too late. Although Lucy had no recollection of laying a hand on Adam, there was a series of angry welts across his neck.

She had been unable to revisit what exactly had happened the evening before when her anger had pulled a red veil over her senses, but the evidence was irrefutable as Adam tugged off his scarf to reveal the scratch marks she had made.

'Adam . . . I think I lost it last night,' she said as she waited for him to put away his things. She heard the click of the closet door closing, but he stayed where he was. 'Actually, I know I did.'

'How have you been feeling today?' he asked when he was ready to face her.

'OK, I suppose.'

'I was worried,' he said, although his tone and expression gave away none of his concern. 'I thought all that hysteria might have done some damage.'

If you were that anxious, Lucy thought, why did you leave me sobbing in the kitchen to clean up the mess on my own? Why did you pretend to be asleep when I went to bed? Why haven't I heard from you all day?

'I have no idea where all that anger came from,' she offered instead.

'But we both know where it was directed,' Adam said, rubbing his neck. 'I accept that I shouldn't have missed the parenting class, and I was ready for the backlash, but that was some way to get back at me, Lucy.'

'I was totally irrational, I know that,' she said, feeling a strong sense of déjà vu. The word *irrational* had featured strongly in their argument.

'Is it still here?'

When Lucy pursed her lips together, her chin wobbled. 'I've been cuddling him all day. He keeps me calm, Adam. I don't want to give him back, but I will if you tell me to.'

'And suddenly I'm the bad guy again.'

Lucy wasn't sure, but she thought his lips were trembling too despite his set jaw. 'I want to make things right. I want to forget all about the argument and if that means removing all evidence, I'm prepared to do it. That's my decision.'

'I used the kitten to explain away the scratch marks at work,' he said. 'I don't think Naomi believed me. She'd love

Ranjit to think my marriage is falling apart while she bangs on about getting engaged. The cat will have to stay so we can keep up the lie you've made me tell.'

Lucy wanted to go to Adam and kiss away the pain but she would feel better if he made the first move. She needed to know that he would remain by her side during this madness – her madness. It was a horrible, horrible word that frightened her, and she needed Adam to pull her back from the brink.

When he shifted position, Lucy took it as an invitation. She rushed towards the arms she was sure would open up for her, but Adam flinched as if expecting her to strike. She buried her head into his shoulder and there was a heart-stopping moment when his arms hung limply by his side, but in the next moment, he was holding her.

'I love you, Adam,' she sobbed. 'I can't live without you.'

'And I love you too,' he whispered. 'I just want my Lucy back.'

Lifting her head, she said, 'I'm here. I'm still here.'

He smoothed the hair back from her forehead and the look in his eyes softened. 'It's not all your fault. I could have reacted better. I should have realized how the kitten was simply another symptom, and the more pregnant you are,' he said, taking a step back to glance at her maternity smock, 'the more likely it is that your moods will be erratic. I think I know where the anger came from and so do you. You're scared that whatever affected your dad is now affecting you and, I have to be honest, it's getting harder to pretend there isn't a connection.'

'If I'd known what I would be like, I'd never have let you marry me,' Lucy confessed. 'I never really gave much thought to what happened to Dad, or at least, not as much as I do now.'

'You've been in denial, that's all,' Adam told her. 'Look at how you used to live your life, pretending you were the same as all those friends who refused to acknowledge how much you were struggling. When you bounded into my life, you acted as if you didn't have a care in the world, but anyone who was willing to take the time to get to know you could have seen through your act. It was inevitable that the past would catch up with you one day. All it was going to take was one trigger. Who knows what it was with your dad, but pregnancy seems to be what might have set you off.'

'But if you knew I was such a screw-up, why did you ever bother with me?'

He kissed the top of her head. 'Because I wanted to. You're my screw-up now, Lucy. I promised to look after you and I will. I've juggled my workload and I'm working from home for the rest of the week. I'll need to lock myself away in the office at some point, but I thought now might be a good time to start on the nursery.'

Lucy followed Adam's gaze to the large carrier bag sitting by the front door. 'What's that?'

'Paint.'

There were two spare bedrooms to choose from for the nursery and Adam had offered to relocate his office to the box room, but Lucy could tell he was loath to do it. If she needed him to stay at home more, it made sense that he should be comfortable, and they could always move the baby into the larger room when she was older.

The question of décor, however, had yet to be agreed.

She planned to paint a mural and had initially dreamt up a gender-neutral scene with forest animals. That had been back when they hadn't known the sex of the baby and Lucy had assumed they would be using her old cot with its squirrel and bunny rabbit motif. Lately, she had toyed with the idea of unicorns dancing on fluffy white clouds, but she had yet to convince Adam about having so much sky blue as the background colour in a little girl's room.

'What colour did you get?'

Adam returned to the bags and pulled out a five-litre pot of silk emulsion. It took all of Lucy's self-control not to pull a face. 'Pink,' she said, flatly.

'Obviously. You were right, it's the only colour we could have picked. I did look at a pastel shade, but it's such a small room and I thought this would make a bigger impact.'

Adam looked so pleased with himself that Lucy had to stop herself from pointing out that the deep shade he had chosen would make the room appear twice as small. She had no idea what had given him the impression she wanted any shade of pink as the backdrop for her mural, but she must have said something, so she concentrated on how she could work with what she had. It was entirely possible that unicorns lived in a world with bubble-gum-pink skies, and she could always make the clouds bigger and fluffier. 'I can't wait to get started.'

Adam shook his head. 'Oh no, you're not coming near it. All that stretching won't be good for you and we can't have you getting paint on your new clothes,' he said, suppressing a smile when he added, 'Although that shirt thing you're wearing would make a good coverall when you've finished with it.'

'You don't like it?' she asked, tugging at the hem and giving Adam a chance to reconsider. It was getting harder to feel attractive and a little white lie was all she needed.

'I was joking, Luce. But if you're feeling *that* pregnant,' he said, glancing at her expanding girth that was emphasized by the smock, 'it's all the more reason not to take on more than you have to. It's rest for you from now on.'

'But I need to paint the mural.'

'Oh, add that at a later date,' he said with a waft of the hand. 'You don't seem to know how to slow down, and I'm sorry, but after last night, I'm putting my foot down. You invest too much of yourself in those pictures of yours and it's been draining you.'

With the memory of their most recent argument haunting her, Lucy wasn't ready for another, and besides, he had a point. 'OK, I will take it easier,' she said, which in her mind didn't mean giving up completely. 'No mural, but I do have to go out tomorrow. I think I've found a buyer for my new paintings.'

'Don't tell me, a housewife with more money than sense,' guessed Adam.

Lucy didn't correct him. Adam might suggest tagging along if he knew she were meeting a strange man on her own, and like he said, he had work to do.

'I promise I won't be out for long, I'm going to the café at Carr Farm garden centre and I'll be as quick as I can.'

'It's probably better that you're not around to distract me.'

As if her presence alone were distraction enough, Adam put down the paint pot and took Lucy in his arms. 'Hungry?'

he asked, and when Lucy smiled hopefully, he laughed and kissed the tip of her nose. 'Later. I need sustenance.'

'Me too,' she admitted as all her anxieties fell away. 'All I've had is a bowl of soup today and I didn't finish that.'

Her ears pricked as she heard a gentle thud from the living room followed by a tiny mewl. Her kitten sounded more like a baby chick than a cat, and his chirping grew louder and more desperate as he searched for someone to take care of him.

'Have we still got steak in the fridge?' asked Adam, only to glance over his shoulder and add, 'Or have you fed it to the cat?'

'He's a kitten, not a tiger,' she said. 'Hey, maybe that's what we should call him. Tigger.'

'Whatever. Your cat, your choice.'

Adam had forgiven her, but not enough to register more than a passing interest in their new addition, and he disappeared into the kitchen while Lucy crouched down to pick up the kitten. She caught up with Adam in time to hear him mutter something under his breath. Her blood ran cold. She could smell gas.

She watched in dismay as Adam raced to the patio doors and flung them open. 'I didn't leave the gas on,' she said with absolute certainty. 'I used the hob to heat up my soup but I definitely turned it off, and I checked it was off I don't know how many times. It wasn't on.'

Adam's eyes narrowed.

Holding the kitten against her chest, Lucy could feel its tiny heart beating as fast as hers. 'I – I suppose it's possible I lowered the burner but didn't turn it off completely. Was there a flame?' she asked.

'No, but it's fine. These things are sent to try us,' Adam said, looking at the cat.

She couldn't read his expression as he approached, and for a split second she felt blinded by a flood of adrenaline – or fear. Holding on tightly to the kitten, she said, 'I'm really, really s—'

'Don't say sorry,' Adam ordered. 'We both know you can't help the way you are, especially when you're so easily distracted.'

With some hesitation, Lucy was drawn into his arms with the kitten pressed between them and temporarily hidden from Adam's sight.

'It could be my hormones,' Lucy offered, preferring the less terrifying explanation for her worsening condition. 'And it won't be for ever.'

'Won't it?'

The draught forcing its way through the kitchen was bitterly cold but as Adam kissed her forehead, Lucy felt a warmth rise up from her chest and she became choked with emotion. 'I'm not my dad and I will do better – for as long as you're willing to put up with me.'

Adam pulled away without giving her the answer she had been searching for. 'You shouldn't stay in here. The fumes won't be good for you or the baby. Go and watch your garbage TV while I get on with the cooking.'

Lucy didn't move. She wanted to tell him that she cared about their baby too. She would never repeat history and leave him with a child to bring up on his own, but to say such a thing would be to admit that the possibility existed. It wasn't that she would ever do anything deliberately but, as the fading scent of gas in the air proved, she posed a real threat to the safety of herself and those around her – including her unborn child.

'Go!' Adam said, his eyes full of playful light.

Her husband seemed to have accepted her carelessness but Lucy knew that now was not the time to let her guard down.

10

Lucy had arrived to meet her potential buyer at Carr Farm but before heading over to the garden centre and the café, she felt compelled to check the boot. To her relief, she hadn't imagined the struggle it had taken to fit three canvases into the limited space, and Mr Judson's trip over from Southport wasn't going to be wasted.

The garden centre was surprisingly busy for an overcast Thursday afternoon, and if Lucy hadn't been there to sell her paintings she might have been tempted to take a look around, not that she would be buying any plants after last year's fiasco. She had tried her best to nurture the raspberry and blueberry shrubs, but her best hadn't been good enough and their leaves had blackened long before they had a chance to bear fruit.

After grabbing a herbal tea and taking a seat where she would be clearly visible, Lucy sent Mr Judson a message to let him know she had arrived. Her photo was on her website and the buyer had her at an advantage, but as the minutes ticked by and no one paid her any heed, she found herself skimming through their exchange of emails.

Satisfied that she was in the right place at the right time, Lucy settled into her seat to watch a couple of mums pushing prams through the maze of tables. Wheels caught on chair legs and coats were pulled off seats, but the women simply made their apologies and were laughing when they sat down. The younger woman, who looked no more than twenty, bent over a pram and lifted up a crying baby. She rested him on her shoulder and with a few pats on the back, her son settled. She made it look impossibly easy.

'Lucy Martin?'

Swallowing the lump of anxiety that had lodged in her throat, Lucy tore her eyes from the mothers and found a disarmingly attractive man standing in front of her. She had imagined her buyer to be a retired executive but Mr Judson was in his early thirties. His clothes were casual but perfectly tailored and, like his cologne, suggested designer labels. He had a kind face with blue eyes that were a shade more violet than Adam's. His features were more symmetrical too, with a strong jaw and chiselled chin, and his dark blond hair was long enough to need sweeping away from his brow as he returned Lucy's intense gaze.

'Sorry,' she said when she realized she had been staring. Extending her hand, she added, 'You must be Mr Judson.'

'Pleased to meet you.'

When he shrugged off his jacket, revealing broad shoulders, Lucy made another apology. 'I've already bought a drink. Can I get you something?'

'How about you finish that, erm . . .' His mouth twitched into a smile as he peered over her cup. 'Sorry, what exactly is that?'

'Lemon and green tea. Would you like one?'

'I'm fine for now, but if we do have a second cuppa, that's what I'll have too.'

Lucy found herself staring again. There was something about the way Mr Judson's mouth curved around the word 'cuppa', as if he wasn't quite used to using it. 'You don't sound like you're from Southport.'

'No, as a matter of fact, I grew up on the Wirral,' he said, which wasn't the answer she had expected from the man with a transatlantic twang. 'But I've moved around a lot since then. Most people say I have an English accent, but can't be specific. It's only when I come home and spend time with my dad that some of his Scouse accent rubs off on me.'

'Come home from where?' asked Lucy as she brought her cup to her mouth and peered at Mr Judson through lemon-scented steam.

'Overseas,' he said, and before she could challenge his evasion, he added, 'So tell me about Lucy Martin. Your paintings are stunning, by the way. There's such emotion to them that I could look at them all day. You have brought them with you, haven't you? Not sold them already?'

'Don't worry, they're in the boot of my car,' Lucy said before doubt crept in again. When she had opened the boot, she had seen the dust sheet covering what she assumed were three paintings. She should have checked properly.

Lucy's grip tightened on her cup as she took a sip of tea to calm herself. From the other side of the café, she heard a baby's cry, more urgent this time, and she noted that the young mum she had envied earlier had become flustered. Returning her attention to her mysterious buyer, she realized he was waiting for more information. She took a deep breath and reminded herself of the passion for her work that this stranger had obviously recognized.

'I've been painting all my life. It was my dad who taught me to draw. He was a brilliant artist and ran a successful marketing company, but designing logos was never going to give him the sense of satisfaction that painting could. I didn't want to make the same mistake,' she said, her eyes dimming briefly. She told herself to focus on their shared love of art that would never be extinguished as long as she painted.

'I went to art college in Edinburgh,' she continued, 'and made money over the summers at festivals by selling very quick and dirty sketches for the revellers.' She was laughing when she added, 'I used to include little details, like non-existent slogans on their T-shirts that my subjects wouldn't notice until they'd sobered up, and plenty came back with friends who wanted me to draw them too. I hardly made a fortune, but it was enough to help me set up a proper business for more discerning customers.'

'But your paintings, or should I say *my* paintings, are so unlike anything else in your portfolio. Why the change?' he asked, his tone serious despite the twinkle in his eye.

Lucy leaned back in her seat to expose her bump but she wasn't sure her latest work should be written off as another side effect of her pregnancy. She recalled the palette knife in her hand as she captured the drama of a gull's wings slicing through sea mist, something that couldn't be achieved with the fine brushes she relied upon for her portraits. Her seascapes reflected the exhilaration she had felt as she splashed colour on to the canvas and the images she had uploaded didn't do the paintings justice. She couldn't wait to show Mr Judson the real thing, although at that moment, he was more interested in the swell of her belly.

'I can only think that motherhood must agree with you because you've captured something in those paintings that makes them breathtaking.'

Lucy's eyes had been sparkling and the urge to cry took her by surprise. She had no idea where the tears came from, or perhaps she did. She wanted to be the woman Mr Judson imagined he was dealing with – the fearless artist and mother-to-be who had dared to put her soul into her most recent work. Lucy wiped her eye casually, but nothing escaped the notice of the man who was watching her. Mr Judson picked up a serviette and passed it to her.

'Sorry about that,' she said. 'I'm at the mercy of my hormones.'

'No need to apologize. Is it the painting that gets your emotions stirred up, or is it life in general?'

'These days, seeing so much as a wilting flower can set me off,' she said, tipping her head towards the small glass vase holding a single gerbera. The points of its bright yellow petals had faded to brown, and she had avoided looking at it from the moment she had sat down.

Mr Judson reached for the vase and, twisting in his seat, placed it on the empty table behind him. 'Is that better?'

'Yes, thank you, Mr Judson,' said Lucy, feeling unabashed despite blubbing like a fool. There was something about her new acquaintance that put her at her ease, something familiar. 'And please, I can't keep calling you Mr Judson. You do have a first name, don't you?'

'Yes, I do,' he said.

From across the room, the baby's wails reached new

heights, but Lucy's gaze remained fixed on her client's hands. He was tapping his fingers against his thumb, back and forth. The air became thick with theories as to why this perfect stranger wanted to remain so, and the answer was surprisingly simple; he wasn't a perfect stranger at all. The family resemblance was subtle but unmistakable. 'Please don't say it's Scott,' she whispered.

'If I say yes, do you promise not to run away?'

Lucy felt the back of her neck prickle as she was caught by an irrational fear that Adam had forgone clearing out the spare room and followed her. She had let him think she was meeting a woman so he wouldn't worry, but the lie, once exposed, would be all the worse when she told him she had met his brother. 'Why are you here?'

'I wanted to meet my sister-in-law,' he said. 'I wanted to meet the woman before being introduced to the wife. I thought I'd get a better understanding of who you were without Adam standing next to you.'

'I would have thought there's little chance of us being introduced,' Lucy said. 'I don't know what happened between you and my husband, but I do know he won't want to see you. He'll be furious that you've got me here on a pretext.' As she spoke, she could feel Adam's anger rising up in her chest. She had taken this man at face value and he had made a fool of her at a time when she was doing a pretty good job all by herself. She couldn't imagine how someone she had known all of fifteen minutes could hurt her so deeply, but he had. 'I have to go.'

'No, please,' Scott said, his open palms motioning for Lucy to stay. 'Let me explain.'

She folded her arms across her chest. If she was going

to have to explain herself to Adam, it would be foolish to leave with half a story. 'Go on.'

'I haven't spoken to Adam for the best part of ten years. I haven't lived with him since I was twelve and what contact we did have was difficult to the point of painful. I don't think it will come as any surprise to know that I'm as reluctant as Adam to pick up where we left off.'

'So why try?'

Scott resumed his finger tapping. If it was meant to make her think he looked nervous and vulnerable, it wasn't working. 'Our relationship didn't affect just the two of us, it affected the whole family. It's always been difficult seeing Mum without raking up the past, and for too many years we didn't try. Inviting her over to visit this spring was my way of healing some old wounds, and I almost had her convinced until Adam got involved.'

'He tried to persuade her to go to New York. *He's* a good man,' Lucy said.

There was a coldness in Scott's eyes that hadn't been there earlier when he said, 'If Adam had wanted Mum to fly over to the States, I think we both know he would have got his way.'

'He did try,' Lucy told Scott firmly, not liking the man emerging from his disguise.

'I didn't mean to suggest . . . Look, I didn't come here to perform a character assassination on my brother. I imagine you love him very much and I hope you're a good influence on him.' He paused to check her reaction. She remained stony-faced.

'What do you want, Scott?'

'My dad had a heart attack last year and nearly losing

him made me re-evaluate my life and the people in it. When Mum and Dad divorced and I opted to live with Dad, I wasn't choosing between them, Lucy. I was choosing where I stood the best chance of being happy, and while that proved to be the right decision for me, it wasn't for Mum. I want to put things right and I thought . . .' He rested his elbows on the table and dropped his head into his hands. Raking his fingers through his hair, he looked up into Lucy's face, beseeching her to trust him again. 'I hoped that, with Adam settled and about to have a family of his own, I could have a little of my mum back. I think Mum hoped the same, but it looks like none of us can escape the past until Adam and I repair the damage, or at least paper over the cracks.'

'And what do you expect from me?'

'To help persuade him to stay when I turn up unexpectedly at Mum's on Mother's Day.'

Lucy's stomach lurched. 'Which would mean I'd have to keep this meeting a secret from Adam for the next week and a half. Do you seriously expect me to do that?'

'Not for me, no,' he said, 'but I was hoping you might do it for Mum.' When Lucy failed to respond, he added, 'All I want is for us to reach a point where she doesn't have to feel like she's taking sides. I don't want to create a scene – and if that does happen, I promise I'll be the first to leave.'

Lucy took a gulp of tea, swallowing hard to dislodge the fear constricting her throat. 'You're still asking me to lie to Adam.'

'I'm asking you to forget this meeting ever happened.'

Lucy picked up her handbag. Scott couldn't know that

she had already lied about who she was meeting. 'It's a deceit, whichever way you look at it.'

'It is,' Scott agreed, 'and I'm sorry for putting you in an impossible position, but if you tell Adam now, you know things are bound to escalate. Adam won't stop at cutting me out of his life, he'll scare Mum into doing the same – again.'

'How could you do this? All that rubbish about liking my paintings. You were conning me,' she said, her voice a harsh whisper as his lies cut into her. She had to get away.

Scott was one step behind as Lucy left the cafeteria. 'I was genuinely interested in your work, Lucy. I *am* interested. I swear I wouldn't have said those things if I didn't mean it. I still want to buy the seascapes.'

'Not a chance,' she said, zigzagging her way through the shop displays in the hope that she would lose her stalker.

Stepping outside, a fine drizzle soaked into Lucy's curly mane and gave her the impetus to hurry across the car park to her Fiat. She was reaching for the door handle when Scott stepped in front of her.

'Lucy, I'm sorry, I didn't mean to upset you. It was a stupid, stupid idea, and you're right, I didn't think things through. Would it be better if I stayed away on Mother's Day?' He paused briefly and Lucy's cold stare gave him the answer. 'Of course, you're right. It would be a disaster.'

Taller than Adam, Scott towered over her. Her glare intensified and he took a step back.

'You remember when I said I wanted to meet you before being introduced to Adam's wife? I wanted you to meet me too. I don't know what you've heard, but the person you met back there,' he said, pointing in the direction of the café, 'the man who would dearly love to buy your paintings, that's the genuine me. That's who I am. I don't expect you to take my word above Adam's, but please don't think too badly of me for trying to make amends.'

'Whatever,' she said. 'Can I go now?'

His smile was tentative when he said, 'I was rather hoping you'd show me your paintings.'

Lucy kept her jaw clenched and her gaze fixed on the car door. She didn't like being played, but she had been so scared when she had posted photos of her paintings online for others to judge. Adam had said they were 'nice', but Lucy wasn't looking for nice, she was looking for the kind of reaction Scott demonstrated when she found herself opening the boot and pulling back the dust sheet.

Scott brushed against her in his haste to take a closer look. 'Can I pick them up?'

The canvases had been placed on top of each other as carefully as Lucy could manage and she was relieved to see that all three were present, and that they had survived the journey unscathed. 'You need to be careful,' she said. 'The paint is quite thick in parts and won't be completely dry yet.'

Wiping a film of drizzle from his face, Scott said, 'And I don't suppose I should get them wet either.'

Lucy collected up the dust sheet and with Scott's help, created a canopy over the boot. Her brother-in-law dipped beneath it while Lucy stood in the rain and watched him devour her work with his eyes. If Scott was play-acting, he was doing a very good job.

'I remember walking across to Hilbre Island when we were kids to see the seals,' he said as he examined the last painting. 'You might find this hard to believe, but we had some good times when we were younger. Although, as I recall, Adam did try to get me to race off towards the sinking sand. I dread to think what would have happened if Dad hadn't kept a beady eye on us both. I'm the first to admit I was a handful, but I never really understood why we grated against each other so much. Our fights were horrendous, but with Adam being three years older, I usually let him win.' He lifted the dust sheet higher so he could offer Lucy a boyish smile. 'Actually, I didn't have much choice.'

Lucy's mind filled with questions. She wanted to know what had turned those fights into battles, and the battles into wars. How bad must it have been for a twelve-year-old boy to want to leave his mum? She imagined the answers each brother would give would be different, and Scott's version of events was not the one she wanted to hear.

'What are we going to do, Scott?' she asked.

'I came back home specifically to see Adam, and while it's not something I've been looking forward to, I have to at least try.'

She shook her head. 'He won't agree to meet you.'

The canopy sagged. 'I'm thirty-three years old, Lucy,' he said, 'and I miss my mum. I don't want to be her guilty secret. All I'm asking is that she feels able to carry on talking to me on the phone when number one son arrives on her doorstep, instead of hanging up – which is what she does now.'

'It'll be a disaster if you turn up on Mother's Day.'

'Will you be visiting Mum any other time?'

'Adam drops by to see her now and again, but it's usually on the spur of the moment.'

'I'll be heading back home in a couple of weeks, which limits my options.'

Neither could think of a single alternative as Scott dismantled the makeshift canopy and set the canvases upright in order to wrap them in the damp cloth. He turned to find Lucy giving him a curious look.

'We had a deal and I am taking them,' he said with a twinkle in his eye that gave Lucy a shiver. 'I swear, I have no qualms about wrestling a pregnant woman for these paintings. They are utterly, utterly amazing and I'm so proud that my actual sister-in-law painted them.'

'I don't know . . .'

'I'll be taking them back to New York with me. Adam need never know,' Scott said before letting his shoulders droop. 'Unless you're going to tell him?'

'If you were planning on making a good impression on me,' Lucy said as she swiped a damp curl from her cheek, 'can I say now that you've failed miserably?'

Her brother-in-law tucked his paintings under one arm and closed the boot. He had that smile on his face again, the one that made him look like he would never intentionally hurt anyone. Lucy's head told her not to trust him but she found herself warming to her brother-in-law despite herself.

Pulling an envelope of money from his pocket, Scott pressed it into her hand and, for a split second, Lucy thought he might kiss her cheek, but he pulled away and said, 'You're underselling yourself, you do know that, don't you?'

Lucy ought to have felt a thrill as she watched a satisfied customer drive off with her paintings, but Scott had left her with a dilemma that filled her with dread. If she told

Adam she had misled him about meeting a woman, he might leap to the conclusion that she knew exactly who she was going to see. But if she kept quiet, how safe was her secret with Scott and what did he plan to do next? She hadn't agreed to anything, in fact she was confused about what the final outcome had been.

In no rush to head home, Lucy returned to the garden centre to use some of the money she had earned to buy gifts for her mum and Viv. She could feel her baby kicking away, but she suspected her impending motherhood wasn't the only reason this Mother's Day was going to be one to remember.

11

The TV chef was explaining what spices he was adding to a bubbling pot but his words floated past Lucy as she stared at the screen. Her laptop had slid off her knee after a morning spent online searching a forum for tips, advice and, more particularly, a little hope from other first-time mums, but it had been to no avail. Not one person complained of symptoms as extreme as hers, and if there were any other terrified mums out there, they were as reluctant as Lucy to draw attention to their inadequacies.

Planting her feet on the floor, Lucy wriggled her toes but couldn't quell the restlessness that started in her fingertips and scuttled through the rest of her body. Her longing to go to her studio had intensified in the week since her ill-fated meeting with Scott but even if she were willing to go against Adam's advice, she couldn't sneak past his office without being heard.

Lunch with her mum in Liverpool city centre might have been an option and was something she had done quite regularly when she had first moved to West Kirby, but her current agitation would make a drive through the tunnel more fraught than ever, and her need for regular toilet breaks ruled out taking the train.

With no choice but to stay where she was, Lucy slumped back against the sofa and almost squashed Tigger in the process. Relocating him to the safety of a cushion, she let her hands explore the rise and fall of her bump. In a matter of months, it wouldn't be a kitten falling victim to her clumsiness but a real baby. Her daughter was already perfectly formed, with eyes that opened and ears that listened, and although there were periods of the day when Lucy knew she was sleeping, this wasn't one of them. Feeling a strong kick, she pressed her hand to the unseen foot and the connection she felt took her by surprise.

'Hello,' she said in a low whisper for fear of being overheard. Was it normal to talk to your bump? Lucy hoped so because it felt right when she added, 'I'm your mum.'

She couldn't know if her daughter heard, but Tigger grew curious and Lucy waited until he was curled up on the summit of her swollen belly before resuming her conversation.

'I love you,' she said. 'In fact I've loved you all my life. Even at school, I used to draw pictures of us together. I knew my first child would be a daughter.' She stopped and pressed her lips together. She had imagined three children in total: girl, boy, girl. Her eldest would be blonde like her daddy – she had got Adam spot on – while her middle child would have jet-black hair for some odd reason. Her younger daughter would be the redhead and Lucy had imagined comforting her when she was made the butt of all the ginger jokes. Not once in all her imaginings had Lucy been anything except the perfect mother.

'I took it for granted that I'd be able to protect you,' she continued. 'And I promise that I will. I'll do whatever it takes, but right now, I don't know what that is. If I can go out shopping and not realize I've forgotten my purse until I get to the till, who's to say I won't come home one day without your pram? I suppose there's always online shopping.'

The laugh caught in her throat and when she swallowed, she tasted the saltiness of tears. 'I keep telling myself to brush them all off as silly mistakes but how many times do you hear of tragedies caused by one momentary lapse? How many people have died because they left the gas on? How am I going to keep you safe?'

'We'll manage.'

Lucy turned towards the sound of Adam's voice. He had crept downstairs unheard and she had no way of knowing how long he had been listening. 'I'm not mad, talking to her, am I?' she asked.

'I must admit, you did have me worried when I heard voices,' Adam said as he knelt down in front of her. 'But if you have to share your worries, I'd rather you shared them with me.'

Lucy had thought she could tell Adam anything and everything, and yet she had kept from him one gigantic, brother-shaped secret that had given her sleepless nights. There had been moments, like this, when she was tempted to confess her sins. She should have told him as soon as she returned home from the garden centre but with each passing day, it had become more difficult to explain, or justify, why she hadn't.

There was something about Scott that made Lucy want

to give him the benefit of the doubt, but what did she know? She prayed that he would decide against showing up at Viv's on Sunday, or if he did, that he wouldn't betray her trust. She had been tempted to contact him again so she would be prepared for what might happen, but she couldn't risk being drawn any deeper into his plans and had already blocked Scott's mobile number and the email account he had set up in a false name. With any luck, he would simply return to New York and Lucy's secret would be safe for as long as she could live with it.

Adam's piercing eyes, which weren't as blue as Scott's, pulled her from her guilty thoughts. 'Sorry,' she said, and only she knew exactly why she was apologizing.

When Adam plucked the kitten from his resting place, Tigger's claws snagged on her jersey dress. Lucy unhooked him and Adam plopped him down on the floor out of sight.

As she listened to the kitten's pitiful cries, she said, 'He loves you.'

'He's a blinking nuisance.'

Lucy smiled. 'I know when you're lying. You love him too.'

Adam leant over and pressed his lips gently against her bump. 'I love this little one more.'

Guiding Adam's hand to the spot where she had been directing her conversation earlier, Lucy said, 'She's been having her own little disco in there this morning.'

'And typical of our daughter, she goes quiet when I'm around. "Nothing to see here, Dad."'

As if to prove him wrong, Lucy felt a limb push against the confines of her womb. 'You must have felt that,' she said.

Adam smiled. 'Hard to miss,' he said. 'I can't wait to meet her.'

Lucy managed to return Adam's smile but she couldn't share his sentiment. Her daughter was safer where she was.

'We will manage, Lucy,' he said. 'Don't lose faith in yourself.'

Dropping her gaze, she said, 'I think it might be too late for that. Promise me you'll never stop loving me.'

'Never.'

'No matter what I do?'

Adam's eyes narrowed. If he asked her now what lay so heavily on her conscience, she would tell him. 'I'd rather that wasn't put to the test,' he said. 'You shouldn't give up so easily.'

'I'm not.'

Lucy could hear scratching as Tigger attempted to climb up Adam's leg. Adam shifted uncomfortably but it wasn't the kitten that worried him. 'Promise you won't keep things from me.'

'Like what?' she asked as Adam's agitation reached her racing heart. Did he know?

'You left your purse when you went shopping?'

Adam had heard her earlier confession to the baby. She tried to relax. 'It wasn't worth mentioning.'

'Everything is worth mentioning if it worries you,' he said. Leaning closer, his eyes widened as he looked into her soul. 'I never want to be in your mum's position. I'm telling you now; I'd never forgive myself if you didn't give me the chance to help you.'

Lucy felt the air thicken as she drew breath into her open mouth. 'That will never happen, Adam. *Never*,' she said sharply.

Adam kissed her stomach. 'I didn't mean to make you angry, but you know I had to say something.'

'I'm not angry,' she said. She was scared. 'I'm more determined than ever to prove that you have nothing to worry about.'

'Good.'

Adam straightened up and looked down at the kitten. There was the sound of snagging as he prised Tigger off his trouser leg and shoved him out of the way so he could stand and stretch his back. 'I'm done with work for now so I'll carry on with the nursery. I should have it finished today, but lunch first. I'm making an omelette, if you want one?'

It felt too early to eat, but unlike Lucy, Adam had risen at an ungodly hour. His latest complaint was how hot she was in bed, and it wasn't meant as a compliment. 'I could manage a small one,' she said.

Adam reached out a hand. 'Fancy helping me crack some eggs?'

'Breaking things is my speciality,' she said as she let Adam lead her to the kitchen.

While Lucy fetched the eggs from the fridge, she ignored the sound of surface cleaner being squirted on the kitchen counter. She had been meticulous in cleaning the kitchen earlier and if there was so much as a crumb, it must have been planted by some evil fairy.

'I used the last of the cheddar last night,' Adam said, 'but if you fancy a cheese omelette, there's grated in the freezer.'

With the box of eggs in one hand, Lucy opened the freezer. She didn't have to pull very hard because the door had been left slightly ajar. 'Shit,' she said under her breath as she looked at the sheet of ice crystals forming around the freezer compartments. Crouching down, she shoved Tigger out of the way and used her fingernails to scrape away the ice as quietly as she could. She gave one of the drawers a hard tug, but it was frozen solid.

'Want me to try?'

Lucy took Adam's hand and stood up without looking at him.

'When did you last go in there?' he asked.

They had both been in the freezer that morning but Adam's automatic assumption was that Lucy had been the one to leave it open. It annoyed her even though he was probably right. 'I used frozen blueberries in my porridge.'

There was a loud crack as Adam broke through the ice and tugged open a drawer. He pulled out the bag of grated cheese and shook it to create a miniature snowstorm. 'We'll have to use up what we can and throw the rest away.'

'But it's only been open a couple of hours, three at most. The food will be fine.'

'Do you really want to take that chance?' he asked. He was doing his best not to sound angry but Lucy could see his jaw twitching.

'I just think . . .'

'Sorry, but you're the last person I'd want to take advice from right now, Lucy,' he said as he slammed the freezer door shut. 'Have you ever had food poisoning?'

Lucy shook her head. She could feel the tickle of a teardrop in the corner of one eye but blinked it away furiously.

'Well I have and it's not nice,' Adam lectured. 'And for a pregnant woman, I'd say it was downright dangerous. I can't believe you would want to take that risk.'

Lucy retreated to the counter where Adam had set out a bowl, and began cracking eggs. 'When did you get food poisoning?' she asked, hoping to redirect the conversation to someone or somewhere else.

'When I was a kid. Mum nearly finished the lot of us off.'

Lucy smashed another egg against the side of the bowl. 'Were you really ill?'

'Not as bad as some,' Adam said, deftly avoiding mentioning anyone by name. 'The fuse box had tripped while we were out and when we came back the fridge freezer was standing in a pool of water. Mum insisted, like you, that it would be all right and she went ahead and switched everything back on. It was about a week later that we got around to eating the twice-thawed pork joint for our Sunday lunch, but in a matter of hours we were queuing up for the bathroom.'

'All four of you?'

'Yep,' Adam said, taking the bowl from Lucy.

Lucy stepped aside, not knowing what to do or how to help. 'There must have been some good times that you remember about your childhood,' she said.

Adam stilled the fork he was using to thrash the eggs into a scrambled mess. 'Yeah sure, and that was one of them.'

Lucy tried to give him a look, but any power she had over her husband was on the wane and he released a sigh of pure exasperation as he turned away. 'I'll sort through the mess in the freezer after lunch. The nursery will have to wait.'

'We can call in at the supermarket on our way back from Mum's tomorrow and stock up.'

'Since when were we going to your mum's?'

'I need to drop off her Mother's Day present,' she said. 'I did tell you.'

'No, you didn't.'

'I did, Adam,' she said, her voice trailing off. They had been watching TV when they had talked about their plans for the weekend. It had been a couple of nights ago, three at most. She had been dozing but she could repeat verbatim their conversation. She had told him they needed to go and he hadn't disagreed.

'We're supposed to be going shopping for nursery furniture,' Adam insisted.

They *had* agreed to shop for furniture but that was going to be the weekend after Mother's Day. Lucy was about to tell Adam as much when another snatch of their conversation floated to the surface of her fallible memory. He had made a remark about not planning too far ahead because she was bound to lose track.

'But I need to see Mum this weekend,' Lucy said. She took a sharp intake of breath as a thought struck her, one that might get her out of another difficulty. 'Could we visit both our mums on Sunday? We could make a quick trip to Viv's in the morning and have lunch with Mum later. She wouldn't mind.'

'Christine might not, but my mum would,' Adam snapped. 'She's been going on about preparing an afternoon tea and has ordered some fancy cakes from the deli.'

‘That’s not like her,’ Lucy said with a sinking heart. It sounded like Viv was expecting an extra special visitor. ‘So what do I do about Mum?’

Eggs sizzled as Adam poured the omelette mixture into the frying pan. So confident was he about what he was doing that he kept his gaze fixed on Lucy until eventually his features softened into something resembling her loving and caring husband again. ‘I tell you what, why don’t you nip to your mum’s for an hour tomorrow while I add the finishing touches to the nursery that I was meant to do today?’

‘Go on my own through the tunnel?’ Lucy asked.

‘Make your mind up. If you don’t want to see your mum, we could always post her present.’

‘No, it’s OK. I’ll go the long way around over the bridge, if you don’t mind me being out a bit longer.’

Adam shrugged. ‘As long as you think you can manage the drive.’

‘I’ll be fine,’ Lucy said, her smile quivering. ‘And I’ll empty the freezer later. You don’t have to do it.’

‘No, I’d rather it was done properly,’ he said. Sprinkling grated cheese on top of the omelette, he added casually, ‘What would you have done if I wasn’t here, Lucy?’

She froze.

‘I have a sneaking suspicion you wouldn’t have told me about defrosting the freezer, like you didn’t tell me about forgetting your purse,’ Adam mused as he continued with his task. ‘I think you would have closed the door and pretended it hadn’t happened. I wouldn’t have known anything about it until it was too late. You could have made us both seriously ill.’

Lucy turned away to hide the fresh tears which had sprung to her eyes. What he said was probably true.

'You could have gone into early labour and the baby might have been born with complications, or worse. How would you have lived with yourself if that had happened?'

'I don't know,' Lucy said, but it was a lie. If she lost her precious baby through her own recklessness, she wouldn't be able to live with herself, it was as simple as that. As her legs began to give way, she went to grip the counter but Adam was already reaching for her.

He cradled her in his arms and brushed the tears from her face. As she looked up into his piercing blue eyes, she felt an ice-cold shock from the coldness of his stare but it quickly disappeared, leaving her wondering if it had been another of the vagaries of her mind.

'Now don't go getting upset,' Adam soothed. 'Nothing happened and nothing will while I'm around. You might not always be able to help yourself, but that's why you have me.' When he was sure Lucy could stand on her own two feet again, he returned to the bubbling omelette. 'If you want to feel useful, why don't I do you a list of what frozen food we need and you can pick it up on your way back from your mum's?'

Lucy's mouth was dry and she had to swallow hard before she could reply. 'I suppose,' she said, attempting to sound normal but not managing it as easily as Adam. 'And what about your Mother's Day card for Viv? I could always get one while I'm out.' She had already bought her mum a card from the garden centre, along with a selection of scented candles and chocolates for both mothers, but she knew how Adam liked to pick his mum's cards personally.

12

Lucy unbuckled her seatbelt and waited patiently for Adam to finish what he was doing. Her eyes felt scratchy and she was tempted to close them. She hadn't slept very well despite going to bed exhausted after another day holding herself rigid as if she were expecting a bomb to explode at any moment.

The argument with Adam that morning hadn't helped. She could have sworn he had said he would get Viv's card, but neither was she surprised when he recounted a different version of their conversation. Someone had said, 'I'll get it,' and Lucy could hear Adam's voice, but why would he insist it was her if it weren't true? As much as she would like to believe that Adam had his fallibilities, the truth was she could have averted another crisis if she had listened properly.

As Lucy waited for Adam to scribble something in the card he had grabbed en route to Viv's, an image came to mind of her pink bicycle with its spinning back wheel. She watched the reflector spin faster and faster until it switched direction. The whirring sound inside her head was deafening and she wanted to be sick.

A finger and thumb snapped in front of her face. 'Earth to Lucy,' Adam said. His tone was soft, his anger and frustration swallowed back for the hundredth time, but there remained a hint of anxiety in his voice. Was he worried that one day she wouldn't snap out of it?

Lucy went to say sorry, but it was a word that Adam was surely sick of hearing. 'Have you written out the card?' she asked instead.

Adam held up a pink sealed envelope. 'Come on,' he said. 'Do you need help getting out of the car?'

'Give me another month and I won't be able to get in, but I'm fine for now.'

It wasn't her growing baby that made it difficult for Lucy to heave herself out of the car but the tension straining every muscle in her body. She rested on the open door for a moment and scanned the neat line of bungalows. Scott had been driving a silver rental car when they had met but she had paid no heed to the make or model. Viv's car was on her drive and of the half-dozen cars parked along the road, only two were silver and both were unoccupied. It was possible that Scott was waiting inside for them. Lucy's urge to throw up intensified.

Adam had taken Viv's gift bag from the boot and came around to Lucy's side. 'Aren't you glad now that we didn't try to visit both our mums on the same day?'

No, Lucy thought, although she had enjoyed a lovely afternoon on her own with her mum the day before. With traffic delays on both sides of the bridge, it had taken Lucy twice as long as it would have done through the tunnel, shortening the time she was able to spend with her mum, but the effort had been worth it. It was as if she had slipped back two years in time. Mother and daughter had curled up together on the sofa to watch one of their favourite programmes on catch-up TV, and for a snatched hour, Lucy hadn't felt like an imposter pretending to be something she wasn't.

'You'd be exhausted by now,' Adam continued. 'In fact you look it already.'

Lucy hooked her arm in his and, as they approached the house, Viv was at the door to greet them. 'I thought for a minute you weren't going to come in,' she said.

Adam kissed his mum's cheek and Lucy followed suit. 'You look nice,' she said, taking in Viv's outfit. The black dress was bias cut to flatter her figure but it was the brightly coloured scarf draped around her neck that stood out from the usual don't-look-at-me style her mother-in-law adopted.

'And you smell nice too,' Adam said, offering the compliment with an accusatory tone.

'A new perfume,' Viv said, taking the gift bag and card from Adam. 'Come on in.'

In the open-plan living room there was no cloying scent of a man's cologne as Lucy had feared, simply the relaxing aroma of lavender from the scented candles burning on the mantelpiece. The cushion resting on the back of the faded armchair where Viv liked to sit was slightly crushed, but all the others were perfectly plumped and the seats empty. The table had been set with a pretty arrangement of spring flowers and a couple of tiered plate stands brimming with carefully arranged finger sandwiches, pastries and cakes.

'I've got a pot of tea brewing but if you want one of your fruit teas, Lucy, I have those too.'

'You really didn't have to go to all this trouble,' Lucy replied.

'Oh, I've had fun getting everything ready,' Viv said, while Adam eyed her with suspicion. When she smiled at him, her eyes remained wide and the overall effect was a little disturbing. She was terrified.

Adam took a seat at the table and examined the spread Viv had laid out as if he were a forensic scientist. He was searching for clues to explain his mother's odd behaviour. There was a stack of side plates with paper serviettes sandwiched between them, six in all. It might suggest that she was allowing two plates per person, or alternatively, it was a ploy to disguise the fact that she expected more company.

Lucy sat down at the table, facing the door as she waited for the inevitable. Like Viv, who had remained standing, Lucy tried to appear relaxed but the more she thought about her posture, the more awkward her pose. She was waiting for Viv to give her a sideways look to let her know that she had heard about the meeting with Scott, but from all appearances, Scott had kept his word.

'Is your back still hurting?' Adam asked when he noticed Lucy grimace.

'Do you want to sit in a comfy seat for now?' offered Viv.

'No, a hard-backed chair is probably better,' Lucy said. She glanced towards the door and wished Scott would put them out of their misery. Adam was going to see through the charade in no time at all.

Viv opened Adam's card with her son looking on, before taking it to the bookshelf to set next to another. Lucy hoped this was a sign that Scott had paid a visit earlier. Viv had dressed up to receive both her sons but at different times. It was going to be fine.

The knock at the door was a playful rat-a-tat-tat and suggested the visitor was a familiar one but the sound gave Viv's body a jolt and she knocked over Adam's card. As Lucy watched it flutter to the floor, she too felt the shock and her blood pressure surged to leave her skin tingling. Watching her mother-in-law scurry out of the room, she tried hard to appear as confused as Adam by Viv's nervousness.

Picking up a side plate, Lucy took a couple of sandwiches from the nearest stand. She didn't care about the filling because she doubted she would be able to force any food down her throat. She could barely swallow as it was.

'Something's going on,' Adam said, too preoccupied by his mum's tangible fear to notice Lucy's tremors.

There were whispers in the hallway that were too low to overhear although the tone suggested that at least one person was voicing last-minute doubts. Shuffling footsteps were followed by a remark that was clear enough to cause Adam to shoot up from his seat.

'It'll be fine, Mum,' Scott had said.

And there he was, looming large in an increasingly small space and sucking the air from the room. His eyes met Lucy's briefly before settling on the one person present who hadn't been expecting him.

'Hello, Adam,' Scott said, extending an arm to shake his hand.

Please accept it, Lucy urged silently.

Viv stood immediately behind her younger son, clasping her hands together in a wordless prayer of her own.

'So this was a set-up?' Adam said, looking straight through Scott to Viv. His voice was cold and his words measured.

'Since I wasn't up to making the trip to New York, Scott offered to come here instead. It's Mother's Day and we thought it might be a good time to bring the family together.'

'We? Sorry, I don't remember that conversation, Mum,' said Adam. He blew air through tight lips like a pressure cooker building a head of steam. 'And I would have thought, since I'm the one who stuck by you, that it would be me you would want to discuss it with.'

Scott continued to hold out his hand. 'This might be the best Mother's Day present we could *both* give Mum,' he said. He cleared his throat before adding, 'Come on, Adam. We're not kids any more. I'll be shooting back to New York in a couple of days, so it's no big deal. Can't we shake hands and let bygones be bygones?'

Adam looked down at the proffered hand. 'No,' he said simply. 'I won't shake hands with you and I won't be inviting you back into the family. You made your choice a long time ago, Scott, and you have to live with that.'

Shoving his hands in his pockets, Scott looked down at his feet. No one could outstare Adam. 'It didn't feel like a choice at the time. You and I both know it was impossible for us to carry on living together.'

'And why was that, Scott?' asked Adam playfully. 'Was it better to have one parent so you didn't have to share? How is Keith, by the way? Now he's all broken, are you looking for a new parent?'

'It's not like that,' his brother said. 'That's not why I'm here.'

Scott made the mistake of glancing towards Lucy. He might have been searching for someone who would understand his intentions, but that wasn't how Adam saw it. 'You keep away from her,' he growled. 'The days are long gone when I'd let you near anything of mine so you could destroy it.'

'I didn't destroy anything!' Scott said, the first to lose his cool. 'You did, Adam. Dad wouldn't have left if—'

'Stop!' Viv cried. Her mouth moved to say more but as she looked from one son to the other, she couldn't decide where her next words should be directed.

Scott pulled her to him, kissing her damp cheek. 'Sorry, Mum,' he said, his words choking him. 'I said I didn't want to rake up the past and I won't.'

'Too late for that, don't you think?' Adam said, spittle spraying from his mouth.

Scott took a couple of breaths that were too shallow to give his voice the power he would need to match Adam's. 'Can't we do this for Mum's sake? She's about to be a Grandma and I'm about to be an unc—'

'Enough! You keep away from my family, Scott,' roared Adam. 'Mum might not be able to see what you're doing but I know what's happening here. I'm the one who's going to tell you to go to hell and walk out of here right now, and I'll be the one who's blamed for keeping the family broken, but don't imagine for a second that I don't know that you came here to fuck it up.'

'No, Adam,' Scott said, raising his hands. 'Stop twisting things. I won't listen.'

'Why would I want a family reunion? You're nothing to me, Scott. You never were.'

Scott shook his head but Adam had already turned his back on his brother. 'We're leaving,' he said to Lucy. 'Now.'

'Adam,' she began. She made a point of glancing towards Viv. 'It's Mother's Day. Couldn't we—'

Her husband's eyes widened in fury but when he blinked, Adam's features took on an altogether different expression. In that moment, Lucy saw who the true victim was and she was so convinced that Adam might burst into tears that she jumped up. She moved a little too fast and her world wobbled. The dizzy spell was over in a couple of seconds but it was enough to have everyone worried. Viv and Scott took a step towards her but it was Adam who was quickest to her side. He put an arm around her waist and held her up.

'What were you thinking, Mum?' Adam said as he guided Lucy towards the door.

'I didn't think . . .'

'No, you never do.'

'I'm fine, Adam,' insisted Lucy. She wanted to pull away to prove she was perfectly capable of walking unaided, but she suspected Adam needed to hold her and Lucy had to at least give him that.

'Maybe you should sit a while,' Scott said.

Adam's brother was doing a good impression of a twelve-year-old boy who wanted his mum, but Lucy hadn't forgotten that Scott had said that he would be the one to leave if things became difficult, not Adam. Lucy wished she could remind him of his promise but to do so would be to expose her own lies, and besides, she didn't think Scott would go. He had engineered the whole thing with the sole intention of hurting Adam and he had used those closest to his brother to ensure that hurt was keenly felt. Lucy had been complicit in what she could see now was a particularly vindictive form of bullying. She should have worked it out sooner and would have done if she were in a more rational state of mind.

Hoping to make up for the betrayal Adam had yet to discover, she said, 'No, Adam's right. We should go. I'm sorry, Viv.'

Her mother-in-law had edged away from her younger son but Lucy imagined she would be drawn back into his arms the moment Adam had left. From what Lucy had gleaned so far about Scott, he was a master of manipulation and Viv hadn't been the only one who had been played today.

'I could drive if you want,' Lucy said after they had left the house.

Adam was too shell-shocked to answer and she pulled the keys from his grasp with little resistance. It was after she had adjusted the seat and steering wheel to reach the pedals of Adam's Lexus that her husband eventually found his voice.

'I can't believe that actually happened,' he said.

Lucy didn't have the heart to feign surprise so kept quiet as she turned the engine and pulled away from the kerb. If they were being watched from the window, she couldn't tell.

'Please don't bend my ear about being rude to Mum again.'

'I wasn't—'

'I bet you think I'm the spoilt brat who doesn't want to share his mum,' he said. 'I'm right, aren't I?'

Lucy took her eyes off the road to meet his gaze. 'I don't think that at all, Adam. No one reacts like you did unless there's something deeper going on inside. I just wish you'd tell me.'

Adam pushed the heels of his hands against his eyes while Lucy was obliged to concentrate on the road. The last thing they needed to happen was for her to wrap the car around a tree, but she was desperate to know more and now felt right. From the corner of her eye, she could see Adam's arms trembling with the effort to suppress emotions he was too proud to reveal.

'Tell me about Scott,' she said softly. 'Tell me as much as you're able.'

'It's hard to explain,' Adam said, relaxing enough to slip a hand on to her knee and squeeze gently. 'And if you're anything like Mum and Keith, you won't believe me.'

'I'll believe you.'

Taking a deep breath, Adam said, 'From the moment Scott was born he claimed centre stage and I learnt early on that I would never be able to compete with my cute little brother, so I didn't even try. Mum loved telling everyone about the funny things he did. I suppose it must have been a relief to have a child who wasn't so awkward.'

Lucy couldn't deny that Adam could be quite stiff in social settings but that was an endearing quality, or at least it was to Lucy. At Ranjit's barbecue, her initial reason for going over to talk to Adam was precisely because he had looked painfully uncomfortable. It had been a refreshing change to approach a man rather than have someone hit on her. She had fallen in love with his serious face and his secret smile.

'I for one am glad you're different from Scott,' she said. 'But you must know how much Viv loves you. Each of her children has a different personality and different needs, that's all.'

'Except as far as Scott's concerned, his needs are so much more important than anyone else's.'

'And he doesn't like sharing,' Lucy said, picking up on what Adam had said earlier.

Adam released a heavy sigh. 'Once Scott was old enough to realize he could take advantage of my weekends away with Dad, that's when the fun and games began. What you saw today was the tip of the iceberg.'

'What did he do?'

'Stupid stuff,' Adam said. 'Honestly, if I told you, you'd wonder what all the fuss was about. He'd hide things from me and break my toys, then burst into tears when Mum or Keith ripped into him for going in my room, making me the villain for not forgiving him. It got to the point where I used to dread coming home from Dad's, and I think that's what Scott intended.'

'He wanted you to stay away for good?'

'Except it had the opposite effect and I had to stop going to Dad's so I could keep an eye on what Scott was up to,' Adam said. 'As it turned out, I'd sacrificed my relationship with Dad for nothing because Scott simply became more devious. He set me up to pass on wrong messages or do the opposite of what I was supposed to until Mum and Keith were not only refereeing between us, but arguing with each other. I tried to warn them that Scott was deliberately trying to break up the family but they didn't want to believe the worst of their sweet little boy. Keith's argument was that Scott wouldn't behave like that if there wasn't some catalyst, and I don't need to tell you who he was looking at when he said it.'

Lucy was spellbound by Adam's story and almost missed the turn into their cul-de-sac, and then she wished she had driven past. She suspected Adam would close down once they reached home.

'And what about your mum?'

'She was less concerned with working out who was telling lies than she was finding a way for us all to make our peace with each other.'

'Which is what she's doing now.'

'I wish she'd accept it's never going to work. Her forgiving nature is the one weakness Scott loves to exploit. Last time she tried to keep us together, it cost Mum her marriage. I wonder what it's going to cost us this time?' he asked as Lucy pulled on to the drive behind her Fiat. 'I'm terrified of what he might do next.'

Pulling the handbrake, Lucy cut the engine and reached across to take Adam's hand. Her heart thumped against her chest as she contemplated her next move. 'He won't come between us, I can promise you that,' she said.

Lucy had become a pawn in Scott's latest game and she would remain so for as long as she kept their meeting a secret. Adam was going to be upset when he found out, but after opening up his heart to her, the least he deserved was her honesty.

Adam tried to pull loose from her grip, but Lucy refused to let go. 'Adam,' she croaked. She licked her lips and tried again. 'Promise me you won't get mad.'

'About what?' he asked as he took in his wife's deathly pallor. 'Oh, no. What have you done, Lucy?'

'Scott tricked me,' Lucy said, the words choking her. She was starting to regret making her confession while they were trapped in the car. She couldn't produce enough saliva to swallow back her growing fear and she wasn't sure how much explaining she could do before her throat closed up. 'You know that buyer I met at the garden centre? It wasn't a woman, it was Scott. He used a fake name and email account.'

Adam's body went rigid and she could feel a coldness seeping into his fingers. She started when he snatched his hand away. 'You met him?'

'I didn't know who he was,' she pleaded.

'So what are you saying? He dressed up as a woman and it's taken until now for you to see through the disguise?'

'No, I knew the buyer was a man. You assumed it was a woman and I let you go on thinking it was. I'm sorry. I didn't want you to worry about me meeting a strange bloke when you had so much work on your plate.'

'I see. So it's my fault because I've been too busy juggling my schedule and letting projects slip to babysit you.'

'No, I just—'

'What other lies have you told?' Adam said. His eyes narrowed into slits. 'When exactly did you work out he was my brother?'

'It was when I got talking to him at the garden centre. I figured something was wrong and then he admitted who he was,' Lucy said.

She had thought herself clever to see through Scott's disguise so quickly. If only she hadn't challenged him, he might have kept up the charade and she would simply be another of his victims. Or had Scott intended her to see through his ruse? Was that part of the trap? Lucy couldn't begin to understand the mind of someone so cruel.

'He said he wanted a closer relationship with his mum but he'd need to make peace with you first,' she continued. 'That's why he wanted my help, and you said yourself how good he is at working people.'

No longer able to look at her, Adam stared straight ahead. 'You came home without the paintings.'

'What?' Lucy said, thrown by the remark. 'Yes, I sold them.'

'Before or after you found out who he was?'

Lucy was confused. She didn't understand why the paintings should be so important. 'After I found out,' she said. 'He seemed genuinely interested in them, and I thought . . .' She stopped. What the hell had she thought? Her mind whirred as she tried to remember and with each sharp intake of breath, she could feel the pressure building inside her chest. 'He said something about papering over the cracks in your relationship. I tried to talk him out of turning up today, but he said he'd leave if it became too uncomfortable.'

'So you gave him your paintings,' Adam said. 'The ones you put so much passion into. The ones that tapped into your very soul.' His head snapped towards her. She expected him to start shouting but his chill words sent a shiver down her spine. 'You gave *those* paintings to my brother?'

'I fell for his tricks. I thought I could trust him,' she said, knowing her feeble excuses weren't good enough. She should have known there was good reason for Adam to erase Scott from his life, but Lucy had been swept along by the thought of repairing Adam and Scott's relationship. He had apologized for putting her in an impossible situation but that was part of his devious plan. He had a history of being a homewrecker. What had she done?

'I didn't know what he was like. You never told me!'

She hadn't meant to raise her voice but it was carried by a swell of panic. Adam flung the passenger door open and the car filled with the sweet scent of freshly mown grass that tasted bitter on Lucy's tongue.

'Adam, I'm sorry!' she cried after him.

By the time Lucy scrambled out of the car, Adam had disappeared inside the house. She was relieved to see he had left the door open wide rather than shutting her out and she stepped cautiously over the threshold. Her ears strained for the sound of movement upstairs as she imagined him storming into her studio to rip up her preliminary sketches of the seascapes and any other evidence of the passion she had transferred into the paintings that were now in Scott's hands. The noise when it came was a thump and a rattle from nearby. It was the sound of the fridge door closing.

'Adam?' she said creeping towards the kitchen.

She wasn't surprised when he didn't answer. He had his back to her and there was a snap and hiss as he opened a bottle of lager. Adam didn't drink very often and the bottles had been lurking at the back of the fridge since Christmas. She had bought them in case they had visitors, and had planned to throw them out if they stayed there much longer.

'Speak to me, please,' she begged.

Leaving the bottle on the counter, Adam turned. 'And

say what, Lucy?' he asked. 'Sorry for letting you down by not telling you how I was bullied by my younger brother? Sorry for being ashamed of how pathetic I am?'

'You have nothing to apologize for. You're not to blame.'

'But I should have told you,' he said, crossing his arms tightly across his chest. 'That's what you said.'

'All I meant was that I didn't know Scott like you do. I fell for his tricks because I didn't realize what a manipulative creep he was.'

'So you do think it's my fault for not telling you?'

'Yes! I mean no,' she said, her blood pressure rising to dangerous levels. 'What I mean is I would rather you had told me. I would have been prepared. I would have understood. I'm your wife.'

'Nice of you to remember. I suppose with your feeble memory, it should come as no surprise that you'd go out looking for another man.'

'No, Adam. I love you. Only you.'

'Until a better version came along,' Adam said with a snarl. 'You fell for Scott, that's what you said. You'd have given him more than the paintings if he'd let you and who's to say you didn't?'

'I wouldn't—'

'How can you treat me like this? I've put up with your mood swings, I've fixed your mistakes and I've looked after you without complaint. I'd do anything for you because I love you, probably more than you deserve,' he said, tripping over his words, 'but the one thing I can't do is take the blame when it's your mess. I've had enough of people pointing the finger at me when I've done nothing wrong.'

Adam's words flew like arrows across the space opening

up between them. 'I know you haven't. It's my fault,' she cried.

'How many nights have you lain next to me knowing what Scott had planned?'

'I thought I'd talked him out of it.'

'But you said a minute ago that Scott promised to leave if things got uncomfortable. That means you must have known he was going to follow through with his plans!' Adam said, his cool composure breaking.

'I didn't! I don't—' Lucy said, but she had already lost track of her thoughts.

Adam's face creased with pain. 'Why are you doing this to me?' he asked. 'You say one thing and in the next breath you twist it into something else. It's like you're deliberately trying to tie me up in knots.'

'I don't mean to. If I sound confused, it's because I am,' she sobbed. She could hear the kitten mewling in the utility room where he was kept safe from mischief whenever they were out. Lucy was tempted to hide away in there too. 'I didn't sleep a wink last night. I was worrying about what might happen today.'

Adam shook his head. 'So it wasn't leg cramps that kept you awake. Another lie.'

'No . . .'

'How am I supposed to trust a single thing you say when you keep changing your story? Did you or did you not know Scott was going to turn up today?'

Lucy felt queasy. She could explain if only she could get her thoughts in order. 'I was scared that he might. That's all,' she sobbed, and as her vision blurred, she saw a tear slip down Adam's cheek.

'You have one meeting with my brother and you're already torturing me like he did.'

'No! I never meant to hurt you, not ever! Please let me explain,' she cried as Adam turned his back on her. 'You have to believe me!'

'I'm sorry, but I can't take this any more,' he said, his voice muffled through his hands. 'I can't do this.'

Lucy felt a rush of emotion that was an explosive mix of fear, panic and guilt and it propelled her forwards. She couldn't lose Adam when she needed him more than ever. Scott had broken up one marriage but he wasn't going to destroy hers. Adam had to listen. She could make him trust her again, but first he had to look at her.

'I won't let Scott do this to us!' she cried out as she grabbed Adam's shoulder and twisted him around.

As tears streamed down her face, Lucy's eyes stung with make-up, her nose became blocked and all she could hear was the pounding of her heart. Her senses were closing down one by one and she was powered by emotions over which she had no control. When Adam yelled at her, she yelled back, words flying unchecked because she couldn't keep up with them. Her thoughts spun faster and faster like a bicycle wheel. Her dad was turning the pedal and the reflector traced a fiery circle of orange until that pivotal point when her stomach lurched and everything changed.

13

The kitten's tired cries for attention from the utility room brought Lucy back to the present. Her chest heaved, her throat was scratchy and her eyes itched. She had no idea how long she had been curled in the foetal position on the kitchen floor but she hadn't been sleeping, she had been sobbing, and long enough to cry herself dry.

Pain bit into her shoulders and neck as she pulled herself up into a sitting position. Her swing dress clung damply to her thigh as she took in her surroundings. Adam had vanished.

She tried to piece together the scattered fragments of her memory. The frothy amber liquid splattered across the porcelain tiles and soaking into her dress triggered the image of a lager bottle spinning across the floor. It had come to rest beneath a dining chair but at the time Lucy had been focused entirely on Adam. She could hear him shouting, telling her to stop but her memory snagged and she couldn't remember what exactly had been happening.

Rising unsteadily to her feet, Lucy's gaze settled on the basket of spring flowers that Adam had surprised her with that morning as her very first Mother's Day gift. The artificial petals glowing in the afternoon sun would gather dust and fade over time but at least she couldn't kill them. She had propped the Mother's Day card next to the bouquet, except now it was lying flat on the table.

'The baby was a mistake,' she could hear herself saying above the sound of a card being torn in two. Or was it Adam's voice she heard and . . . Had he torn the card? No, it must have been her, but the pieces of her memory wouldn't fit. She needed to find Adam but as Tigger's futile attempts to attract attention faded, the house fell silent.

Beads of sweat pricked Lucy's brow as she shrugged off the denim jacket that gave her a reason, if not a desire, to leave the kitchen and hang it up. Her damp dress slapped against her leg but she heard no other sound as she entered the hall. She held her breath as she opened the closet. The jacket Adam had been wearing earlier was hanging in its usual place. He hadn't left her, not yet.

Lucy felt a rush of relief but managed to swallow back the sob in time to hear a noise from the living room. The door had been left ajar and she moved closer to the shadows stretching across the threshold.

Lifting her hand, Lucy resisted the urge to knock before entering. She pressed her palm against the door and it opened with a whisper. The room was filled with an eerie glow from the sunshine reflecting off the tightly closed blinds. Adam was perched on the edge of the sofa with his elbows on his knees and his head in his hands. His blond hair was sticking up in awkward peaks and the shirt he had ironed so carefully that morning was creased. His sleeves were rolled up and there appeared to be a tear in a shoulder seam. With the shadows playing across his body, he looked beaten.

'I can't do this,' he whispered.

His words gave Lucy's mind a jolt as well as her body. He had said the exact same thing while she had been screaming at him. 'Please, Adam,' she said as she crept forward.

Planting a hand on his knee for support as she knelt down, Lucy wasn't surprised when he flinched. She took a deep, juddering breath and tugged his hands away from his face.

'I don't know what happened,' she said as she searched her husband's face. His eyes were bloodshot and the creases around his nostrils were painfully red. When he opened dry lips to speak, she realized she didn't want him to fill in the gaps. Quickly, she added, 'I'm scared. I know I lost control again, and I feel sick thinking about how much I've hurt you. I can't begin to imagine what you're going through right now, but I need you to know that I won't give up on us without a fight.'

Adam looked at her hands clasped around his. His thumb played across the ridges of her knuckles. 'I think I already know that,' he said in a whisper, 'but what you did, Lucy, it was unforgivable.'

'I know.'

'And yet somehow I'm going to have to forgive you, aren't I? What other choice do I have?'

'None, because we will get through this. I made a massive mistake but I promise, I'll never, ever speak to Scott again and if he does try to get in touch, I'll tell you. We'll work out what to do together. I wish I could get the paintings back too but I don't want him to know he has something over us. That's why I told you about our meeting. I thought he might blackmail me.'

Adam pulled free of her grip and cupped her face. 'You really don't know what happened just now, do you?' he said in a wondering tone. He skimmed a thumb across her cheek, his soft skin rasping against the salty flakes of her dried tears.

'N-no, not exactly,' she said, faltering. 'I know I said things that I didn't mean and I truly, truly regret it, but we're both calmer now. Let's put it behind us and start again.'

As Adam straightened up, he held out his arms and Lucy's heart lifted. She was about to wrap herself around him when her attention was caught by the shadows mottling his forearms, except it wasn't shadow at all, but bruising.

'I didn't—' Lucy began, but immediately clammed up. It was time to stop accusing Adam when she was the one at fault. She could smell the spilt lager clinging to her dress and she could remember it being swept off the counter. There had been a blur of movement and hands balled tightly into fists. She could hear Adam begging her to stop. 'Oh, Adam. What have I done?'

'Maybe it's my fault,' he tried. 'Maybe if I hadn't yelled back, if I'd accepted this is how you are now, it wouldn't have gone so far this time.'

Lucy's cheeks burned and fresh tears welled in her eyes as she looked down at her hands. Her fingers felt stiff but she had assumed it had been caused by holding her body so tense. She had hit the man she loved and it wasn't the first time. 'What's wrong with me? How could I do something like that to you?'

Adam hooked a finger under her chin and forced her to meet his gaze. 'If you want me to stay then something has to change,' he said. 'I can take the beatings but I'm worried about the baby. I wish you would stop and think about her too.'

The mention of the baby made Lucy gasp. She had felt sluggish and encumbered as she had picked herself up off the floor but she hadn't given a thought to the child she carried. She had been in shock but still, why hadn't her daughter been her first thought and not her last? Splaying her hands across her belly, she made a belated attempt to protect her precious child. 'Oh, god. I haven't felt her move.'

Adam leapt into action while Lucy concentrated on what might or might not be happening inside her body. He helped her to her feet and guided her to the sofa. She lay down and four hands smoothed over the creases of her dress, coming to rest on the rise of her stomach.

'Please be safe, little one,' Adam whispered. 'I swear I'll protect you as much as I can. You *are* wanted, you really are.'

Lucy squeezed her eyes shut and a heavy tear slid down her cheek and into her ear. Please don't be dead, she silently begged. You're not a mistake.

'Do you think we should go to the hospital?' Adam asked.

'I don't know,' Lucy said, torn between seeking help and not wanting to face her shame. 'What if the doctor realizes what's been happening?'

The lines furrowing Adam's brow deepened. 'If they find out you've been hitting me, they might never let you take the baby home.'

'Oh, Adam,' Lucy sobbed.

'But what if that's what it takes to keep her safe?'

Lucy pushed the image of the torn Mother's Day card to the back of her mind. 'This isn't me, you know it isn't,' she said in a hoarse whisper. 'I don't want to excuse what I've done but it has to be the hormones.'

'And if it isn't? Think about what happened with your dad, Lucy. What did he do that was so terrible that he couldn't carry on?'

'It won't be like that. Once I've had the baby, things will get back to normal.'

Words alone were not enough and as their hands stilled, the world slowed to a stop. Lucy breathed in through her nose and out through her mouth in a slow, steady rhythm. *Wake up, baby girl*, she told her daughter. *Don't be afraid.*

Adam rested his forehead gently against Lucy's abdomen as he too transferred his prayers to their daughter.

A sob burst from Lucy's lungs before she could hold it back. 'Did you feel that?' she asked. 'She's OK, Adam. She's moving. Can you feel her?'

Adam kissed the spot where Lucy had directed his hand. 'Thank God,' he whispered.

'I promise I won't let anything like this happen again,' she said as she took Adam's hands in hers.

'I don't think you should be making any promises you can't keep,' Adam warned. 'It's going to take time for me to trust you again and I'll be watching you like a hawk. If you don't like that idea then say so now, because it's the only way I'm prepared to move forward.'

'I'll do anything you ask as long as you stand by me. I'd be nothing without you,' she said, feeling a shudder run down her spine as if she had heard those words before, as if Adam had said them.

But it was true nonetheless, and for a moment, she wondered if Adam were being too generous with his love. She had known he had suffered in the past but never imagined that she would be the one to inflict more pain. It was all wrong. He shouldn't be looking after her or worrying about the baby. If today had proven anything, it was that he wasn't as strong as she had thought. She wished she could heal him, and if there was a way, it wouldn't be by making secret plans behind his back. She had learnt her lesson.

14

Lucy's breath was laboured as she made the short journey from the car to her mum's front door. Before knocking, she glanced over her shoulder and caught Adam giving her an odd look. She froze. 'What's wrong?'

'Nothing,' he said softly, his face blank again. 'You're doing fine, Lucy, but maybe we shouldn't stay too long. I don't want you exhausting yourself.'

Her husband's words failed to soothe her. 'But why were you smiling?'

Adam looked abashed. 'When?'

'Just now?'

'Was I?' Adam asked. He looked pointedly at her hand raised in mid-air. 'Are you going to knock or should we turn around right now?'

Three weeks had passed since Lucy had found herself sitting on the kitchen floor too scared to remember what she had done, and since then, she and Adam had withdrawn into an impenetrable bubble of denial. Adam had told his boss that Lucy needed bed rest and he had worked from home almost continuously, and on the days that he had needed to go into the office, they had remained in constant touch via texts and calls. It had taken a while for Lucy to feel safe in her own company and she still wasn't quite there. She didn't know what she would do without him.

It was only with Adam's encouragement that Lucy had left the house at all during her self-imposed confinement and he had been by her side when she had attended her antenatal appointment. It was a relief to be told that the baby was developing normally despite the stress Lucy had put her through, but there were fresh fears with which to wrestle as Lucy entered her third and final trimester.

The midwife had wanted to discuss her birth plan and Adam had held Lucy's hand tightly as she was forced to contemplate the day her baby would enter the world. Lucy had liked the idea of an epidural as there was less chance of her lashing out at Adam unexpectedly when the pain of childbirth became unbearable, but Adam had started asking questions about the effects the drugs might have on the baby. The midwife had said it was perfectly safe and Lucy would know what level of pain she was willing to endure. It had taken one look from Adam to remind herself that the worst pain of all was bringing harm to her daughter and so they had opted for a natural birth. Her mum had managed well enough without drugs apparently, but she made motherhood in general look so easy. Unfortunately, it wasn't her mum that Lucy took after.

Before Lucy had the chance to knock, or turn and run, her mum was pulling open the door. 'I thought it was you two lurking outside,' Christine said. She was wearing cropped linen pants and a lace vest-top that revealed toned arms and shoulders warmed by the sun. She lifted her prescription sunglasses to squint at them. 'Isn't it a gorgeous day? I thought we'd sit outside, if it's warm enough for you.'

Lucy played with the zip of her hoodie. She was wearing a T-shirt over a pair of maternity jeans that made her feel drab and dreary next to her mum. 'I'll be fine.'

As she stepped across the threshold, Christine put one hand on the small of Lucy's back and the other on her bump. 'Oh my goodness, look how you've grown. Not long now.'

As Lucy soaked in some of the excitement lighting up her mum's face, she almost said, the sooner the better, but she couldn't summon the courage.

'And she's started to waddle like a duck,' Adam said. He had been left on the doorstep, unable to pass the two women blocking his entry.

'Is that why you were smiling before?' Lucy asked, giving him her sternest look but secretly relieved to know he had been toying with her earlier.

'Ah yes, and whatever you do, don't laugh at her,' Adam said to Christine, but he was already chuckling.

'I swear, you test my patience sometimes,' Lucy said, eager to join in the joke.

Despite the bright April sunshine, Adam's eyes dimmed. Lucy wanted to apologize immediately but her mum was ushering her through the house with Adam trailing behind.

Stepping into the garden, Lucy was immediately reminded of her dad. This was the place where they had had the most fun when she was growing up, and although decking had been constructed over the patio she remembered her dad and uncle labouring over one long hot summer, she continued to think of it as their place.

The garden furniture had been warming in the sunshine and Lucy sank into the swing seat, allowing enough space for Adam to join her. If her husband was smarting from her stupid remark, he hid it well as he helped his mother-in-law bring out refreshments.

Leaving Adam to pour glasses of fruit punch from a large jug speckled with condensation, Christine flopped down next to her daughter. 'It's so lovely to see you,' she said. 'But you do look tired, love. If traipsing over here is getting too much for you, I don't mind coming over to you.'

Ice cubes clattered against the side of a highball glass as Adam dipped his head beneath the fluttering canopy and handed the first drink to his wife. 'We like coming here and getting fussed over,' he said to Christine. 'And try as I might, I'd never compete with one of your roast dinners.'

'I don't mind doing the cooking,' Christine said. 'I'd rather that than not see you at all.'

The dig didn't go unnoticed. 'I've missed you too,' Lucy said, 'but I was completely wiped out and needed some time out to build up my strength.'

'But you are better now?' asked Christine, lifting her sunglasses again to scrutinize Lucy's pale features.

'The midwife says she's doing fine,' Adam said as he pulled his garden chair closer. 'In fact, she said she was blooming.'

Lucy stopped herself from suggesting that it had been Adam who had said that, or mentioning how the midwife's expression had been similar to the one appearing on her mum's face. 'And I've opted for a natural birth,' she said.

'There was nothing I could do to persuade her differently,' Adam added. 'Although I am going to invest in some protective clothing for when she blames me halfway through labour that it was all my fault.'

'It is all your fault,' Christine said with a chuckle, but the joke fell flat. Feeling her daughter tense, she took hold of Lucy's hand and gave it a quick squeeze. 'Childbirth is always a bit of a shock, so maybe now would be a good time to concentrate on what's going to happen after the baby's born. I know you won't want to travel far in those early days, so I intend to pay regular visits whether you like it or not.' Turning to Adam, she added, 'You'd better make plenty of space in your freezer because I'll be bringing supplies.'

Lucy hung her head and folded her shoulders into herself as she waited for Adam to make some comment about the freezer having been cleared out relatively recently. She stared at her husband's shadow stretching across the sun-bleached decking, his foot tapping out a silent tune, but he said nothing.

Noticing the pause, Christine said, 'Or am I stepping on your mum's toes? I expect she'll be eager to help too.'

Adam swirled the ice cubes in his glass. 'I wouldn't know what Mum's planning at the moment.'

'You're still not speaking?' asked Christine, having been told, with Adam's blessing, the barest of facts about the family rift.

It had taken a week for Adam and Lucy to build up the courage to sit down and talk rationally about what had happened, and even then his pain had remained raw. He had admitted that seeing the closeness Lucy shared with her mum would feel like rubbing salt into the wound and that was why they had put on hold their usual trips to Liverpool. He had, however, come around to the idea that Lucy needed her mum, although there was no telling when he would recognize that he needed his.

'She hasn't tried to get in touch,' Adam said, his tone revealing hurt and disappointment in his mum that Lucy hadn't heard before.

'I expect she wants to give everyone a chance to simmer down,' offered Christine. 'It must be hard for her though. Whatever problems there are between you and your brother, you're both her sons.'

'What was Nan like when Dad fell out with Uncle Phil?' asked Lucy. She looked to Adam for a sign that she had been right to steer the conversation away from Scott, but he was staring into his glass

'That was different.'

'Different how?' asked Lucy.

When Christine rubbed her arm, Lucy could see fine dark hairs standing on end. 'Their falling out didn't last long.'

'Because Dad died,' Lucy said in a whisper, afraid to disturb old ghosts, but knowing she had been treading softly over her father's grave for far too long. If she could peer into her dad's mind, it might provide the route map to her own personal minefield of thoughts and emotions. 'The argument was over the business, wasn't it?'

Christine simply nodded and looked to Adam. 'I really hope you sort things out with your mum, but I don't mind filling the breach if it doesn't happen as soon as you would like. I'm saving my holidays this year especially for you two.'

'You're not going away?' he asked. 'What about your annual trip to the Algarve with the girls?'

Christine wrinkled her nose. 'It's a month after the baby's due and I'd rather stay close to home.'

'We'll be fine, Christine.'

'No, honestly, I need to save my money for other things. Like that, for one,' she said as she tipped her head towards a large hole in the fence at the far end of the garden.

Adam craned his neck to inspect the damage. 'It looks like it's only a handful of slats that are missing. The rest looks sturdy enough.'

'They blew off into next door's garden during that last storm.'

'Do you still have them?'

Minutes later, Adam was hammering the splintered slats back on to the fence.

'He's a good lad,' Christine said.

Lucy rested her head on her mum's shoulder, not knowing whether to smile or weep. 'Yes, he is.'

'It must have been some fight with his brother for them to be at loggerheads all these years. Adam's always come across as someone who keeps his emotions buried. I can't imagine him losing his temper.'

'I remember you and Dad arguing.'

Lucy felt her mum's chin press against the top of her head. 'We had our moments.'

'I could hear you through the walls, whispering like crazy at each other, but what was it like when I wasn't there?'

'How do you mean?'

Lucy closed her eyes. 'Did Dad ever lose it?'

'I think we both did at times.'

'No,' Lucy said. The cold drink in her hand had numbed her fingers but the rest of her body tingled with fear. 'I mean, did he ever lose control? Did he ever hit you?'

As Christine's body stiffened, Lucy prepared for impact. At long last she had stumbled upon the answer to a twenty-year-old question. Had her dad been unable to keep his feelings in check or his fists to himself? Was that why he couldn't live with himself? Was Lucy doomed to the same fate?

'No, of course he didn't hit me. Not ever,' Christine said. She leant back and lifted Lucy's chin. 'Why are you asking these questions, Lucy? What's wrong? And don't say you're fine because I can see perfectly well that you're not.'

Lucy wanted to tell her mum everything but it wasn't only her secret to tell. Adam didn't want anyone to know. He said it was because he wanted to protect her, but Lucy suspected there was also an element of shame to it. What would people think if he confessed to being beaten up by his pregnant wife? His boss was already concerned and his colleagues suspicious. His bruises had been spotted by the eagle-eyed Naomi.

The possibility that Lucy was a husband-beater would never cross Christine's mind but she was willing to consider another horrifying scenario. She flinched when her son-in-law hammered a nail into the fence. 'Does Adam hit you, Lucy? Is that what you're trying to tell me?'

'No, *he* would never hurt *me*,' Lucy said, willing her mum to listen to the inflection and turn the statement on its head.

'Then what?' Christine persisted. 'So much for

blooming, you look like you'd be knocked down by one wrong look.'

'It's hormones,' Lucy said, pulling her chin free to escape her mum's scrutiny and nestling back into her shoulder.

'I was reading somewhere that you can get postnatal depression before the birth,' Christine said, as if she hadn't purposely trawled the internet. 'I'm surprised the midwife hasn't spoken to you about it.'

'I'm not that bad,' Lucy said. She and Adam had been careful about what they told the midwife. Adam had said they would be better off without any interference from prying eyes. He would look after her.

'It's all fixed,' Adam said, dropping the hammer and a box of nails on to the decking before filling his tumbler with warming fruit punch. He took a long gulp before adding, 'Which means you don't have any excuse now for cancelling your holiday to the Algarve.'

'You're a star,' Christine said, 'but that wasn't the only reason why I'm not going away.'

'It was the only valid reason,' Adam said firmly. 'Tell her, Lucy.'

Curled up like a child in her mother's arms, Lucy felt suddenly self-conscious. Adam had made a comment recently about not smothering their daughter so she would be better prepared for life as an adult, and although he hadn't made a direct comparison with Lucy and her mum, the inference was there. Pulling herself into a sitting position, she said, 'Adam's right. You worry too much, Mum. We're more than ready for parenthood, aren't we?'

Adam gave Lucy an approving smile then turned to his mother-in-law. 'You should see the nursery, Christine.'

Lucy reached for her phone. 'Here, I have photos.'

'It's very pink,' Christine said after a long pause. 'I thought you were going to paint a mural?'

'I'm not lifting a paintbrush until after the baby's born.'

'And probably not even then,' Adam said to Lucy, as if he were reminding her of something. 'She's worried it would be difficult, if not dangerous to keep the baby with her in the studio while she absorbs herself in whatever she's painting.'

'I'm really sorry I can't look after the baby as much as I'd promised,' Christine said. 'With any luck, I'll be able to cut back my hours next year.'

'You don't have to any more,' Adam assured her. 'If anything, it's been a blessing in disguise. Lucy wants to be a full-time mum and if it means I have to work that little bit harder to give her what she wants, I will.'

'Adam's right,' Lucy said as she held his gaze. She was finding it difficult to keep up with the conversation while trying to recollect the discussion she must have had with Adam. It sounded right that she would want to devote all her time to the baby when her abilities to multitask were non-existent, and from the smile on her husband's face, she had given the correct answer.

'You say that now, but I bet you'll keep sketching,' Christine said as she turned to Adam. 'I can remember what a major catastrophe it was if ever she spotted something interesting and didn't have her sketchpad with her.'

'I'm not doing *anything*,' Lucy said before Adam could answer. It was her decision.

'But you love drawing,' Christine said.

'She says it's too emotionally draining.'

'No, that's surely wrong, Lucy,' Christine said. 'It's always had such a positive effect on you. Could this be why you've been feeling down in the dumps?'

Lucy had to admit that she often fought the urge to escape the pressures of real life by retreating to her studio, but wasn't her disconnect from reality part of the problem? Of more concern to her right now was that her mum had indirectly suggested that Adam had lied. There was an uncomfortable pause as she waited for Adam to smooth over the awkwardness.

'Maybe your mum has a point,' he said at last. 'I did tell you that you'd be mad to give up painting.'

Lucy's eyes widened in shock. 'D-do you think so?'

'Am I ever wrong?' Christine asked with a smile. 'Those paintings you had on your website of the seagulls and the Dee were like nothing you've painted before, and now the weather's improving, you should take yourself off to the beach and fire up your passion again.'

'No,' Lucy said quickly, unable to meet Adam's stare. She had long since removed the photo images from her portfolio and, in echoes of Adam's attitude to his brother, preferred to carry on as if they had never existed. 'If I was to do anything, it would be that portrait for Hannah's grandad. She's been dropping hints again.'

'Really?' asked Adam, looking more surprised than he should.

Hannah had been in touch earlier that week under the guise of checking up on Tigger, but she had spoken at length about her grandad's grief. Lucy had told Adam how she felt guilty putting her off again, and although he had simply shrugged, she had definitely told him. Was it possible that

Adam was being deliberately obtuse to punish her? It would be no less than she deserved.

'I always liked Hannah,' Christine was saying. 'And it sounds to me like you have the perfect excuse to get yourself out into the world again. It can't be good being cooped up at home all day and the portrait will give you a new sense of purpose. Don't you think so, Adam?'

Adam's expression remained carefully neutral. 'I can only think that Lucy's raised the subject for a reason.'

Lucy's skin broke out in goosebumps. She shouldn't have mentioned Hannah. Adam would be worried her friend would lead her astray again. 'No, it was a stupid idea. I don't have a photo to work from yet and by the time we got around to agreeing on one, the baby would be here.'

'There's plenty of time,' Christine insisted. She looked to Adam once more for support.

'Stopped doubting yourself, Lucy,' he said with a smile that made Lucy think she was being paranoid. 'Do what feels right.'

Painting felt right. Immersing herself in a world she could control with the stroke of a paintbrush felt right.

'Text her now before you change your mind,' Christine said when she caught the sparkle that had been missing from her daughter's eyes. Hauling herself off the swing seat, she turned to her son-in-law and added, 'Meanwhile, would you like to help me sort out dinner? I can give you some pointers so you know what to do when I come to yours for Sunday lunch.'

'I thought you said you'd do the cooking.'

She winked at him. 'I'll take that as an invite then.'

Lucy composed her text but didn't have the courage of

her convictions to send it and was still cradling her phone when Adam returned from the kitchen. He sat down next to her and hooked his arm around her shoulder, inviting her to curl up next to him as she had done with her mum.

'Are you sure I should send this?' she asked.

'Your mum seems to think it will give you a much-needed purpose in life,' he said, his tone measured.

Lucy tried to read between the lines. 'I'm happy with the purpose you gave me when you asked me to marry you,' she said as an image came to mind of Adam on bended knee.

They had been together less than a year when Adam suggested a return visit to Heart's Leap where he was to make the surprise proposal. The first time she had stood on that precarious sandstone shelf looking out towards Liverpool Bay, she had quaked with fear, but on that glorious spring day, she had felt grounded.

'What if I'm simply asking for trouble?'

Adam's chest rose up then deflated with a sigh. 'It's your funeral, Luce. What's the worst that could happen?'

15

Lucy breathed in the scent of linseed oil and felt her heart soar. She couldn't wait to get started on the portrait, but arranging a suitable time to meet up with Hannah and her grandad was proving more difficult than she had envisaged. Hannah had wanted to wait until after the Easter holidays and Lucy preferred a day when Adam would be in work. Today would have been perfect, but Adam hadn't known until the night before that he was needed in the office and there had been no time for Hannah to find a babysitter for her youngest.

With nothing to do except keep out of trouble, Lucy locked herself away in her studio. The oversized shirt she used as a coverall no longer met in the middle and her bump protruded over the leggings she had rolled down to allow free movement. Bright sunlight reflected off the floorboards, toasting her bare feet and heating up her entire body. She wished she could open the balcony window but Tigger was curled up on the armchair where Lucy liked to sit and plan her compositions, and she was afraid he would use it to climb out on to the roof.

After twenty minutes of standing in front of her easel, her shirt had developed a pattern of sweat stains while her canvas remained stubbornly blank. Her palette was also bare because she had yet to settle on a subject. She had considered painting Tigger but as she debated how best to capture her little fur ball, he had stretched and yawned, picked himself up and disappeared downstairs. As she waited for fresh inspiration to strike, a tiny limb pushed itself against her taut belly. Beneath a network of blue veins, she thought she could make out the impression of a foot.

'Now if you could just hold that pose,' she told her daughter. Promptly, the foot disappeared and after several minutes of waiting patiently, she realized her baby had also grown weary of her prevarication and fallen asleep.

In desperation, Lucy grabbed a handful of paints from her supply box and squeezed oily globs on to her palette. She would paint a still-life portrait of the crumpled tube of cobalt blue in her hand if she had to, but as she looked down at the colours on her palette, her heart froze. She had thought she was adding a random mix of colours but the blues, greens and purples she had selected were a perfect match for the ones she had used for her seascapes.

Lucy sucked thick, stale air into her lungs and told herself this was not her subconscious dredging up memories she would rather forget. It was simply happenchance. The last tubes of paint she had used had been uppermost in the box and first to hand.

'I am going to paint,' she said aloud as her hand played across the jars of paintbrushes. She stroked flat and filbert brush heads in her search for the perfect tool, stopping when she felt the point of a palette knife prod her finger.

Plucking it from the jar, Lucy lifted the steel tip to the light where it shone clean and bright. She opened her palm to examine the handle and her gaze settled on splashes of the ocean that had soaked into the woodgrain. Her hand tipped forward and the palette knife clattered to the floor.

The urge to give up was almost as strong as the one that had brought her up to her studio but she wasn't ready to throw away the chance to still her mind for a few short hours. Grabbing a rag and wiping the palette clean, Lucy squeezed fresh paint on to its surface, selecting earthy tones of raw umber and yellow ochre that would ground her. As an afterthought, she dared to add crimson and magenta to lift the palette but still she had no subject. Her eyes darted around the studio and eventually settled on the natural wood of the window frame and the fingers of light poking through the panes. She would paint the spring sunshine.

Picking up her prepared thinner, Lucy shook the bottle before holding it to eye level. She could see globules of linseed oil floating in the turpentine and as she drew the liquid into the pipette, she tried to recapture the enthusiasm she had felt earlier when Adam had said goodbye and she had raced upstairs.

Her stomach rumbled as she mixed her paints and her hand shook when she lifted her brush to the canvas. Sweat trickled down her spine and as she released the breath she was holding, it sounded too much like a sob.

'I should have had breakfast first,' she said and, looking to her bump, added, 'Are you hungry?'

Telling herself she would return to her studio once she had eaten, Lucy made her way slowly down the two flights of stairs. The air was cooler on the ground floor and when she stepped into the kitchen, it was decidedly fresh. The patio doors were wide open but she didn't understand how that could be. They had been closed when Adam had kissed her cheek goodbye.

She sifted through her memory in search of potential gaps. The weather was warm but the only window she had considered opening was in her studio, and she had decided against that because Tigger might escape.

'Tigger!' she cried, her heart leaping into her throat. She raced through to the utility room. He wasn't in his bed.

Returning to the kitchen, Lucy approached the open doors with dread before stepping outside. Adam had pulled up the shrivelled fruit bushes, but the empty planters were high enough to help a determined kitten climb on to a fence. Tigger was too young to explore the outside world and if he jumped into a neighbouring garden, there was a chance he wouldn't be able to climb back.

'Tigger, come on, sweetheart,' she called in a soft tone that belied her fear.

The returning sound was the heavy beat of her heart and birdsong floating down from the nearby beech tree. Reassuring herself that the blackbirds wouldn't announce their presence if there was a cat on the prowl, she turned on her heels and raced back inside. She flitted from room to room, floor to floor, and was breathless by the time she reached the impenetrable heat of her studio. Racing past the empty armchair, she slapped her hands against the window and pressed her forehead against the warm pane. She could see sections of their neighbours' gardens but no sign of the kitten.

Closing her eyes, Lucy's first thought was that she wanted

her mum. It was a childish impulse and she pushed it to the back of her mind. She refused to sob because that could all too easily lead to hysteria, but one tore from her throat nonetheless when she heard the doorbell ring.

Lucy ran so fast that she almost stumbled down the stairs. Someone had found Tigger, but who? Neither she nor Adam knew their neighbours particularly well, and she doubted anyone nearby would know they had a cat. But if it were Lucy who had found a kitten, she would knock on all the neighbours' doors until she found the owner.

Hitching up her leggings, Lucy pulled open the door and barely registered Viv's worried expression. She stared at her empty arms.

'I'm sorry for calling,' Viv began.

'Where's Tigger?'

The crow's feet around Viv's eyes deepened. 'Lucy? Are you all right?'

'Oh,' Lucy said, as a different kind of fear rose up to steal what little breath she had left. 'You haven't come about the kitten, have you?'

As she stepped back from the woman who wasn't supposed to be there, her gasping became more pronounced. She didn't know how she was meant to deal with this. Her first thought was to run and hide until Adam came home, but she couldn't phone him until she caught her breath, and that was becoming increasingly difficult. Feeling dizzy, Lucy bent over to rest her hands on her knees. Her bump pressed against her chest, reminding her that she wasn't the only one being starved of oxygen.

'I think you need to sit down,' Viv said. 'Here, let me help.'

Lucy lifted a hand in objection but the movement unbalanced her and it was Viv who stopped her from sinking to the floor. As her mother-in-law led her through to the kitchen, Lucy's fight for air became more fraught. How was she going to explain this to Adam?

Lucy tried to speak. 'I need – I need to phone – Adam.'

'Let's get you settled first,' said Viv, guiding her to the dining table. 'You have to slow your breathing, Lucy. I think you're hyperventilating. Have you got a paper bag?'

With her fingers in spasm and curling into claws, Lucy gestured to a drawer where Viv retrieved a brown paper lunch bag.

'Take slow breaths,' Viv said as she lifted the bag to cover Lucy's mouth.

The paper crackled as Lucy sucked air in and out of the bag. Her lips tingled and, fearing she might pass out, she kept her eyes open wide. She listened to Viv's soothing words of encouragement, focusing on the present battle for air rather than what would happen once she had regained control of her body. She had let the cat out. And she had let Viv in.

Eventually, Lucy's breathing eased and her muscles began to relax. 'Adam,' she said, thrusting the word into the paper bag. Her mobile was in her shirt pocket but she hadn't recovered her motor skills sufficiently to use it. 'Ring him. Please.'

'In a minute,' Viv said. She smiled. 'You're doing great, Lucy. Keep breathing slowly and let me do the talking.'

There was something about Viv that jarred, and only now did Lucy realize it was her appearance. Her mother-in-law's white fitted blouse set off her tanned skin and she wore a touch of blue-grey eyeshadow and mascara that defined her eyes. Her silver hair had been cut into a mid-length style that made it look as strong and healthy as the woman herself. For a mother at the centre of a family feud, she appeared well rested if not completely at ease in the home of the son who had ostracized her.

'I've driven past your house countless times,' Viv said, which was some feat given that they lived in a cul-de-sac. 'I was waiting for Adam's car to disappear. Is he in work?'

Lucy nodded out of politeness. Her primary concern was to bring her breathing under control so she could look after her baby and reach her husband.

'I'm not here to cause trouble. All I want is to make sure that you and Adam are OK. You most especially. I know that Scott came to see you,' she said, before quickly adding, 'Not at the time, I should say. I never wanted you to be caught up in their war. Believe me, I know how that feels.'

They were silent for a moment, the only sound the crackling of a paper bag. As the noise lessened, Viv pushed on. 'I went on holiday with my sister and, for the first time in a long time, I was able to think for myself without . . .' She paused as she struggled to find the right word. 'Interference, I suppose. I'd like to say I came up with the perfect solution but I'm as stumped as ever by my boys. They are a riddle I've never been able to figure.'

The paper bag deflated slowly and Lucy took a chance and pulled it away from her face. 'I won't talk – about this. Not without Adam here,' she said.

'I know I can't change who they are,' Viv continued as if Lucy hadn't spoken. 'Or how they behave with each other, but I was hoping I could still be of help to you and the baby. She's what matters, isn't she?'

Lucy smoothed a hand over her belly and could feel her daughter's spasmodic hiccups. She had been unsettled by her mother's latest bout of hysteria but she was alive and kicking. With one fear settled, Lucy prepared to face a second. Having abandoned hope that Viv would make the call, she fished her mobile from her pocket. Viv didn't attempt to stop her.

'Adam?' Lucy said when the call connected. 'I need you – to come home.'

She could hear a radio in the background and the hum of traffic. 'I'm on my way to see a client. What's wrong?' he asked. She could tell he was doing his best to sound sympathetic but his tone gave away what he was really asking: What have you done now?

'Tigger got out,' she said quickly. 'I can't find him.'

'How did you manage that?'

Lucy lifted the brown paper bag in readiness as she felt her chest tighten. Ignoring his question, she said, 'And your mum's here.'

'What?'

'I was looking for Tigger.'

'Stop going on about the fucking cat. He'll turn up when he's hungry,' Adam said tersely. 'Are you telling me Mum is there with you? In the house?'

'Yes.'

'What's she said?'

'Nothing,' Lucy said. 'I told her I won't talk unless you're here.'

'Make sure you don't,' he replied. 'You know what you're like, you'll agree to anything. I'm on my way.'

After Adam cut the call, Lucy placed her phone on the table next to the silk flower display that she secretly loathed. It symbolized everything she hated about herself. The flowers weren't real and neither was she. She was pretending to be a competent wife and mother-to-be and failing miserably at both.

16

The incessant birdsong floating in from the garden made it difficult for Lucy to listen out for the sound of faraway miaows, or worse still, a dog's snarls or the screech of brakes. The task became impossible when the kettle her mother-in-law had been watching began to bubble and boil. When it switched off, Lucy thought she heard a car door slam. She forced herself to take slow, steady breaths but the tremors running through her body rattled her teeth when she heard the jangle of Adam's keys. He had made it home at breakneck speed.

'He's here,' Lucy said, wanting to stand but knowing she didn't have the strength. She watched as Viv lifted the kettle, making no acknowledgement of Adam's arrival.

Adam reciprocated by ignoring his mum as he rushed in and knelt in front of Lucy. He pushed back the curls that had fallen over her face when she had pressed her chin to her chest. 'Are you all right?' he asked.

'I'm sorry.'

'It's not your fault,' he said, taking her hand and pressing it to his lips. His brow creased as he detected the scent of oil on her fingers.

'I was upstairs – in my studio. I left the patio doors open – didn't realize,' she said, her shortness of breath returning. 'Tigger got out. I was looking for him – when your mum knocked.'

'It's OK,' he whispered. 'You don't need to explain. This is what happens when you get wrapped up in your painting. I know I made a joke about it being your funeral, but let's hope it's not going to be the cat's.' He tried to tempt a smile from her with one of his own. Giving up, he added, 'Do you want to go and have a lie down while I talk to Mum?'

'No,' she said, shocked at the suggestion. 'I have to know Tigger's safe.'

'Even so, I'd like you to try,' Adam said, raising himself up and bringing Lucy with him. 'I'm not sure you'd make it upstairs so why don't you lie down on the sofa for a while?'

'But—'

Ignoring her protests, Adam led Lucy past Viv, who handed her a cup of tea. Rather than one of her usual herbal drinks, this was milky and probably sweet, but Lucy accepted it gratefully with trembling hands.

'Here, I'll take that,' Adam said.

With one hand never leaving the small of her back, Adam guided Lucy through to the living room where she sat down carefully on the sofa as if something inside her might break. That something pushed against her womb, telling her to stop worrying, but Lucy wasn't so quick to forgive. She had been irresponsible as she raced up and down the stairs looking for Tigger, proving once again that she wasn't fit to be a mother.

'She's kicking away,' she told Adam.

'Good,' he said. 'Now don't you worry about a thing. I'll find the stupid cat.'

'What are you going to do about your mum? I didn't invite her in, Adam. It was just that I'd got myself worked up and I couldn't breathe. I couldn't stop her.'

'It was probably a good thing she came when she did. Who knows what I might have come home to?' Adam said. He kissed the top of her head and gave her one last instruction before he left. 'Don't move.'

'I won't,' she promised.

Lucy stared at the firmly closed door as she sipped her tea. She felt as if she were a child again, sitting on the stairs listening out for the heated exchanges between her parents, but there were no raised voices floating in from the kitchen. She wanted to believe that this was a good sign, but her parents had inflicted wounds with whispers and so might Viv and Adam.

Putting down her drained cup, Lucy followed the rise and fall of her abdomen with her hand and wondered what lay in store for her daughter. With Lucy setting the example, her little one was going to face some serious challenges unless she found a way to stop this madness. She had to keep fighting if she was going to prevent her father's legacy from being passed on to the next generation, and she wasn't going to do that by hiding away. She had to get up and be the strong person she had once been, so that was what she did.

Taking tentative steps, Lucy crept towards the door and opened it without a sound. The flow of conversation coming from the other side of the house drew Lucy across the hall.

The kitchen door was slightly ajar and the air not as cool as it had been earlier, suggesting Tigger had been locked out. Fighting an impulse to sneak outside to find him, Lucy chose instead to eavesdrop on the conversation from which she had been excluded.

'Do you think I don't know how hard it is for you?' Adam was saying. From the echo of his voice, he was at the far end of the room and Lucy imagined him sitting at the table opposite Viv, two heads clashing over trembling silk flowers.

'I'm not sure you do, Adam,' said Viv. 'You expect too much from people sometimes. You seem to think I can cut Scott out of my life as easily as you did.'

'There was nothing easy about it, Mum. I had to do it for my own sanity,' Adam said. 'And I'm not asking you to take sides. I accepted a long time ago that you were never going to see Scott for what he is.'

'He says the same about you.'

'So you have spoken to him?'

'I've answered his calls,' Viv said, her voice stronger than Adam's. 'And I've said to him what I'll say to you. I won't live like this any more. If you love me as much as you say you do, you have to keep me out of your fights.'

'I wasn't the one who set up the surprise appearance, was I?'

'It might have been Scott's idea but he did it with my blessing,' countered Viv. 'I want him back in my life, Adam. He's been on the sidelines for too long.'

'That was his choice,' Adam said in a low growl. 'He didn't care about you then. Remember?'

'He was twelve years old, Adam. If anyone's to blame

for his choices, it's me,' Viv said, her words twisted with anguish. 'I let him go without argument. We all opted for the easy solution.'

'And Scott was perfectly happy with that until he realized Keith wasn't going to be around for ever,' Adam insisted. 'That's why he's forcing his way back into our lives.'

'My life,' Viv corrected. 'And it's time I let him.'

'Can't you see how you're being manipulated?'

'Keith isn't in the best of health and Scott needs me. I want to do this. You've had the lion's share of my affection for long enough, and you're settled now with a family of your own. It's time I got to know Scott better.'

Lucy rubbed her arm. They sounded like Scott's words.

'He's ready to move on,' Viv continued. 'He's even talking about getting therapy to help him resolve his feelings about, well, everything. I know it's the thing to do in America but I did wonder if it might help you too.'

'Me? Is this an idea that's just crossed your mind now, or by some chance was it planted there by Scott? In case you hadn't noticed, I'm the only sane person around here,' he said. His voice had risen but his breath was unable to keep up with him, making him sound more vulnerable than Lucy would like. She barely caught his next words. 'If anyone needs help, it's Lucy. She's getting worse and I don't know what to do any more.'

There was the scrape of chair legs and Viv's voice was muffled when she said, 'Oh, sweetheart, it's all right. I'm here now.'

'I don't like falling out with you, and if we can find a way for me and Scott to live our separate lives without upsetting you, I'll do whatever you want. I'll do anything,

Mum,' He stopped to take a deep, juddering breath. 'I need you.'

Lucy wrapped her arms around herself as she imagined Viv holding her son.

'I don't know what to do for the best,' he said in a whisper, as if he knew Lucy was close enough to hear. 'I'm terrified every time I go to work in case something happens, and little wonder. You saw what she was like today.'

'Have you taken her to the doctors?'

'I'm scared, and she is too,' he admitted. 'What if he says she's an unfit mother?'

'Are things really that bad?'

If Adam answered, it was with a nod of the head. 'I wouldn't be surprised if they put a social worker at the door when she gives birth to stop us bringing the baby home.'

'But if she needs help, son . . .'

When Lucy heard sharp heels clicking on the porcelain tiles, her eyes darted towards the living room. She didn't think she could make it back without being seen, and she had to stop rushing around while she carried her precious cargo. The footsteps paused and there was the sound of running water.

'Here, drink this,' Viv said.

Lucy slowed her breathing, the air making a soft whooshing sound.

'We start proper parenting classes next week and part of me thinks we should raise it then, but . . . I don't know. Lucy doesn't want to draw attention and I'm tired of arguing with her.'

'I'm no expert but there must be treatment available,'

Viv said. 'It could be something as simple as a pill to help sort out Lucy's hormones. And even if she can't take medication while she's pregnant, we can all be ready when she has the baby.'

'What if it's not her hormones?' Adam said, his voice lifeless. 'What if . . .'

Lucy's heart thudded as she waited for Adam to voice his fears, but there followed an eerie silence. She pictured him sharing a knowing look with his mum. They had already talked through other possibilities and it wasn't too difficult for Lucy to guess what they might be.

Adam released a deep sigh. 'Do you still think I'm settled and happy?' he asked. 'All I wanted was to buy a house and make a family, but it keeps going wrong. My home life's a sham and if I'm not careful, my career's going to nosedive too. I was *determined* not to make the same mistake I made with Rosie. I thought with Lucy I could keep work separate, but I'm struggling to do my job and look after her at the same time.'

'You can't compare Lucy to Rosie. Rosie used you.'

'And Lucy needs me,' Adam added, as if it were the same thing.

'She needs to see a doctor, Adam, if only to rule out anything else.'

'You have no idea how headstrong she can be,' he said. There was a pause followed by the sound of a glass being set down on the table. 'This is killing me.'

Ashamed of what she had been putting him through, Lucy decided to retreat. She had taken a step back when she heard a gasp from Viv and the sound of the patio doors sliding open.

'And where do you think you've been?' asked Adam in response to a distinctive mewl.

'Oh, Lucy's going to be so relieved.'

'Or more worried,' said Adam. 'It would kill her if something happened to him, even though she can't help the way she is. She does things unconsciously and that's where the danger lies. Leaving the patio door open isn't even the worst thing she's done. She begs me to stay with her all the time, but how can I?'

'Oh, Adam. How are you going to manage with the baby?'

'We'll have to take each day as it comes.'

Adam was doing his best to regain his composure but the crackle of emotion in his voice remained. Lucy wanted to run, but couldn't decide if that should be into his arms or as far away as she could get. Adam didn't deserve this.

'I'll help as much as I can, son.'

'Can I trust you?' Adam asked. 'I don't want Scott hearing any of this. He'd make something of it, you know he would.'

'I promise I won't tell,' Viv said, sounding very much like her old self.

In the background, Lucy could hear Tigger crying for attention. She should have felt relief that a disaster had been averted but Adam was right, she still posed a danger and not just to the kitten. She would destroy her family one way or the other, and for the first time in her life, she considered the possibility that her dad had done the right thing.

'There is something you could do,' Adam said to Viv, pausing as if he wasn't sure he should continue. 'Do you think you could look after the cat for a while?'

'I'd be happy to,' Viv said, 'but what will Lucy think?'

Lucy pulled back her shoulders and lifted her chin. After months of making mistakes, she had the opportunity to show Adam she could do something right. She stepped through the door.

'I think you should take him,' she said.

Adam and Viv were at the patio doors and it was her mother-in-law who held the mischievous kitten. Tigger glanced in Lucy's direction briefly before tipping his head back to allow his new guardian to scratch his chin.

'You will look after him, won't you?' Lucy asked before Adam or Viv had recovered.

'I haven't had a cat since I was a girl, but I'll take care of him, Lucy. I'll love him as you would.'

Lucy wanted to thank Viv but the words stuck in her throat. It was going to be a wrench letting Tigger go, but that wasn't what cut deepest into her heart. If she didn't pull herself together soon, it wouldn't only be a kitten that had to be removed for its own protection.

17

Lucy was lying on her side when she heard Adam creep into their bedroom. She had gone to bed early, exhausted after another day pretending to be happy and normal while questioning her every move and emotion. There was a time when she would have been the last one to bed, but in the weeks since Tigger had been taken from her, Lucy had developed the habit of scurrying upstairs the moment she saw Adam stretch and yawn. She couldn't trust herself to lock up for the night, and Adam had made no comment on her change of habits.

She had seen a doctor, or at least the happy, normal version she projected of herself had paid a visit to the GP with Adam. She hadn't mentioned the hysteria, or the physical abuse, and had managed to sound more curious than concerned about her forgetfulness. The doctor had listened with mild amusement and had made a joke to Adam about his own wife never listening to him, but he had been thorough in his examination, testing her reflexes and shining a light into her eyes. The only treatment he could provide was a reassuring squeeze of her hand and a sympathetic look to her husband.

Closing heavy lids, Lucy felt the duvet lift and the mattress dip as Adam slipped into bed. When he switched off the bedside lamp, the length of Lucy's spine tingled as she waited for him to draw his body close to hers. She felt his weight shift as he settled into position, which he did without touching her. She couldn't remember the last time Adam had held her with passion instead of pity.

She knew he was tired. She knew his energy had been spent helping her through another day without disgrace, but she needed that little bit more from him. 'Adam?'

The mattress creaked. He had been facing away but his voice came closer as he whispered, 'I thought you were asleep.'

'You do still love me, don't you?'

A hand slipped around her waist and came to rest on her bump. 'What kind of stupid question is that?' he asked sleepily.

She tugged his arm, pulling him closer until she could feel the warmth of his minty breath on her neck. The cotton sheet beneath her tugged as she wriggled her body back towards his, searching for the perfect fit but not quite finding it.

'It will get better,' she said. '*I'll* get better.'

'You're doing fine.'

'Am I?' she asked, not ready to be reassured. In the darkness that existed behind her closed lids, she searched for the missing pieces that dropped out of her consciousness on a daily basis. What had she missed today?

'You don't think so?'

Lucy scrunched her nose. She didn't need to see Adam to know his eyes were boring into the back of her head.

With her conscience prodded, she said, 'Let me know if you come across my china cup. I haven't got a clue where I put it.'

'Is it in your studio?'

'No, I haven't been up there,' she said.

Lucy's last visit to her studio had simply been to collect a sketchpad so she could doodle away the hours while Adam was at work, and he was working at the office more often than she would like. There was a limit to the excuses he could give Ranjit for staying at home and it made sense to hold back further requests until after the baby was born. That was little more than a month away, she reminded herself as her stomach flipped.

'Have you given up?'

The whirr of thoughts inside Lucy's brain was at odds with the stillness of the room and the steadiness of Adam's breath. 'No, not ever,' she said quickly.

She felt his chin on her shoulder. 'I meant painting.'

'I said I'd do the portrait for Hannah, and I will. The problem is that every time we try to arrange a meeting, something crops up.'

When Adam's body stiffened, Lucy bit her lip. There had been plenty of opportunities to see Hannah and her grandad now that Adam was back at the office. In truth, the only thing that had cropped up was Lucy's nerves.

'Sorry, that's not exactly true,' she confessed. 'I think I'm just scared of making a fool of myself. I like that there are people out there who don't see me as a complete flake and I'd rather keep it that way.'

Adam was quiet for a moment. 'Then why didn't you say that? I can't look after you if you don't tell me what's going on inside your head,' he said, his tone soft despite the sting of the accusation. He pressed a kiss against her neck and his voice was muffled by her curls when he added, 'Don't start hiding things from me again.'

'I wouldn't,' she promised. 'So do you think I should tell Hannah that I can't do it?'

'I'm starting to think you never wanted to take the job in the first place. Another one of your mum's bright ideas that you go along with to keep her happy.'

'But I did want to do it,' Lucy said.

'Did?'

'I mean, I do.'

'Then why the hell are you asking me?' He sounded tired when he added, 'I can't be here twenty-four hours a day telling you what to do, Lucy. I wish I could but I swear, I don't have the strength.'

'I will get better.'

'So you said,' Adam replied. 'But if things don't improve, maybe you should go back to the GP and tell him the truth this time.'

Lucy twisted around so she could guage Adam's expression but in the dim light she could make no sense of the shadows. 'What do you mean?'

'About your dad, for a start,' he said. 'And I don't mind coming with you, so long as you don't shut me up this time. I know you don't want to hear about the possibility that you're carrying a faulty gene, but how else will we get you the help you need?'

'I didn't—' Lucy began, stopping while her brain went into overdrive as she replayed the consultation with her doctor. He had asked about her medical history, and it had been Lucy who had started to speak first. She had intended to explain about her dad but Adam had shot her a look. She had thought he was telling her to keep quiet but had she misread him? Had she talked over him? Had she been too eager to gloss over the problems she had inherited from the past? 'Did I?'

Adam sighed in frustration. 'You need to ask? Seriously, Lucy, do you have to play dumb *all* the time? You knew exactly what you were doing. You know what's wrong with you but you don't want to admit it because . . . Well, who cares why? I'm at my wit's end and I'm really sorry but I'm too tired to have this conversation right now.'

'I'll mention it next time,' she promised, but Adam had lost interest. He attempted to turn away but she kept hold of him. 'You do still love me, don't you?'

'You already asked me that,' Adam replied, deftly avoiding the question a second time.

Ignoring a flutter of panic, Lucy raised herself up on to an elbow. 'I need you show me,' she said.

'I'm here, aren't I?' he said. 'Now stop winding the both of us up and go to sleep. I'm in Manchester tomorrow in case you've forgotten and I'll need an early start.'

Lucy ignored the latest hole that had been exposed in her memory and stroked her hand across Adam's chest. There had been times early on in their relationship when she would have climbed on top of him and demanded his attention but that was back when she had been sure of a favourable response. Now, he lay exhausted by the constant demands of a neurotic wife, and found no rest in the night while she fidgeted or snored.

'Would it be better if I slept on the sofa?' she asked.

There was a sharp hiss as Adam exhaled. 'I'm hardly going to let my pregnant wife sleep on the sofa, am I? Fine, I'll move. I assume that's what this has all been about?'

'No,' she said, forcing the word past her constricting throat. 'I don't want you to go. I just thought you might not want me disturbing you if you have an early start. I don't mind sleeping downstairs.'

Adam snapped back the duvet and swung his legs over the edge of the bed. 'For someone who's concerned about my sleep, you're doing a good job of keeping me awake. I don't care where I sleep now as long as it's away from you.'

'No, Adam,' Lucy called after him, but the door was already closing. 'That's not what I meant.'

As she listened to Adam pull blankets from the airing cupboard, Lucy lay flat on her back and fought against the panic rising from the pit of her stomach. She closed her eyes and tried to understand how she had driven Adam from her bed when all she had wanted was to be held and loved. She didn't blame him for growing tired of her constant demands for reassurance and attention. It was her fault, it always was.

18

The Railway in Meols was on the same road as the garden centre where Lucy had met Scott, and as she pulled into the pub car park, her skin itched with embarrassment at the thought of how she had allowed her brother-in-law's charm and flattery to blind her. Her passion for art might be her strength but it was also a very real weakness, and as she prised herself out of the car and stretched her spine in perfect synchronicity with her baby, she continued to question her decision to meet Hannah and her grandad.

She had told Adam that morning that she was excited by the prospect of painting again and had gone so far as to warn him that she might be locked away in her studio when he came home. He had made some remark about sweeping away the cobwebs before she set to work, but at least he hadn't told her she shouldn't do it. She wanted her mum to be right. She needed something to lift her spirits.

Rubbing what felt like the heel of her daughter's foot, Lucy left behind the spring sunshine and stepped into the darkened pub. The tables were spread out across different levels with columns and corners that made it difficult to see if Hannah had already arrived. Pausing to check her phone, she overheard the elderly gent at the bar make a comment to the barman about football. He had a strong Scouse accent and a gravelly laugh that reminded Lucy of her Liverpool home. Abandoning the text she was about to write, she stepped closer.

'Leonard?'

The man with fine silvery hair turned with a smile on his face and a pint in his hand. He glanced briefly at Lucy's olive-green smock that wasn't as roomy as it had been when she had first worn it, and his smile broadened.

'You must be Lucy.'

In the time it took Lucy to figure out whether to shake Leonard's hand or give him a peck on the cheek, he had brought his hand to her face and pinched her cheek. 'You look a picture,' he said. 'Can I get you a drink?'

'No, no, I'll get these.'

'You will not. Now, what do you want?'

The blush rising in Lucy's cheeks warmed her entire body. In her misspent youth, she could make a fiver last all night, but it had been a long time since a stranger had bought her a drink. The yearning to go back to those times took her by surprise and she laid a guilty hand over the swell of her belly. 'I'll have a lime and soda, please.'

Leonard winked before glancing over his shoulder, 'A lime and soda for my friend, if you'd be so kind, barman. She's the famous artist I was telling you about.'

As the old man escorted Lucy towards a quiet corner of the pub, she tried to imagine what she and Adam would be like in their eighties, free of the dramas of making babies and pursuing careers. A moment later she spied Hannah stacking up her grandad's treasure trove of family albums and felt her heart tug. She prayed that, when the time came, Adam would be the one left grieving for her rather than the other way around.

'You found us then?'

'I know, I'm late – again,' Lucy said, not mentioning that she would have been early if she hadn't turned around halfway to the pub to give in to a nagging doubt that she had left the iron on. She was struggling with a new niggle that she hadn't locked up properly after her fool's errand but she forced a smile. 'If you can believe it, Leonard, I used to be the one left nursing a pint while Hannah and the others were applying another layer of slap.'

'Not everyone can be blessed with your natural beauty,' he said, to which his granddaughter poked her tongue out at him.

'Oh, this isn't natural,' Lucy joked. She had broken the crusted seal on a bottle of foundation before she left the house in an effort to brighten her sallow complexion. Unfortunately, there was little she could do to hide the puffiness around her eyes.

'Still finding it tough?' Hannah asked, the playfulness in her eyes ebbing away as she took a closer look at her friend. 'You look like you've lost weight.'

'You must be joking,' Lucy said, pushing out her belly.

Hannah watched her closely as Lucy repositioned the surrounding chairs to create enough space to sit comfortably at the table. She could feel the pressure building at the back of her nose, a sure sign that there would be an eruption of tears the moment someone made a well-meaning remark about how she was supposed to be blooming.

'How long is it now?'

'Five weeks,' Lucy said, her fingernails digging into her palms.

'Wow, she'll be here before you know it. Are you ready?'

'I think so. We had the nursery set out perfectly, until we started storing all the other paraphernalia we've collected along the way. It's going to take me a week to read through all the instructions,' Lucy said. She took a breath but it wasn't deep enough to push away the pressure building against her chest. She had already made a start working out how to use the bottle sterilizer and the breast pump, as if she were cramming for an exam; one she wouldn't be allowed to fail. 'The one thing we haven't got yet is the pram, but we're going to test drive a few at the weekend.'

'And how are the antenatal classes going?'

'I didn't bother in the end,' Lucy admitted, as if it had been a simple decision taken casually rather than the full-blown panic attack she had experienced in the car park while her fellow mothers-to-be and their partners streamed past. Adam had held her hand tightly, telling her over and over that he wouldn't let anyone take her baby away, but the fact he had to mention the possibility at all had sent her nerves spiralling out of control. Lucy's smile wobbled when she added, 'I've already had a tour of the hospital and I've read up on everything else. You said yourself how you forget half of what they tell you. If I want to know about breathing techniques, I can look it up on YouTube.'

'Are you getting nervous about it?' Hannah asked, as if it wasn't glaringly obvious.

'It doesn't help that you make it sound like she's about to face a firing squad,' Leonard said. 'You'll be fine, love.

Annie always said having babies was the easy part. The trouble starts when they're old enough to run rings around you, not to mention the grandkids who come later.' He shot a look at Hannah.

'Now who's making her nervous?'

Blinking rapidly, Lucy pulled the largest of the photo albums towards her. The cover was dark ebony with a mother-of-pearl inlay and silk cord tassels. The chipped edges suggested it was well-thumbed and the smell of must confirmed she had picked the oldest set of photographs. 'Can I?' she asked.

Leonard shuffled his chair closer so he could look over her shoulder as she opened the album and took a peek into his life. 'That was back when we were courting,' he said as he laid a finger gently on the black-and-white photo at the top left of the page.

The style of clothes looked to be from the fifties, while the couple's awkward pose suggested they weren't familiar enough with each other to show their affection in front of a camera. The image was a two-inch square and the figures were tiny against the backdrop of an overgrown garden with what looked like a dilapidated Anderson shelter in the background. The adjacent photos were of similar quality and although Lucy was eager to continue her search for an image that might serve her purpose, she waited for Leonard to finish with the introductions before turning over the page.

Peeling back the brittle lining sheet, Lucy revealed a large portrait photograph with a white scalloped border.

'That's my Annie.'

'Gosh, she's beautiful.'

'Now you know where I get it from,' Hannah said brightly, only to clear her throat as they all fell silent.

Leonard's eyes glazed over as he stared at the image of his wife, who was no more than twenty at the time. Annie had dark brown eyes that looked towards something or someone out of camera shot. 'She went to a proper photographer and I tagged along,' he said. 'She'd been pouting for the camera, pretending she was Jane Russell, but I didn't want some imitation movie star. I wanted a photo that caught that smile of hers, but Annie hated the gap between her teeth. She didn't understand that it was her perfect imperfections that I loved most, so I made her laugh and she couldn't keep her face straight after that.'

'I was thinking we could use that one for your portrait,' suggested Hannah.

The photo was faded and didn't have the depth of detail that Lucy would prefer, but it had something special that she hoped she had the skills to capture. 'I'll give it my best shot,' she said to Leonard. Realizing he had been quiet on the subject because he wasn't able to speak, she added, 'How about we go through the rest of the photos and then decide? I might be able to incorporate some of the detail from other images so I get the colour of Annie's eyes and her skin tone right.'

When Leonard nodded, Lucy turned a page and peeled back another layer of his life. There were more professional photographs, except this time her subject was wearing a white, tea-style wedding dress.

'It was all the rage,' he said. 'I tried to tell Annie she'd regret not having a full-length dress, but she knew best.'

'She had a mind of her own, my nan,' Hannah added.

'And did she regret it?'

Leonard chuckled. 'Oh yes, and she blamed me for not talking her out of it, but that was my Annie. She was always scolding me.'

'I think you called it nagging, Grandad.'

The old man sipped his pint and swallowed back the hard lump in his throat. 'Whenever anyone asked me what the secret was to a happy marriage, I told them straight: my wife was always right even when she was wrong.'

Lucy trailed her finger down her glass, collecting droplets of condensation until they fell like tears. 'So you did argue?'

'Yeah, we had some right set-tos, but we never went to bed on an argument,' he said, then laughed. 'Sometimes that meant staying up half the night until one of us gave in out of pure exhaustion, but it worked.'

If Leonard were giving her the perfect recipe for a happy marriage, Lucy feared she lacked too many of the essential ingredients. The arguments with Adam weren't the kind of disagreements that could be debated. There was no chance of compromise or backing down because they had invariably been caused by things that couldn't be undone or unsaid. And there was no risk of going to bed on an argument; Adam was still sleeping downstairs.

Leonard's wrinkles deepened when he realized how intently Lucy was listening to his wise words. 'What made my marriage work was that I had the good fortune to marry the most loving, self-sacrificing and fiercely protective woman I have ever met. Annie said what needed to be said, but she listened too. I'd like to think she'd say the same of me. Give and take, that's what it's about.'

'Remember the time Nan wanted to take up pottery?'

Leonard chuckled to himself. 'It was after we'd both retired. Annie decided we needed a new interest we could share, so she signed us up for pottery classes. I think I've still got a couple of the pots we made in the cupboard somewhere.'

Pushing aside a mental image of Leonard and Annie in the iconic pose from the film *Ghost*, Lucy thought again about her own marriage. Their shared interest had been walking, but since the wedding, Lucy would be hard pressed to recall any long treks other than the ones Adam's firm organized. Adam had threatened to take her rock climbing but she had become pregnant before anything had been arranged. She wasn't particularly interested in technology, and although Adam had once expressed an interest in learning to paint, he had so far refused to pick up a paintbrush.

As Lucy's mind turned, so did the pages. There followed photographs of christenings, holidays and more weddings as Leonard and Annie's family expanded. Annie's hemline shortened through the sixties, lengthened again in the seventies, until she settled into her own style. In the most recent photos, she wore expandable trousers and polyester tops that pulled across her bosom; the slender girl who had been too shy to hold her beau's hand had transformed into a handsome woman who was proud of the wrinkles that mapped out a life well-lived. Halfway through the last album, the photos came to an abrupt end and they all stared at the empty pages until Leonard found the courage to close it.

Once they had agreed which photos Lucy would take with her, Leonard offered to buy lunch and refused to take no for an answer. Lucy chose a sandwich, something light and quick that wouldn't delay her return to her studio for too long. Leonard's passion for his late wife had given her the desire to pick up a paintbrush again and she needed to know she could do so without shaking in fear.

'While Grandad's at the bar ordering our lunch, we need to discuss money,' Hannah said.

'I told you I'd do it for free,' Lucy replied, ignoring the voice in her head that reminded her she needed the cash.

Adam had told her not to worry about finances and while it was one expression of his love that she could quantify, there was something about not earning her keep that jarred. When they had married, Lucy had been determined to keep some independence and they each kept their own bank account with a joint one for household bills. Adam had insisted he continue to pay the mortgage, but in every other respect, they contributed equally, or at least they had.

In the last few months, Lucy's contributions had diminished along with her savings pot, and she didn't know what she would do when it was all gone. She didn't want to have to ask Adam if she needed extras like clothes and toiletries. She was demanding enough and soon she would be putting in requests on the baby's behalf too. She would put it off until it was necessary – or until she could find a means of paying her own way again. She was beginning to regret saying she would be a full-time mum, and couldn't remember why she had said it at all, but if Adam was happy to support her, it was the right thing to do.

Pulling out an envelope, Hannah said, 'I've checked your website for prices but if it's not enough, tell me. And don't look so awkward, it's not my money I'm handing over. The whole family's contributed and we'll be offended if you don't take it.'

With her hands resting on her stomach, Lucy made no move to take the cash. 'I haven't done anything yet, and while I'd like to think I'll have it finished before the baby comes, I can't rush this, not after hearing such wonderful things about Annie. I refuse to take a penny until you have the finished product, Hannah. There's still a chance I won't produce something worth selling.'

Hannah's fingers tapped out a tune on the envelope. 'Is this putting too much pressure on you? You don't look well, Lucy. Are you eating enough? I have some great tips for heartburn if you need them.'

'I've been eating fine,' Lucy said and, as subtly as she could manage, she puffed out her gaunt cheeks and smiled.

'Then what's wrong? You haven't killed the kitten, have you?' Hannah said, her playful smile quickly falling away. 'Oh, my God, is that it? Has something happened?'

'No,' Lucy said. 'Honestly, he's in safe hands.'

'But not your hands,' Hannah concluded when the heat rising through her friend's body reached her cheeks. She rolled her eyes. 'I knew Adam would talk you out of it. He talks you out of everything.'

'No, he doesn't,' Lucy said sharply. 'Why would you even say that?'

Hannah winced and her tone was softer when she said, 'I just mean it's a habit you seem to have gotten into. I was hoping after our turn around Marine Lake that we might hook up a bit more…'

'It's difficult to find the time when I'm still working out

how all this settling down and being married is supposed to work. You were exactly the same, Hannah.'

Her friend could have cited various examples to prove the contrary – including the time a pregnant Hannah had left her husband with two kids for the weekend to join Lucy for what was to be their last music festival. Instead, she showed some rare diplomacy and simply shrugged. 'I suppose,' she said. 'If I'm being snarky it's only because I miss you, Luce.'

'And I miss you too, but I need Adam more. You have no idea how much,' Lucy said as she glanced towards the bar. Leonard would know exactly how she felt. 'I swear I'd be a danger to myself – and others – if it wasn't for him. I left a door wide open for Tigger to escape. I thought . . . well, I can't tell you what I thought, but thankfully he came back and now my mother-in-law's taking care of him for a while.'

'Hardly cause to have him confiscated.'

'He wasn't confiscated. I asked her to take him,' Lucy said. 'I couldn't cope.'

'If you think a kitten's hard work, you're in for one hell of a shock when—' Hannah said, but managed to stop herself mid-sentence. She didn't see the tears welling in Lucy's eyes because she was too busy squeezing hers shut. 'Shut up, Hannah.'

'You're not saying anything I'm not thinking,' Lucy said as she nudged the envelope towards her friend. 'You'd better put that away, Leonard's on his way back.'

Slipping the money into her bag, Hannah said, 'Are you absolutely sure about the portrait? I don't want to make things worse.'

'You're not,' Lucy said. 'I need to do this.'

19

The tip of Lucy's paintbrush didn't so much as quiver as she offered it to the canvas. It had taken a week to bring her tremors under control but she had become adept at ignoring the armchair where Tigger used to make his bed, and the steel-grey drops of ocean splattered on the legs of her easel. Her focus remained on the photograph clipped above the canvas in a protective sleeve.

Having blocked out the shape of Annie's head and shoulders in muted shades of burnt umber, Lucy had added fresh colours to her palette. The violets, oranges and yellows were not an obvious match for her subject's skin tone but Lucy had been experimenting and, comparing the mix with later photos rather than the faded one she was working from, she was confident she would get the balance right.

'And what are you smiling at?' asked Christine, her voice floating out of nowhere and giving Lucy a start.

Wiping off paint she had smudged on her vest top in fright, Lucy said, 'Where did you come from?'

Christine stepped closer, moving slowly to analyse every

detail of her daughter's present state. 'You weren't expecting me?'

The anxiety in her mum's face reflected the kind of fear Lucy had spent the best part of the morning pretending wasn't there. 'Why? What's Adam said?'

'Nothing,' replied Christine, only to pull a face. 'Although, he did mention the mix-up with the pram yesterday.'

A mix-up was such a benign description and nothing like how Lucy remembered it. Adam had forgone their usual Saturday together so that Lucy could get on with her painting. There had been some suggestion of catching up with his old mates at the rock-climbing club but, of course, Lucy had got it wrong.

While Adam was out, she had taken a break from her studio to do a little online shopping. Using the last of her savings, she had found the pram they had been considering and phoned the store to negotiate what she thought was a particularly good deal. The travel system had a bassinet that could be used in the house so they didn't have to bring the crib downstairs during the day, and came with a free base for the car seat.

She had been looking forward to telling Adam and had been horrified when he had returned home with a huge box that had an image of a jogger-style pram on the side.

'But we didn't want a three-wheeler,' she had protested.

'Yes we did. It's the one we were looking at last weekend,' he had said slowly. 'We talked about taking the baby out for long country walks.'

'But we never go on walks any more,' she had replied, smarting from her own stupidity and the prospect of having to tell Adam what she had done.

'What is your problem? I thought you'd be pleased.'

'I've bought a pram too,' she had said, dropping her gaze to stare at the floor.

'After me saying I was going out to buy one?'

'Yes,' she had been forced to agree. Adam had commented that morning how the baby was due in less than a month, and it was this that had prompted her to look online. Unfortunately, Lucy had missed the point entirely about Adam going out shopping and to top it all, their choices couldn't have been more different.

She had shown him the store's web page, which she had purposely left open so she could boast about haggling with the shop assistant, but it had turned out to be a humiliating confession.

'Why are you getting upset?' he had asked. 'You can cancel the order.'

'And tell them what? That I was too stupid to remember that my husband had gone out shopping for a pram on the same day?'

'It's not something I particularly want to advertise either,' Adam had muttered. 'You don't have to tell them anything.'

'But the assistant was so helpful and not explaining would be plain rude. What if he thinks the baby's . . .' She hadn't been able to finish that thought. She hadn't wanted Adam to finish it either.

'People change their minds all the time,' he had said. 'It would take someone with a twisted mind to jump to the conclusion that something bad had happened.' His eyes had narrowed. 'Why would you even think that?'

Her cheeks had become scorched with guilt as she tried

to think up the right response but her mind simply whirred. 'I don't know.'

'You do want this baby, don't you?'

'Of course!'

'It wasn't that long ago you said it was a mistake,' Adam had reminded them both as his mind began to turn in time with Lucy's. 'And how often have you put the baby at risk with your forgetfulness, or your hysteria for that matter? Were you actually hoping something would go wrong? Are you so worried about what you might be passing on to her that you'd rather she didn't survive?' His eyes had widened and his mouth fell open. 'Oh, Lucy. I'm right, aren't I?'

'No!' she had cried, raising her voice loud enough to block out that small voice in her head that was agreeing with him. Could that be what she had secretly wanted? Who would blame her for not wanting to bring another tortured soul into the world?

The paintbrush in Lucy's hand trembled as she told herself it wasn't too late to make things right. 'I do want this baby, Mum.'

Christine rubbed her daughter's back. 'I know you do, love. And buying two prams certainly goes to prove how excited you both are.'

'I'm not cancelling my order. Both prams have car seats so we can have one for each car.'

'Not a bad idea,' Christine said a little too brightly.

Lucy set down her paintbrush before she dropped it. 'Have you been here long?'

'Not really. I thought I'd say hello first before helping Adam with the Sunday lunch.'

'Do you need me to do anything? I promise not to go near the oven, but I could be trusted to peel the veg.'

'No need, all the hard work's done. I roasted the beef and the potatoes this morning so I could spend more time with you. There's not much left to do now, although I'm not sure if Adam was impressed or disappointed that he wasn't going to keep me trapped in the kitchen with him. I've told him he can still be my sous chef and I've given him a long list of things to get on with once he's finished the housework. He wants so much to be of use. You've got a good one there, love.'

Lucy wanted to explain how she had risen early to clean the house before her mum's arrival, but if Adam needed to finish the job, it must be because she hadn't done it properly. Adam wasn't a good one, he was the very best, and so she held her tongue. She was learning it was usually the better option.

'So if you don't mind, I'll stay here and keep you company while you paint until Adam needs me,' continued Christine as she slipped behind Lucy to peer over her shoulder. 'It's wonderful.'

Lucy glanced at the muddy smears on the canvas. 'You can't possibly tell that yet.'

'Of course I can, and it has nothing to do with what I see now, but what I know you're capable of doing. I know what you're like.'

Christine's clumsy attempts to shore up her daughter's crumbling confidence had the opposite effect. Even Lucy didn't know what she was capable of, and while it was Adam who had been the first to make a connection between Lucy and her dad, it would be impossible for her mum not to see it too. Had she given him the same advice she had given her daughter, to lock himself away in the back room and paint to lift his spirits?

Taking a deep breath, Lucy asked, 'And how well did you know Dad?'

'That was different,' Christine said, tensing slightly.

'But what was he like in those last few months when his business was failing?'

'Lucy, listen to me,' her mum said, a clear sign she was about to retreat from the subject. 'I don't think it's doing you any good dwelling on the past. We got through it, didn't we? If anything, it made us stronger and I'm so proud of the woman you've become. You shouldn't lose sight of that.'

'But it's not healthy to pretend it didn't happen either,' Lucy insisted. 'Please, Mum. Were there any signs of how depressed he was?'

Christine continued to look over her daughter's shoulder, finding it easier to direct her answer to the stained canvas. 'With hindsight, perhaps there were, but at the time I didn't know that much about depression and your dad wasn't one to talk about his feelings.'

'Did he ever see a doctor about it? He might not have wanted to worry you, but maybe . . .'

Her mum was shaking her head. 'He kept everything to himself – and I mean *everything*. If I asked him how he was, he always said he was fine. It reached the point where all he would give was one-word answers, and maybe that was the symptom I missed. At the time, I thought it was me he'd lost interest in, not life itself.'

None of this was close to the answer Lucy was searching

for and she continued to pick at the scab covering an old wound. 'He must have let some of his feelings out when you argued. Was he angry? Was he scared? What made him think the unthinkable?'

'Lots of things, although I do think part of your dad's problem was that he confused his fears with reality. When he fixated on something, there was nothing I could say or do to reassure him.'

Lucy stared at the canvas until her brushstrokes melded into a murky mess and the picture began to sway. She made a grab for the easel, thinking it was about to topple over but it was her mum who had to catch Lucy. It wasn't only the canvas but the entire room that was moving.

'Lucy, are you all right?'

As her mum guided her to the armchair, Lucy said, 'He was like me.'

Christine opened the balcony window before kneeling down in front of her daughter. 'No, what's happening to you is not the same, it really isn't. You must leave this alone.'

'But I can't leave it alone, can I? I get fixated on things. My fears are turning into reality,' Lucy said, describing her father's symptoms.

'I used the wrong words,' Christine said. 'What you have is baby brain mixed with last-minute jitters, that's all.'

When Lucy splayed her hands across her bump, Christine followed suit and together they encircled the next generation that was meant to give them hope. Lucy loved her daughter, in the same way that her dad had loved her, but that comparison gave her no comfort.

'I know you don't want to hear this, Mum, but what if

there's a link? What if I've inherited a yet-to-be diagnosed mental illness?' she asked. 'I need to know.'

Christine took hold of Lucy's hands, breaking the connection with her unborn grandchild. She waited until Lucy could hold her gaze. 'OK, this has gone far enough' she said firmly. 'There was good reason for your dad's paranoia.'

An electric current ran through Lucy's body but it was the creak on the stairs that made her jump.

'I thought you came up here to encourage Lucy to paint, not distract her?' Adam said as he appeared at the top of the staircase. He had been wiping his hands on a tea towel but they quickly stilled. 'What's wrong? Lucy? Are you all right?'

'She had a bit of dizzy spell,' Christine explained. 'I think I might stay with her a while if you can get on with lunch?'

Adam had drawn closer. 'Ah, there might be a problem with that,' he confessed. 'I've been trying to make the stuffing from the ingredients you brought but I think I've made a mess of things. Do you mind coming to check?'

He was holding out his arm and reluctantly, Christine let him guide her to her feet. 'Do you want to come down with us, love?' she asked her daughter.

No, Lucy thought. I want us both to stay here so you can finish what you were about to say.

'I'd be told off if I tried to drag her away from her painting,' Adam said before Lucy could think of a more considered answer. 'But if you're feeling unwell, love . . .'

'No, I'm fine now,' Lucy said. 'You go down, Mum. We can catch up later.'

Lucy sat in her armchair nursing the glass of water her mum had fetched before she was dragged away by Adam.

She didn't know what her mum had been about to tell her, but she wasn't as frightened by the prospect as she might expect. At least now she knew there was an answer close to hand and although the parallels in her father's life were unnerving, she was getting to know him better by the day and it made her feel less alone. Taking a deep breath, she let the familiar scent of oil paint transport her back to her childhood, which she viewed with fresh eyes.

The last days and weeks with her dad had been unremarkable at the time, but she could recall sneaking into the back room to watch him paint. He was rarely happy with his work and often reused canvases, so she hadn't questioned why there was a stack of stark white surfaces where once there had been landscapes, still-lifes and portraits. Later, everyone had assumed this had been her dad's first step to erase himself from their lives, but what if there was another reason? The blank canvases might have been a last-ditch attempt for him to make a fresh start – to press the restart button on his life. She was sure he hadn't wanted to abandon her, in the same way that she wouldn't want to abandon Adam, or their baby, but if she knew anything about her illness, it was that its effects were unpredictable.

As she returned to her easel, the walls didn't bend and bow as they had before, and Lucy's hand steadied surprisingly quickly. She spent the next half-hour working on the structure of Annie's face and found herself envying the delight captured in her subject's eyes as she looked to her future husband. Longing to feel something similar and hoping that whatever her mum was about to tell her would mark the start of a healing process for her mind and her marriage, Lucy set down her tools of distraction and headed downstairs.

Her steps faltered on the very last step as she picked up the hushed tone of Adam's voice coming from the kitchen. She didn't make a sound as she drew closer and pressed her ear to the closed door.

'Oh, Adam, I'm sorry for blubbing like an idiot. I don't know where that came from,' her mum was saying. There was a pause as she blew her nose.

'You've been holding back those feeling for far too long,' Adam said, his voice soothing and melodic. It was a tone he had often used with Lucy, using gentle words and probing questions to dig deep into her soul. 'It must have been so hard for you to keep something like that to yourself.'

'And I never thought I'd tell anyone, not ever,' Christine said, her words catching but her voice was growing stronger. 'But if I can tell you, I can tell Lucy. She's expecting an answer and I've kept it from her for long enough.'

'Perhaps you're right, but is now the time for her to hear something like that?'

Lucy reached for the door handle. It came as no surprise that Adam would be the one to coax the long-awaited answers from her mum, and whilst Lucy would have preferred to have heard it first, if Adam knew the truth about her dad now, it would at least save her the agony of breaking the news to him. They would know what was wrong and together they would fix it. Her fingers wrapped around the cold steel handle but it was Adam's next words that sent a shiver down her spine.

'You've seen what she's like, Christine. Something like that could push her over the edge,' he said. After a nervous cough, he added, 'Sorry, that was a really bad choice of words.'

'You don't think . . .'

'Please, never think that. Although . . .' Adam paused and Lucy held her breath. 'We can't ignore the parallels. I'm beginning to understand exactly what you went through with your husband. Lucy's been pushing me away too. She won't even let me sleep with her any more, and I'm sure she'd lock herself in her studio permanently if she could. You've seen how she's letting everything else go. Her appearance, the house, me. Sound familiar?'

'Was I wrong to encourage her to paint?'

'You were trying to help, and if it keeps her safe, it's no bad thing.'

'But is it enough? Do you need me to come and stay for a while? I don't mind sleeping on the couch.'

'I'm not sure there's room for two of us,' Adam said. Despite his attempt at a joke, there was no hint of a smile behind his words when he added, 'I know how much you love your daughter, but I love her too, and I want to be the one to look after her. She's refusing to go back to the doctors or mention how this obsession with her dad has affected her, but from what you've said, is there really any point? We will get through this, Christine. I'm not going anywhere, and I'd like to hope that all of this will make us stronger. I won't let anything happen to Lucy, or the baby. You have my word.'

Lucy relaxed her grip on the handle as her husband's words sunk in. Adam wanted to protect her, even if that meant protecting her from the truth, and whatever he had heard had given him the confidence to think they could work on it together, without outside involvement. She believed him when he had said he would keep her and, more importantly, the baby safe. And in the meantime, she would do what she could to help. She hadn't meant to push him away, and perhaps this was one aspect of her father's mistakes that she didn't have to repeat.

As Lucy backtracked upstairs to wait until she was called down for her dinner, she clung to the words that she had been longing to hear. He still loved her and she wasn't as close to the edge of the world as she had feared.

20

Lucy's body ached after another night tossing and turning in an otherwise empty bed. She trudged downstairs in search of her husband and found him peering at the contents of the fridge. He looked up and smiled.

'So you still remember how to find your way downstairs? I thought you'd go straight up to your studio to spend another day with your beloved Annie.'

Placing both hands on the small of her back, Lucy stretched her spine. 'I know where the kitchen is and I also know it's Saturday,' she hit back before she could stop herself. She hadn't meant to challenge him. 'What I mean is, I've only got a couple of weeks to go and I don't want to give up one of our last weekends as a couple. Annie can wait.'

Adam's smile evaporated. 'You really don't like the idea of it not being just the two of us, do you?'

Cursing herself for another stupid remark, Lucy's slow, steady pulse began to quicken. 'Not at all.' Was that the right answer? In a rush, she added, 'I thought we might go out for a walk. We could scout around for a route to take the baby in her new pram.'

Adam's features continued to darken. 'Is that another jab about me getting the wrong pram?'

'I was the one who got the wrong one,' Lucy said, wishing she would learn to think before she spoke. 'I thought . . . OK, if not a walk, we could go for a pub lunch somewhere.'

'I'd rather you concentrated on finishing the portrait. Due dates aren't set in stone, Lucy, and you don't want your best mate Hannah breathing down your neck to finish it while you're getting to grips with a new baby.'

'She wouldn't—' Lucy clamped her mouth shut before she found herself correcting her husband a second time. 'If she tries, I'll tell her she'll have to wait. I promise.'

'Even so.'

Adam closed the fridge and as he turned, she stepped in front of him. She lifted her head so that her lips were ready to meet his. 'We could go back to bed,' she whispered, aiming for a seductive rather than a desperate tone but missing the mark.

Adam gave her a brief peck. 'I hate to say this but I already have plans with a Mr Sainsbury. I thought I'd make one of my lasagnes. We can double up and put some in the freezer, ready for the post-birth chaos.'

Not liking being turned down for a lasagne, Lucy said, 'Mum's going to make lots of meals for us to freeze. You don't need to bother.'

'But I want to bother. I know your mum resents the fact that I took you away, and would like nothing more than to make me redundant in your life, but don't I deserve some credit for picking you up every time you fall to pieces?' Adam said as he sidestepped her. 'Why do you keep pushing me away?'

Lucy had thought she was doing the exact opposite. She tried again. 'OK, if you want to stay in, why don't we do something else? I could always teach you how to paint.'

'I think you're mistaking me for my brother. He's the one interested in art.'

Lucy could feel a swell of panic. 'But remember how you said you wanted to learn.'

Now the confusion was Adam's. 'You mean like you said you wanted to go rock climbing? We made a lot of promises when we were trying to impress each other, Lucy. They were never meant to be taken seriously,' he scoffed. 'I'm making lasagne and I need to go shopping. Go lock yourself away in your studio. I'm perfectly capable of amusing myself.'

Lucy's churning stomach refused to settle. Was Adam saying he didn't mind, or didn't care? She was trying to close the distance that had opened up between them but what if it was too late? Why didn't he want to spend time with her? 'There's mince in the fridge, and milk and cheese,' she said. 'What else do you need? If we've run out of lasagne sheets, you could do a pasta bake instead with the penne.'

'What is this? Aren't I allowed to go out? Don't you trust me?' Adam said. Mild amusement transformed to disappointment when he added, 'Is this because I keep mentioning Naomi? Are you worried because she's broken off her engagement? Has your little mind been working overtime?'

'You hate Naomi. I know that,' Lucy said, glossing over the fact that she had no recollection of Adam mentioning the break-up. Was her insecurity a reaction to information she had wanted to bury? Was she jealous?

Adam rolled his eyes. 'Wherever did you get the idea that I hated her? I'd be in deep trouble at work by now if she wasn't covering my back while I'm here playing nursemaid to you. I can understand why you might feel a bit intimidated knowing I'm around someone that beautiful and way more clever than any other woman I know, but that's no reason to distrust me.'

'I do trust you, Adam,' she said, the words forced out by a timely kick from her daughter. She had to remain calm. She would cause a scene if she wasn't careful, and the last thing she wanted was to push her husband into the arms of another woman. 'And you're right, you deserve some time to yourself. It'll be chaos here in a couple of weeks and we both need to recharge our batteries. You go, I'm being silly. Please, Adam. Ignore me.'

She pulled a face to let him know she was fully aware that she was being irrational – again – but that it was under control. To her relief, he smiled.

'Can I rely on you to stay out of trouble while I'm out?'

'I'll make myself a cup of tea and take it up to my studio. You won't hear a peep out of me for the rest of the day.'

Adam kissed her forehead. 'That's my girl,' he said. He was halfway to the door when he added, 'It's the farmer's market in St Andrew's today so I might be some time, assuming I'm allowed to go?'

'Of course you are, I'll be fine,' Lucy said, a mantra she continued to repeat to herself on a loop as she made her tea and carried it up to her studio, the echo of the closing front door following her. Suppressing unpleasant thoughts about what her husband might have planned without her, Lucy removed the dust sheet draped over her easel.

Annie's portrait was taking shape and Lucy was currently working on the background. She had sketched the outline of a table that would hold symbols of the couple's long and happy marriage, and her next task was to add the pots Leonard had mentioned throwing in their pottery classes, using photos Hannah had managed to acquire in secrecy.

Lucy took her position in front of the easel as her mind ran through a checklist that would unshackle her from her surroundings. Realizing she hadn't checked the kitchen before heading upstairs, she told herself she didn't need to. She hadn't used the hob, or taken anything from the fridge freezer, and what did it matter if she had left open a window or door? Tigger was having a whale of a time with his new mum and had all but ignored Lucy when she had last visited Viv.

Her reassurances were futile, and she made the slow trek down two flights of stairs to find the kitchen as she would hope to find it – except, on closer inspection, there were greasy smears on the cupboard doors. She polished them before dragging herself back upstairs, pausing on the first-floor landing to catch her breath after a well-aimed kick in the ribs from her daughter. She consoled herself with the satisfaction of knowing with certainty that all was as it should be, as long as she didn't allow herself to worry about what Adam might be up to.

Resuming her position in front of the easel, Lucy returned the smile on the face emerging from the canvas. She could imagine Leonard standing somewhere behind them, making his wife's eyes sparkle, but she wouldn't be distracted again and ignored their imaginary onlooker. Stretching up to pin the photos of the pots next to the original portrait photo, Lucy froze. Annie wasn't there.

She whirled around, scanning the paint-splattered floor and spinning so fast that she made herself dizzy. Unable to find where the photo might have fallen, she turned in a wider circle then stooped down to pick up the dust sheet. She ignored the next wave of dizziness as she straightened up and shook the cotton out. Her ears strained for the sound of the plastic sleeve containing the photo fluttering to the ground, but all she heard was a whooshing sound against her eardrums.

As she turned in another fruitless circle, it was Lucy's thoughts that began to spin. She hadn't moved the photo since clipping it to the easel when she had first started the portrait. Where on earth could it have gone, and what would she do if she didn't find it? Leonard had entrusted her with the original and it was irreplaceable. Why hadn't she warned him that his trust was misplaced? It was possible that she could finish her painting from memory with the help of her preliminary sketches, but it wouldn't be perfect. Leonard had already lost his wife and this would be like losing another piece of her.

A sob tore from Lucy's throat as she searched every nook and cranny in the studio. She found all of the other photos Leonard had given her in a folder where she had kept them for safekeeping. It was only the single most important one of all that she couldn't find and as the minutes ticked by, she realized she had been looking in the wrong place. Sinking to the floor, Lucy closed her eyes and replayed her movements in the studio the day before. She had been working on the background and hadn't needed to look at the photo. Was that why she had moved it? But where to? The answer was beyond her grasp.

Lucy wanted to stay calm for the baby's sake, but it was already too late. She could feel her breath catching as her lungs refused to take in sufficient air. Panicking made the task twice as hard and she grabbed her phone while she could still speak. What if Adam didn't answer? What if he was too busy with someone else? What if that somebody wasn't Mr bloody Sainsbury, but bloody Naomi?

'Adam?' she cried when the call was answered after two rings. 'Thank God, thank God. You have to come home. I'm sorry. Please, I need you.'

'I'll be right there,' Adam said. The phone went dead.

Knowing he was on his way, Lucy managed to slow her breathing and her thoughts. She retraced her steps again in her mind. She had said goodnight to Annie as she covered her with the dust sheet, but it was the painting she recalled covering and not the photo. She had done a quick tidy up and there had been scraps of sketches she had thrown away . . .

When Adam arrived home, Lucy was kneeling in the courtyard amongst a sea of household waste and an upturned recycling bin. She had found the discarded drawings. 'It's not here,' she sobbed. 'I've lost Annie's photo, Adam. Leonard's going to be heartbroken.'

Adam set down the shopping bags he hadn't thought to drop as he rushed through the house to find her. 'It must be in your studio.'

'It isn't. I've looked everywhere.'

'I'll look.'

Lucy stayed where she was while Adam took up the search. She had hiccups, as did the baby, but otherwise all was still. She dreaded telling Leonard what she had done but she would complete the portrait. She would fix this.

'Is this what you're looking for?'

Adam was framed in the patio doors. He had taken off his jacket and the glare from his white T-shirt was almost as strong as the glint of sun reflecting off the plastic sleeve dangling from his hand. Lucy struggled to her feet and squinted as she took a step towards the missing photo.

'Where was it?' she asked as her body flooded with relief.

'Clipped to your easel.'

'No it wasn't,' she snapped, as a different kind of emotion swelled inside her. 'I looked there.'

Adam's reaction was just as quick. He let his hand drop and, as he turned away, he flung the photo across the dining table.

'No, wait,' Lucy pleaded as she hurried after him. 'Honestly, Adam, I looked. It wasn't there.'

He spun around. 'How am I supposed to respond to that, Lucy? I can't change the facts to suit. Or do you want me to start lying to you?'

'It wasn't there, Adam!'

'Then I apologize. It must be me who's losing my mind.'

'I am not losing my mind!' she shouted. 'It—'

'It wasn't there,' he snarled. 'Yes, I think I got that. I'm the liar. I must be, because you're back to questioning everything I do.'

'I'm not questioning you.'

'Then what was this morning all about? Would you like to check the shopping bags to see what I've bought and where I've been? Was this whole crisis with the photo simply a trick to get me back home?' Before Lucy could answer, he added, 'Well, here's another little puzzle for you to ponder over. Work out where I'm going now.'

As Adam went to grab his car keys from the counter, Lucy lunged at him. Her eyes were wide and the rational voice inside her head that was meant to soothe and calm her was all but drowned out by the doubts and fears she had been trying to ignore. 'You can't leave,' she cried. 'I won't let you.'

Adam snorted a laugh as he shook himself free from her grasp. 'And how do you propose to stop me? Are you going to make another pathetic attempt to seduce me? Look at you, Lucy. Look at the hovel you live in,' he added as he swept his arm across the spotlessly clean kitchen and pointed an accusing finger towards the rubbish she had scattered across the courtyard. 'You're a mess.'

'I'll clean up,' she promised, clawing at his arm. 'I'll make everything right. I'll do whatever you want, Adam. I'm sorry.'

'Let go of me,' he said, glaring at the fingers digging into his flesh. 'I'm not talking to you while you're like this.'

'But you can't go. We have to talk. You *know* why I'm like this,' she said, tightening her grasp.

'Do I?'

'Yes, Mum told you!' she yelped, feeling the ground shake beneath her feet. She had decided she didn't want to know the truth, but Adam was meant to be helping her, protecting her. Why wasn't he? What was she doing wrong? 'What did she say about Dad, Adam? What's wrong with me?'

Adam yanked his arm away. 'Do you seriously want me to tell you?' he asked, his voice infuriatingly calm. 'Aren't you crazy enough as it is? Look what you've done, Lucy.'

He twisted his arm so she could see the marks she had left from gripping him so tightly. 'I don't know about you, but I'm not sure I can take much more of this.'

'Don't say that. I'm sorry,' she cried. 'I'm sorry.'

While Lucy continued to sob, Adam spun around to grab something from the rack. 'Here, why don't you do the job properly?' he said, holding out a carving knife.

'No, Adam, please. I don't want to hurt you,' she pleaded, but her eyes were drawn towards the flash of the blade. She wanted everything to stop and her mind turned as she fought to find a way out of her madness. With each repetition, she heard the click of bicycle spokes until her thoughts became a blur. She grabbed him again. Pleaded with him. Argued. But her words kept tripping her up and very soon she was retreating into herself. She sank to the floor, her emotions draining away to leave her spent and confused.

Lucy had no idea how long she stayed there but when she crept out from the corners of her mind, she found she was alone. Using the back of her hand to wipe away tears and snot, she attempted to lift herself into a sitting position but an intense pain pulled across her abdomen and she fought for breath. When the pain eased, she shuffled along the floor so she could rest her back against a cupboard. The tiles were wet and slippery beneath her and, recalling the last time she had found herself in a puddled heap on the kitchen floor, she looked around the deserted kitchen for an upturned beer bottle. What she found was a knife and blood spatters.

Another pain rippled across her stomach and she glanced down expecting to find herself in a pool of blood but the liquid she had trailed across the floor was clear. Her waters had broken.

'Adam!' she screamed.

What had she done? She couldn't remember. Did she grab the knife? If she had, why wasn't she bleeding? The details were hazy but she was certain she hadn't intended to hurt anyone, or at least not Adam. They had struggled and then . . .

She released a moan. He had tried to get away from her but she had clung to him. What was too terrifying to remember? She didn't want to know. All she wanted was Adam.

'Don't give up on me,' she whispered.

Before she could call out for him again, she gasped with fresh pain. She panted in the vain hope that she could slow her contractions. She was about to have her baby and she was all alone.

'Adam!' she screamed. 'The baby's coming!'

21

There were too many people crowded into the tiny hospital room but no one except Lucy seemed aware that the walls were closing in around them. She was desperate to go to the toilet but couldn't get out of bed wearing only her smock and the pair of disposable knickers the midwife had given her.

'Are you all right, love?' her mum whispered.

Lucy refused to lift her gaze from the delicate pink bundle asleep in the transparent crib next to her bed. If everyone would just hold their breath, she might be able to hear her baby's gentle snores. Her little girl had downy blond hair, blue-grey eyes, and precisely ten fingers and ten toes. How Lucy had been able to bring something so perfect into the world was nothing short of a miracle.

'Lucy?'

'I'm fine, Mum.'

When she did look up, Lucy found three sets of eyes upon her. Christine and Viv were vying for position next to the crib and it had yet to be settled which of the grand-mothers would hold their granddaughter first. Faye, the midwife, was happy to take a step back, having already had that pleasure. She had brought the baby into the world to the accompaniment of a cry that tore at Lucy's throat and transformed into a sob the moment her daughter was placed on to her chest.

'Is she mine?' Lucy had said.

It was a stupid question but much better than the one she had wanted to ask: Can I keep her?

'Isn't it usually the father who asks that?'

Adam's face had been inches from hers as the family of three snuggled together. 'I love you,' she had told him, and this too was an edited version of what was on her mind. Don't leave me, was what she had wanted to say.

The fact that Adam was there at all should have been answer enough. He had come rushing into the kitchen when Lucy had started screaming and it had almost been a relief to see him panicking as much as she was. The contractions had come thick and fast and an ambulance had been called. It was a close thing and she had given birth within ten minutes of arriving at the hospital. There had been no time for the pain relief she had thought she would be begging for when the time came, and the birth had been entirely natural.

'I'll leave these two lovely ladies to look after you,' Faye said, 'but I'll be back to chase everyone out in say, ten minutes?'

'Will Adam be back by then?' Viv asked.

'Judging by the way he raced out of the hospital, I should think so,' said the midwife.

Adam had been sent home to fetch all the supplies that Lucy should have had the presence of mind to pack weeks ago. She had been ill-prepared for an early delivery and couldn't quite believe that the baby was actually here. Her body felt strangely empty – with the exception of her bladder.

'Can I go to the toilet?' she asked Faye before the midwife could leave.

'Of course you can.'

Faye helped Lucy to her feet while the grandmothers busied themselves rummaging through their shopping bags. They had each grabbed bottles of juice, sandwiches and chocolates during their dash to the hospital, but whereas Viv had brought flowers, Lucy's mum had a selection of Liz Earle toiletries to pamper the new mum.

Lucy shuffled to the edge of the bed and pulled back the blanket to expose bare legs smeared with watery blood. Faye grabbed the hospital gown Lucy hadn't had time to change into earlier and wrapped it around her waist as she stood on wobbly limbs.

'It'll probably sting quite a bit but that's normal,' Faye said as they reached the door to the en suite.

'Am I going in by myself?' Lucy asked when she realized Faye wasn't following.

'I have to get on but honestly, you don't need me. You're doing fine,' she said. 'If there are any problems, pull the emergency cord and I'll come running. Once your husband comes back with your things, you can have that shower too.'

Lucy watched the midwife leave then glanced towards Viv and Christine who gave her matching smiles of encouragement. The pink cotton bundle remained perfectly still and Lucy wanted to tell them not to disturb her, but she held her tongue and closed the door without a word.

Sitting on the toilet, Lucy dared to put her hand on her deflated stomach. Her daughter was a few feet away in the next room but the sense of separation was surprisingly intense. Lucy had told herself over and over that she would look after her baby, but it felt like such an impossible task. The doctor had said she was perfectly healthy but it hadn't lessened Lucy's guilt for giving birth ten days early. It might have been a natural delivery but it had been far from a natural labour. Her behaviour that morning was unforgivable.

Faye was right about the stinging but the tears in Lucy's eyes were already there. She had lost control again and, just hours before her daughter had been born, she had thought fleetingly about taking her own life. Why else would she have fought Adam for the knife? What kind of mother was she? Pressing the heel of her hands against her eye sockets, Lucy told herself it wasn't too late and, if Adam was willing, they would start their new life with a blank canvas. She had to hold it together if she was to be allowed to leave hospital with her daughter, although right now she was in no rush to go home. Faye had suggested she could be discharged as early as tonight as long as the baby had started feeding but the very idea made her tremble in fear. She couldn't do it. She wasn't sure she even had the courage to leave the en suite. She could hear whispers on the other side of the door, and then . . .

The baby's cry was no more than whimper but it released a set of emotions that Lucy had never experienced before, beginning with a flooding of warmth in her chest. She cleaned herself up quickly, fumbling as she slipped on the disposable knickers and a sanitary towel that was bigger than a whole pack of the ones she hoped Adam would remember to pick up.

The baby found her voice and her cries became more urgent, as did the cooing sounds from the grandmothers, but Lucy forced herself to pause and wash her hands carefully before rushing out. Each move she made had to be a conscious one. She would get every detail right.

Viv was holding the baby and looked decidedly guilty when she said, 'Sorry, we couldn't resist.'

'I think she wants you,' Christine said with a sparkle in her eyes that reflected all of the delight Lucy felt about the new addition to their family, but none of the fear.

Lucy settled herself in bed and, holding out her arms to take the baby from Viv, prepared for her daughter's cries to intensify. To her surprise, her daughter settled immediately, soothed by the familiar pounding of her mother's heart.

'See, I told you you'd be a natural,' Christine said in response to Lucy's shocked expression.

Her mum spoke too soon because, although the baby had stopped crying, she refused to be soothed back to sleep. She pulled an arm free of her swaddling and nuzzled the side of the blanket.

'I think she's hungry,' Christine said. 'Do you need to feed her?'

Lucy felt a swell of pride at being asked the question, as if she would know the answer. 'I think so,' she said.

Lucy had made an attempt to breastfeed soon after the birth under Faye's watchful eye, but the baby had fallen asleep before she had latched on properly. The midwife had reassured her that she would feed when she was hungry and Lucy had tried not to think of it as a failure. There would be no room for error this time.

'Do you want us to leave, sweetheart?' her mum asked when she noticed Lucy's reticence.

Lucy nodded and the gaggle of grandmothers gathered up their things. They planted kisses on the cheeks of mother and baby and were heading for the door when it was flung open. Adam's cheeks were flushed and his hair stuck up at odd angles as he struggled through the door with a sports holdall that wasn't the Cath Kidston overnight bag Lucy had been expecting. His packing had been rushed and the holdall was partly unzipped with its contents spilling out. He had picked up the wrong outfit for the baby, and what looked like a pair of paint-splattered leggings she would rather not be seen wearing in public.

'Thank you,' she said, her lips trembling with gratitude. It was enough that he was there.

'Are you off?' he asked Viv.

'She's about to feed the baby.'

Adam craned his neck around the door as he checked the room. 'On your own? Where's Faye?'

Christine was laughing when she said, 'Don't look so terrified. Lucy knows what she's doing.'

From Adam's clouded expression, he didn't agree.

'I'd like to give it a go,' Lucy said. 'Unless . . .'

With doubt setting in, Lucy's voice trailed off, but no one noticed as Viv and Christine switched their attention to Adam.

'We'll leave you to it,' Christine said. 'But let me know when you bring her home and when you're ready for a proper visit. You don't want everyone overwhelming her but Lucy needs mothering too remember, and I'm always on call.'

'Thanks, Christine,' Adam said, giving her a peck on the cheek.

'I wish you'd hurry up and decide on a name,' Viv said. 'Everyone's asking.'

'Everyone?' asked Adam, pulling back from the kiss he was about to plant on his mum's cheek. Even from a distance, Lucy could see his jaw twitch.

Heat bloomed in his mum's cheeks but she dared to hold her son's gaze. Since that awful day when Tigger had gone missing, Viv had maintained a degree of confidence that had previously been lacking in her mother-in-law. Her voice was firm when she said, 'I'm allowed to tell people I'm a grandmother, Adam.'

Her son's lips cut a thin line as he glanced at the phone clutched in her hand. 'Have you been taking photos?'

'Tonnes of them,' Christine said brightly in an effort to break the tension. 'To be honest, it was us that woke the baby up.'

On cue, the baby released what was a proper cry this time. She had become frustrated suckling Lucy's finger and could no doubt smell the mother's milk that made Lucy's breasts tingle. Eager to join his wife, Adam gave his mum a stiff hug.

'He doesn't see the photos,' he told Viv and she nodded her agreement.

'Sort out that name!' Christine called out as Adam let the door close on them.

Their unnamed baby wriggled in Lucy's arms as she finished unbuttoning her smock. Fortunately, the maternity bra she had been wearing doubled as a nursing bra, so at least she hadn't been completely unprepared.

'Are you sure you should be doing this?' asked Adam as he came alongside her.

'I'm going to have to learn fast if they're expecting us to go home tonight.'

When Adam sat down on the edge of the bed, Lucy leant her shoulder against his chest. He smelled of shower gel and had swapped his stained white T-shirt in favour of a long-sleeved cotton jumper that hid the gash to his forearm. The makeshift dressing had been the first thing Lucy had noticed when he had rushed into the kitchen to hold her hand as another contraction took hold. The second thing had been his red, puffy eyes.

She felt those eyes upon her now as she attempted to latch the baby on to her breast. Holding her nipple between her fingers exactly as the midwife had shown her, she was determined to prove she was up to the task, but she gasped in pain.

'You're not ready,' Adam said, slipping off the bed.

Lucy wanted to try again but Adam was right. She wasn't ready and her daughter's next heartfelt cry crushed her.

'I'll get a midwife,' he said. 'And don't worry about going home. I'll talk them into letting you stay longer. They can't make you leave once they realize what you're like.'

'You're not going to tell them, are you?' she asked. 'About this morning, I mean.'

'I would never do that to you, Lucy,' he promised. 'I'll simply explain how insecure you are right now. That's all.'

'Does it hurt?' she said, gesturing to his arm.

Adam pressed a hand to his wound. 'Once I've got you

sorted, I might nip to accident and emergency to get a couple of stitches, but it's nothing that won't heal. I shouldn't have argued with you. I feel like it's my fault.'

'No, Adam, you can't blame yourself. I should never have questioned you,' Lucy said. 'And I promise I'll never do it again.'

Adam smiled at her. 'Good girl,' he said. 'Now try not to panic while I'm gone.'

Left alone with her baby wriggling in her arms and too afraid to make a second attempt to feed her, Lucy placed the baby on her shoulder so that they were cheek to cheek.

'I love you,' she whispered, testing out the words and the emotion. It felt real. Why had she been so afraid that it wouldn't?

Sitting cross-legged on the sofa with a nursing pillow propping her up at precisely the right angle, Lucy took a long swig of ice-cold water. As she set the bottle down, the sound of gulping continued and she looked down in wonder at her sleepy daughter with her milky wet lips suckling her breast. When she lifted a tiny hand with her finger, the baby's grip was fierce.

Feeling unexpectedly content, Lucy allowed herself a smile as she closed her eyes and leant her head back. Adam had been right to insist she stay in hospital that first night, although she hadn't slept a wink. A midwife had popped her head around the door every once in a while, but for the most part, Lucy had enjoyed the sense of semi-seclusion. There had been a few momentary panics when she had fought the urge to pick up the phone and call Adam, but he deserved time to himself to search for his own peace and she hadn't wanted him to think she was checking up on him. She trusted Adam more than she trusted herself.

There had been a terrifying moment when they had left the hospital and she had glanced over her shoulder expecting to find a security guard chasing after them. It didn't seem possible that she should be allowed to take the baby when it was obvious to even a casual observer that she wasn't ready. Why else would her husband have pleaded with staff to let her stay overnight? And yet here she was, muddling through four days later.

Feeling herself drift, Lucy straightened up to find Adam standing in the doorway. She had been listening out for his car but perhaps she had nodded off after all.

'Were you asleep?'

The fear in his voice made Lucy's heart leap and her head snapped towards her daughter, whose face remained pressed against her breast. Despite the baby's rosy cheeks, she was deathly still and the cry Lucy was about to release lodged in her throat when the suckling started up again. Lucy released the sob anyway as Adam's shadow loomed over them. Taking a juddering breath, she offered him a trembling smile. 'She's fine,' she whispered.

'But you're not,' he said as he sat down next to her. 'You're exhausted, Lucy, and I know it's to be expected but you shouldn't fall asleep while you're nursing. All you had to do was lean the wrong way and you could have suffocated her.'

Lucy had followed the guidelines to the letter when she had positioned the nursing pillow and she had only intended to rest her eyes. She wanted to reassure Adam that she hadn't put the baby in danger but the fact was, she had been asleep. 'Sorry,' she said. 'I'll be more careful.'

Adam glanced around the living room and the stack of baby paraphernalia Lucy had managed to put into some sort of order while he was out. She had mopped the floor and dusted too, wanting to prove to Adam and the midwife, who was due later in the afternoon, that she was functioning.

'We need to get more organized,' he said. 'All this mess can't be good for your state of mind. Maybe you should go to bed while the baby's sleeping and I'll make a start clearing some space.'

'I've managed to find homes for all the presents,' Lucy said.

There had been many well-wishers but all had been warned not to overstretch the new mum. Christine had been the most persistent and, having failed to secure clearance from Adam, had turned up unannounced the day after Lucy left hospital. Viv, not wanting to be outdone, had appeared the day after that, and Ranjit had dropped by briefly with a car full of presents from friends and colleagues.

Hannah had phoned to order Lucy to keep away from Annie's portrait. Her friend didn't need Adam telling her that she could do with one less visitor but, in truth, Lucy wouldn't have minded. She would have liked to swap notes on motherhood with her friend, but Adam had warned against taking advice from someone who might not have the exacting standards expected of a modern-day mum.

'I think we should start changing her in the nursery. What's the point of buying a changing table if we're not going to use it?' he asked. 'And it's doing my back in, crouching down on the floor.'

'I used the nursery this morning when I gave her a bath,' Lucy replied proudly.

In the silence that followed, Lucy racked her brain to work out why Adam should look so horrified. 'What's wrong?' she asked.

'Lucy, are you sure you should be bathing her while I'm not around?'

'I was careful.'

'You mean like you were a moment ago?' asked Adam. He covered his face with his hand. 'Sorry, I didn't mean to snap. I guess the lack of sleep is getting to us both. I'm worried, that's all. I want you to feel comfortable around her as much as I do, but these things can't be rushed. Bonding obviously takes more time for some mums than others. It's nothing to be ashamed about.'

'Sorry,' Lucy said as she took in Adam's stricken features and the enormity of the risk she had taken. She could have zoned out, or fallen asleep, or felt her frustrations rise up and make her do unthinkable things. 'How could I be so stupid? I didn't think.'

Adam leant over and when he kissed the top of her head, she heard a sharp sniff. 'Let me do the bathing for now, and meanwhile, you might want to have a proper wash yourself before the midwife gets here.'

'I will,' Lucy said, attempting to smile without spilling her tears. She was being ridiculously emotional, another score for her hormones. 'Did you get everything sorted at the registry office?'

'Yes, all I need to do now is put away the birth certificate before it goes missing,' he said. 'I suppose you've told everyone?'

'You did say I could, didn't you?' she asked, biting her lip as she waited for Adam's answer.

Her husband gave her a lopsided smile. 'As if I could stop you.'

Relaxing, Lucy lifted baby Eva gently off her breast and watched her smack her rosebud lips before settling back to sleep. As Lucy fastened up her shirt, she felt a vibration run along the sofa. Adam rummaged beneath a cushion and picked up her mobile.

'It's a text from your mum,' he said.

'What does she say?'

Lucy was lifting Eva up to rest on her shoulder when she noticed the frown. 'What is it?'

'Eva?'

Lucy felt a rush of panic. Had she disappeared inside her own thoughts again while Adam's words floated over her head? 'What about her?'

'That's not the name I've registered,' he said carefully. 'Or did I get it wrong?'

Lucy held herself taut. They had spent the pregnancy discussing a long list of names that had gradually shrunk to three by the time the baby arrived: Lily, Eva, and Ava. It had taken until the day before to come to a final decision but when Adam had left for the registry office, she had told baby Eva to say goodbye to Daddy, and Adam hadn't corrected her.

Adam continued to wait for an answer, although he wasn't asking her a question as such. He was testing her response and it was time for Lucy to prove she had learnt from previous mistakes.

'It was between Eva and Ava,' she said, realizing how easily the two names could be confused. 'I got it wrong, didn't I?'

'Oh, Lucy, you really are struggling. Why don't you go and have forty winks and I'll wake you up in time to have a shower before the midwife arrives. I can look after Ava,' he said, emphasizing the name in case it wasn't yet fixed in Lucy's brain.

'But I've told everyone her name's Eva,' Lucy said. The hollowness of her voice matched the emptiness she felt when Adam took the baby from her.

'I'll text them now,' he said. 'We can blame it on autocorrect.'

Lucy walked through the house as if in a trance. Focusing on each tread of the stairs, she kept her mind on a singular path that allowed no space for anger or frustration. She couldn't bear to acknowledge the crushing humiliation she felt for announcing the wrong name and concentrated on the minor victory of not letting the situation deteriorate into another bout of hysteria.

Sunlight streamed through her bedroom window and played across the fresh duvet cover Lucy had changed while the baby – Ava – gurgled in her crib. She had wanted Adam to come to bed later and notice the freshly laundered sheets so he would know how much it meant to have him sleeping next to her again. She was loath to contaminate the clean bedding without showering first but the effort alone of undressing was enough to sap what little energy she had left. She climbed into bed and when she closed her eyes, her tears felt cool against her burning cheeks but she ignored them. She would get better. She *was* getting better.

22

When Lucy awoke, she was confused by the rain drumming against the window – it seemed only hours ago that she had felt the sun warming her face as she settled down for her nap but the days were merging into each other. She wouldn't be surprised if she had slept through the seasons, but by her groggy calculations, Ava was now ten days old.

There was a tap at the door, louder than the one Lucy realized had tugged her from her dreams. As she pulled herself up, Faye poked her head around the bedroom door. Lucy had been under the care of several midwives during the course of her pregnancy and it was the first time she had seen Faye since leaving hospital.

'Can I come in?'

'Yes, of course. Or should I get up? Ava must be due another feed by now,' Lucy said, picking up the edge of the duvet but not able to commit to flinging back the covers.

'Your husband has it all in hand. I hear you've become an expert at expressing milk.'

Lucy looked down at her pyjama top with two dried circular stains. She used pads to soak up the leaks but they were never enough to stem the flow completely. 'I'm doing my best,' she said as she imagined Adam nursing Ava with a quiet confidence she envied. He was doing more than his fair share of the feeds and Lucy knew she should be grateful, but she felt like a cow in a dairy using the breast pump. At least it didn't matter if she fell asleep using it, as Adam had rightly pointed out.

'You're doing brilliantly.'

'Am I?' asked Lucy. 'Is Ava OK?'

'Yes, I had a quick peek at her and she's fine. Did I detect a hint of copper in her hair?'

It was hard to tell the colour of Ava's hair from the soft layer of down covering her scalp. It was a golden blonde at first glance but, in a certain light, it looked like Lucy had passed on the ginger gene that she had inherited from her father. 'I hope not,' she said sourly. 'I'd rather she took after Adam.'

Faye came over and perched on the edge of the bed. 'When Liz saw you the other day, she put in her notes that you said you were feeling quite low. How are things now?'

Liz had been the midwife who had called on the day that Lucy had made the mix-up with the names and she had offered one kind word too many. 'Better, I think. I've been catching up on sleep when I can,' Lucy said to explain why she was in bed at two in the afternoon when she should have known the midwife was due. 'Adam was supposed to wake me up before you arrived.'

'Oh, don't worry about it. Count yourself lucky,' Faye said. 'Some husbands wouldn't notice there's a new baby in the house until they reach for the remote and pick up a dummy instead.'

'Adam has to go back to work next week.'

'Which is all the more reason to make the most of him,' advised the midwife. 'How do you feel about managing on your own?'

Lucy shrugged. If only she could trust herself, she would love to have some time to herself with Ava.

'Have you been getting out at all?'

'We took Ava for a walk along the prom yesterday.'

'Oh,' Faye said, not sounding as impressed as Lucy had hoped. 'OK, that's a good start.'

Beginning to panic, Lucy thought back to their stroll around Marine Lake. She had felt like a fraud and a failure, but she had done her best not to let it show as she smiled at the smug families parading past them. Had she done something wrong? 'What is it?' she asked.

'Your husband said you stayed in bed yesterday, that's all.'

'Did I?' asked Lucy, her mind clouding over as was its habit whenever she was challenged. 'I must have lost track of the days. It happens a lot.'

'You do know I'm due to discharge you today?' Faye asked slowly. 'I believe one of the health visitors has been in touch to arrange a visit.'

'Yes, I spoke to someone the other day,' Lucy said, already embarrassed by the unnecessary tears welling in her eyes. The health visitor had made several failed attempts to see Lucy before Ava was born and her persistence had finally paid off. Lucy hadn't wanted an extra pair of eyes to judge her, but the woman had sounded very nice on the phone and had invited Lucy to a mums' group. It had to be a good thing, listening to other mums sharing their anxieties and complaints, but how could Lucy possibly compare?

Faye had a tissue to hand as if she had been expecting her patient to blub. Rubbing Lucy's back, she said, 'I think I can delay discharging you for a day or two while we work out what's going on. By all accounts, you've been finding it difficult for quite a while.'

'Adam told you?'

'Why don't you start by telling me how you really feel?' Faye said gently.

Sniffing back tears, Lucy tried to find the words to encapsulate how she felt in a way that would be palatable to an outsider. 'Lost, I suppose. I think I'm doing fine and then I go and do something stupid. I hate being like this but I can't seem to find a way out.'

'You will,' Faye said, 'but don't think for a minute you have to do it on your own. It's time you had a proper chat with your doctor. No more pretending you're managing when you're not. It won't do you or the baby any good.'

Lucy doubted she could pretend even if she tried. She would tell the doctor everything, but what then? Hadn't Adam said to her mum that there was little point in seeking help? 'They won't take Ava away from me, will they?'

Faye didn't look as taken aback by the question as Lucy expected. 'I've looked after plenty of mums in my time, and some have had quite severe postnatal depression, but not one of them had their children taken away.'

'Is that what you think it is? Postnatal depression?'

'It's probably too soon to jump to conclusions. Your hormones are still settling back down after the shock of giving birth and it can take longer for some mums than others. That's not a reflection on you, Lucy. Everyone's different and we'll take it one step at a time. Are you OK for me to speak to your GP and arrange an appointment?'

Lucy couldn't meet the midwife's gaze as she nodded obediently. The lifeline Faye offered felt more like a death sentence, and that thought alone sent a shudder down her spine. 'What if it has nothing to do with my hormones?' she asked, lifting her gaze but not her head.

'What else do you think it could be?'

Lucy held her breath until the air in her lungs turned toxic and forced out her confession. 'Did Adam tell you my dad committed suicide?'

Faye pursed her lips. If Adam had shared his own worries, Faye was keeping his confidence. 'I'm so sorry to hear that.'

'I was eight at the time, and it was a while before I was told it wasn't an accident. Dad took himself off to the Lakes one day, walked halfway across a footbridge and decided he couldn't go any further. His business was in trouble, but it still made no sense,' she said, pleased to have kept her tone level and her pulse slow as she recounted the facts as she knew them. 'Some questions will never be answered because he didn't leave a note, but I've become more and more convinced that he must have had a mental illness that went undiagnosed – he never tried to get help. All I know for sure is that there's more to it than I know.' What Lucy didn't add was that her mum and Adam held the answer to the questions that might tip her over the edge.

Faye pursed her lips while she thought. 'Did you ever talk to anyone about it, like a counsellor?'

'No, it didn't seem necessary at the time. I had to be strong for Mum and she had to be strong for me. We got each other through it, and I swear I thought it was behind us.'

It was only after meeting Adam that she had come to appreciate how traumatic an experience it had been. She could recall the concern on his face when they had stood on the craggy outcrop they would christen Heart's Leap and, with gentle coaxing, she had explained exactly why her fear of heights wasn't a simple case of vertigo. She hadn't known Adam particularly well at that point, and it had felt more like a leap of faith to reveal something so intimate so soon, but she had been right to trust him.

'I know the stats,' Lucy continued. 'Children of a suicidal parent are three times more likely to take their own life, but that wasn't who I was.'

'And now?' Faye asked.

'That isn't who I am,' Lucy said, correcting her mistake. 'I wouldn't abandon Ava like my dad abandoned me. Whatever happens, I promise you, I won't do that.'

'It's natural for you to compare and contrast your life to your dad's, especially now that you have a daughter of your own,' Faye said. 'Do you think it's affecting how you've bonded with Ava?'

Lucy wasn't sure what bonding was supposed to mean. Every time she held her daughter, she searched for that elusive connection without knowing what that missing element was meant to feel like. 'I do love her,' she said, and that at least was true. There were times when she knew in her heart that she loved her child more than life itself, but nothing else about motherhood came naturally to Lucy. Adam could see it and from the cloud crossing Faye's face, she could see it too.

'Do you think you could explain what it is about bathing her that makes you feel uncomfortable?'

Lucy shook her head. 'I don't feel uncomfortable because I *don't* bathe her,' she said. 'We agreed it was best if Adam did it for now.'

Faye cocked her head as if, once again, what Lucy said jarred with the information she had been given. 'It's understandable that you would feel anxious holding a slippery baby, especially if you've already had one little mishap, but you'll be growing in confidence every day, even if you don't recognize it yourself.'

'Oh, there hasn't been a mishap. Honestly,' Lucy added as she caught the tiniest twitch of the midwife's eyebrow. Her cheeks burned. 'I would never do anything to put Ava knowingly in danger, *never*. I don't care what happens to me, she's more important.'

'For the record, Lucy, I care what happens to both of you and so does your husband. Talking about your feelings instead of bottling them up would be a good start, and your doctor can help you decide the best way forward. In the meantime, take whatever help is on offer. I believe there's talk of Ava's grandmother coming to stay when Adam goes back to work.'

'Yes,' Lucy said, thinking of the open offer from her mum. It had been refused, but if Adam had mentioned it to Faye, he was clearly having doubts about trusting Lucy on her own. 'Do you think I should?'

'It can be a mixed blessing, but it really depends on what kind of relationship you have with your mother-in-law.'

'You mean Viv?'

Faye looked momentarily confused. 'Have I got that wrong? She lives in Moreton, doesn't she?'

'Yes,' Lucy said, rubbing her forehead. She couldn't be sure, but she was fairly certain that Viv hadn't made a similar offer to stay. 'Do you think it should be my mum instead?'

'Mum's can be a little overpowering,' Faye said as if speaking with authority. 'Everyone wants to do their bit, I'm sure, but it's entirely your choice. The most important thing is that you recognize when you do need a helping hand, but don't be afraid to tell people when they've overstayed their welcome either. This is about what's best for you and Ava. Don't be afraid to speak up.'

Faye couldn't know that speaking up was at the root of Lucy's problems and had already caused untold damage to her marriage, and to Adam especially. Not speaking up was how they would all survive the coming months.

23

Stepping on to the landing, Lucy was temporarily blinded by the midday sun that had been excluded from her bedroom. Her restlessness had exhausted her in the last few days but not enough to find sleep. She had been warned that the antidepressants she had been prescribed would take a week or two to take effect, but she hadn't been prepared to feel worse.

It had been Adam who had done most of the talking during their short consultation with the GP, and although her husband had provided a fuller answer to Lucy's family history, to her relief, he hadn't felt it necessary to offer the information her mum had shared. Lucy, meanwhile, could do no more than nod as she held back her sobs, although she had managed a little better at the baby clinic where Faye had spoken to her at length. Lucy must have said the right things because the midwife had discharged her and the one person she might have been able to open up to was lost to her. She was someone else's problem now.

Ava's cry floated up from the living room but Lucy didn't feel the familiar tingle of milk in her hard and sore breasts;

her body no longer reacted to her baby's needs. There followed the sound of her mum singing a lullaby, which meant it was Adam rattling pots and pans in the kitchen as he prepared Sunday lunch. He had told Lucy to stay in bed but she could no longer endure the suffocating weight of the duvet while pretending she was trying to sleep rather than simply hiding. They had invited Christine over to tell her of the new arrangements for Ava's care, and Lucy had no way of knowing if she had stayed out of sight long enough for Adam to break the news.

As she began her descent, Lucy didn't feel her anxiety build as much as she had feared. Her medication had created a crash barrier between her thoughts and emotions, but it made the decision she needed to take when she reached the foot of the stairs no less difficult. Should she turn left or right? The matter was settled with a baby's cry.

'Hello,' Lucy said, coming to a stop at the living room door where she tried to gauge her mum's mood. It was a complicated task, given Lucy's dampened senses and the camouflage of her mum's smile.

Rocking Ava gently, Christine had a muslin cloth draped over her shoulder and an almost empty feeding bottle in her hand. 'Adam said you were sleeping.'

'I did try,' Lucy said, stepping closer to give her mum a peck on the cheek while resisting the urge to take the baby she was longing to hold.

'Isn't the medication helping?' Christine asked.

'It will,' Lucy said, accepting no other outcome. 'Or else giving up breastfeeding will have been for nothing.'

'You could have carried on. Adam mentioned the doctor had said it was fine.'

'Yes, but what if . . .' Lucy let her voice trail off. She and Adam had gone through a range of 'what if's' that had terrified her. It came down to choosing between her baby's health and her own, and she had cried for hours after taking the first antidepressant that brought an end to the one thing she could do for Ava that no one else could. 'The good thing is we've built up a stock of breastmilk in the freezer and Adam's suggested we spread it out and use it for one feed a day until we run out. '

'You know best,' Christine said, her smile a distant memory.

Lucy remained quiet as she watched her mum place a dozing Ava in her bassinet. Christine set down the baby bottle on the coffee table and began folding the muslin cloth, but there was only so long she could keep herself distracted from the conversation they needed to have.

'Are you sure this is what you want, Lucy?' her mum asked, taking a seat and inviting her daughter to sit next to her.

Lucy's mind was too sluggish to work out the nuances of the question. 'Do you mean about the antidepressants?'

'No, I mean about Viv looking after you both. I wish you'd told me, love.'

'It's not that I don't want you here, Mum,' Lucy admitted. She did want her, but apparently not enough to make a forceful argument. Adam was making a huge compromise by accepting help from anyone and it was right that he should choose who that person should be, and Lucy had to agree that Viv wouldn't take over in the same way that her mum would. 'It makes sense for it to be Viv because she lives so close. She isn't moving in or anything, she'll just be here when Adam's at work. It wouldn't be so easy for you. Viv doesn't have the same work pressures and apparently her boss has been really supportive about her taking an extended break.'

'An extended break?' repeated her mum. 'Exactly how long is she planning on being here?'

'Not very long,' Lucy replied, hoping Viv's month-long sabbatical was a worst-case scenario, although Adam talked as if the arrangement were indefinite.

'I could have managed,' Christine said. 'I know I live further away but as far as I'm aware, there are no plans to brick up the Mersey tunnels.'

Guilt and fear rose up through Lucy's body and trickled through her defences. Her eyes were glistening when she said, 'I'm sorry, Mum. I wish I didn't have to rely on anyone, but Adam has to go back to work tomorrow and we needed to do something.'

When Christine put her arm around her daughter and pulled her close, they were both shaking. 'I hate to see you like this,' she whispered. 'I wish there was something I could do to make everything better. I want to help – you have no idea how much – but I'll go along with whatever you want, Lucy. Don't ever think you're imposing on me if you need me to do more.'

Adam cleared his throat. He was standing in the doorway with a wooden spoon in his hand. 'We're lucky to have both our mums offering help, and believe me, it was hard for Lucy to choose between you both,' he said. 'If anything, it was the kitten that swung the decision.'

'Oh, so I've been passed over because of a blinking cat,' Christine said, prodding her daughter playfully.

Lucy's tears evaporated at the sight of her husband's smile. Adam had a special knack of getting everyone on his side. 'It might have been a deciding factor,' she admitted, and it was true that she was happy at the thought of Tigger returning home on occasional day release when Adam had to work long days and the kitten would be left alone for too long.

'If it becomes a struggle for your mum, you will let me know, won't you?' Christine said to Adam. 'It might not be as easy for me to take leave at the drop of a hat, but my family will always come first.'

'I can't see there being a problem, Christine. Mum can't wait to become a full-time nan, and if I'm honest, it's a title that suits her better than you.' Before his mother-in-law could object, Adam added, 'For the life of me, I can't see you as a granny yet and it would ease Lucy's conscience, and mine too, if you didn't let us stop you from enjoying what has to be a better social life than the rest of us put together.'

When Adam looked at Lucy and raised an eyebrow, she felt momentary panic. He was expecting her to say something. They had talked the night before about how much they appreciated their mums. She had been paying attention, she had made sure of it, and with a rush of relief, she remembered what it was he expected her to say.

'Mum, I hate that you're missing out on your trip to the Algarve because of me, and if there's a chance you can sort out a flight and a hotel room in the next couple of weeks, I think you should join the others.'

'I don't know about that, Lucy. Yes, I could always bunk in with someone, it's been done before,' Christine said, 'but—'

'But nothing,' Adam insisted. 'It might be a bit too much for Lucy to keep an eye on the house while you're away, but I don't mind stepping in. You work hard and you deserve the break.'

'I suppose I could go for a long weekend.'

'Nonsense,' Adam told her. 'You know you'd hate to drag yourself away after a few short days, and you need to look after yourself too, don't forget. It has to be the full hit.'

Christine's grip around Lucy's waist loosened a fraction. 'Oh, I don't know what to do now,' she said.

Lucy closed her eyes in case Adam noticed her resolve weakening. She didn't want Viv, she wanted her mum, and while the heart palpitations that tickled the back of her throat could have been a side effect of her medication, they were more likely caused by a surge of adrenaline. She heard Faye's voice telling her to speak up and she opened her mouth to beg her mum to stay.

'Do you think you can keep an eye on Ava while your mum helps me in the kitchen?' Adam asked before Lucy could get the words out. He made a stirring motion with the wooden spoon he was holding. 'I'm another one who needs constant supervision.'

'Will you be all right on your own?' asked Christine when she noticed Lucy coming with her as she went to stand.

The thin line of Lucy's mouth quivered as she gave a polite nod and sneaked a look towards the bassinet. She had been told that holding the baby too much would stop her from learning to settle on her own, but once Adam was out of sight, Ava was soon in her arms. It was a timely reminder that Lucy was more than her mother's daughter, she was a mum herself. Taking ownership of the words Christine had given her, she whispered, 'You will always come first.'

As a cloud passed across the benevolent face of the sun, the summer breeze whipped up and Lucy's dress billowed out like a parachute. She stepped off the kerb and was halfway across the road when her grip on the pram tightened and her steps faltered. She looked left and right in search of the oncoming car she might have missed, but with an encouraging smile from her mother-in-law, she made it to the other side.

'Greengrocer's first,' Viv said, pulling a shopping list from her pocket and leaving Lucy to concentrate on weaving the pram between shop displays and passers-by. 'Just don't let me buy more than we can carry.'

It had been Lucy's idea to walk to the shops. After two weeks of popping pills, she and her medication had reached a truce, and whilst it wasn't the road to recovery she would have liked, she felt less anxious about what lay ahead; in fact, she felt a little less of everything.

Stopping at a tiered display of artfully arranged fruit and veg, Viv asked, 'Do you want to stay out here while I go in? There isn't much room in there and I know what we need.'

Viv had taken over Adam's role as chief cook with surprisingly few complaints from her son. She kept to traditional dishes but she did them well and her shepherd's pie was Lucy and Adam's favourite by far. Viv had given Lucy step-by-step instructions so she could make it herself come the day that she could manage without a chaperone, something Lucy suspected Viv wanted as much as she did.

'Here, take my bank card,' Lucy said, as she double-checked that the card she was handing over was for the joint account.

Lucy's personal account had been drained of funds after buying the pram, and her dire financial state was another reason why she had suggested the walk. She didn't want Viv driving them around all the time and her faithful Fiat was running on fumes. She preferred not to ask Adam if she could use the household fund to refuel and, with little prospect of making her own money now that she was committed to being a full-time mum, she was going to have to get used to walking more. As a last resort, there was the money Hannah had offered for the portrait of her nan, but that would mean tearing herself away from Ava and returning to her studio to finish it. Adam had already advised against it but she didn't need him to tell her she wasn't ready.

As she waited outside the shop, Lucy took advantage of some precious time alone with her daughter. Ava was one month old and becoming more aware of her surroundings by the day. It wouldn't be long before she offered her very first smile and Lucy longed to be the one to receive it. As she leant over the pram, a tiny hand made a grab for a coil of her mother's hair and Lucy used it to tickle Ava's face.

'Hello, beautiful girl,' she whispered. 'Where's my smile?'

Ava's eyes opened wide and her legs jiggled. Her rosebud mouth opened but she couldn't replicate the smile that quivered on her mother's lips.

'Come on, you can do it,' Lucy whispered, a little too desperately, she realized. Feeling self-conscious, she looked up to find Viv emerging from the shop. Her mother-in-law had a shopping bag hooked over one arm and was carrying a tray of bedding plants.

'I thought these might help brighten up the garden.'

'I'm no good with plants, Viv.'

'You're better at more things than you give yourself credit for,' Viv said as she squeezed the tray into the shopping basket beneath the pram. 'Pansies are easy to look after and I'll help you fill the pots. All you have to do then is keep them watered. It'll be a nice surprise for Adam when gets home.'

Adam was more likely to complain about wasting money on something that Lucy was bound to kill off eventually, but he was coming home later and later, and with any luck would be too tired to care. Despite promising to work from home at least one day a week to give Viv some respite, Adam had been practically living at the office. He had to make up for lost time and was reluctant to ask for another favour so soon after taking paternity leave. Lucy wasn't the only one whose confidence had been knocked.

After a couple of other short stops, they found themselves at the supermarket. Adam supervised the weekly shop but they weren't there to pick up groceries and headed straight for the pet aisle. Tigger often accompanied Viv on her daily trips to babysit her son's wife and the kitten was struggling to adjust to not being centre of attention. Lucy scanned the shelves for the cat milk she hoped would win back his affections, and was as much as she could afford, while Viv checked out some new toys.

'He loves these,' Viv said, holding up a feathery creature that had been packaged with what looked like a tube of dried herbs. 'It's catnip. Have you tried him with it?'

Lucy checked the price tag. 'I haven't brought enough money out with me,' she confessed, not needing to explain that Adam would have something to say if she used the bank card on frivolities for the cat.

'It's my treat,' insisted Viv. 'And while we're here, I might ask if they sell cat flaps. I've been letting Tigger have a bit of an explore outside the bungalow. He doesn't roam too far and he's managing to climb fences with no problem at all.'

'But our fences are much higher than yours,' Lucy said. She felt a distant thud and realized it was her heart thumping against her breastbone as she recalled Tigger's great escape.

'I've let him out in your garden too,' Viv said. Patting Lucy's hand, she added gently, 'He was out this morning while you were sleeping. He's fine, Lucy and if there's a problem at all, it's that he's going to get confused about where he lives. I don't see any reason why you can't take him back, and I know you want to. If we can put a cat flap in the utility room door, he'll more or less look after himself.'

Before Lucy could allow her hopes to build, she said, 'I need to check with Adam first.'

'Cutting a hole in the uPVC door should be straightforward. I've got a hacksaw and drill that would do the job,' Viv said. She stopped to take in Lucy's wide-eyed expression. 'Except you need to run it past Adam first.'

Lucy manoeuvred the pram through the checkout, too embarrassed to watch Viv pay for the cat toy. What she couldn't ignore, however, was her mother-in-law's most recent attempt to lessen the burden that had been placed on her shoulders.

'I'm sorry for being a nuisance,' she said when Viv joined her outside. 'You want your life back, don't you?'

Viv's shoulders sagged. 'It's not that I don't want to help, and it's been nice seeing so much of Ava, and you,' she added.

'But?' Lucy asked as they fell into step.

'I wish I could split myself in two, if not three, but the truth is I can't carry on doing this for ever.'

'No one's expecting you to.'

'I think Adam might be, and I know the whole debacle over Mother's Day was as much my fault as anyone's, but I didn't know it would have such a terrible impact on your health.'

'You can't think you're responsible for me being like this,' Lucy said, not sure what 'like this' meant.

'I didn't exactly help, Lucy, and I really do want to make amends, but I still have to make a living. I don't have much in savings and I simply can't carry on without an income.'

'You're not getting your wages?' asked Lucy. There was a pulling sensation across her chest that was a down-graded version of the anxiety she knew she should be feeling. 'Are you saying you've lost your job?'

'No, not at all,' Viv replied as she strolled past the shops that had been on her list. 'My sabbatical is unpaid,' she said gently.

'I – I didn't know.'

'Sorry, I presumed Adam would have told you.'

'He likes to protect me.'

'Ah, yes. That's something my son does best,' Viv agreed, her brow creasing when she added, 'Both of them, actually.'

Viv left a pause as she waited for Lucy to agree, but any

softening towards Scott would be a betrayal of Adam. Viv hadn't mentioned her younger son's name since making her peace with Adam, and although she had made it clear at the time that she had room for both of them in her life, Lucy had been hoping that her silence on the subject had meant she had let her relationship with Scott drift after he had scuttled back to New York. With her skin crawling, Lucy headed for the pedestrian crossing and pressed the button. She wanted to go home.

'I want to do the right thing, but I don't know how,' Viv said. 'Adam isn't the only one who needs me right now.'

Lucy opened her mouth to speak, wanting to know what crisis Scott might have conjured up to make Viv feel so guilty, but she was too scared to ask. Whatever Viv told her, Lucy would be duty-bound to repeat to Adam with or without Viv's agreement. The last thing she wanted was to be the holder of information that might damage what was already a fragile relationship between mother and son.

'Viv, can we please talk about something else?'

'It's not easy for you either, I know that,' Viv continued as if Lucy hadn't spoken. 'But I've been watching you over the last couple of weeks and I see nothing that suggests you're not capable of looking after yourself or Ava. I know what it's like to be too afraid to do anything in case you get it wrong, but it's a habit you can break out of, Lucy.'

'You're not with me all the time,' Lucy said. 'You don't know what I'm like.'

The traffic had stopped but neither Viv nor Lucy reacted to the signal announcing it was safe to cross. Viv reached out and took Lucy's hand. 'Look at me, love. You haven't once left open a door or misplaced something, and as far as I can tell, you've not been confused or given me one minute's concern about your behaviour.'

'But – but I do make mistakes, Viv,' Lucy said. 'It could be that the medication is helping a little.'

'Maybe that's true. You have no idea how much I want to believe that there's a simple medical reason for how you've been and that things can get better,' Viv said. 'For all our sakes.'

There was something behind Viv's words that made Lucy shudder. Looking down at her sleeping daughter, she couldn't imagine ever doing harm to her family, but what if Viv's belief in her was misplaced, motivated by her need to be somewhere else? Lucy wished more than ever that she had had the courage to speak up and ask her mum to stay in Viv's stead, but it was too late. Her mum had sent a text the night before to let Lucy know she was enjoying her first cocktail in Portugal.

'If it's money you need, we could sort something out between us,' Lucy said, her mind turning in slow, lazy circles. If Viv agreed to carry on looking after Ava, Lucy might be able to resume taking commissions. Everything she made could go towards paying Viv for her time.

'It's not as simple as that,' Viv said. She paused as if to consider what she might say next, but said nothing at all.

Lucy's mind turned another half circle and returned her thoughts to Scott, who she suspected was once more vying for a stake in his mother's affection. 'No, it never is.'

Viv didn't answer.

24

Lucy stretched an arm across the bed, pressing her palm flat against the warm sheet where Adam had been sleeping. Through the darkness, she heard Ava's cries rise up from the kitchen, impatient to be fed, no matter the time.

Adam had told her to go back to sleep but Lucy couldn't rest and pulled herself into a sitting position to await his return. She felt the house settle into stillness until it was broken by the gentle creak of the stairs. Adam was feeding Ava as he pushed the bedroom door open with his shoulder and it took a moment for him to notice the shift of shadows on the bed.

'What are you doing?' he whispered. 'I told you I'd feed her.'

'But you're in work tomorrow, you need your sleep.'

Adam skirted around the bed and sat down in the armchair they had brought down from the studio for Ava's night feeds. 'Not nearly as much as you do,' he said. 'Go back to sleep, Lucy.'

She felt her shoulder turn towards the mattress but she stopped herself from lying back down. 'I need to learn to manage.'

'I know you do,' Adam said softly, 'but I'd rather you

slept through the night so you're not nodding off in the day. Mum can only do so much.'

'I know, we had a talk today,' Lucy said as her fingers picked at the exposed flesh on her arms.

'You mean yesterday.'

Lucy glanced at the clock showing that the new day was four hours old, but she wouldn't be distracted. If she were to stand any chance of getting back to sleep, she needed to start the conversation she had put off several times already since Adam had come home from work. 'Tigger's big enough to climb fences now,' she said, losing her nerve at the last. 'Your mum's been letting him out and we were thinking we could install a cat flap so we can keep him here for good. Viv said she'll have a go at installing it. She's a woman with power tools.'

'If anyone's going to be cutting holes in one of our doors, it's going to be me.'

Lucy pulled at the fine hairs on her forearms to wake up her groggy mind. 'Will you?'

'Do we really need to have this conversation now?' asked Adam. He pulled the teat from Ava's mouth and, ignoring her protestations, lifted her to his shoulder. He patted her gently on the back as he scrutinized Lucy's features through the shadows. 'What's this about, Lucy? Has something happened?'

'No,' she said. 'Honestly, Adam, I'm feeling so much better, even your mum's noticed. She thinks I'm ready to start looking after Ava on my own.'

'It's too soon.'

Ava burped loudly and Adam settled her expertly in his arms to continue her feed.

'But it's not fair on your mum. You didn't tell me she was taking unpaid leave.'

'Didn't I?' he challenged. 'I suppose you also forgot how I told her I'd make up the difference in her pay and she refused. Do you really think I'd expect her to be out of pocket?'

There was hurt in Adam's voice. She had phrased it wrong. 'Of course not,' Lucy said, pinching herself hard. 'The problem with your mum is that she's used to being independent and I'm sure my mum would feel as torn.'

Torn was the perfect word to describe her mother-in-law, Lucy realized. Viv had spent the best part of thirty years being pulled in two opposing directions, and this latest tug of war showed all the signs of ending badly.

'What else did she say?'

'Nothing,' Lucy said, not daring to speculate. She would leave Adam to draw his own conclusions.

'Why am I even asking you?' Adam asked with a sigh. 'I'll talk to Mum myself. This isn't your problem. I should be able to get someone to cover for me and get off early tomorrow.'

Lucy briefly wondered if he would ask Naomi, a name that had haunted her since their argument on the day Ava had been born. 'I don't want you to get in trouble with work,' she said.

'Go to sleep, Lucy. Let me deal with this.'

It was late afternoon and Ava was far more amused by her mother's slow, circular sweeps of the living room than the bluebirds dangling from a rainbow arch above her baby bouncer.

'Daddy home soon,' Lucy told her daughter when her gurgles transformed into whimpers.

She had said something similar to Viv when she had left her pacing the kitchen. Lucy had made the mistake of mentioning that Adam would be home earlier than usual and Viv had seen it as an opportunity to escape and catch up on errands. She was preparing to leave the moment Adam arrived and Lucy couldn't tell her that he was expecting her to hang around, not without explaining why. The last thing Lucy wanted was to be dragged into a family matter that had anything to do with Scott.

With her daddy officially late now, Ava was growing tired of watching her mother's anxiety rise above the levels her medication could contain. Not wanting Adam to contend with a crying baby as soon as he came through the door, Lucy opted for a pre-emptive move and had the baby cradled in her arms as she stepped into the hall. She was about to open the kitchen door when she heard Viv's voice on the phone.

'I'll have to drop the kitten off at home but I'll be as quick as I can,' she was saying.

Lucy rested her lips on the soft down of her daughter's crown. She could either back away or make her presence known before she heard something she would rather not, but it was already too late.

'I can't leave Lucy on her own, son,' Viv said. After a pause, she added, 'How can it be deliberate when Adam doesn't even know you're in the country? I hate doing this to you but I promise I'll get to the hospital before the end of visiting hours.'

Ava let out a cry, which was followed by a gasp from

Lucy. She took a step back but before she could turn, the door swung open. Viv had her phone pressed to her ear.

'I have to go,' she said. 'I'll see you later.'

Lucy slipped past her mother-in-law with her head down. 'Ava needs feeding.'

'I take it you heard some of that.'

Lucy's hand shook as she switched on the kettle. 'You need to talk to Adam about this,' she said, chancing a look in Viv's direction. 'And please don't ask me to keep it from him. I can't go through that again.'

'I wouldn't ask you to,' Viv said.

They worked silently as a team to make up Ava's next feed and as Lucy dropped the freshly made bottle into a jug of cold water, she heard the jangle of keys. The sound prompted both women into action, although neither knew exactly what to do other than to appear busy. Lucy turned the bottle to help it cool down while Viv wiped away the dusting of milk powder on the kitchen counter.

'Have you eaten already?' Adam asked when he stepped into the deathly quiet kitchen. He looked disappointed not to be presented with one of his mum's home-cooked meals.

'I thought I'd be eating at home,' Viv explained, picking up the kitten, who had been winding himself around her feet. 'Lucy said you were coming home early.'

Adam pulled a face at his wife. 'No, I told you I was going to check on your mum's house. That's where I've been.'

'But I thought . . . Last night . . .' Lucy stammered, and then stopped. She couldn't repeat the previous night's conversation in front of Viv, and besides, now was not the time to challenge Adam when there was already a ticking time bomb in the room that had Scott's name written all over it.

Adam tilted his head as if he could hear it too, or at the very least the thumping of Lucy's heart. 'If you're referring to the conversation we had in the early hours of *this morning*, I said I'd get off work early *tomorrow*,' he said slowly. 'Tomorrow's still tomorrow, Lucy.'

'It's an easy enough mistake,' Viv offered.

'I know, but I'm sorry if it's upset your plans?'

The question mark Adam had appended to his statement hung in the air, unclaimed.

'It's not a problem,' Viv said as she hurried to the dining area where her things had been readied for her departure, 'but I really should be getting on.'

'No, wait,' Lucy said quickly, not wanting to be the one left to break the news about Scott. 'You can't go yet.'

Tigger's claws caught on the door of the pet carrier as Viv placed him inside. When she checked her watch, Lucy imagined her balancing one competing priority against the other. 'I have to,' she said.

Adam looked from Lucy to Viv, then back again. He remained at the doorway with his legs slightly apart and his arms folded. 'Is someone going to tell me what's going on?'

Ava's wriggling allowed Lucy to sidestep the question by picking up the feeding bottle. Milk squirted across the baby's arm as Lucy popped off the cap and went to test it on the back of her hand. She wasn't sure if it was the hot liquid or the smell of milk that made Ava howl.

'Mum?' asked Adam as his wife made desperate attempts to soothe the baby, who was going to have to wait a little longer for her feed.

'If you must know, I've made arrangements to see Scott and I'm already late.'

'He's over here?' asked Adam. 'And you didn't think to tell me?' He shot a look at Lucy, who had made the mistake of glancing up after dropping the bottle back in the water jug. 'Did you know?'

Lucy's medication had been eviscerated by the adrenaline coursing through her veins. Her heart pounded. 'I—'

'Is that what last night was about?' Adam said, firing off another question he wouldn't allow her time to answer. 'How could you not tell me?'

'She didn't know, Adam,' Viv said, raising her voice.

'I overheard Viv on the phone just now,' Lucy said, giving Viv what she hoped was a look of apology. 'Scott's in hospital.'

Adam rubbed a hand across his face. 'What have you been telling him, Mum?'

Unable to watch Viv squirm under the intensity of her son's stare, Lucy looked down at Ava. The connection between them was immediate and the baby's cries subsided long enough for Lucy to test the temperature of the milk a second time. Gently, she offered the teat to Ava's searching mouth and was rewarded with a sense of tranquillity that remained her daughter's alone.

'Scott's visiting Keith,' Viv was saying. 'I told you he was going in for a triple bypass, Adam. I tried to talk to you about it the other week, and I would have mentioned Scott's plans if you'd given me the chance.'

'Maybe I had other things on my mind, Mum.'

'I know, you were worried about Lucy,' Viv said. Catching Lucy's eye, she added, 'It was when Adam called over to talk through how much he should tell the midwife about you, but I was on the phone to Keith. It was such bad timing and as soon as I started to explain what was going on, Adam *said* he didn't want to know.'

'Lucy doesn't need to hear this.'

Viv turned to her son. 'Not everything is a conspiracy to hurt you, son,' she said softly. 'I've been trying not to let either you or Scott down, which is why I have to go. Keith's op is tomorrow and I said I'd visit.'

'I'm curious,' Adam said, sounding anything but. 'At what point did it become necessary to tell Scott that Lucy had mental issues?'

'I didn't . . .' Viv began, but the lie fell away with a sigh. 'I had to explain why I was here so often.'

'And once again, my brother is demanding you be somewhere else. Why didn't you phone me when you realized I was late? Why didn't you let me know you had plans? I can't second-guess every move Scott makes,' Adam said. 'If he needs you, go.'

Viv didn't move other than to rest her handbag on the table as if its weight were too much to bear. 'I don't want to leave like this.'

'I know you don't. You want to stay and tell me how none of this is your doing. It never is, Mum, but whose fault is it that you can't see Scott pulling your strings? I bet he's behind all those ideas you've been planting in Lucy's head about her managing without you.'

'Please, Adam, it's not like that. I genuinely believe Lucy is well enough to look after herself. She might make little mistakes now and again, but who doesn't? Can't you leave her alone?'

The room fell deathly quiet and Adam tipped his head slowly to the side. 'And what exactly does that mean?'

Viv's voice was shaking when she said, 'Sometimes you expect too much of her. You expect too much of us all.'

'And there I was thinking that having you here would bring us closer,' Adam scoffed. 'I didn't realize it was Scott I was letting in. I can see his handiwork a mile off.'

In the lull that followed, Lucy could almost hear the strain of a tug-of-war rope as her mother-in-law's loyalties were tested beyond breaking point. There had been a time when she might have stepped in to remind Adam that he only had one mum and he needed to accept that she was fallible, but Lucy had learnt that her place was on the sidelines.

'OK, I'll admit Scott has made me think hard about our situation, and that includes all the problems of the past that never got resolved,' Viv said at last. 'I keep asking myself if it was right to defend you both whenever something went wrong. One of you had to be bending the truth. You couldn't both have been in the right.'

Adam's face contorted into a snarl. 'And I suppose you're going to tell me that it was me telling tales.'

Tears welled in Viv's eyes as she cast a glance at Lucy and her granddaughter before making a final plea to her son. 'I think we should sit down and talk about why there's so much in your life that's gone wrong and I'm not simply talking about what happened between you and Scott. There was that whole mess with Rosie, and yes, with me too.'

'I'd love to, Mum but apparently you have somewhere else to be,' Adam said. 'It's time you left.' His voice was clipped and he took a step away from the door to give his mum an obstacle-free exit.

'Son . . .'

'Goodbye, Mum.'

Tears slipped down Viv's cheeks as she collected up her things. She gave Lucy and Ava trembling kisses before moving towards her son. 'I'll come back tomorrow.'

'No, you won't,' Adam said, pulling the pet carrier from her grasp. 'And we'll look after the cat from now on. Sorry, but I've had enough. You seem to think we can manage without you and we will.'

'Please, Adam . . .'

'Go,' he hissed, and that single word propelled his mother out of their lives.

'What do we do now, Adam?' Lucy asked when she heard the soft click as the front door closed.

'We manage.'

'I'm so sorry. I could tell Viv wasn't happy coming here, but I didn't know why, I swear,' Lucy said. She swallowed a lump of fear as she waited for Adam to accept her explanation.

Drawing closer, he cupped her face in his hand and used his thumb to wipe away the tears. 'I believe you.'

'I don't want you to fall out with your mum again because of me.'

'Didn't you hear her? She blames me, not you.'

'But I created this whole stupid mess.'

'You can't help how you are, Lucy. If anything, it's my fault for inflicting my family on you.'

'I'm sorry,' she repeated.

'Here, you're doing it all wrong,' Adam said, lifting Ava deftly from Lucy's arms. He pulled the bottle from the baby's mouth and placed her on his shoulder to pat her back. 'Once I've finished feeding Ava, I'll take a trip to the retail park to buy a cat flap so it's one less thing for you to worry about. Can you manage on your own? And I don't just mean later. I'll get home as early as I can tomorrow, but you'll still be taking on an awful lot. Forget the ideas my mum's been feeding you. Think about how you feel. Can you cope alone?'

'I wish Mum was here,' Lucy said as she came crashing down from her earlier adrenalinee rush.

'Maybe it's for the best. You wouldn't want her taking over, would you? You have to start believing in yourself, Lucy.'

It was exactly what Viv had told her, but Adam had said to ignore what his mum had said. Lucy didn't know who to believe, which was confusing because they were both saying the same thing. As her thoughts became muddled, her eyes flicked to the kitchen drawer where she kept her medication. She wasn't due her next dose but she needed something to dampen the worries and fears that bubbled and fizzed in the pit of her stomach. 'I'll try,' she said.

'Take an extra one of those tonight,' Adam said, following her gaze. 'I'll do the night shift so you can be at your best tomorrow. The most important thing is that you don't let your guard down again. Mum and Scott stay out of our lives. Agreed?'

'Agreed.'

25

Lucy had worn a cardigan to ward off the early morning chill on her walk to the baby clinic, but much like her mood, the day had brightened. As she strolled home, the blue sky had been left with just a few thin stretch marks from the clouds that had bothered her earlier, and the sun warmed her shoulders.

Almost a week had passed since she had been obliged to take full responsibility for Ava's welfare and if her visit to the clinic was anything to go by, mother and baby were doing well. Ava had passed her six-week health check with flying colours and had been a little angel while Lucy chatted to the other mums. It transpired that Lucy wasn't that different after all; in fact, one mum had been genuinely impressed when Lucy had mentioned returning to her studio to work.

In truth, Lucy had managed to grab less than an hour in the loft the day before, and most of that had been spent settling Ava in her bassinet, but she had enjoyed some time in front of her easel. It had been long enough to reassure herself that her medication hadn't snuffed out her creative spark, and she had almost built up the nerve to resume working on Annie's portrait when the baby had woken.

Not to be thwarted, Lucy had held on to her paintbrush while she cradled the baby in one arm, and for possibly five whole minutes, her daughter had been enthralled by the new sights and smells until an entirely different smell had overpowered them. Lucy had taken Ava to the nursery to change her, and that was that. She had sneaked upstairs later to clean her brushes, and soon after Adam had come home and caught the smell of turpentine on her fingers. He had narrowed his eyes at her half-hearted attempts to reclaim a little of her old self, and had asked one too many questions about it being safe to take Ava up a steep flight of stairs, but Lucy remained hopeful that she would adapt to her new way of life, albeit slowly.

Her new normal included a set of estranged in-laws and while Lucy refused to dwell on how Viv must be feeling, it would be foolhardy to block Adam's family from her mind completely. It had taken Scott thirty years to turn his mum against Adam, but who was to say he would stop there? As Lucy turned the last corner, she scanned the handful of cars parked in the cul-de-sac. There were none she couldn't account for, but Adam had warned her to remain alert.

Pushing the pram to the front door, Lucy made sure she had applied the brake before slipping past her snoozing daughter. Her house key was at the ready but there were certain insecurities that had become embedded and she tested the lock first. To her horror, the handle turned without resistance.

Prodding the door open with a finger, Lucy remained on the doorstep. It didn't make sense that she would be so careless about something so obvious. Her thoughts were being held to a sluggish pace by her pills, but that had made everything she had done that morning mindful and deliberate. She had given herself plenty of time to leave for her appointment and she could remember looking up at the leaden sky as she pushed the pram out of the house. She had flicked on the brake and locked the front door. She had tested it. Twice.

Lucy leant forward, her senses alert for clues that the house was not as she had left it. Tigger had settled into a routine of night prowling and he had been fast asleep in the utility room when she had locked him in there. She sniffed the air. There was an absence of a breeze that might suggest an open patio door and there was no smell of gas.

Probing her memory again, Lucy recalled having second thoughts about not wearing a jacket as she stepped outside, but if she had erased the memory of returning to the house, where was the jacket? Unable to accept that she had suffered a fresh lapse, Lucy followed one conclusion to the next. If she hadn't left the door unlocked, someone else had opened it.

Adam was in Manchester and the only people trusted with spare keys were their mums. Christine was in the Algarve for another week and, although Viv was much closer geographically, Lucy couldn't imagine her wanting to sneak back to cause another argument. A thief wouldn't need a key but there was no sign of forced entry, which meant it *had* to be Viv . . . or someone who had access to her keys and was devious enough to find a use for them.

Before Lucy could process where her mind was taking her, she heard a clatter and her head snapped upwards. The landing was in shadow, but she wasn't expecting to find someone lurking there because the noise had come from higher up in the house. Whoever was in there, had an interest in her art, confirming her worst fear.

Lucy backed away, circling the pram until she was level with her handbag dangling from the handle. Her phone was in the front pocket but if she phoned Adam now, whoever was in the house might hear her. Her first priority was Ava's safety. Leaving the front door ajar, Lucy snapped off the brake but as she began to back away, a shadow spread over her shoulder and across the pram, accompanied by the crunch of gravel behind her.

'Don't be angry with me.'

Lucy's knees almost buckled but her grip on the pram tightened and she remained standing. 'Go away, Scott,' she hissed, not daring to glance behind her.

'I need to talk to you, Lucy. I won't leave until you've heard me out.'

Keeping her back to her brother-in-law, Lucy's eyes darted left and right. The garden on one side of the house was enclosed by a six-foot hedge and her car blocked her in on the other. 'You're wasting your time. We have nothing to say to each other. Please, go. You can't do this,' she told him as she turned the pram 180 degrees so she could pull it into the house. Except she couldn't go inside, she realized. There was still someone in there. Her last remaining option was to force her way down the path but unless she was prepared to use her daughter as a battering ram, she was trapped.

'I know you're scared, Lucy, and I understand why,' Scott continued. 'If you'd just let me explain, then I promise I'll go. Can we go inside?'

'No!'

Scott was about to say something else when there was another clatter from upstairs, louder this time. 'Is there someone else at home?' he asked.

Lucy had her back to the door and her skin crawled as she imagined the unknown intruder sneaking downstairs. Her daughter was exposed to attack on both sides, but what could she do? Her palms were slick with sweat as she prepared to push the pram at Scott. Her shoulders began to shake. She couldn't do it. She squeezed her eyes shut.

'I don't know who's in there,' she sobbed.

As he raced past, Scott thumped into Lucy hard enough to knock her over, but his arm steadied her as he passed in a blur. He took the stairs two at a time and the sound of doors being flung open was followed by silence.

Lucy picked up Ava as gently as she could and held her to her chest. With each thunderous beat of her heart, her medication proved once again to be ineffectual against the extremes of her emotions. Its residual effect still managed to keep her thoughts slow, but it was at a time when she needed to think fast. She could make a run for it, or take a chance that the car had enough fuel to reach safety, but she did neither. The silence was complete and it worried her. Scott hadn't attacked her. He had rushed into the house to face down what might be a knife-wielding lunatic. She couldn't leave him, or at least she couldn't leave until she knew why he hadn't returned.

Taking one step over the threshold, Lucy searched the shadows playing across the wall along the staircase. 'Scott?' she called up.

She heard a creak that might have been the door to her

studio opening. The air moved slightly and he appeared soon after at the top of the stairs cradling a ginger kitten.

'I'm afraid he's been in your studio,' Scott said. 'It's a bit of a mess up there.'

'But I locked him in the utility room,' Lucy replied, forgetting it was Scott she was talking to. She was at a loss to understand how her meticulous preparations for leaving the house that morning could be undone so completely. Had she imagined locking up, or had she blanked out the memory of going back inside to sabotage all her hard work. Neither scenario was as terrifying as the man coming down the stairs.

'I need to phone Adam. I want Adam,' she mumbled, dropping her gaze as Scott leant across to close the door. Her pram, her handbag and her phone remained outside and out of reach.

'Not yet,' he said as he scratched behind Tigger's ear, making the kitten purr loudly. 'Do you want to sit down?'

Before Lucy could object, Scott set down Tigger and took hold of her elbow. With Ava in her arms, Lucy put up no resistance as he guided her to the living room and motioned for her to sit.

'Why are you doing this?' she asked. 'Why can't you leave us alone?'

'I wish I could,' said Scott, taking his place on the other side of the L-shaped sofa so they were almost facing. He reached out to stroke Ava's head, but Lucy blocked him by raising an elbow. Pained by the rejection, Scott pinched the bridge of his nose with his finger and thumb. 'Where do I begin?'

While he considered his next move, Lucy noticed that Scott wasn't as sharply dressed as he had been that first time they had met. There was a small cut on his chin from what looked like a haphazard attempt to shave. His eyes were sunken with purple bruises beneath that reminded Lucy of her own reflection in those weeks and months of sleeplessness. He didn't fit the image of a cruel manipulator, but wasn't that what he wanted her to think?

'None of this is your fault, Lucy.'

'I know it isn't,' Lucy replied, her voice stronger than his. If she were clear about anything, it was that Scott was obsessed with his brother's life and she couldn't be held responsible for his actions.

Either Scott didn't realize she was shifting the blame, or he didn't care. 'Mum's told me a little about what's been going on and the rest I can kind of guess. Maybe you should tell me what happened this morning. You said you locked the cat in the utility room?'

Lucy clenched her teeth and held her body taut.

'OK, maybe I should do the talking,' he said, but left another pause. The only sound was Ava's snuffled breaths as Lucy held her close to her breast, and then, 'I should start with an apology. It was wrong to trick you into meeting me. No, actually it was cowardly. I wanted to face Adam and at the same time, I didn't. He could always out-talk me and I wanted more people on my side when it happened. The truth is, I was scared.'

Scott coughed to clear his throat then wiped a hand across his face. His hand was trembling. 'That's how it's always been with Adam and, until recently, I never really understood how he could provoke such a strong reaction in me. I've been seeing a therapist for a couple of months and I wasted the first few sessions trying to convince him

I wasn't lying about all the things that had happened between me and Adam. It turned out it wasn't him I needed to convince but myself. Do you know what it's like not to trust your own memory?'

Lucy pressed her back against the sofa as he leant forward.

'I think you do,' Scott answered for her. 'Of all the people I've tried to explain this to, I have a feeling you'd know *exactly* what it was like for me. That's why I'm here, Lucy. If I can understand what's happening to you, I might be able to stop questioning what happened to me. You said you locked Tigger away, and I'm guessing you checked that all the windows and doors were closed and the gas was off. You didn't leave until you were satisfied that you'd done everything right.'

Lucy's already burning cheeks disguised fresh humiliation. Viv hadn't told Scott *a little*, she had told him everything.

'There was a time when I felt exactly as you're feeling now,' Scott said. The twitch in his jaw wasn't dissimilar to the one Adam had whenever he trawled through painful memories, but Lucy suspected Scott wasn't thinking back to his childhood, but recalling a story he had recently concocted. 'When I was younger, I thought it was normal to have an alternative version of myself that I never got to meet, the version that broke my brother's toys and trashed his room when he was at his dad's for the weekend. In my mind, I could see Adam snapping the head off some action figure or other, but I accepted it when Adam said it was me. It was my therapist who made me realize I'd been conditioned to believe what were false memories implanted by my big brother. Does any of this ring true?'

The shake of Lucy's head was imperceptible. One wrong movement and something Scott said might take root in her mind.

Edging closer, Scott said, 'When I was little, I tried to defend myself to Mum and Dad, but it was hard for them to believe me when there were so many inconsistencies in my cover stories, which were a screwed-up version of Adam's reality and my own. I swore I didn't do anything but, when pushed, I always admitted it *must* have been me because nothing else made sense.'

Lucy's jaw began to ache. She wanted to tell Scott to shut up, but to do so would be to give a reaction and that was exactly what he wanted.

'Dad had a gut feeling Adam wasn't the innocent victim he claimed to be. I've had some long chats with him since his op, although I've had to be careful what I say while he's still recovering.'

'But you've spoken to Viv,' guessed Lucy, thinking back to the confrontation the week before when she had told Adam to leave Lucy alone. It all made sense now, she thought bitterly.

'When Mum mentioned how she was spending her days with you, I couldn't put off talking to her any longer,' Scott said. 'Of all of us, Adam's been able to fool Mum for the longest. What mother would believe her child capable of going to such extremes to break up her family and destroy her marriage?'

'Viv, by all accounts,' Lucy said.

'To be honest, I don't think she's quite there yet. All I know for sure is that this has broken her. It's a bitter pill to swallow, but she's seen enough of Adam's manipulation techniques to know there are questions to be answered,' Scott said. He tilted his head and scrutinized Lucy's features when he added, 'She thinks the real reason Adam asked her to come and help you was because he'd realized she was back in touch with Dad. He senses a tug in one direction and he pulls in the other. Did you want Mum to be with you all day every day, or were you persuaded it was what was best for you?'

Lucy blinked; adamant that she wouldn't give any other response to Scott's speculation. Adam *had* spoken to his mum and Faye before she was even aware of the suggestion that Viv would be helping out, but even if Adam's actions had been a result of old jealousies involving his stepfather, it didn't make him a monster.

Scott shifted uncomfortably. He knew he was losing his captive audience. 'Do you want to check the damage in your studio?'

'No, Scott. I've listened, and now it's time for you to leave.'

'I will,' he said, standing abruptly. 'But indulge me one last time.'

'And then you'll go?'

'Yes, you have my word,' he said and, pre-empting Lucy's response, added, 'For what it's worth.'

When they reached the first-floor landing, Scott rattled the handle on the door leading up to her studio. 'Let's assume you did leave the utility door open. Would this door also be left ajar? And if it was, how do you think Tigger managed to close it behind him?'

'It's easily done,' Lucy said, answering all of his questions. 'Is that it?'

'Not quite.'

'In that case, let me put Ava down,' Lucy said. She didn't want to be separated from her baby but if Scott were going to continue with his character assassination of her husband, she wanted the opportunity to retaliate, and the sort of thing she wanted to say was not for delicate ears.

Ava's neck was damp with sweat as Lucy laid her down in her crib but she wasn't the only one who had become hot and bothered. Lucy's loose-fitting dress was damp against her skin and, as she left the bedroom, she peeled it away to hide the post-baby bulges Adam had a habit of poking with a finger when he thought he was being playful.

The landing was empty and the door to her studio wide open. She found Scott waiting at the top of the stairs, playing a silent drumbeat with his fingers and thumb. He stepped aside to allow her to inspect the damage Tigger had caused. The dust sheet had been pulled from the easel and the noise she had heard had been the canvas clattering to the floor. The strong smell of turpentine was explained by an upturned jar on her workbench that she used to clean her brushes. Lucy picked up the canvas and set it back on the easel while the unrepentant kitten wound himself around her leg. As she picked up the dust sheet, Tigger launched himself at its centre and was quickly lost within its folds.

'He's a bit a handful, isn't he?' Scott said. 'Someone would know he'd get up to mischief if he were locked in here.'

'Tigger's not normally like this,' Lucy said, falling for Scott's trap of defending her husband when she should have simply ignored the remark.

Dropping her gaze, she tugged at the dust sheet and

watched as Tigger head-butted the material and ground his shoulder to the floor. It was an odd behaviour but one she had seen before – except she couldn't quite remember when.

'Does Adam resent the time you spend up here painting?' Scott asked. 'Would he care if your work were destroyed?'

'Adam supports me more than anyone,' Lucy snapped.

'Good,' Scott replied although he didn't sound convinced. 'All I want is for you to question what's happening, Lucy, and listen to that inner voice. I can come up with my own theories, but you're the one who has to make the leap.'

As Lucy flicked Tigger off the dust sheet, she heard what sounded like fine grit raining down on to the timber floor and her mind made the sort of leap that would make Scott proud. She had seen Tigger's contortions when Viv had given him the toy she had bought from the supermarket. A sprinkling of catnip on anything could send Tigger into feline ecstasy.

'Is the painting damaged?' asked Scott, before Lucy could replace Annie's shroud.

'It's fine,' she said. Thanks to Ava, Lucy had applied very little paint to the canvas the day before and there wasn't so much as a smudge.

'It's more than fine,' Scott said. 'It's amazing.'

Refusing to be courted by Scott's flattery a second time, Lucy said, 'Are we done?'

'I know I'm making a mess of this,' Scott admitted. 'But if I was that good at explaining myself, my childhood might have turned out quite differently. Only you can spot the knots Adam's tied you up in, and only you can untangle them. Trust what you see, Lucy, and not what you've been told.' He tapped the photograph clipped to the easel. Despite his dishevelled appearance, Scott's fingernails were perfectly manicured. 'Objects don't move of their own accord.'

'You seem very well informed,' Lucy said. 'Viv described you and Adam as a riddle she couldn't work out, and I can understand what she means, but don't make the mistake of thinking I'm as gullible as your mum.'

Taking Scott's advice, Lucy trusted what she saw, which included the green flecks of catnip scattered across the floor. 'When I thought there was an intruder, it crossed my mind that you might have taken Viv's spare key, and who's to say you didn't? You seemed to know your way around my house pretty well and just because you stormed inside to face a potential intruder, doesn't mean you didn't know exactly what you'd find. It's easy to get a cat all excited if you sprinkle around enough catnip.' She waited for Scott's feigned confusion, before adding, 'It was Viv who introduced Tigger to the stuff, and I expect she's still got some at home somewhere.'

To Lucy's surprise, Scott smiled. 'If nothing else, I'm glad your first assumption wasn't that it was you who left the doors open. Deep down, you know you're not as dysfunctional as some would have you believe. You're not your dad, Lucy.'

Lucy's shock was quickly overtaken by her anger. 'Don't you dare!' she yelled. 'You don't get to exploit my family for your sick games. Get out, Scott. Get out, now!'

To her relief, Scott backed away. 'I'm sorry, I shouldn't have said that. I promised to leave you alone and I will,' he said, although his reluctance showed as he paused at the top of the staircase. 'For Ava's sake, keep asking those questions, Lucy. Not everything can be explained by me travelling across the Atlantic to mess up your life.'

When Scott searched her face for confirmation that his attempts to seed doubt had worked, she wished she could have closed her ears as easily as she closed her eyes, but she was grateful for the sound of Scott's retreating footsteps. When he reached the carpeted treads of the main staircase, it became more difficult to follow his progress, in fact she couldn't hear him at all. Her eyes snapped open. 'Ava,' she whispered.

Hurling herself down the first set of stairs, Lucy crashed into the rails on the landing and used her momentum to push herself towards her bedroom. She had closed the blinds but she could see Ava lying on her back in her crib with her arms stretched over her head. Her closed lids flickered in reaction to the reverberation of the front door being pulled shut.

Lucy tried to bring her emotions into check but what little strength she had left wasn't enough. Her chest heaved as she returned to the ground floor to find Ava's pram in the hallway. With each exhalation, Lucy released a sob, gentle at first but soon they racked her body. She pressed her back against the door and slid down. Why couldn't Scott leave them alone? How could she find the truth when there were so many lies? He had said to trust what she could see, but the idea terrified her and she didn't know why. It was all too much. She couldn't go on like this.

26

When Adam arrived home, Lucy was sitting on the living room floor rattling a teething ring above Ava's head – it disguised the strange noises coming from her throat each time she took a breath. Their baby girl kicked her legs excitedly as her daddy's shadow stretched across the play mat.

'Have you calmed down yet?' Adam asked.

'I didn't mean to let him in. I was coming back from the clinic – and when I opened the door – I heard a noise,' she said, her words broken by sharp intakes of breath. When she looked up, Adam's expression was as clouded as her thoughts. 'I thought someone had broken in – I thought it might be Scott – but he was behind me. I don't know why I followed him into the house. I was stupid – but I told him – I wasn't going to fall for his tricks. I didn't.'

Lucy waited for Adam to crouch down beside her and kiss away her tears but he remained out of reach. 'Are you sure about that?' he asked.

'Yes,' she replied, but she couldn't hold his gaze.

After phoning Adam and begging him to come home,

the small voice Scott had planted in Lucy's head had grown louder. It reminded her that there had been a time when she too had blamed Adam for her mistakes, but she had gradually learnt not to trust herself. Had she been wrong?

'Jesus,' Adam said. 'You're actually considering whatever it is he's told you.'

When he crouched down, he ignored his wife and swept their daughter into his arms. Ava let out a brief cry but settled quickly in her father's embrace. Lucy was slower to rise and followed in the wake of Adam's heavy footsteps. As she entered the kitchen, he was pulling open the patio doors. He stopped in the centre of the yard and lifted his head briefly towards the warmth of the sun before turning to face her.

'Are you going to tell me what he said?' Adam asked. 'Do I at least get the chance to defend myself?'

Giving Adam the space he needed, Lucy kept to the shade of the house. She tried to tell herself it was the sunlight making Adam's eyes glisten. She didn't think she could cope if he cried; she was too close to not coping at all. 'You don't need to defend yourself,' she said. 'He just repeated what you'd already told me about breaking your toys.'

'And?'

Unable to escape Adam's intense stare, Lucy said, 'He claims he didn't do it, but it was all nonsense, you don't have to tell me that.'

'And what other tall stories has he been telling you?'

Lucy was afraid to answer. If she repeated Scott's latest theories, it might sound as if she were voicing her own suspicions. From the way Adam was looking at her, it was precisely what he was expecting. 'You don't have to hear this,' she tried. 'I don't believe any of it.'

'Humour me,' Adam said, smiling at Ava as if they were sharing a secret joke at Lucy's expense.

Praying she could earn back her husband's trust, Lucy said, 'The front door was unlocked when I got home and Tigger had locked himself in my studio. Scott said you'd set it up because you didn't want me to paint. I told him it was more likely that he was responsible.'

'More likely,' Adam repeated, feeling the words as they rolled over his tongue.

'I mean definitely,' Lucy said, her voice trembling. 'I wasn't suggesting it was you, Adam. Never you.'

'Oh, Lucy, if that's the case then why are you getting so agitated? Are we back to not trusting me again?'

'No,' she pleaded. Beads of sweat pricked her brow and her fingers tingled. 'I'm scared of upsetting you, that's all.'

'Scared?' he asked with a shake of the head. 'I'm not upset, Lucy. I'm disappointed. You might kid yourself that you haven't been manipulated, but he's got to you.'

Thinking she might faint, Lucy clutched the patio door to steady herself. 'If he's got to me, it's because he knew everything about me. He even knew about Dad.'

Lucy had wanted Adam to be as shocked by this revelation as she had been, but he seemed more interested in the bright purple flowers of the clematis creeping over their neighbour's fence. He reached for a bloom and Ava's eyes danced for her daddy as he plucked it from its stem and held it aloft.

'What if he's done it before, Adam? What if it's been him all along?'

Adam shrugged. 'Assuming it is Scott.'

'I know, none of it fits,' Lucy said, eager to agree. 'I could understand how he'd be able to sneak in and turn the gas on or open a door, but what about all the other stuff that's been going on? I can't blame Scott for the times I've zoned out of conversations, or when I've lost it so badly I can't remember what I've done.'

As Adam held the delicate purple flower in his hand, an unpleasantly large spider crawled from behind one of the petals and on to the heel of his hand. There was a sharp intake of breath, but it came from Lucy. Adam didn't flinch as he crushed the spider and flower in his palm.

'Scott wasn't there, but I was,' he said. 'Is that what you're saying?'

'No,' Lucy said as she began to cry. 'You're not listening. It was me! I know it was me!'

'But a minute ago, you were convinced someone had deliberately set you up today and you seem keen to give Scott the benefit of the doubt. Who else would it be?'

'Me! It must still be me,' she tried, but it was of no use. Adam was right. Scott had succeeded in making her consider the impossible, if only to dismiss it.

When her husband took a step towards her, Lucy's heart lifted.

'I love you, Adam,' she said. 'I'm nothing without you.'

'I know you're not,' he said, 'and do you have any idea how draining that is?'

Adam swept past her before she had time to react. He strode into the kitchen and took a carton of ready-made formula milk from the cupboard. Grabbing a sterilized bottle, he glanced back. 'You're stopping me from being the father I know I can be because I'm constantly on edge. Every time I think you're getting to grips with being a mother, something like this happens. Scott's taken advantage of that, but you're right, you can't blame him for everything. You have to take responsibility for your own failings, unless of course you can offload them on to me, which is exactly what you're trying to do now.'

Following him into the hall, Lucy watched as Adam shoved supplies into Ava's changing bag. 'Where are you going?' she asked.

'Anywhere. I need to clear my head and you need to sort out yours. Why don't you go for one of those long walks you keep complaining we don't take? Make it a *very* long walk.'

'I don't want to,' whimpered Lucy, thinking of her dad and wishing she hadn't.

As she took a fumbling step towards him, Adam glared at her. 'What?' he demanded.

Her sobs were deep enough to make Ava's lip tremble. 'Please, don't leave me,' she begged.

Adam leant in close so that he could kiss Lucy if he chose. 'I know I can't fucking leave you. I have to put up with all of this shit for Ava's sake.'

'I know you do and I'm sorry. I swear I didn't believe Scott, not for a minute.'

'Yeah, but maybe for a second,' Adam said, the intensity of his stare making her quake as he probed her conscience. 'See, I was right. You truly are sick, Lucy, and those pills of yours are next to useless. Go take another one. Take more than one.'

As she listened to Adam's car reversing out of the drive,

27

'Lucy?'

The knife stilled in Lucy's hand but she didn't turn. She didn't trust what her ears were telling her.

'Lucy, love, it's me. I'm here,' the voice said, close enough for her to feel the warmth of her mum's breath against her ear.

The knife was pulled from her hand and set down on the chopping board. She felt a tug on her shoulder as she was turned around to face her mum. 'But you can't be,' Lucy said slowly, her tongue feeling too big for her mouth.

'I couldn't stay in Portugal, not after what happened.'

There was fear behind her mum's eyes, glimpsed briefly as Lucy was clasped in a bear hug. She could detect the faint whiff of sun lotion. 'You came home?'

'I flew into John Lennon Airport a couple of hours ago, dropped off my case and packed another one. I'm staying here for as long as you need me.'

'I can't let you do that,' said Adam.

Lucy was too numb to feel the fear that tightened around her chest. Adam had followed Christine into the kitchen and his expression offered no clue to his thoughts.

'In that case, I'll take Lucy home with me,' Christine said as she turned towards her son-in-law and, in the process, shielded Lucy from his scrutiny. 'You can't manage on your own, Adam, and Lucy needs me.'

'I know you mean well, Christine, but she has to learn to manage on her own if she's ever going to bond with Ava.'

'This isn't open for debate. If you insist, I'll go, but I'll take Lucy and the baby with me,' she said. In a more conciliatory tone, she added, 'I have another week until I'm back at work, and if I'm needed for longer, I'll take unpaid leave. After the fright she gave me, I'm not letting Lucy out of my sight until I know she's OK.'

Lucy could recall only brief snatches of the desperate call she had made to her mum. She had been sobbing uncontrollably, having managed to squeeze herself beneath the dining table. She could remember looking for refuge, somewhere safe from harm, but the greatest threat to Lucy had been herself. Her weapon of choice had been the pills she had had the good sense to leave on the kitchen counter after taking what she hoped was enough to weather the storm without being swept off the edge of the world. It was Ava who had saved her, the name her mum had repeated over and over again until Lucy could think of nothing else. If she had passed on a genetic death wish to her daughter, she couldn't leave her to face it alone.

'Why don't I make a start by cooking dinner?' Christine said as she steered Lucy away from the knife.

'Adam?' asked Lucy.

Her husband's features remained etched in stone and the connection between them was no more than white noise, as it had been since Adam had returned home the evening before with their over-tired daughter. Lucy had ignored the scent of a floral perfume on her baby's clothes and had fed Ava as Adam instructed. Leaving her asleep in her bassinet, Lucy had gone in search of her husband and found him at the dining table with his arms folded and his back pressed against the chair, glaring at the lengthening shadows on a day that refused to end.

'What have you been saying to your mum?' he had asked without looking at her.

'I don't remember.'

'Did you tell her about Scott? Have you been spreading his lies?'

'No, Adam, I wouldn't,' she had said, although her over-medicated mind was too clouded to be sure. 'All I want to do is forget about it.'

'Easier for you than me,' Adam had retorted. 'I had hopes for us, Lucy, I really did. Our marriage was meant to be a new beginning, but you brought your past with you and now you're dragging mine into our lives too. Today it felt like I was back home with Mum and Keith, having to justify myself. You have no idea how much you've hurt me. I could put up with the physical abuse, but this?' When he turned, the fading light deepened the shadows beneath his eyes. 'You don't need a knife to cut me.'

Lucy had taken tentative steps towards him. 'I didn't mean to . . .'

'No, you never do,' he had said. 'But thanks to you I've just had a barrage of abuse from Christine. You must have told her something.'

'I was crying,' Lucy had said. Her pills had doused her

emotions but the tears had become a habit she couldn't break. 'I told her Scott had been in the house, but I didn't repeat what he'd said. Do we have to talk about this? Please, Adam, I'll do anything. We can change the locks and keep everyone out. All I want is for us to get back to normal.'

'Normal?' Adam had asked with a bitter laugh. 'There's nothing normal about you.'

'I know, I'm sorry,' she had said, creeping closer as he returned his gaze to the shadows. 'What can I do to make it up to you?'

'Nothing, it would seem,' he had said, the chair legs scraping against tiles as he stood.

Lucy had made a fumbled attempt to grab Adam before he could escape. Despite her dulled reflexes, she had managed to wrap her arms around his neck while Adam attempted to push her away. 'Don't leave me, I'm begging you. I'll be good from now on. I won't speak to anyone you don't want me to.'

She had pressed her chapped lips to his cheek but Adam twisted away before she could plant a kiss on his mouth. 'Please, I'll do anything,' she had begged.

Realizing she had been clawing at his skin, Lucy released him with a gasp and then it was Adam grabbing her. 'How about being the wife you promised to be?' he had asked, his features contorted by the pain she had inflicted. 'Do you think you can do that?'

Lucy hadn't resisted as he spun her around and bent her over the table, but she had been shocked by his roughness as he pulled up her dress and snagged her pants. They hadn't made love since Ava's birth, or a long time before that, and although she hadn't been ready and it had hurt, she had been overcome by a ridiculous sense of gratitude. Adam still wanted her to be his wife. He still loved her.

That love was apparent now as Adam acceded to Christine's demands and painted on a smile. 'I've made such a mess of things, Christine,' he said. 'I never meant for you to cancel your holiday. Lucy doesn't have a monopoly on having meltdowns. I can't cope with much more of this.'

Lucy was transfixed by the tears welling in her husband's eyes, her mind too shocked to react, and it was her mum who reached him first. She cupped his face in both her hands, 'Hush now,' Christine said. 'I could have handled it better too and I'm sorry for shouting at you on the phone. No wonder you don't want me here. Do you forgive me?'

'There's nothing to forgive.'

Only when Christine had secured a smile that reached Adam's eyes, did she let him go. 'Why is your brother so hell-bent on hurting you and Lucy?' she asked.

Lucy shuddered. Adam wasn't looking at her, but she felt his eyes boring into her memory. Had she told her mum more than she should?

'He likes being centre of attention,' Adam said. 'I used to joke about him being the number one son, but it's true. After years of sitting on the fence, Mum's picked her side. We needed her here but she chose to walk away and give Scott all the ammunition he needed to attack us. He failed at charming his way into Lucy's life so now he's trying to exploit her weaknesses. Did Lucy tell you he used Mum's spare key to break in and cause a mess?'

'That's what I guessed, but it was hard to make sense of what she was saying,' Christine said, glancing briefly at her daughter.

'Don't ask me why he does it,' Adam said. 'I've spent most of my life wondering the same thing. It's a sport to him. It's as simple as that.'

'And your mum? She can't see it?'

'Believe me, I've tried, but who wants to believe their son's a psychopath? I know you must think I'm terrible for cutting her out of our lives, but what else could I do?'

'I don't think badly of you,' Christine said. 'As long as you don't cut me out of your lives too.'

'I have a feeling I couldn't if I tried.'

'Does that mean I can stay?'

'For as long as you can put up with the sofa,' he told her. 'Unless we make up a temporary bedroom for you in Lucy's studio. We could buy or borrow a foldaway bed from somewhere.'

'I don't think so,' Christine said. She crossed the kitchen to stand shoulder to shoulder with her daughter but continued to direct her conversation towards Adam. 'I want to see Lucy back in her studio painting.'

'Of course. So do I,' Adam said, countering one of the many accusations Scott had made.

'Although, I suppose we should get some medical advice on that first,' Christine added. 'She needs to go back to the doctor urgently, or have you made an appointment already?'

'Not yet.'

'Then why don't you do that while I sort out dinner?' Turning to Lucy, Christine said, 'What were you making, sweetheart?'

Lucy stared at the mounds of chopped carrots, onions and celery she had amassed. She had wanted to prove to Adam that she could take care of her family, but she couldn't remember what it was that he had told her to make. 'Soup, I think.'

Adam gave a short laugh. 'It must be my mum's influence. It looks like you arrived in the nick of time, Christine.' He kept his smile until his mother-in-law turned to the chopping board. The light in his eyes dimmed as he looked at his wife.

Lucy took a deep breath and waited for her body to still. The house was silent except for the steady beat of her heart and the occasional gust of wind through the eaves. Adam was at work and her mum out visiting a friend so that Lucy could finish Annie's portrait in peace.

She had resumed her painting the day after blubbing like a fool in front of her GP. Her tears had erupted simply because Adam was holding her hand, one of the few times he had allowed her to touch him in the last week. The pressure of his grip had increased when she had confessed upping her meds, but rather than chastise her, the doctor had simply increased her dosage. The expression her GP wore had scared Lucy as she watched him make call after call until he had secured an appointment for Lucy with a therapist in two weeks' time.

Lucy didn't want to think about how therapy might help, or what she would do if it didn't. Her mind focused on the half-dozen bristles teased into a fine point on the tip of her paintbrush. With a stroke of titanium white, Lucy added the final touch to the reflection in Annie's eyes that glimpsed the man who was never to leave her side.

It was testament to Lucy's skills that she had captured the depth of Annie's emotion, but rather than take a step back and applaud her work, she searched for imperfections.

She couldn't decide if the gap in her subject's teeth needed a touch more light or shade, a sure sign that it required neither, but she wasn't ready to say goodbye to Annie. What would she do next?

As Lucy considered her options, the stillness of the house unsettled her and she longed for the sound of her daughter's babbling. Ava's first smile was well overdue and she would hate to miss it. It was time to accept that she wasn't going to find salvation painting a version of someone else's happiness, no matter how much her mum would like to think it would. Rolling Tigger off the dust sheet, Lucy covered Annie's face one last time.

As she unbuttoned her oversized shirt, she recalled the swell of her stomach that had made it impossible to fasten. She couldn't imagine surviving the complications of another pregnancy, if indeed that was behind her failing mental health. Her doctor had applied the label of postnatal depression and she was doing her best to make it stick, but the drugs couldn't stop her from peeling back the corners of other possibilities.

The house shuddered as the front door opened and closed, making Lucy blink. She didn't know how long she had been twisting her shirt into a tight knot, but she was relieved to be rattled from her thoughts. Ava was home.

Tigger raced ahead and, reaching the hall, the cat sniffed Ava's teddy print jacket left draped over the empty car seat by the door. Lucy took a deep breath too, hoping to catch the first hint of her baby's scent, but it was an intense and decidely acrid smell that filled her nostrils. When a shrill alarm rose up, she rushed into the kitchen to find it filled with thick, black smoke.

The grill pan was resting on the counter with the smoking embers of what looked to have been two sausages. Lucy's eyes streamed as she checked the oven, but her mum had managed to switch everything off with the exception of the smoke alarm before escaping through the patio doors. She was at the far end of the garden with Ava in her arms.

'Lucy, come out here where you can breathe,' she called.

Lucy coughed and spluttered but she wouldn't join her mum until she had checked she hadn't left the gas on too. She swept a hand across the hob, which had been warmed by the heat rising from the oven but wasn't hot.

'I don't know what happened,' Lucy said, holding out her hands to take Ava the moment she joined her mum.

Staring at the smoke billowing out of the patio doors, Christine clung on to her granddaughter until Lucy prised her from her grasp. 'Sorry,' she said when she realized she was in the midst of a tug of war. 'I had such a fright. If I hadn't come home when I did . . .'

'I was on my way downstairs,' Lucy said, attempting to defend herself.

'What happened?'

Lucy's stomach twisted. She didn't remember switching on the grill, she didn't even recall feeling hungry. 'It's fine, Mum. It's not like I left the gas on too,' she said, only for a thought to strike at the same time as her mum's eyes widened in horror. What if a burner had been turned on but not lit? How long would it have taken for the fire in the grill and the gas to create an explosive mix. 'I didn't, did I?'

'No, but—' Christine began. 'Oh, Lucy. I'm scared.'

Lucy tipped her head towards the bruised sky and felt

droplets of rain splash against her cheeks. She put so much effort into proving herself trustworthy but it was getting harder. She felt the weight of Ava in her arms and noticed how cool her skin had become. 'This dress is too thin. She needs her jacket.'

'Don't go back in there,' her mum said, as if they had escaped a haunted house, but Lucy was already returning Ava to the safety of her grandmother's arms.

Taking a deep breath, Lucy raced back through the house. The alarm continued to wail but the smoke was settling as a thin layer of soot on the kitchen surfaces. It could have been so much worse. One day it might be.

When Lucy returned, she slipped the jacket on Ava, wrapped her in a blanket and then her arms in a pathetic attempt to protect the child she continued to endanger.

'Do you actually remember using the grill?' Christine asked.

Lucy trawled her memory and shuddered as she pictured herself standing at the top of the stairs twisting the shirt in her hands. 'No, but I got lost in my thoughts. It's what I do.'

'Is it?'

Lucy dropped her gaze to the dark splodges appearing on the flagstones as the rain grew heavier. 'It's no use blaming anyone else, Mum,' she said. 'I can't use Scott as an excuse this time because we've spent a fortune changing the locks.'

'I'd agree with you there,' her mum said solemnly as she slipped off her linen jacket and held it over their heads as a makeshift canopy. 'It wasn't Scott.'

'Do you think we can clean up the mess before Adam gets home?'

'Are you scared of him finding out?'

'No,' Lucy said too quickly. 'It's just that he feels so powerless. He can't control what's happening and, as you can see, neither can I. This is who I am, Mum. This is what I do. There are chunks of my life that disappear down a rabbit hole.'

'I wish you could remember putting the grill on, or at least be sure that it wasn't you. You have to trust your instincts, Lucy,' said Christine. Her jacket had become sodden and rivulets of rain ran down her face. 'And I have to trust mine.'

From the kitchen, the alarm persisted with its warning but it was the familiarity of her mum's words of wisdom that made Lucy's skin crawl. It wasn't quite the advice Scott had given but it was close. 'And what are your instincts telling you?'

The alarm stopped and from beyond the linen canopy obstructing their view, Lucy heard the distinctive patter of rain against a taut nylon umbrella. Her mum let her jacket slip and raindrops splashed across Ava's face until her daddy arrived to shield her.

'Who burned the toast?'

'It was sausages,' Lucy said as she attempted to give her memory another nudge, but to no avail.

'Oh, Lucy,' Adam said with such despair.

He opened up his jacket, inviting Lucy and Ava to snuggle into him. For the briefest moment, Lucy felt safe and warm, and then she glanced at her mum. It was hard to distinguish the rain from her tears but the fear in her eyes was unmistakable.

28

Returning to the house, they worked in silence to make order of the chaos. Adam prepared hot drinks while Christine changed Ava and put her down in her bassinet. Lucy went to her room to change and there was a moment when she considered staying there. When she did find the courage to return to the kitchen, Christine and Adam were sitting at the dining table. Spent raindrops glistened in the sunshine as they trickled down the window panes, but the storm had yet to pass.

'As horrible as Scott's accusation is, I think it's something we need to talk about,' Christine said, glancing towards Lucy as she approached.

'I thought you said you didn't tell her?' Adam said, following his mother-in-law's gaze.

'She didn't.'

Adam ignored Christine and continued to glare at Lucy. 'Sit down, I think you need to hear this,' he said, pulling out a chair and positioning it next to him so they could both face her mum. 'Apparently we have someone else who thinks it's me driving you crazy.'

'That's not what I said, Adam. Of course I don't believe that – it's too horrible for words – but there must be something that's made Scott and Viv believe it's true.'

Confusion creased Adam's brow. 'You seem very well informed about what my family seem to think, Christine. How is that?'

'I went to see your mum.'

Despite the tension in the room, Lucy felt a brief sense of relief. She wasn't going to be blamed for blabbing.

'She was the alleged friend you were visiting?' Adam asked. 'You went behind Lucy's back and lied about where you were taking the baby?' He looked to his wife, who nodded to confirm it had been against her wishes.

'Viv invited me over,' Christine explained to her daughter. 'I didn't realize Scott would be there too.'

Adam had picked up one of the three steaming cups of tea and blew softly over the rim. 'Oh, it gets better. I don't suppose it crossed your mind to leave when you realized you'd been set up?' he asked. 'I can't believe you'd betray Lucy's trust like that. I welcomed you into our home because I thought you of all people would want to protect her, not inflict more pain.'

'I am trying to protect her,' Christine said. 'But if I'd known what Scott had been saying, I might not have agreed to see Viv. You should have told me.'

'So you could start questioning my every move when, as we can all see,' he said, flicking his hand towards the soot-smeared kitchen, 'it's Lucy we need to watch?'

'When I left Viv, I was happy to dismiss every word Scott had said,' Christine said. 'But that was before I walked in here and found the place full of smoke. Having seen first-hand how meticulous Lucy is about switching everything off, I'll admit, I did doubt you. I want you to put those doubts to rest, Adam. That's all I'm asking.'

'And what about you, Lucy? Do you doubt me?'

'No,' she said, directing her answer to her mum and pleading with her to stop.

'Have you *ever* doubted me?'

'No.'

To Christine, Adam said, 'Satisfied?'

'Of course I'm not satisfied! There could have been a fire. Lucy could have been trapped in her studio.'

'Do you think I don't know that? Has it ever crossed your mind that maybe, subconsciously, Lucy actually wants to harm herself? You know how obsessed she's become about her dad.'

Lucy shifted in her seat.

'No, you're wrong. She wouldn't,' Christine said. Her eyes flicked to her daughter. 'I know you too well, love.'

'You don't exactly have a good track record of recognizing suicidal tendencies though, do you, Christine?'

When Adam and Christine locked eyes, the temperature in the room dropped and Lucy shuddered.

'I'm not blinkered, Adam. I know how fragile my daughter is, which is why she's coming home with me until we can work out what's going on here.'

Adam clenched his jaw and the veins at his temples pulsated. 'Scott is what's going on,' he said.

'Scott was waiting for me when I arrived at your mum's and he was still there when I left. I think we can at least agree that he didn't try to burn the house down. Where were you, Adam? Why are you home so early?'

'I said it would be a short day at the office.'

Lucy sunk lower in her chair as she waited for someone to ask if she remembered him saying that, but her body language alone told them she didn't. Her mum pushed her glasses up the bridge of her nose. 'That must be a conversation both Lucy and I missed. Not listening obviously runs in the family.'

'It always did,' answered Adam.

Christine refused to take the bait and pressed her lips tightly together.

'So let me get this straight,' Adam continued. 'You don't think it was Scott, and you don't think it was Lucy. You also claim not to believe the lies Scott told you about me, and yet you want me to provide an alibi for my movements. It sounds to me like you're as confused as your daughter.'

'I said I left Viv's not believing your brother,' Christine said. 'But I can't help wondering why you're being so defensive.'

'Could it be that I feel as if I'm under attack? I've been bullied before, Christine, and I've learnt to hit back.'

There was something about the calmness of Adam's voice that made Lucy's pulse race. Her eyes widened as she silently implored her mum to stop. Viv had been expunged from their lives for siding with the wrong brother and Lucy didn't want her mum to suffer the same fate.

'I don't want a fight,' Christine said, taking note of her daughter's growing anxiety. 'I accept that there are two sides to every argument. Tell me your side, Adam. Help me understand.'

'He hasn't done anything wrong, Mum,' Lucy said, finding her voice to plead Adam's innocence. She placed a hand on the table as she prepared to stand up. 'Can we please stop this now?'

Adam reached for Lucy's hand before she could move.

'I wish we could but I have a feeling your mum isn't going to rest until she finds someone else to blame for your problems,' he said. 'It eases your conscience, doesn't it, Christine? I doubt there's anything I can say to change your mind now that you've been charmed by Scott. You always did fall for the wrong brother, didn't you?'

'Don't do this, Adam,' Christine said, her voice trembling as much as the cup she had tried to pick up. 'Don't put Lucy through any more torment. Let this end now.'

'*Me* torment her?' asked Adam. 'You're the one who sat back for decades and watched her struggle to come to terms with what her dad did. You could have put her out of her misery a long time ago but you couldn't even tell her the truth when she'd convinced herself she'd inherited the family madness.'

'We agreed,' Christine said quickly. 'I trusted you, Adam, and I relied on your judgement. You said it would be too much for her to deal with and that still stands.'

Adam looked nonplussed. 'As I recall, you were the one who lost your nerve about telling her.'

'Does it matter?' Christine exclaimed. 'This isn't about what happened twenty years ago. It's about what's happening now.' She looked to her daughter when she added, 'Please, love, think about all those conversations you don't remember. You never did it with me, or Viv. Is there anything that can't be linked back to Adam?'

To her shame, Lucy had asked herself the very same thing on the day that Scott had made her doubt her husband, and there had been one instance she could recall. 'I lost my car keys that night after we'd been to the antenatal class,' she reminded her mum.

'They'd slipped out of your coat pocket, that was all. It proves nothing.'

Christine reached for her daughter's free hand, but Lucy recoiled. 'Stop it,' she said. 'Adam's been hurt enough. Can't you see how cruel you're being?'

'She doesn't know any better, Lucy,' Adam said, hugging his wife to him. 'She pushed your dad over the edge and now she's pushing you.'

'What happened, Mum?' Lucy asked, not knowing if she could cope with the answer but certain that ignorance was no longer an option.

Christine's mouth gaped open, leaving Adam to make the confession on her behalf.

'Your mum told you that she'd stopped speaking to your dad, but what she didn't tell you was that she had found *comfort* elsewhere.'

This time Christine did manage to answer. 'Oh, Lucy, I didn't want you to find out like this.'

'You didn't want her to find out at all.'

Christine glared at Adam before returning her attention to her daughter. 'I opened up to your uncle Phil,' she said, flinching when Adam gave a short laugh. 'I thought he might know why your dad had become so withdrawn, or at least help him snap out of it. I didn't know at the time that depression didn't work like that. Phil was struggling to keep the business afloat and I helped out where I could, but your dad didn't see it that way. He accused me of having an affair long before anything happened. It was almost as if he was expecting his life to fall apart.'

'You and Uncle Phil?' Lucy said as it slowly sank in.

'It wasn't an affair, Lucy. It was one mistake and I hated

myself for it,' Christine said. Her chest rose as she inhaled but her body remained deflated. 'I told your dad about it, thinking it would shock him into fighting for me, but it had the opposite effect. He walked out and I never got the chance to tell him I was sorry.'

'No,' Lucy moaned as she pressed her face against Adam's shoulder so that she didn't have to look at her mum.

'But don't you see?' her mum continued. 'There were reasons why your dad did what he did. He suffered from depression, yes, but it was what I did that triggered what happened. That's what I was going to tell you months ago but Adam talked me out of it. Maybe it's for the best that you do know now. Think about it, sweetheart. What's been happening to you isn't the same as what happened to your dad. The connection you thought was there doesn't exist, which means there has to be another reason why you are the way you are.'

Lucy's voice was muffled when she asked, 'What about the way *you* are? How could you do that to Dad? I don't know you any more, Mum. Why did you let me go on for years thinking there were no answers?'

'Because you were too young in the beginning, and . . .' Christine said, her words falling away. When she was ready to continue, it was in a whisper. 'We were doing fine, and despite what Adam would have you believe, you weren't suffering.'

Lucy's head snapped towards her mum. 'How would you know? We didn't talk about it, Mum! You should have told me.'

'Your mum felt understandably guilty,' offered Adam. 'Although I can't help wondering why she would tell a man who was so obviously on the edge of despair that she had been unfaithful. Unless she wanted to push him to the point of no return.'

Christine jumped up, knocking over her chair as she did so. 'No, you don't get to do this!' she cried. 'Lucy, you know I wouldn't lie to you, not now. I accept I haven't been as open as I should, but I loved your dad. What I've told you is the truth. We can talk about it all you like. Just come home with me. Give yourself the time and space to think clearly.'

'No!' Lucy cried, loud enough to drown out the whirr of her mind turning from one revelation to the next. Her mum *had* lied. She had made up a story that very morning about showing Ava off to her friend.

'I can't leave you and Ava here,' Christine said as she stepped closer. 'I won't.'

Her arms were open in the hope that her daughter would come to her but Lucy clung to Adam as if she were on the edge of a precipice. He was the only one left she could trust.

'Can't you see what you're doing to her?' Adam asked.

'Me?' asked Christine. 'Scott was right. You've brainwashed my daughter into thinking she's incapable of any independent thought. You're not, Lucy. You're clever and talented and you have to believe in yourself. If you don't come with me now, I'll have no choice but to contact the police and tell them you're being abused.'

'You can't do that!' Lucy said, untangling herself from Adam. She lunged at her mum and grabbed her by the arms. 'If the police find out what I've done, they'll take Ava away.'

'You've done nothing wrong,' Christine said. She went to push the damp loose curls from her daughter's face, but Lucy jerked her head away.

'I do stuff far worse than switching on the cooker and forgetting about it, Mum. I lose it completely. I do things I'm ashamed of,' Lucy said, glancing over her shoulder to see the tears welling in her husband's eyes.

'You don't have to do this,' Adam said in a tone that managed to be both soothing yet steely.

For once, Lucy ignored him and turned back to her mum. 'I attack Adam.'

'What?' asked Christine. 'No, I don't believe you.'

Adam stood and with one tug, brought Lucy back to him. 'I'm afraid it's true. Even a cursory glance at my medical records would reveal the signs of abuse. Remember the gash to my arm the day Ava was born? It was no accident, Christine. It happened during one of Lucy's meltdowns.'

'Now do you see?' Lucy said, and from the look of shock and confusion on Christine's face, she did. 'I hate myself for what I've done to him. I'm not who you think I am.'

'You don't mean to hurt me,' Adam replied, choking on his words. He cleared his throat as he faced Christine one last time. 'She's not responsible for her actions when she gets upset, and my job is to make sure that doesn't happen. If I'm guilty of anything, it's not protecting her from people like you. You've betrayed Lucy's trust once too often, Christine. I'd like our spare key back and then I'd like you to leave.'

29

Staring at the bedroom ceiling, Lucy fought against the nothingness her medication was pulling her towards. She waited until Adam had slipped into bed and switched off the bedside lamp before asking the question she had wanted to ask all night. 'What do we do now?'

'How am I supposed to know?' he hissed. He was lying on his side away from Lucy, and kept his voice low so as not to wake the baby sleeping in her crib. 'Why is it me who has to sort out everyone else's problems? It turns out your family is even more fucked up than mine. Can we leave it at that?'

'Am I allowed to see Mum again?'

The mattress shook as Adam twisted around. 'Allowed? Christ, Lucy, you make me sound like the tyrant your mum's painted me to be. Is that what you really think?'

'No. I didn't mean it to sound like that.'

'I could almost forgive your mum behaving like she is if you've been saying stuff like that to her.'

'I'm sorry.'

'If you're so sorry, why even ask about seeing your mum?

You really are a selfish bitch sometimes. If you had any feelings at all for me, the answer would be obvious,' he said, shifting on to his back so he could join her in staring at the inky blackness above their heads.

Lucy sensed him waiting for the promise that she would never see her mum again, but she wasn't sure she had the strength to give it. She was bereft but she was angry too. Whether it had been deliberate or not, her mum had sent her dad to his death. It was hard to imagine how she had lived with that level of guilt for so long but, as Lucy was now discovering, her mum was used to keeping secrets.

Why had she gone behind her back and spoken to Scott? How could she be so gullible when it wasn't that long ago she had trusted Adam enough to tell him all those things she had been keeping from her own daughter? Lucy wanted to pick up the phone and remind her mum of this but fear and shame prevented her. 'Do you think Mum will go to the police?'

'I hope she does,' he said. 'I'm sorry, Lucy, but maybe it's time to accept that you're not a fit and proper person to look after our daughter.'

'No!' Lucy cried out in a hoarse whisper. Her fear gave her the courage to wrap an arm around Adam and cling to his unyielding body. 'Please, don't say that. It's going to be OK. You said I needed to learn to manage on my own and I will.'

'In amongst all the drama, you seem to have forgotten that you nearly set fire to the house today. Were you cooking? Do you even remember going into the kitchen?'

'No, I thought I'd stayed in my studio.'

'I should have guessed you'd be up there. You let yourself become too absorbed in someone else's life to care about your own. What happens next time, when Ava's there with you? Will you forget about her too?'

'I won't paint again, not ever. I've finished my last portrait and once I've handed it over, that will be an end to it. I'll put all my energy into looking after you and Ava. You have my word.'

When Adam moved, it was to unhook Lucy's arm from around his chest.

'I love you, Adam,' she pleaded, grabbing hold of him again. Her mind flashed back to the night when he had pushed her over the dining table. She was desperate for him to want her again and slipped her hand beneath the waistband of his boxer shorts.

'Stop it!' he hissed, pulling her hand away. 'Do you really think I want you after this? God forbid you might get pregnant again. I'm telling you now, if that happened, I'd be happy to slit my own wrists rather than wait for you to do it for me.'

'Please, don't say that, Adam. I need you.'

'I know you do, and it's too fucking much, Lucy,' Adam growled. 'It's only because of Ava that I didn't pack your bags along with your mum's. It's your fault I can't do my job properly and if I didn't have Naomi covering for me, I hate to think where we'd be. Thank goodness there's at least one woman in my life who isn't trying to destroy me.'

'You do still love me, don't you?' Lucy asked, knowing her life wouldn't be worth living if he gave the wrong answer or, worse still, proclaimed his love for someone else. An image of her dad standing on a footbridge came to mind. She could see him holding out his hand, ready for her to take it.

'Can't you think of anyone but yourself?' answered Adam. 'No wonder your mum had an affair if your dad was this bad.'

Balling her hands into fists, Lucy could contain her terror no longer. 'Don't say that!' she yelled.

Ava let out a startled cry, and soon Lucy was crying too. She had forgotten the baby was there.

Adam snapped back the covers. 'For f—'

'It's all right, I'll see to her,' Lucy said, jumping out of bed and wiping her eyes.

'Can I trust you downstairs?'

'I'll be good,' she promised as she picked up the baby.

'Take another tablet while you're down there,' Adam called out as she left the bedroom. 'After today, I think we both deserve a peaceful night.'

30

As Lucy parked up behind the pub, she recalled the young mums who had disturbed the other customers in the café at Carr Farm and wondered how she would fare by comparison in the Railway. Unlike Hannah, she hadn't been able to call upon anyone to babysit, but that was fine. She and Ava had been inseparable in the last couple of weeks.

Her daughter slept soundly as Lucy disengaged the car seat from its base and hooked the carrier handle over her arm. She grabbed the changing bag before attempting the trickier task of removing the canvas from the back seat of her three-door car. The painting had been too big for the boot and it had been a struggle to squeeze it behind the driver's seat. It was now wedged firmly, although Lucy's efforts to remove it were less than enthusiastic. Annie had become a role model of sorts and it would be a wrench to lose her.

The portrait captured a rare moment of joy that framed Lucy's own hopes for the future. Her life at present, however, remained bleak and it was likely to stay that way unless she found a way of healing herself and, in doing so, prove the accusations against Adam false. For this, Lucy accepted full responsibility and so, when she hadn't been caring for Ava, or attempting to rid the house of the persistent smell of smoke, she had scoured the internet for any information that might help improve her mental health.

Unlike her mum, Lucy hadn't completely discounted the connection between her dad's problems and her own. Whatever the circumstances that had led to his death, her dad had been ill and it remained a possibility that they shared a predisposition for depression. Frustratingly, her research failed to find information on symptoms as baffling as her own, so she had moved on to postnatal depression in the vain hope that her GP's diagnosis had been correct after all. The conclusion she had reached was that her experiences didn't quite fit here either, which begged the question why was she taking drugs that were meant to fix a different problem?

Unbeknownst to Adam, she had begun palming the pills he pressed into her hand, which he did more often than she would like. When that small voice planted inside her head asked why he was so eager to dose her up, she ignored it. Doubting Adam's intentions was a cancer that had been cut out of their lives. They both wanted her to get well, they simply had different ideas about how that should happen.

The side effects of her withdrawal were even worse than the ones Lucy had suffered when she had first taken the medication, but so far, Adam hadn't been around enough to notice. He had taken to sleeping on the sofa again and missed the night sweats and restlessness, and during the day, he found other occupations either at work or at play. Having freed themselves from family obligations at weekends, Adam had reconnected with his old rock-climbing club and Lucy told herself that the arrangement suited her fine.

She liked having Ava to herself after craving it for so long. There were some things that she didn't quite trust herself with, like giving Ava a bath, and she preferred to use ready-made formula milk when Adam wasn't around to supervise, but she kept her baby clean, safe and warm, and one day, she would prove herself worthy of calling herself her mother.

'Do you need some help with that?'

Lucy let out a yelp. She had been distracted by the tug of war with the dust sheet that had snagged on the headrest to give much thought to who might be creeping up on her.

'Jesus, I didn't mean to scare you,' Hannah said when Lucy spun around.

'Sorry, I didn't realize it was you.'

It wasn't just Scott who Lucy feared these days. Her mum had practically camped outside the house in her car during that first week and regularly showed up for a lunchtime vigil now that she was back at work. She had sent countless text messages to remind her daughter that she was there whenever Lucy was ready to talk, but Lucy had no intention of taking her mum up on the offer while she still believed the ridiculous conspiracy theories about Adam. Lucy refused to leave the house whenever her mum showed up and had been forced to cancel a trip to the baby clinic for Ava's first inoculations when she had found herself trapped. It wasn't that Lucy didn't want to talk to her mum – she was desperate to hear a full account of what had happened immediately preceding her father's death – but she refused to betray Adam by consorting with the enemy.

‘We were standing at the bar when you drove in,’ Hannah continued. ‘I didn’t think you’d be this early.’

Lucy’s cheeks pinched into a smile that was more a muscle memory than a response to any feeling of pleasure. She ought to be proud of her precision planning that had ensured she had arrived at the allocated time, but she hated that leaving home should be a military manoeuvre.

‘It’s lovely to see you,’ Hannah said with a wide grin. She made being a yummy mummy appear effortless, with her hair pulled back in a haphazard ponytail and smoky eyes that were a combination of yesterday’s make-up and her natural colouring. The only colour on Lucy’s face was the dark circles beneath her eyes, which were impossible for Hannah not to notice, but her friend smoothed away her frown. ‘Grandad’s ordered you a lime and soda, I hope that’s OK.’

‘Perfect,’ Lucy said as she held out her arm for Hannah to take the baby’s car seat. She felt a measure of relief when her friend’s attention was drawn away from her gaunt features to her sweet baby girl with her cupid bow lips.

‘Oh, Lucy, she’s beautiful,’ gushed Hannah. ‘I’m so glad you brought her with you, although I bet she’s a little monster during the night. Are you getting much sleep?’

‘She’s not so bad.’

‘Yeah, right. Let’s get you inside before a light breeze blows you away.’

When Leonard gave Lucy a hug, he pretended not to notice the canvas she was holding. His first priority, once they had found a table in a quiet corner, was the return of the precious photos Lucy was happy to relinquish.

‘You’ve taken good care of her,’ Leonard said as his eyes devoured the photograph.

Lucy recalled snatches of the day it had gone missing but said nothing. It was a battle for her conscience and not his. 'Are you ready?'

Leonard didn't answer immediately. He straightened his back and waited for Hannah to stop stroking the baby's cheek. When she looked up, he gave Lucy a stiff nod. She took hold of the dust sheet and loosened the folds so she was sure she could lift it off in one movement. Her knuckles turned white as her hand froze. She should have checked the painting one last time, and would have done if Hannah hadn't appeared next to her in the car park. What if it had been damaged in transit? What if she had sabotaged her own work and erasaed the act from her memory?

'This isn't the *X-Factor*,' Hannah cried. 'Stop keeping us in suspense!'

Lucy felt her stomach lurch as she uncovered the painting. With her eyes tightly closed, it was impossible to tell if the gasps she heard were the good kind. She sneaked a peek, expecting the worst, but even Lucy could recognize happy tears.

Leonard cleared his throat. 'That's my Annie.'

'Do you like it?'

The old man took a folded handkerchief from his pocket and dabbed the corners of his eyes. 'If I'm honest, I was worried that I wouldn't recognize her and I'd have to live with this stranger in my house just to keep the family happy, but this is something else, Lucy. Annie was her worst critic, but even she would love it. You're a very, very gifted young lady, but I doubt I need to tell you that.'

Hannah released a second gasp. 'Look at the table in the background, Grandad. Do you recognize the pots you and

Nan made? That's why I was helping you clear out your cupboards a while back.'

Leonard's laughter turned into a sob that somehow caught in Lucy's throat. Hearing her mother's distress, Ava let out a brief whimper that was silenced by the shock of seeing a stranger's face staring down at her

'Can I pick her up?' Hannah asked, already releasing the straps.

'She'll be hungry. I'll ask the staff if they can heat up her bottle.'

Leonard heaved himself up. 'I'll do that,' he said taking the carton of formula milk and empty bottle Lucy had retrieved from Ava's changing bag. He chanced another look at the canvas propped up on the back of a spare chair before leaving.

'Is he all right?' asked Lucy as she watched Leonard wipe at his eyes again as he weaved through the tables. 'If the painting's too much for him, I could take it back until he's ready.'

'You'll do no such thing,' Hannah said, holding Ava in the crook of her arm as if she belonged there. 'He loves it, Lucy, and I'm so proud of you. You can't tell me it was easy with the baby and everything, but you did it. You've delivered another masterpiece.'

'It was a pleasure to paint her, despite all the chaos at home,' Lucy said before casting a guilty look at Ava. She hadn't meant it to sound as if she resented the baby. She *did* love her daughter.

'It took a lot out of you, though, didn't it?' asked Hannah.

Lucy pulled at the edges of her denim jacket to cover her sagging boobs. She didn't need Hannah to tell her how awful she looked, Adam's disinterest was proof enough that her body was repulsive. 'One of my next jobs will be to get back into shape. I've found some good workouts on YouTube and it's cheaper than the gym.'

'As long as you don't try to lose any more weight. You need to build up your strength.'

'I eat when I can,' Lucy said, although she was happy to skip meals if it meant shifting the baby weight Hannah pretended not to see. 'I don't know how you manage with three kids.'

'It took a while to get used to, and post-birth I always had plenty of visitors who brought dishes so I didn't have to cook. Are you getting help? Do you need me to send food parcels?'

'No, I'm fine,' Lucy said as she looked over to the bar where Leonard was chatting to the barman. 'But enough about me. How's your grandad doing?'

'Much better than you,' Hannah said, her focus fixed on Lucy. 'You're not leaving here until I've seen you eat something.'

Lucy grimaced. 'I forgot my purse,' she said, although in truth it was languishing at the bottom of her bag. The loose change in her pocket was left over from money her mum had given her. She had used it to fill up the car, and what was left would stretch to buy a round of drinks but no more. It wasn't that Lucy couldn't ask Adam for money, but the time never felt right when her husband was dealing with all her other demands.

'That reminds me,' Hannah said, reaching for her handbag. When she slid an envelope across the table, it looked thicker than when Lucy had last seen it. 'No arguments this time.

Looking at that painting, we should be paying you twice as much.'

'I can't.'

'Take it,' insisted Hannah.

Lucy's fingers stretched towards the envelope. She hadn't bought any new clothes since the baby was born and while she had managed to fit back into some of her old wardrobe, there were some things from her misspent youth that she would never wear again, not without Adam laughing at her. At the very least, she could invest in some shapewear. 'I don't know what to say,' she said. 'Thank you.'

'Don't make it sound like you're doing me a favour,' Hannah told her. 'You deserve it, Lucy. You're a bloody brilliant artist and I can't help feeling you've forgotten that.'

'Like most things,' Lucy muttered as she slipped the envelope into Ava's changing bag.

'Still convinced you have baby brain?'

Lucy picked up a beer mat and began picking at its edges. 'I'll have you know I found both my boots in the closet today.'

'But you are struggling,' Hannah persisted.

'I was diagnosed with postnatal depression,' Lucy confessed. She hoped it would embarrass her friend into shutting up, but she should have known that sublety didn't work with Hannah.

'Do you still have gaps in your conversations with Adam?'

Surprised that Hannah should focus on this one symptom, Lucy simply nodded.

'Maybe you should try recording him. I did it with Jamie once. He was always persuading me to be nice to him and let him go to the pub, and in return he was supposed to get up with the boys at the weekend. He'd get what he wanted and, lo and behold, he'd have no memory of his side of the bargain. I used an app on my phone to record his promises and it worked a treat. It didn't matter how bad his hangover, he was the one getting up at five thirty.'

'I don't know. I can't see how it would be of any use to me.'

Ava began to wriggle as she realized the stranger holding her wasn't going to feed her. Hannah remained unfazed. 'It would prove that you're in the right,' she said.

Lucy swept up the confetti surrounding what was left of the beer mat and hid it behind a menu. 'But I already know that I'm not,' she replied. 'Here, let me take her.'

Ava wasn't impressed when she realized her mum didn't have her bottle either and released a particularly high-pitched squeal that made it difficult to hear Leonard as he came to the rescue.

'Is it safe for me to come back yet?' he asked his granddaughter.

As Lucy grabbed the warmed bottle, she caught the look Hannah gave her grandad and it brought her out in a cold sweat. She was getting better at spotting attempts to manipulate, and for one horrible moment, she wondered if Scott had got to her friends as well as her family.

She watched Leonard as he returned to his seat but the old man had shrugged off the chastisement and adjusted his chair so he could look at the portrait. Stop being paranoid, Lucy told herself. Leonard had simply stayed away long enough for Hannah to hand over the money.

With her baby content in her arms, Lucy began to relax.

'Tigger's back home,' she told Hannah quietly, not wanting to disturb Leonard's moment of reflection with his wife.

'So you said.'

'Did I?' Lucy asked. She had spoken to Hannah over the phone a number of times to arrange the handover of the painting but, due to various demands of parenting on both sides, their conversations had been brief. She didn't remember mentioning it.

Hannah chewed her lip. 'Erm, maybe not. I probably thought you'd get him back once he was big enough to go outside, and assumed it had happened.'

Lucy smiled at her friend's weak attempt to save her embarrassment. 'It's all right. I probably did tell you and it's gone out of my head,' she said, happy at least that this was one gap in her memory that Adam couldn't be accused of implanting. 'See what I mean?'

Ava dribbled milk on to her bib as Lucy sat her up so she could take a proper look at her new surroundings.

'Look, Grandad,' Hannah exclaimed. 'She's looking at you.'

'She's a beauty,' he said, drawing his watery eyes from the painting. 'And she takes after her mum, if I'm not mistaken.'

'God, I hope not,' Lucy said with enough conviction to make the old man frown. She offered a weak smile. 'I'll have to dig out the photos of me when I was a baby to compare.'

'It's a wonder your mum hasn't already,' Hannah jumped in. 'She must adore Ava.'

'I suppose.'

It wasn't difficult for Hannah to gauge from Lucy's

expression that something was wrong. 'Has something happened?' she asked.

Lucy felt two sets of eyes on her but refused to raise her gaze beyond Ava's strawberry-blond crown. 'We had a bit of a falling out,' she mumbled.

It was Leonard who found his voice first. 'No, you can't do that, love,' he said. 'Life's too short, and if there's one thing my Annie wouldn't stand for, it was a family rift. Friends, and sometimes spouses, come and go, but your family is your bloodline. Whatever it is, fix it.'

'I'm trying.'

'How?' Hannah asked. When Lucy offered a simple shrug, she added, 'Talk to her, Lucy. Answer her calls or nip round to see her. You don't have to tell Adam. Bloody hell, if Jamie knew half the things I get up to, there'd be trouble.'

'It's complicated,' Lucy said, using the same words her mum had so often relied upon to avoid difficult conversation. 'And for the record, I'd never go behind Adam's back. We're not like that.'

'More's the pity,' Hannah said quietly as she let Ava wrap a chubby hand around her finger. 'Your mum's heartbroken.'

The impact of Hannah's unintentional confession was immediate and Lucy jerked Ava away. 'You've spoken to her?'

'She phoned me, and I'm glad she did. She wants you to know that she'll agree to whatever it takes to get you back in her life. And if you won't speak to her, talk to me. We can have play dates with the kids – the boys love babies and it would be good for Ava too,' Hannah said, speaking as fast as she could because she knew Lucy was about to stand up. 'Don't let yourself become isolated, Lucy. No one's trying to break up your marriage. We just—'

Lucy was on her feet. 'Of course you are. Was it Mum's suggestion to tape the conversations with my husband, by any chance?' she asked. 'Mum has the cheek to suggest I've been brainwashed, but if you ask me, it's Adam's brother who's been brainwashing everyone else. It's sick, Hannah. You have no idea what you've been dragged into, so keep out.'

Grabbing the rest of her things, Lucy was about to leave but the changing bag snagged on a chair.

'Lucy, please wait, love,' Leonard said, and the old man's desperate words carried enough weight to stop Lucy in her tracks. 'I don't pretend to know what's going on, but I trust my Hannah's judgement and I'm guessing there was a time when you trusted your mum's. Listen to them.'

'Would Annie stand by and let everyone accuse you of horrible things when all you were trying to do was protect her from herself?' Lucy asked, her eyes full of pleading. Of everyone, Leonard would understand.

'No, I don't suppose she would,' he said, 'but if I were truly trying to protect my wife, the last thing I'd want was to cut her off from her family.'

Leonard's parting shot played on Lucy's mind as she drove home. It was easy for someone on the outside to sit in judgement, but she was the one living the nightmare, and it was a nightmare. She and Adam had to put each other first and after the stunt her mum had pulled recruiting Hannah, any guilt she might have felt about ignoring her attempts at reconciliation had vanished. Adam was right. Her mum had fallen under Scott's spell and their combined efforts made Lucy feel as if she were under siege. She longed to be home.

Turning into the cul-de-sac, Lucy noticed her mum's car parked outside a neighbour's house. She would know where Lucy had been, and there was a good chance she had been informed that her latest attempt to undermine her daughter's marriage had failed. Lucy was tempted to phone Adam but she didn't want to disturb him at work while he had other battles to fight – like keeping his latest project afloat – and it wasn't yet a crisis that Lucy couldn't handle.

After parking up, Lucy raced around the car to release Ava's car seat. She slammed the passenger door shut, only to hear its echo further up the road. If there were approaching footsteps as she unlocked the front door without testing it first, she couldn't hear above the whooshing of blood and adrenaline coursing through her veins, and she didn't look back as she tumbled into the house and slammed the door shut.

Lucy's relief was short-lived as she noticed the trail of foamy slime on the hallway floor, followed by the smell of bile and undigested cat food. She had stopped locking Tigger in the utility room, partly because tracking him down hampered her exit, but also because it was one less thing she could chide herself for when she got it wrong.

'Tigger?'

She kept her voice low, not wanting to disturb Ava any more than she had already. The baby blinked sleepily as she watched her mother slip the newly installed security chain on the door before setting the car seat gently on the floor. Creeping slowly away, Lucy waited until she was out of her daughter's sight before racing towards the utility room.

With fear twisting her insides, Lucy wanted to believe she was panicking unnecessarily, but it was as if there was something buried deep inside her psyche that was preparing her for the worst. She found a Tigger-shaped indentation on his bed but no kitten and was about to continue her search elsewhere when she spotted his food bowl, complete with the remnants of congealed meat and savoury jelly. She had fed Tigger that morning but she had thrown away the scraps and washed the bowl clean. *Why* would she feed him again?

Returning to the kitchen, Lucy glanced briefly out of the window, already knowing that the vomit trail suggested Tigger had retreated deeper into the house. Her ballet shoes slapped against the kitchen tiles but her pace slowed again as she crept past her daughter and into the living room. The cat wasn't there either.

Exertion and fear made Lucy's breathing ragged as she headed upstairs. She hadn't quite reached the top when she spotted the tightly balled kitten in front of her closed bedroom door. He had gone looking for her and she wanted to offer him comfort now, but as Lucy crouched down, Tigger didn't look up. Trembling, she made a clumsy attempt to stroke his head but the kitten gave no response.

Pressing her palm gently on the curve of his spine, she said, 'Please, don't be dead.'

Tigger's fur was warm to the touch and as she slipped a hand beneath his tummy to pick him up, she felt the rapid flutter of his heart. He remained limp as she lifted him into her arms, foam dripping from his mouth. She needed to take him to the vet but as she carried him downstairs, she remembered her mum was outside. What would Adam's objectors make of Tigger's plight? Would they accuse him of deliberately poisoning a defenceless animal?

Adam's alibi was airtight. He was sixty miles away in Manchester this time, which begged the question, who else would, or more pointedly, *could* do something so despicable? There was only one other person with a key to the house.

As Lucy held the dying kitten in her arms, it wasn't the thought of facing her mum that prevented her from opening the front door. It was the fear of being uncovered for the heartless monster she feared she had become.

31

Lucy was sitting at the dining table when Adam arrived home. There was a homemade shepherd's pie resting on the counter ready to slip into the oven and Ava was gurgling contentedly in her baby bouncer having been recently fed. Her feeding bottle was in the dishwasher amongst the pots and pans Lucy had used to make dinner and Tigger's emptied food and water bowls.

As Lucy stood to greet Adam, he backed away. 'What's wrong?' he asked, not fooled by the display of domestic bliss. 'Since when did you make dinner?'

'I thought you'd be tired after a long day.'

'Is that a dig about me working late?'

Lucy pressed her lips together, the corners of her mouth pulling down despite her best efforts. 'I wanted to surprise you, that's all. It's shepherd's pie, like Viv used to make.'

Adam watched impassively as she pulled open the oven door. 'Have you been overdosing on your medication again?' he asked.

'No.'

The casserole dish was in her hand when he said, 'Maybe you should.'

The dish clattered on to the wire shelf as Adam loomed over her. She looked up, wide-eyed.

'You need to preheat the oven first,' he said with a sigh that was strong enough to make Lucy sway as she straightened.

'But I'm only browning . . .' Her words trailed off as Adam stepped in to remove the dish and set the oven.

Ava flinched when her daddy slammed the oven door shut. He folded his arms and pressed his back against the counter. 'Are you going to tell me what's going on?'

Having spent the last few tortuous hours going over her movements on a continuous loop, Lucy had found no evidence of the gaping hole she knew must be there in her memory.

'I can't be trusted with Ava,' she blurted out.

'Oh for God's sake, is it because I'm going on the Sandstone Trail this weekend? Is this another way of trapping me at home?'

'No, it's not that.'

'Then what?'

'Tigger's been poisoned,' she said, unable to look Adam in the eye as she took a step back. 'I came home after meeting Hannah and he was really sick.'

Adam didn't need to ask who was responsible. His jaw dropped. 'You've killed the cat?'

'He might be OK,' she said, recalling his lifeless body as she had wrapped him in one of Ava's blankets before leaving the house.

Her mum hadn't been waiting, and there had been nothing to prevent Lucy from reaching the vet's surgery except her own conscience. She could at least find some solace in knowing that she had done the right thing, although she hadn't mentioned the half-eaten food to the vet and he had presumed that the kitten had accidentally ingested rat poison during a mid-morning prowl.

'I left him at the vets. They've managed to stabilize him but the next twenty-four hours are critical.'

'How could you do something like that?'

'I don't know for sure that it was me,' came Lucy's strangled reply. 'I don't remember putting more food in his bowl, or what I might have put in it. There's all kinds of insecticides and fertilizers in the utility room, I checked.'

'Before or after you added them to his food?' Adam said. 'Jesus, Lucy.'

'That's why I can't be trusted.'

'Too bloody right,' Adam said, picking up the casserole dish and dropping it in the bin. 'I'm not taking any chances.'

Lucy wasn't in the least bit offended. 'I was thinking, if Tigger's OK, he should go back to your mum's.'

'Yeah, I can see that conversation happening,' he mocked.

'We don't have to speak to her. I could drop him off in his pet carrier outside her house.'

'And whose doorstep do we leave Ava on?'

Rather than respond, Lucy brushed her hand over the darkened screen of her mobile phone resting on the kitchen counter.

'And if you're about to suggest we find a childminder, forget it. We can't afford it,' Adam said as he stormed over to Ava, whose babbling had transformed into loud demands for attention. With a handful of reassuring words, he settled the baby down to watch the slow simmering war raging between her parents.

'I know, but I thought . . .'

'That I'd be the mug to look after her,' Adam answered for her. 'What you seem to forget is that someone has to earn the money you're quite happy spending. How much is today going to cost me, by the way?'

'It's all right,' Lucy said. 'We have insurance.'

'So it's OK for you to go poisoning animals as long as we can make a claim?' he asked. 'There'll still be excess to pay.'

'It won't cost you anything,' Lucy insisted as she felt the conversation slipping away from the reasoned discussion she had wanted to have. 'Hannah paid me for the portrait. I can use that to cover it.'

'But not the premiums, which will skyrocket after we've made a claim.'

'There's enough for that too,' Lucy told him, drawing his gaze towards the envelope on the table. With Adam's attention diverted, Lucy pressed her finger against the control button on her phone and the screen came to life.

There was the rustle of paper as Adam examined the contents of the envelope. 'There must be a thousand quid in here. Since when did you charge that amount of money for a painting?'

'I didn't know it was that much,' she said, her expression giving away her unease. She doubted it was a coincidence that the envelope had grown in thickness after her mum had become involved in the transaction. 'Hannah said she wanted to pay what she thought it was worth.'

'And she thinks one of *your* pictures is worth a thousand quid? That doesn't sound right.'

Lucy could feel another confession bubbling in the pit of her stomach. She told herself to remain calm whatever happened. 'I don't think it all came from Hannah. Some of it might be from Mum. She knew how I was struggling for money.'

'Hold on,' Adam said. 'How does your mum have anything to do with this?'

'She knew I'd be in touch with Hannah, and she tried to get her to help me.'

'Help?' demanded Adam. 'So you've poisoned the cat and yet *you're* still the victim in all of this?'

'I didn't mean it like that,' Lucy said, her fingers trembling over her phone. She had opened the voice recorder app and the red record button glowed like a beacon that would help her find a way back through her memory should she need it.

'Oh, really?' challenged Adam. 'Do you mind explaining why your mum would suddenly think you're a pauper? Have you been telling her I can't provide for my family?'

'No.'

'Then why would she think we needed the money?'

'I don't – I don't remember,' Lucy said, her breathing becoming rapid to keep up with her racing heart.

'Oh, that's convenient! I suppose you've also forgotten how I've been working twice as hard to make sure we can afford all your fuck-ups – and I'm not just talking about insurance premiums. Do you ever look at the bill when we buy all those readymade cartons of baby milk? And buying two prams wasn't exactly cheap.'

'But I bought one of them!' Lucy yelped as she pressed her finger to the button on the screen. The fear and frustration in her voice showed up as a series of sharp spikes.

Covering the phone with a tea towel, Lucy turned to face Adam. She had been prepared for his glowering expression but it was Ava's shocked features that cut deepest. Her daughter's eyes were wide as if she too could see the chasm that had opened up beneath Lucy's feet.

32

'You can't leave, Adam,' Lucy said as she rushed downstairs to intercept him in the hallway. It was an hour before dawn and she had been waiting for the first sounds of him rising from his makeshift bed on the sofa.

Ignoring the wild-eyed apparition that followed him into the kitchen, Adam switched on the kettle and began heaping coffee granules into a travel cup.

'You know how bad the last couple of days have been for me,' Lucy said, her voice breaking. 'You can't leave me alone with Ava for a whole weekend.'

When Adam continued to ignore her growing agitation, Lucy closed the kitchen door and pressed her back against it. She didn't want her daughter to hear another of her mother's meltdowns. 'You said you wouldn't go if I didn't think I could cope, Adam. I – can't – cope!'

When her husband looked her up and down, she didn't need to read his expression to know she looked a mess. Her hair was frizzed and her pyjama shorts exposed the ugly dappling of cellulite on her thighs.

'Walking the Sandstone Trail isn't just about raising

money, Lucy. Do I really need to explain that?' he asked, shaking his head. 'After everything that's been happening – because of you – I need to prove to Ranjit that I'm still part of the team. Backing out now because you *can't cope* would be the ultimate humiliation, but I'm starting to think that's what you want. You want me to fail. You're as bad as everyone else.'

'No, I'm not. Please, Adam,' Lucy said as she wrapped her arms around her body to shield it from his scornful gaze. 'Can't you at least come home tonight? The halfway point isn't that far away and you don't have to stay at the hotel with the others. I could pick you up and take you back in the morning.'

'So that's it. You don't trust me.'

'Of course I do, but you'll be with them during the day, isn't that enough?' she said, choosing to refer to the group as a whole rather than single out the individual whose name was the source of her sudden fit of jealousy. Naomi.

'You don't get what being part of a team means, do you?' Adam said as he continued to make his drink. 'No wonder our marriage is a joke.'

'Don't say that, please. I am trying. I know how bad it's been lately but I have my appointment with the therapist next week. It won't be like this for ever.'

'It?' Adam said, rounding on her. 'There's no *it*, Lucy. You're the problem, or have you forgotten?'

To jog her memory, Adam pulled up his T-shirt so she could see her latest handiwork. The deep gouges running down his chest had scabbed over in the last couple of days but the shame remained raw. Overwhelmed by her anger, Lucy had come out of her fugue crumpled on the kitchen floor as usual. What wasn't so usual was that Ava had been nestled in her arms. The baby had been sleeping but her delicate eyelids had been red and crusted with tears.

'I know it's me,' she said, as an image came to mind of fingernails digging into flesh. She squeezed her eyes shut and pushed away the memory.

If Lucy wanted to relive the argument, she could simply listen to the recording she had made. The app had shut off automatically at some point, but even if it had stored a snatch of her madness, it would be too much.

'I will get better,' she said, opening her eyes to discover that Adam had lost interest and was rooting around in a drawer.

When he approached her, there was contempt in his eyes. 'Here, take these,' he said, forcing a sleeve of pills into her hand. 'All you have to do is feed and change Ava without poisoning her. Do you think you can manage that?'

No, was the simple answer. Tigger had survived, but it had been a close call. After a carefully worded text to her mother-in-law, Viv had agreed to pick up the kitten from the vets. Lucy had received a flurry of messages from her mum soon afterwards, asking what had happened to him. It was a question Lucy still asked herself.

'How can you trust me? Please, I'm begging you. Don't go. Let's spend the weekend together. We could go on our own mini-trek with Ava and meet up with the others somewhere,' she said, her eyes lighting up like a distress flare. 'We could go to Heart's Leap and show Ava where you proposed to me. We could add her name to where we carved ours.'

'Why on earth would I want to go back there, Lucy? It wasn't one of my best decisions and, knowing you, I'd say the wrong thing and you'd shove one or both of us off the ledge.'

'I'd never do that,' Lucy said, but she wobbled slightly as if she were already standing on the precipice. 'We will get back on track, Adam.' Correcting herself, she added, '*I'll* get back on track.'

'What's the point?'

'Of what?'

Adam snorted. 'The point of you,' he said, taking her by the shoulders and removing the obstruction blocking his way. 'I'm going upstairs to change and pack a few things, but if you really want me to come home tomorrow night, you're going to have to stop being so fucking pathetic. Get on and do the one job you have left: look after your daughter.'

'I'm your wife too,' she called after him, but Adam's footsteps didn't falter.

Lucy's back was pressed against the wall as she craned her neck to peek out of the nursery window. The sun had risen and her mum's car was parked in its usual spot further up the road, effectively trapping Lucy inside for what might be the entire weekend, knowing her mum. Lucy didn't want to stay indoors. She didn't think she could last another day fighting the urge to play the recording and exhume the memories she had buried with good reason.

Wearing a hooded dressing gown over the short pyjamas she doubted she would change out of all weekend, Lucy pulled her mobile from her pocket. The screen was blank and she had no idea how long she had been staring at it when a message flashed up.

I can see you, Lucy. I know you want to talk. Let me back into your life xxx

Lucy felt the garish pink walls closing in on her. She hated this room. If the colour had been her decision . . . She cut off that thought. Criticizing her husband was a habit she had to curb if she wanted to keep him.

Her teachers had described Lucy as headstrong in school reports. It wasn't intended as a compliment but she had taken it as such, and so had her mum. Lucy's response to her father's death had been to set out to prove that she would never be that weak.

Except her dad hadn't been weak, he had been ill. And Lucy was far from headstrong.

She had been lying to herself then, and she was lying to herself now. She wasn't afraid of listening to the recording and confronting the monster within, in fact, she would almost welcome having tangible proof that she could share with Adam's dissenters. What Lucy feared most was that the recording would give a different answer to the one she was expecting.

What if Scott had been telling the truth? What if there was a reason she could so easily understand what he claimed to have gone through as a child? Was it even possible for Adam to plant false memories, as Scott had described? Lucy thought back to her teachers' remarks. How could someone who was apparently self-assured and stubborn become so fucking pathetic?

Halfway down the stairs, Lucy slumped under the weight of those questions. She pulled the hood of her dressing gown over her head and rested her forehead against the banister. She had left Ava asleep in the living room after her first feed. The door was ajar and she would hear her if she woke up, which shouldn't be for another hour unless she was disturbed by whatever Lucy's reaction might be in the next telling minutes.

Holding herself taut, Lucy stared at the rows of apps displayed on her mobile. She let her finger hover over the voice recorder icon before releasing a sigh of exasperation. She opened up her messages and tapped out a reply to her mum's latest text.

Don't go anywhere x

She wasn't sure how her mum would react to her breaking radio silence, but it made Lucy feel a little less alone. 'Oh, shit,' she whispered as she pressed play on the recording.

Her voice, when it came, made Lucy flinch.

'I bought one of them!'

Her outburst was followed by the gentle rustle of a tea towel being draped over the phone. She pictured herself turning to Adam. He was angry, or shocked, or disappointed – she couldn't quite recall, although she wasn't sure she had been able to read him at the time. What she could remember was Ava's startled expression, and Lucy's body jerked as the scene she was recalling flooded with detail. She was tempted to stop play and delete the file, but for now, her nerve held.

'I don't want to keep spending your money, Adam. What if I started painting again? If work's getting too much for you, I could be the one who provides for us!'

'Hold on, are you suggesting I give up my job and we rely on you?'

'I told you, I can't *look after Ava!'*

'Then maybe you should have said that before you decided to have a baby.'

'It was you who said we should have one. I was only giving you what you wanted.'

'So you're finally admitting it. You don't want her.'

There was disbelief in Adam's voice and who could blame him? Why had she said that? Ava deserved a better mother than she could ever be. Lucy dropped the phone on to her lap and wrapped her fingers around the staircase spindles to stop from falling.

'Of course I want her, Adam. I love her. All I'm saying is I'm not sure I was ready, and, maybe, all this stuff that's been happening is proof of that.'

'My God, Lucy. Is everything you say a lie? Have I been that stupid? You made me think you were beautiful and smart, but look at you. You're a mess. You don't even try to hide it any more. You don't care what you wear or how you look, because you've trapped me. You didn't want Ava, and you probably didn't want to marry me. All you were after was some mug to look after you.'

'No, it wasn't like that!'

Above her raised voice, Ava's cry had risen up like an air-raid siren, but Lucy's outburst continued unabated.

'I wanted to marry you more than anything. I wanted to be your wife and the mother of your children.'

'Wanted? So it's not what you want now?'

'Yes, it is. I do.'

'But a minute ago you said you didn't want kids – ever.'

'I never said that. What I meant was—'

'Don't waste your breath. I can't believe anything you say any more. I have to go on what I see. How long has Ava been crying? You haven't even flinched.'

Lucy *had* heard Ava's cries but she had been so confused that her mind couldn't process the information. Her thoughts had been turning, turning, turning and she had needed to make Adam understand. She had raised her voice each time Adam lowered his, hoping that the words spilling out of her mouth would make sense.

There was a pause in the argument while the combatants repositioned themselves. Adam had taken a step back from Ava so he could observe Lucy in action. She had lifted her daughter out of the baby bouncer to cradle her, but the baby's cries intensified. Lucy could hear herself making choking sounds that were meant to soothe but had simply added to the baby's distress.

'Are you neglecting our daughter while I'm at work too? Is that why she's so terrified of you?'

'No, I take good care of her.'

'But you still won't bathe her, will you?'

'You said I shouldn't . . .'

'No, you *said you shouldn't. And why is that? What are you so afraid of, Lucy? Do you think you might drown her?'*

'N-*no.'*

'Would it even bother you if she did die? Is that why you missed getting her inoculated?'

'Mum was outside. I couldn't go out.'

'No, *that's an excuse and a pretty pathetic one at that. You don't care. I think you're waiting for the day that something does happen, just like you were waiting for something to happen to the cat.'*

'I would never hurt our baby.'

'Then who the hell said you couldn't be trusted with her? Was it me?'

'No. . .'

'But somebody said it, not ten minutes ago in this very room. Come on, Lucy, think. Who said you couldn't be trusted with her?'

'Me.'

Lucy's eyes were closed as she listened to mother and baby sobbing, but they snapped open again as Adam finally lost his composure.

'Yes, you! It's a wonder poor Eva has made it this far.'

'Eva means everything to me. I would never, ever do anything deliberately to hurt her, Adam. My life's nothing without her.'

'Eva?'

'What?'

'Jesus, Lucy. Can't you even remember her name? Our daughter's called Ava.'

'I know she is! I didn't call her Eva.'

'Here we go again. I'm *the liar.'*

Lucy lunged for the phone resting in her lap and pressed the pause button. She didn't need to rewind the recording. She had picked up immediately when Adam had mistakenly called their daughter Eva. She knew she had simply been repeating the mistake, but this revelation wasn't worth celebrating because her heart had flooded with fear of what came next. Her memories remained confused but she recalled quite clearly how she had felt, and what had led up to the moment Adam had received his injuries. Her heart thumped against her chest so hard that she could feel it reverberating against the back of her throat, making her feel sick.

Racing upstairs, Lucy almost dropped her phone down the toilet in her haste to lift up the seat. A mixture of bile and curdled tea spattered across the toilet bowl and her nose and throat burnt as she retched. When there was nothing left, she collapsed on to the floor, pulling a stream of toilet paper with her. The smell of vomit was overpowering, but Lucy was only vaguely aware of her surroundings. She was back in the kitchen where she had sunk to the floor clutching Ava to her chest while fresh accusations flew from Adam's mouth like a swarm of angry bees.

She recalled accusing him of an affair at some point and although it wasn't the first time she had felt threatened by Naomi, she had taken her fixation to a new level. In the midst of her hysteria, she had convinced herself that Naomi would take her place, and not only in her husband's heart but in her daughter's life.

It was fortunate for Adam that she hadn't been within easy reach of a knife because she was sure she had thought about it. As it transpired, she had used the nearest weapon available to her; Lucy's fingers tingled as she relived the moment cruel fingers raked down his chest.

In amongst the masses of crumpled toilet paper, Lucy found her phone. There was a new message from her mum. She could be there in a matter of seconds. All Lucy had to do was open the door.

'Oh, Mum,' Lucy whispered. 'You're better off without me. Everyone is.'

Lucy didn't know how Adam had put up with her for so long. What would he think if he knew she had recorded him? It would surely be the end of their relationship and she had to delete the evidence – but first she had to listen to it all. She deserved to be punished.

'So go on. Tell me how this is all my doing again.'

'No. I know it's not.'

'More fucking lies. Why bother denying it? We both know where this is leading. Come on, Lucy. Do your worst!'

'No, I take it back. I take everything back. Please, don't do this.'

'Look at you, you're hysterical. I bet you're already constructing an alternative reality where I'm the abuser, because anything is better than confronting what you really are. It doesn't matter that it was you who said

you didn't want Ava. You'll plant the blame on me anyway. You always do. No wonder everyone thinks the worst of me. It's all because of you.'

'I – I've never blamed you.'

'Are you sure about that?'

'No.'

The phone clattered to the floor as Lucy lurched towards the toilet bowl again. Her head was spinning, a blur of bicycle spokes and flashes of orange until the reflector became a fiery circle. The sensation was nowhere near how she had felt lying on the kitchen floor, gagging on her tears and holding on to Ava but, then as now, she could hear a low whine as her blood pressure surged.

'See! You're admitting it. Not that it'll matter. Come tomorrow you'll deny it all again. I know what you're like, Lucy. Trust me, I know you better than you know yourself.'

There were footsteps and the sound of Adam's soles squeaking against the porcelain tiles as he crouched down in front of his wife.

'Let me tell you what's going on in there.'

Lucy could see Adam reaching out a hand, but she couldn't be sure if he had swept away a rogue curl from her damp, snotty face, or if he had knocked his index finger against her temple. She rubbed the side of her head.

'That faulty brain of yours, the one you inherited from your dad, is taking every message it receives and turning it into something evil and twisted. You see my sad expression and the tears welling in my eyes. You see my arms reaching out to you, imploring you to put the baby down, promising that, whatever happens, we'll get through this together, and all the while your twisted mind is putting horrible, nasty words in my mouth. I'm begging you to get help, but you're cowering because all you can hear is me telling you what a worthless piece of shit you are.'

'Stop. I need you to stop.'

'If I could get away with it, Lucy, I'd stick you and all your ugly, fat-girl clothes in the wheelie bin and have you dumped in a landfill, or better still, tipped over the ledge at Heart's Leap.'

'Don't say that, please.'

'But I'm not saying it, Lucy. Haven't you been paying attention? These are your words, not mine. You know you're worthless, and you need to hear it. It might be my voice, but these are all your thoughts. Every one of your nasty insecurities is coming back to haunt you. I'm the one begging you to love our daughter, but all you can hear is someone telling you that you resent her for making you crazy as fuck. She deserves to suffer for what she's put you through.'

'I love her. I swear I do.'

'Stop lying. You hate the two of us because you know we'd be better off without you. You know you're about to lose everything. Watch my lips, Lucy: you already have. You know I can't stand to look at you,

and who would blame me? Naomi certainly doesn't. She's horrified by what you've been putting me through, and she can't wait to give me what you can't.'

'No, I don't believe you.'

'Between you and me, she's ready to step in whenever you want to step out. It's only a matter of time, wouldn't you say? She'll be a better mother to our daughter than you could ever be. You say you love Ava? Wouldn't you want her to have a mother who was funny and smart and beautiful? Maybe it's time you did the right thing, just like your dad.'

'I'll never let anyone take my baby! I'd rather us both die first!'

'Give her to me.'

'Get off! You're not taking her!'

'And if I try, what's going to happen? Will you grab a knife from the drawer and do something about your suicidal thoughts? I can see you're thinking about it. Would you like me to get a knife for you? Ah, no, I'd best not do that. You might use it on me instead.'

'I wouldn't.'

'You already did! Don't you remember slashing my arm? You were laughing at the time. How can you not remember something like that, Lucy? Why can't you remember putting poison in Tigger's food? Why can't you remember doing something like this?'

Lucy was overcome by something akin to vertigo. The spinning wheel of her thoughts gathered momentum, spinning faster and faster until it seemed to change direction. In a split second, the illusion showed Lucy's life from an entirely different perspective – all she had to do was find the courage to face the horrors being revealed.

Gripping the toilet bowl, Lucy released a scream that mirrored the one captured in the recording when she had watched Adam lift his T-shirt and scrape deep gouges down his chest with his own fingernails. He hadn't even flinched as he inflicted this pain on himself, but simply curled his lip at her horrified expression.

'You're pathetic. It makes me sick just to look at you.'

It was as if Adam could see her curled up on the bathroom tiles amongst the spatters of vomit and crumpled toilet paper, and she was relieved to hear his receding footsteps. Left with only the sound of Ava's mournful cries on the recording, echoed by the sobs of a mother who couldn't comfort her, Lucy rose unsteadily to her feet.

33

As Lucy wrenched open the front door, her hair and face were dripping wet. She had hastily swilled away the vomit before giving in to the more pressing urge to hold Ava, whom she had found kicking away happily in her bassinet. The baby hadn't needed to cry out for her mother, which made Lucy want hers all the more.

'Oh, Lucy,' was all Christine could manage. Her complexion was sallow and there were shadows beneath her eyes that matched her daughter's. She reached out tentatively to touch Ava's grasping fingers but Lucy recoiled as if her mother had been about to snatch the baby from her.

'I'm sorry,' her mum said. 'I didn't mean to—'

'Do you want to come in?' Lucy asked.

Lucy had yet to process what she had heard but instinctively she led her mum through to the kitchen, choosing a room that offered more than one exit. The home that was meant to be her refuge wasn't safe. It never had been.

'Has Adam gone on the Sandstone Trail?' asked Christine, her trembling voice giving away her own nerves.

'He'll be back late tomorrow.'

It was possibly the one fact on which Lucy could rely. Adam would leave his car at the starting point at Frodsham and even if he wanted to sneak home in a cab to do the kind of things that Lucy was just beginning to fathom, he couldn't do so without being missed. He wasn't at the office now, and couldn't make up some spurious excuse about meeting a client. His colleagues would notice his absence, and he was probably too enthralled with Naomi to think of his wife anyway.

Lucy blinked hard. How was it possible to think of her husband in those monstrous terms? This was Adam, for pity's sake; the socially awkward, oftentimes vulnerable, but fiercely protective man who had captured her heart.

'I love him, Mum,' she said as she stared at the cupboard she had opened. She looked beyond the glasses lined up on the shelf and searched her tattered mind for scraps of evidence that the man she had married might still exist.

'I know you do,' Christine said. She had come to stand next to Lucy and reached past her to take two glasses from the cupboard. 'Do you need some water?'

'Yes, please.'

'Does Ava need feeding?'

'No,' Lucy said sharply as she turned her back on her mum. If Ava had needed her next bottle, it would have been the first thing Lucy would do. She settled her daughter into her baby bouncer and sat down so she could use her foot to rock her.

Christine's head was bowed as she filled their glasses without a word before taking a seat facing Lucy. 'I'm not going to interfere,' Christine said. 'I've learnt my lesson, you can tell Adam that. I'll accept whatever terms he offers, as long as I'm allowed to see you and Ava. You can tell him that too.'

Lucy took a sip of water. 'I can't.'

'Please, Lucy. I know how much I've hurt you, and I know I should have been more honest about what happened with your dad, but I was ashamed. I was scared it would damage our relationship and I wanted to protect you. I still want to protect you.'

Lucy wiped the water dribbling down her chin. 'From Adam?'

'I'm not here to talk you into anything you're not ready to accept.'

'But you do think Adam's behind all of this, making me think I'm going crazy? He's the one who leaves doors open and the oven on. He mocks me for forgetting conversations that never happened. He plants ideas in my head and makes me believe they're my own,' she asked, only to realize she wasn't posing questions but making statements. 'He's the one who poisoned Tigger.'

Christine splayed out her fingers on the table, reaching tentatively towards Lucy to test her reaction. Tears welled in her eyes when this time her daughter didn't retreat. 'I want you to be happy and safe, that's all,' she said. 'Maybe you don't think you need me, but I'm damned sure I need you.'

Holding her breath, Lucy listened for the first crack in the world Adam had constructed around her. 'I do need you, Mum. I'm scared.'

Christine held her gaze but, to Lucy's relief, didn't ask her to speak her fears aloud. What would Lucy say? It wasn't the truth alone that terrified her but the compelling urge not to confront it. It had been repeatedly demonstrated that she couldn't function without Adam and she suspected that still held true. Dismantling a false reality wasn't going to be easy when Lucy didn't know what was real and what was pure fabrication. It might even be her undoing.

'I have to do what's best for Ava,' she said at last.

'You look after your daughter and let me look after mine,' her mum replied. 'Please.'

'Will you catch me?'

Christine's features paled. 'Sorry?'

Holding back the sob took more energy than Lucy thought she had left. 'I think I'm about to fall.'

'Tell me what to do, love.'

Lucy scrambled for the phone that had been a heavy weight in her pocket. 'I need you to listen to this.'

34

Lucy stood in the courtyard beneath the weight of a cloudless sky as her mum listened to the recording. The tendrils of the clematis creeping over the fence continued to offer blooms but the pots and planters she and Viv had filled with a rainbow of colours had been allowed to wither and die. Lucy hadn't noticed them shrivelling under the glare of the sun, but she saw them now.

Christine put a hand on Lucy's lower back but didn't speak.

'I didn't imagine it, did I?' asked Lucy, resting her cheek against Ava, who was snoozing on her shoulder. The sunhat, grabbed as she fled the sound of Adam's voice rising up from her phone, was a pitiful attempt to protect her daughter.

'No, you didn't.'

Lucy pressed her lips together hard enough to make her chin quiver.

'You need to pack your things.'

The song of a blackbird carried on a breeze that was filled with the scent of sweet summer blooms. All around them, life went on as normal whilst remaining impossibly out of reach.

'Lucy, I'm not leaving you here,' warned Christine when her daughter failed to respond. 'Not a second time.'

'Why did he do it, Mum?'

'No,' Christine said, the growl in her voice drawing Lucy's gaze from the fathomless sky. 'Don't try to understand him, not yet. I've spent the last couple of weeks talking to Viv and Scott, and even they would be shocked to hear what I've just heard. For now, all you need to do is accept that you and Ava are in danger if you stay here. And so that we're absolutely clear, that's not an option.'

'I know,' Lucy whispered.

'Do you? One of the first things you said to me when I arrived was that you loved him. After listening to the things he said to you, Lucy, how could you possibly say that?'

'Because I don't know any better,' Lucy said. 'Or because I don't deserve any better? Adam didn't give me a magic pill that made me fall under his spell, Mum. I fell in love with him and he became the centre of my universe. I know it doesn't make sense that I can't let go, but I don't know who I am any more.'

'You're in shock,' Christine said, giving Lucy's back a firm rub as she became more disturbed by Lucy's lack of response. 'It could be your medication numbing your reactions.'

'I stopped taking my antidepressants. Adam was feeding them to me like sweets,' she said. 'God, I knew, didn't I? I knew something was wrong but I refused to face it.'

'None of this is your fault,' Christine told her. 'I can't imagine what it's going to take for you to make sense of everything, but you will. This first step will be the hardest but please, for Ava's sake, pack some things and let's go.'

The blackbird fell silent and although her mum's mouth moved, Lucy couldn't hear what she was saying. Her world had imploded and she was pulled into a vacuum where only one thought reached her: this was how her dad had felt.

The pressure of her mum's hand on her back increased as Christine stopped rubbing and began pushing. Birdsong erupted and the first thing Lucy felt when she entered a new world was the weight of the baby in her arms. Her mum was right, now was not the time to make sense of what had happened.

She had been mentally and emotionally abused but that knowledge alone wasn't going to undo the damage that had been done. She felt sick at the idea of telling Adam she was leaving him, but if she knew anything about her husband, it was that he wouldn't let her go willingly. She was going to have to be prepared for a fight.

'It's going to take a few trips,' she said. 'I'm not leaving anything behind.'

Extracting Lucy from her former life took time, and the day-old sun skimmed the rooftops as she and her mum emerged from the house with the last of her belongings. Christine had suggested calling in reinforcements but Lucy preferred fewer witnesses to her humiliation and they had managed on their own using both cars.

Their first trip across the river had been a circuitous route over the bridge, but to save time, Lucy had managed the second trip to Liverpool by tailgating her mum through the tunnel. Although she rationalized that Adam's concern about her competence as a driver had almost certainly been a tool to isolate her, it was still going to be a battle to reclaim her confidence.

'Are you sure that's everything?' Christine asked after forcing a box of paints into the footwell of her car while avoiding the easel protruding through the gap in the front seats.

'I'm having second thoughts about leaving the cot,' Lucy said, having previously agreed that it would take too long to dismantle.

'We can always use your old one in the garage when Ava's too big for her crib,' Christine said, her smile not quite disguising her pained expression when she added, 'Remember how sure you were that it was there?'

'It seems such a long time ago,' Lucy said as she wrapped her cardigan around the brightly patterned playsuit she had found languishing at the back of her wardrobe. She had gone crowd-surfing in it once but had stopped wearing it after Adam had made a comment about her looking like a schoolgirl with bad dress sense. That had been last summer, not long after they had married.

'Are you ready?' Christine asked, her eyes narrowing as she checked the road – the one way out of the cul-de-sac was also the way in. 'I'm not going to relax until you're both home with me.'

Lucy glanced back at the house. There was nothing left that she wanted to take. She had packed all the baby's things, along with her personal belongings. She had even taken her maternity wear, not because she had any intention of having another baby, or another relationship, for that matter, but because she didn't want to leave any part of her with Adam. The two exceptions had been the drugs he had tried to force down her throat, and the faded silk flowers that were as artificial as their life together.

Checking the deepening shadows, Lucy imagined that Adam would have finished the first leg of his trek by now and would be ensconced in the hotel bar with his colleagues – and they were definitely colleagues rather than friends. Adam engendered only those relationships that offered something to him, and Lucy couldn't help but wonder what it was that he had thought he could take from her.

She wanted to know why he had set out to destroy her so completely. Had he started out with hopes for their future? Had Lucy messed up? Would Naomi do any better? Assuming she could believe anything Adam told her, he had managed to turn his colleague from foe to friend, and Lucy hadn't imagined a woman's scent on Ava's clothes the other day. As Lucy had become more of a burden, Naomi had become an asset. Was it possible that she had been set up as an eventual replacement, as Adam had suggested?

'Lucy,' Christine said as she took hold of her daughter's arm and tugged her loose from her thoughts. 'Can we go?'

'I need to lock up.'

'I'll do it if you want to go ahead. Ava's bound to wake up any minute.'

Lucy had reversed her car into the drive and the passenger door was ajar. Ava was sleeping soundly in her car seat, having tuned out of the hustle and bustle that had been going on around her all day.

'No, you go. I want to be the one to close the door on this part of my life,' Lucy said, not fooling herself that turning a lock would bring closure. If the first step was leaving, the second would be confronting Adam. 'And I'd like to drive back to Liverpool by myself.'

'No, we're going together.'

'It's OK, Mum. Adam is miles away and he'll be too busy charming his boss to worry about me.' When it looked like her mum would refuse again, she added, 'Please, I need to do this. I need to be this strong.'

'You're sure?' Christine asked slowly as she too considered all the risks. When Lucy nodded, she took some cash from her purse and added, 'Take this in case you need to refuel again.'

Lucy made a show of going to the front door with her keys in her hand as her mum drove away. Christine kept glancing back, not quite believing that her daughter would follow through with their plans. She needn't have worried. There wasn't a hole in Lucy's memory big enough to expunge what she now knew about her husband.

As her mum disappeared from view, Lucy's hand was steady as she turned the key in the front door. She was about to walk away but, out of habit, she tested the lock first. Her hand tightened around the handle. Was she ever going to untangle herself from the web of Adam's lies?

With her pulse racing, Lucy scurried away and was sitting in the driving seat before she realized she was doing it all wrong. She didn't want to flee. If she was going to stand up to Adam, she was going to have to walk out on him with her head held high. Her breathing slowed.

When Lucy stepped back into the house and closed the front door, she had Ava's car seat hooked over her arm. She poked her head into the kitchen first and was surprised to find it relatively unaffected by her imminent departure. The baby equipment was missing, making the kitchen appear tidier, but whatever imprint Lucy had made on the heart of their home had been negligible. The living room was much the same.

It was only when Lucy reached the last stop on her tour that she noticed a pronounced difference. Resting Ava's car seat on the studio floor, she stretched her back and took in the bare shelves and empty floor space. She hadn't left so much as a paintbrush and if she'd had the time, she would have scrubbed away the splatters of paint on the floor too.

This was the place where Lucy had fought hardest to retain some of her former self, and as she took a deep breath, she stopped thinking about what she was running away from and concentrated on what she was aiming for. She crouched down in front of her sleeping daughter and trailed a finger across a rosy cheek, provoking a flutter of eyelids.

'I do love you,' Lucy whispered.

She took hold of her daughter's hand, hoping against hope that the day's revelations might help her find the missing something that was preventing them from bonding properly. Ava's warm skin provoked a feeling of warmth in Lucy's chest that was reminiscent of the moment she had held her daughter for the first time. As the feeling spread, Lucy's heart soared and at last, she remembered herself. She remembered that she wasn't the product of Adam's twisted imagination. She loved Ava purely and simply. There was nothing missing. There never had been.

The surge of emotion rising up through her body was unstoppable and for once, it wasn't an unpleasant sensation. Leaning forward, Lucy's lips broadened into a smile as she kissed her daughter's forehead. 'I – love – you,' she said between more kisses. 'I love you so much, my sweet, precious girl.'

Ava released a whimper and when she opened her eyes, she looked at Lucy as though about to cry but her body stilled. Her eyes widened briefly and, as if it were the most natural thing in the world, she smiled her first smile at her mummy before the muscles in her face relaxed and sleep caught her again.

Sitting back to stare in wonder at her baby, Lucy stifled her laugh before it could transform into a sob. She loved her daughter with every beat of her heart and every ounce of the strength she would need to face Adam. She wished she could see the expression on his face when it slowly dawned on him that she had left him. He would phone her, and eventually she would pick up.

Lucy's brow furrowed. No, that wasn't how Adam's mind worked. He wouldn't pester her with calls. Adam would force her to wait, using time as a weapon until her feelings of dread had built to unbearable levels. It didn't have to be like that, she told herself as she pulled her phone from the shoulder bag strapped across her chest.

Adam had sent a couple of texts during the day and had made no reference to the hurtful things he had said that morning. He told her he missed her, and went as far as to suggest they could bring Ava on the trail when she was old enough, spinning her the lie that they were destined to have a long and happy life together. Her replies had been simple assurances that she and Ava were having a quiet weekend. She told herself the 'x" at the end of her message wasn't a kiss, but a cross to cancel out every loving thought she had ever had for that man. She wished it were that easy.

She and her mum had made no comment on how the battle for custody might go, but there was no doubting it would be a battle, which was why she had to be the one to tell Adam what she had done. It wasn't good enough to let him work it out for himself, and sending a text felt too much like wimping out. Adam's number glowed in the failing light but, feeling him closing in on her, Lucy knew instinctively she should be in sight of an exit before pressing the detonator on their marriage.

Ava's eyes flickered open as her mum picked her up and the corners of her mouth pinched into another beatific smile. It was all Lucy needed or wanted.

Returning downstairs, Lucy was about to sit on the last step and make the call when she felt an involuntary shudder run down her spine. She could feel the hairs rise on the back of her neck and she glanced towards the kitchen. The door had been left ajar, exactly as she remembered leaving it five minutes earlier. There were no gaps where she might have gone back into the kitchen to open patio doors or switch on the oven.

So why did she smell gas?

35

Lucy kept tight hold of Ava in her car seat as she stepped into the kitchen. Every cupboard door was open and her medication had been lined up in a neat row of bubble-packs along the counter. Every dial on the gas hob and oven had been turned to the highest setting and fumes filled the kitchen at an alarming rate.

Despite her thumping heart, Lucy kept her composure as she turned off the gas and escaped through the patio doors. It was only when she felt the tingle of fresh evening air on her pink cheeks that she allowed her thoughts to catch up. If it had been the day before, she might have closed her eyes and retraced her steps, searching for the slightest flicker that would suggest a carefully edited gap in her memory. Today, she knew why she would never find one.

Her phone slipped in her sweaty palm as she composed a text message.

I know you're here and I know what you've been doing. It's over, Adam, so go back to your hotel and fuck whoever you like.

It took no more than seconds for Adam to respond.

What the hell? Lucy, what's wrong? You're scaring me. Please don't do anything stupid xxx

The only stupid thing I did was trust you.

Although Lucy had typed out the last message, she stopped herself before she could send it. It was pure folly to engage with a man who knew all her weakness while she knew nothing of his. Slipping her phone into her handbag, she left the patio doors open and carried Ava quickly through the house and out of the front door, which she also left ajar. Locking up was of no concern of hers and besides, Adam wasn't too far away.

With that thought foremost in her mind, Lucy secured Ava's carrier on to its base on the front seat. She had circled the car and was pulling open the driver's door when she heard Adam's voice.

'Lucy, what are you doing? What's wrong?'

Adam had appeared from the side of the house, his dark clothes converging with twilight shadows. As he drew closer, Lucy held the car door in front of her as if it were a shield. 'Stay away from me.'

Adam stopped some ten feet away and shook his head as he took in the youthful attire that didn't belong on the version of Lucy he had created. 'I knew I shouldn't have left you alone. You're hysterical. You need to come into the house.'

'I'm not going anywhere with you,' Lucy said. 'Why did you come back, Adam? Why do this to me? I don't understand.'

'I jumped into a taxi because I was worried. I was telling Naomi earlier how scared I was that you might do something unthinkable. Christ, I'm right, aren't I?' he asked, taking a step towards her.

'Don't come any closer!' she screamed.

'Please, Lucy,' Adam said, his voice catching with emotion that might once have sounded convincing. 'What will the neighbours think? If they phone social services, it'll open up an investigation. I'm trying to do my best here. I don't want anyone taking Ava away from you, but you need to listen to me. You have to come back inside.'

'I'm leaving you, Adam,' she said, keeping her voice low this time. 'Please, just let me go.'

'But I love you.'

When Adam's face crumpled, Lucy saw beyond the false persona of the man she had married. 'How can you say that when you've been abusing me from the day we met?'

'I've never laid a finger on you.'

'You didn't need to!' she hissed.

Adam shook his head. 'Who's been filling your mind with these ridiculous thoughts?'

'You! You're the one who's been playing games, Adam. That's why you came home. Were you hoping I'd take an overdose? Did you even care that your daughter might have been blown up in an explosion?' Lucy said, placing one foot in the footwell as she prepared to slip behind the wheel.

'You're getting worse, Lucy.'

'No, you are. I know you're the one who's been driving me—' she began, but couldn't finish the sentence.

'Insane?' Adam asked as he positioned himself in front

of the car so that she would have to mow him down if she dared drive off.

'Can't we call it quits?' she begged. 'You don't want me, so let me go. I'll walk away with nothing and you can do whatever you want, with whoever you want.'

Adam squinted as he took in the black bin bags crammed into the back seat of the car, but his gaze settled on the top of the baby's car seat when he said, 'It doesn't look like you're walking away with nothing. If you want to go, then go, but Ava stays with me. My conscience won't allow you to take her, and no court in the land will give you custody with your history of mental illness and violence.'

Lucy's wedding ring rattled against the door frame as she dared herself to smile. While it didn't quite reach her eyes, it was enough to make Adam shift uncomfortably in front of her tiny car – it might be small but it was big enough to cause significant injury at the hands of a determined driver.

'They will when they find out what you're really like,' she said. 'I recorded you.'

The street lamps flickered on and beneath their orange glow, Lucy could see a vein throbbing at Adam's temple.

'Recorded what exactly?'

'Our last argument. Would you like me to remind you of what you said?' she asked, enjoying the upper hand despite her rising fear. 'You told me how paranoid I was about Naomi taking my place and then you lifted your shirt and scratched your fingernails down your chest.'

'Don't be silly, Lucy. Whatever crazy ideas you have are yet another symptom of your madness,' he said, but his voice had wavered.

'And yet I have a recording of you saying and doing exactly that on my phone – so no, it's not "my" crazy idea after all. I don't want to use it but I will if you try to take Ava away.'

'I can't believe you're doing this to me,' Adam said, and this time when his voice cracked, the emotion sounded genuine. 'You're breaking my heart.'

'You don't have a heart,' Lucy replied, her smile slipping. She yanked her wedding ring from a sweaty finger and flung it at Adam. 'I don't belong to you any more.'

Adam scoured the driveway for the gold band. He saw something and kicked it away before saying, 'Fine, if that's how you feel.'

To Lucy's surprise, Adam stepped to the right of the car and waved his arm theatrically as if to direct her out of his life. Lucy jumped into the car and slammed the door shut. She let out a sigh of relief as she reached for the lock-door button only for a shock of cool air to hit her face as the passenger door swung open.

'No!' she screamed, grabbing hold of the car seat handle at the same time as Adam.

While Adam attempted to release the car seat's locking mechanism, Lucy used her free hand to locate the key in the ignition. It was a race to see whose fumbling would win first and as she turned the engine, the car seat wobbled free.

There was a stunned expression on Ava's face as she opened her eyes to find her parents fighting for possession of the carrying handle above her head. Lucy's fingers pressed against Adam's but, having reached a stalemate, neither was ready to initiate the tug of war.

'I can't let you take her, Lucy,' Adam said calmly. 'You don't want her. You never did.'

'They're not my thoughts, they're yours!' Lucy seethed. 'I won't leave her with you. Get your hands off my daughter!'

'So much anger,' Adam observed. 'And you say you're not a danger to Ava? Where's the love, Lucy? Do you even know what that word means?'

Adam's taunts passed over her head as Lucy concentrated on bringing her emotions under control, knowing that if she couldn't, Adam would be the one controlling her. She loosened her grip on the car seat to allow the cool air to dry her sweaty palms while pressing her foot down slowly on the clutch. She would have to act fast and didn't want her hand to slip on the gear stick when the time came.

'Why couldn't you just love me?' she asked. 'What happened? What did I do wrong?'

'How about secretly recording me?'

'I had to – you drove me to it!'

'Are you sure about that? I can't imagine what people will make of this recording you have, but there are two sides to every story. I'm the one who's had to endure your irrational behaviour throughout our entire marriage, and during that time I've tried my best to look after you. If I came across badly in an argument, it's because you made me that way.'

'No, you were already sick and twisted,' Lucy said. 'Scott will vouch for that.'

The anger in Adam's eyes burnt brighter. 'So he's behind all of this? I can't believe you're destroying everything we had because of your infatuation with a devious manipulator.'

'*You're* the manipulator, Adam, and I've had enough,'

Lucy cried. Her hand flew to the gear stick and the moment the car was in gear she brought up the clutch and floored the accelerator. As Lucy reached back for the handle of the car seat, the car lurched and stalled, and her hand found empty space where her daughter had been.

'It might be an idea to take the handbrake off,' Adam said above Lucy's cry. He was no longer leaning into the car but had straightened up. Lucy couldn't see his face but she detected the smile in his voice as he held Ava out of reach.

'Please, give me the baby,' she sobbed. 'You don't want her. You're doing this to hurt me.'

Adam crouched down so he could see the face that matched the broken voice. She had been right. He was smiling – a cold hard smile. 'And what do I get in return?'

Wiping the snot collecting on her upper lip, Lucy glanced towards the house. 'I'll do whatever you want. I'll be whatever you want,' she said, hoping she would simply be playing for time. 'Please Adam, anything.'

'No, no, no,' he said, stopping Lucy before she could pull open the door. 'If Scott's stupid enough to want damaged goods, let him have you.'

'This isn't about Scott.'

'Isn't it? Did you share the recording with him?'

'No.'

'With anyone else?'

'Mum listened to it.'

'But the only copy is on your phone?' he asked. From the pitiful nod of Lucy's head, he seemed satisfied with the answer. 'Shall we do a swap?'

Lucy's tongue pressed against the roof of her mouth as

she prepared to refuse. Without evidence of Adam's abuse, she risked losing any future custody battle, but the future was a problem for another day. At the present time, the power lay in a precarious balance between them and knowing this gave her the courage to put the car in neutral and turn the engine again. 'Give me Ava first.'

There was a look of disdain on Adam's face as he glanced down at his smiling daughter. 'Here,' he said, balancing the car seat back on its base without fixing it in place. He kept hold of the handle. 'Now give me the phone.'

'You'll let us go?' she asked.

With one hand staking his claim on the car seat, Adam reached over with the other, his palm upturned. 'You have my word.'

After two years of being conditioned to take Adam's word before her own, Lucy was surprised how quickly she recognized the insincerity of his promise, but she had no option but to proceed with the trade. Cautiously, she slipped the car into gear and released the handbrake before pulling her phone from the bag still strapped across her shoulder.

Lucy kept the phone temptingly out of reach and nodded towards Adam's other hand. What happened next happened at lightning speed. Adam let go of the handle, and as she floored the accelerator, he made a grab for the phone. Lucy let him take it so she could hold on to the car seat as the car lurched forward.

She heard a grunt as Adam's shoulder hit the side of the car but she was more concerned with keeping Ava's seat from toppling over as she sped off the drive and on to the road. The car's momentum was enough to pull the passenger door to, but it swung open again as she reached the mouth of the cul-de-sac with the engine straining in first gear.

Having forgotten to blink, Lucy's eyes stung as she checked her rear-view mirror. The road behind was empty. She stretched across Ava to close the door then hit the lock-door button firmly before fixing the car seat securely on to the base. She kissed her daughter's brow before straightening up.

She glanced again in the rear-view mirror as she fixed her seatbelt. Adam had appeared in front of the drive, his arms folded across his chest. He was watching her with mild bemusement, and she knew she would spend the entire journey home to Liverpool wondering what his next move would be.

36

When Lucy pulled up outside her mum's house, Christine was standing at the living room window, the lights blazing and a phone pressed to her ear. She brought a hand up to her mouth before disappearing from view. The front door opened soon afterwards and Christine raced towards them. Circling the car, she pulled open Lucy's door.

'Oh, thank God, I've been sick with worry.' she said. Checking Ava and realizing she was asleep, Christine lowered her voice and added, 'Is there something wrong with your phone? I've been trying to call, but whenever it connected, there was this weird silence. Why did you take so long?' When she received no answer, she looked from Lucy's pale features to her white knuckles gripping the steering wheel. 'Lucy?'

'I've seen Adam,' Lucy said with a rasp that hadn't been there earlier. 'I told him, Mum. I told him I was leaving.'

'Adam came home? But why? What happened?' her mum asked. When the only response was a series of hiccups, she added, 'Oh, sweetheart. What has he done to you?'

Christine prised her daughter's fingers from their

anchoring point on the steering wheel and pulled her from the car. She guided her gently towards the front gate but came to a sudden stop when Lucy's pliable limbs transformed to granite.

'I'm not leaving Ava here.'

'Go into the house. I'll get her.'

Ava let out a wail as her grandmother thumped and bumped the car seat as she removed it from the car with distinctly less expertise than her son-in-law. Lucy hadn't moved and it was left to Christine to bundle a fractious baby and her catatonic daughter into the house.

Lucy was aware of a shawl being draped around her shoulders, and at some point a mug of tea was forced into her stiffened hands. The ice in her fingers burnt against the hot surface of the mug until Lucy was forced to feel it.

She looked around, surprised to find herself sitting in her mum's living room where the lights had been turned low and the curtains drawn against the night. Christine sat in the armchair opposite, feeding her granddaughter while watching Lucy's tentative return from whatever dark place she had been hiding.

'He's going to take her away from me, Mum.'

'Over my dead body,' Christine said with misguided confidence.

'And mine,' said Lucy. 'And it might have to come to that.'

Her mum's face fell. 'I was going to call the police and I still think we should. Adam can't be allowed to come near you or Ava again.'

Lucy shook her head. 'He'll win in the end.'

'Don't talk like that, Lucy. You are the best mother Ava

could wish for and when the time comes, we'll prove it to anyone who cares to listen. You're already proving it now. You left him. Whatever Adam has made you feel about yourself is false, never lose sight of that.'

Lucy's head dropped and she stared at her bright pink fingers that screamed with pain from the heat of the mug. All she had to do to stop the hurt was to put it down, but there was a deeper pain she couldn't escape from.

'What happened, Lucy?'

'He sneaked back in while I was doing one last check upstairs. He turned on the gas and . . . I don't know, maybe he hoped to do a better job of blowing up the house this time,' she said as if Adam's sabotage were a banal, everyday occurrence – but perhaps it had been. 'I sent him a text to say I knew what was going on and he came back. I still left him, Mum. I got Ava, and I left.'

'But you've been missing for over two hours.'

'Have I?' Lucy asked without surprise. She could recall exactly where she had been and what she had been doing. 'I had to pull over. I parked up in a lay-by for a while.'

'Doing what?'

Images flashed across Lucy's mind of her fingernails digging into the steering wheel while she tipped her head back and released one silent scream after another. It had been Ava's whimpers that had saved her, which Lucy hadn't been able to ignore. Her instinct had kicked in and she had responded as a mother should.

'I held Ava,' she said, her voice scratching against torn vocal cords. 'While I still can.'

'She'll always be yours,' her mum said as she stood with Ava in her arms.

Placing the empty bottle on a side table, Christine waited for Lucy to put her mug on the floor. Lucy flexed her fingers but it was only when she took hold of Ava that the pain eased.

'No one's going to believe me,' Lucy said. 'I'm the one with a track record of mental illness and physical abuse and, up until this morning, I doubt even I would have argued that Adam should have sole custody.'

'Things are different now. We have proof. We have the recording.'

Lucy's lips trembled as she pulled her gaze from her precious little girl as if it would be for the last time. 'No, I don't. Not any more. He took Ava off me and he wouldn't give her back until I gave him my phone. I had to, Mum. I wasn't going to leave her with him, not even for a minute. Do you think there's a chance he might leave us alone? He doesn't really want Ava, does he?' Lucy said, wrestling with the questions that had tortured her in the darkened lay-by. It had been a small miracle that she had made it back to her mum's at all; there had been a moment when she had thought she wouldn't.

'No, he doesn't want Ava, but he does want to hurt you,' Christine said. Her anger coloured her cheeks when she added, 'Well, if that fucking bastard thinks I'm going to stand by and let him destroy my family, he has another think coming. He doesn't know who he's dealing with, but he's about to find out.'

Turning on her heels, Christine retrieved her phone from the mantelpiece.

'No, Mum,' Lucy said. 'Don't make him angry.'

Her mum took a deep breath to compose herself before

pressing redial. She switched to speakerphone and they listened in silence as the phone rang out. Lucy flinched when the call connected.

'I know you're listening,' Christine said. 'What is this, Adam? Are you too scared to talk to me?'

'No at all,' Adam said playfully. 'You sound rather upset, Christine. Is everything all right?'

'I couldn't be better, now I have my daughter back where she belongs,' Christine replied, her voice more controlled and level this time. 'I phoned to tell you that if you come near Lucy or Ava again, I will personally make sure everyone knows what kind of man you are. You deserve to be locked up for what you've done.'

Lucy pulled Ava closer as Adam's laughter travelled down the line.

'I don't know what kind of story you think you're going to spin,' he said, 'but do you honestly expect anyone to believe a lush like you? You're no more capable of looking after Ava than your daughter. It was bad enough that you turned up pissed for one of Lucy's antenatal classes.'

'I suppose it was my drink problem that forced you to throw me out of your house?' asked Christine. She didn't understand how Adam could twist an element of the truth and turn it into a weapon, but Lucy did, and her stomach heaved.

'You're such a fool, Christine and if you're not careful, you're going to cause more harm than good. Did you not listen to the recording Lucy made?'

'Of course I did. It was horrific.'

'And you still want me to leave the baby with her?' he asked. 'Thankfully, it won't be you who makes that decision.

All I need to do is play back the part where Lucy threatens to kill herself and Ava and I don't think any judge will let her near the child again.'

The colour drained from Lucy's face and she bowed her head. There was no doubt that her words would have the power to shock when taken out of context. As she had feared, all was lost.

'You had placed her under immense duress,' Christine said, her voice quaking in sympathy with her daughter. 'She didn't know what she was saying. She'd never hurt Ava.'

Lucy would like to agree, but those words – that sentiment – had haunted her during the hour or so she had spent sobbing in her car, and if it hadn't been for an overly zealous dog walker strolling past one too many times, she might have talked herself into carrying out her threat. She couldn't fight Adam and she couldn't condemn her daughter to a life as his next victim. What other option was there?

'I must admit, though,' Christine said, 'you make a compelling argument. I'll have to listen to the recording again.'

Lucy's head snapped up, and Christine winked at her.

'You don't have a copy,' Adam said.

'Oh, not only do *I* have a copy, but I've sent one to your brother. He's flying home as soon as he can and he's as determined as I am to stop your horrible little games once and for all. Sorry, Adam,' she said, preparing to cut the call. 'You lose.'

37

Lucy peeled open her eyes and was neither confused nor disoriented when she found herself in her old bedroom. Whether it had been the illusion of returning to her life before Adam, or pure exhaustion, she had slept peacefully and woken only once at dawn to feed Ava. Letting her arms drape over the sides of the single bed, she allowed her eyes to adjust to the dappled light playing across the ceiling.

The paisley curtains were too thin to halt the rising sun but thick enough to trap the warm air pressing against her chest. Lucy took a deep breath and was surprised how quickly the weight shifted. Stretching her fingers, she touched the side of Ava's crib but as she turned towards her daughter, she found the crib empty.

Lucy jumped up, clasping a hand to her throat to suppress a sob until rational thought could replace irrational fear. She grabbed the towelling robe draped over the end of the bed and hurried downstairs where she could hear the rumble of voices behind closed doors.

When Lucy stepped into the living room, the conversation stopped and all that could be heard was Ava's contented gurgles. Her baby bouncer faced the sofa where both grandmothers sat shoulder to shoulder with an iPad held between them.

'Viv. I didn't know you were coming over,' Lucy said numbly.

'Oh, love. I've been so worried about you and Ava. I hope you don't mind me dropping by to make sure you're OK. I'm on my way to take Keith shopping; he still can't drive after his op,' she explained. 'I won't stay long. I don't want to overtire you. I just thought . . . Are you OK?'

Unable to give the reassurance her mother-in-law was hoping for, Lucy swivelled the baby bouncer around so that she could kneel in front of Ava and soak up her daughter's smiles.

'You could have slept in, Lucy,' Christine said. 'You need to build up your strength.'

Lucy sat back on her heels. 'Why? Do you think there's still going to be a fight?'

Christine and Viv shared a look, and it was Viv who made the first attempt to predict her son's next move. 'Even with the recording, I'm sure Adam won't want to admit he's done anything wrong.'

'Have you listened to it?' asked Lucy, still not sure how she should feel about her mother-in-law. How long had she known what Adam was like? Why had she left it to others to warn her?

'Not yet, but I will. I have to,' Viv said with a shake of the head as if to break free of their nightmare. 'I'm so sorry you had to go through this. It's my fault.' Seeing what might have been a look of agreement from her daughter-in-law, she added, 'I tried to convince myself that what was going on with you was separate from what had happened to Scott. I should have stood up to Adam a long time ago. I know that. I'm sorry.'

Christine rested her iPad on her lap and patted Viv's knee. 'He fooled us all, Viv, and you're as much a victim as anyone.'

'But he's my son, Christine. What did I do to make him this way?' Viv asked. 'I'm ashamed of myself as much as him.'

'You must have some idea of what went wrong,' Lucy said, too tired to be diplomatic.

'Scott can explain it better than I can,' Viv said. 'You need to talk to him.'

'She will,' Christine reassured her.

'But what do you think?' asked Lucy, pushing for an immediate answer, no matter how uncomfortable it made Viv feel.

Twisting in her seat, Viv said, 'Adam was still a baby when his dad and I divorced. I thought he'd adapt easily enough when I married Keith, but I'm not sure Keith was ever the problem.'

'It was Scott he took issue with,' Christine added sagely.

'I'd agree that things started to go wrong for me and Adam around the time Scott came back into your life, Viv,' Lucy said. She had had time to trace the fault lines in their relationship back to the spring before they were married, which also happened to be around the time Keith had had his heart attack. Poor, insecure Adam had felt threatened and had started off with subtle ways of wrong-footing her, establishing the foundations for a life of isolation. He would rather break her than let his brother get close.

'It seems too simple to call it jealousy,' Viv said. 'The

boys couldn't have been more different from the start. Adam always had to work hard for what came naturally to Scott. He didn't like to show his feelings, but I think he learnt through watching Scott that he could get more through charm than he could with sullen silences. I used to think it was sweet that he would mimic his brother's behaviour, right down to his mannerisms,' Viv said, holding up her hand and tapping her fingers against her thumb to demonstrate. Her hand stilled and then it shook.

'I never saw him as a charmer,' Lucy said as she was forced to revisit one of the countless memories she would have to reframe. 'If anything, Adam came across as slightly vulnerable when I first met him.'

'I think he puts on a different show for different people, depending on what he's after,' Christine said. 'I still can't believe how he persuaded me to tell him about your dad. He makes you think your world's about to fall apart and that he's the one who can save you, when all the while he's using you for his own sick purposes.'

'But what did he want from me?' Lucy asked. She was looking at Viv again.

'Only Adam can answer that,' Viv said, 'but I'd like to think that deep down he did want to be loved.'

'Viv's been in contact with one of his old girlfriends,' Christine said.

'Rosie?' asked Lucy. There was hardly a long list from which to choose.

'It was Scott who tracked her down actually, and she wouldn't tell him much. I don't think she quite trusted him and she was more concerned with the possibility that Adam might try to get in touch next,' Viv said.

'What did she say?' asked Lucy.

'Enough, I think,' Viv replied. 'You know how Adam always made out that it was Rosie who took credit for his work, and that she was the one who talked him into buying a house so they could move in together?'

'And when he started having second thoughts, she sabotaged the project they were working on so they were both asked to leave,' Lucy finished for her. 'Let me guess, it didn't happen like that.'

'She was the one who broke up with him,' Viv told her. 'Which must have been a bitter pill for Adam to swallow because Scott wasn't around back then to take the blame for his life falling apart. Apparently, Rosie never wanted to move in with him. She was tired of covering for his mistakes and he repaid her by getting her fired. I don't think he cared that setting her up to fail meant he would be forced to resign too.'

Christine rubbed her arm. 'It looks like he enjoys taking revenge.'

'I will try to talk to him, for all the good it will do,' Viv said. 'I did go over to the house first thing but he didn't answer.'

'I'm guessing he would have gone back to finish the Sandstone Trail,' Lucy said, trying to see the world from Adam's point of view. 'He'll want to keep up appearances for as long as he can. He'll be looking for allies.'

'You may be right, but I want you to know that I'm not going to be one of them,' Viv said, reaching out to take Lucy's hand, but she was too far away and simply let her arm drop. 'I've promised your mum that I'll give whatever statements you need to keep him away. If I can, I'll persuade

Adam to get help, but I won't make the mistake of trusting him again . . . I can't believe how scared I am of my own son.'

'I'm scared of him too,' Lucy said with a trembling smile. She was trying to be angry with Viv but it was no use. Her mum was right, she was a victim too.

Viv swallowed back a sob. 'It's Ava we have to protect now.'

'And we will,' Christine said. When she looked at her daughter over the rim of her glasses, the spider web of lines around her eyes deepened. 'I've already spoken to social services.'

'What?' Lucy asked, hoping she had misheard. 'On a Sunday morning?'

'I wanted to make sure we got to them before Adam. It was only a general enquiry, but I've been told we should be able to get an emergency appointment with a social worker tomorrow.'

'I can come along too, if it would help,' suggested Viv.

'It will,' Christine said before Lucy could offer an opinion. 'And Scott wants to speak to them too.'

'Have you spoken to him since sending him the recording?' Lucy said, trying not to make it sound like an accusation. She didn't want to appear ungrateful, but she had been both elated and appalled the night before when she realized her mum had sent herself a copy of the recording without Lucy's knowledge – and then forwarded it on again without her consent. It was true that her mum's intervention had prevented what might otherwise have been a fatal blow to Lucy's life but still, she should have asked before sending it halfway around the world.

'I spoke to him first thing this morning, although it was the middle of the night over there,' Christine said, oblivious to her daughter's scratched nerves. 'He said he couldn't sleep and he'd been arranging a flight. His plane arrives in Manchester early tomorrow morning so he'll probably be too exhausted for the meeting with social services, although I'm hoping he'll come along when we see our solicitor.' She paused to tap her iPad. 'Viv and I have drawn up a short-list and I think it's best that we get some advice before deciding whether or not to involve the police.'

Lucy looked away from her mum and rattled a teething toy over Ava's head. Taking a deep breath, she reminded herself of why they were doing this and who was most at risk if they made a slip-up. 'And what should *I* do?' she asked.

'Concentrate on yourself,' Christine told her. 'Let us worry about the rest. Why don't you go and have a nice soak in the bath?'

As Lucy rose obediently to her feet, her mum turned the baby bouncer back around so that they could watch over Ava. Lucy wasn't needed. She took a step towards the door, telling herself it was right that her mum should take charge. It was going to take time to work out how she was meant to feel and think without Adam's puppet mastery, and until then, she remained a liability. She might say or do the wrong thing and any mistake could play into Adam's hands.

As her fingers wrapped around the door handle, it occurred to her that it wasn't only the past, but the present that needed to be reframed. Adam had convinced them all that she was incapable of looking after herself, let alone a baby, but that wasn't the real Lucy. She loved Ava and it was her job to protect her. Her job – no one else's. If she wasn't allowed to do that, then what did she have to live for?

'No,' she gasped as anger bubbled up from the pit of her stomach.

'Did you say something, love?' asked Christine over her shoulder.

Lucy returned to the middle of the room but this time she didn't kneel down in front of her mother and mother-in-law. 'I need you to stop.'

'I don't understand?' Christine said with growing alarm. 'Stop what?'

'You! All of this!' Lucy cried as she pointed an accusing finger at the iPad. 'Stop moving me around like I'm a marionette without feelings. I have a heart, and I have a brain too.'

'I know you do, sweetheart.'

'Do you?' snapped Lucy. 'You phoned social services, Mum! That should have been my job, my decision! Or are you worried that Ava might be at risk from both her parents? Are you trying to finish Adam's job for him?'

'No, of course I'm not!' Christine said, loud enough to startle the baby. Her tone was more conciliatory when she added, 'No one is trying to take Ava away from you.'

Lucy's eyes were no more than slits. 'Aren't you forgetting Adam? If he's going down, he'll want to take me with him. He'll tell them what I'm like – and don't forget, the recording condemns me too. I had Ava in my arms and I ignored her cries.'

'No one will see it like that, Lucy.'

'I lost control, Mum,' Lucy said. She managed to hold

back the tears but the burn at the back of her throat made her croak when she added, 'And who's to say I won't lose control again? Look at me! Aren't you just a teeny bit worried that I'm a bad mother?'

When Ava let out a cry in response to Lucy's harsh words, all eyes turned to the baby and although Viv and Christine twitched, neither of them reached for her. Lucy lifted Ava into her arms while her question hung in the air unanswered.

Lucy awoke with a start. Her eyes were gritty from crying herself to sleep, which didn't seem that long ago. She and her mum had exhausted the day raking through the past, and the safest place to start had been Lucy's life before Adam. After twenty years, Christine had finally been ready to answer her daughter's questions and Lucy's first one had been brutal:

'Were you in love with Uncle Phil?'

'No, I loved your dad, even after he'd fallen so deeply into himself that we'd both lost sight of who he was,' her mum had told her as she watched Lucy make up Ava's next feed with a confidence that was hard fought.

'Then why?'

'Phil hadn't long been divorced, and I know it's a pathetic excuse, but we were both lonely.'

'I do understand, Mum,' she had replied. 'And I can see why you wouldn't want to tell me about the affair, but why take so long explaining how much Dad was struggling?'

'Because he was always perfect in your eyes, and he tried his hardest in front of you. I didn't want you thinking it had been an act. It wasn't. He loved you, and it was my fault that he thought he was losing us both. I killed him, and that truth has been my punishment and my shame to bear.'

'Oh, Mum. You can't blame yourself. It's obvious that he was living with depression, although I doubt even he knew to give it a name,' Lucy had said as she glimpsed life through her father's eyes and found the view a familiar one. 'Do I remind you of what he was like? It's not like all my symptoms have been imaginary.'

'I don't think anyone could endure what you've been through without being affected. The important thing is to be honest about your feelings,' her mum had told her. 'Don't hide them away like your dad did.'

It was good advice but Lucy suspected that the dark thoughts that had wrestled her from sleep would terrify her mum. In the silence of her room, she turned her back on Ava's crib and spied her phone glowing in the dark on the bedside table. She rubbed her eyes and in that hazy place between sleep and wakefulness, realized it had been a missed call vibrating in silent mode that had woken her and not fear of the oblivion she had felt her mind pulling her towards.

She blinked hard as she tried to focus on the screen. The letters were no more than a blur but the outline of the words was a familiar one. She let out a gasp as the phone buzzed again but she didn't give in to the terror that her husband's name evoked. She rested her head back on the pillow and pressed the phone to her ear.

'What do you want, Adam?' she asked, keeping her voice low so as not to wake the baby.

'Sorry, did I wake you?' His voice sounded scratchy and hollow and it gave Lucy hope that she might be strong enough to take him on.

'Seriously, what do you want?'

'To give you one last chance to put things right.'

'That's what I'm doing,' she replied. 'It's not the ending you had in mind, but I'm going to survive this. I'm going to survive you.'

'You're killing me, Lucy. Do you know that?' he said, his words wet with emotion that was no more real than his love for his wife. 'I've got nothing left to live for. Is that what you want?'

'It's no more than you deserve,' Lucy said, horrified that she had understood what her husband had implied and not reacted to it. She refused to follow his script. 'I don't have to put up with this any more. Goodbye, Adam.'

A smile tugged at the corners of her mouth and she was about to pull the phone from her ear when Adam asked her one final question, almost as an afterthought.

'Aren't you wondering how you managed to get your phone back?'

38

Lucy sat bolt upright in bed, her heart pounding a frantic beat of pure fear and panic. As she scanned the room for unwelcome shadows, the small part of her mind that wasn't spinning told her that Adam's voice had come from the phone and nowhere else. He couldn't be in the house. She had watched her mum lock up and Lucy's spare key was in a box amongst the rest of her belongings waiting to be unpacked. Except . . . except Adam had been the last one to use the key when her mum had gone away on holiday. She should have checked it had been returned to the box, but it was too late. The damage had been done and Lucy was about to find out how grave that mistake had been.

A whimper escaped as she reached for the bedside lamp before turning towards the crib. The bundle she had taken to be her sleeping daughter was an empty blanket.

'Have I got your attention now?' came Adam's voice from the phone she had dropped amidst the bedclothes.

Lucy picked up her mobile and held it to her head as if it were a gun. 'Where is she?' she gasped.

'Not so loud. I'm on speaker phone and the last thing I need is for you to freak out and upset Ava any more than you have already,' he said. 'And it would be advisable not to wake your mum either.'

'I want my baby back. NOW.'

'You know that can't happen, Lucy. I said you had one last chance to put things right and you've just blown it. I think we were saying our goodbyes, weren't we?'

'Don't do this, Adam. You don't want her, not really. Please, give her back.'

'And why would I do that? Because you're hurting? You didn't seem that bothered about me when *I* was hurting a minute ago,' he reminded her, his voice lowered to a hiss. 'After all I've done for you, how dare you walk out on me. I looked after you and gave you everything you could possibly need and you threw it back in my face. This is your fault. I want you to know that.'

Lucy pressed a finger and thumb to her eyes to stem the tears and halt emotions that wouldn't save her daughter. 'What are you going to do?' she asked, not sure if she wanted to know the answer.

In the silence that followed, she could hear the hum of passing traffic.

'Talk to me, Adam, please,' she begged, not caring what words spilt from her mouth as long as the line stayed open. Her legs wobbled as she got out of bed and crept to the window. She pulled back the curtain, hoping to see Adam's car stained yellow beneath a street lamp. The road was empty. After a frantic few moments with nothing except her panicked breaths for company, his voice finally came back on the line.

'Fine, what would you like to talk about? I could tell you what a great time I had on the Sandstone Trail. I finished it, in case you were wondering, and it was worth all those blisters. It gave me the chance to open up to my friends and tell them about everything you've been putting me through. Ranjit didn't think it was safe letting you keep Ava, and I'm inclined to agree. You're never going to see her again.'

'You're taking her away?'

'I'm doing the right thing,' he said, 'because you obviously won't.'

'No, Adam. Please don't hurt her,' Lucy begged as she sank to the floor. The only reply was a wail from Ava, who had heard her mother's heartbreaking plea. 'I'm sorry. I never wanted this to happen. Please. I'll do anything.'

Adam waited for Ava to quieten. 'How many times have I heard your empty promises? You don't love me, and you certainly don't love Ava. How could you, when you swapped her for a phone? Is that how much she's worth to you? Well, aren't you a lucky girl, you have your phone back.'

'But it was you who wanted the phone,' she said, feeling a tug from Adam's familiar manipulations.

'Goodbye, Lucy.'

'No, don't go,' she yelped.

'It's too late. The damage is done,' Adam said, a theatrical sob tearing from his throat.

Lucy ignored Adam's feigned pain and strained her ears for the delicate sound of her baby's breaths, not knowing if or when she would hear them again. There was a bond between them, a pull so strong that it might have toppled her if she hadn't already been on her knees.

'Let me come to you,' she said. 'Please, Adam. Give me one more chance.'

Adam sniffed. 'Can I trust you this time?'

'Yes.'

He cleared his throat, but left an anxious pause before he proceeded to set out his terms. 'Then this is what's going to happen . . . ' he began.

39

As Lucy drove along Speke Boulevard towards the bridge, she fumbled to open the route planner on her phone. She had expected Adam to invite her back to the house, but her husband was in a sentimental mood and wanted their reunion to take place at the spot where she had promised to love him until her dying day.

After confirming her destination, Lucy was dismayed to find that Heart's Leap was over half an hour's drive away, but logic dictated that Adam would need to travel a similar distance. Guessing he would have phoned minutes after taking Ava to avoid the risk of Lucy waking up and raising the alarm, she tried to reassure herself that, for the time being, her daughter would be tucked up safely in her car seat, oblivious to the danger Adam posed.

'I'm coming, sweetheart,' Lucy whispered as she floored the accelerator.

Driving across the bridge, Lucy glanced down at the Mersey slithering like a dark snake beneath her and felt a crushing sense of hopelessness. Her little Fiat was no match for Adam's powerful Lexus and as the car began to judder under the strain, she imagined him extending his lead.

Her grip on the steering wheel was fierce and when her phone suddenly vibrated, her body jerked enough to make the car swerve into another lane. Thankfully, the roads were all but deserted and she straightened up before checking who was calling.

'Shit,' she said under her breath. Her mum had presumably found the note and Lucy could only imagine what was going through her mind. Adam had given explicit instructions about what to write.

I'm so sorry. I have to go to him.

'You bastard, where's Lucy?' yelled Christine. 'What have you done?'

'Mum,' Lucy said gently. 'It's me.'

A sob exploded down the phone. 'Oh, sweet Lord. Oh, Lucy, I thought . . . I saw the note and I thought,' she stammered. 'Where are you? What you doing?' There was a sharp intake of breath and a pause. 'Are you with Adam?'

'No.'

'Then how did you get your phone back? Where are you? Are you driving?'

Lucy had pulled on to a roundabout and was temporarily distracted by the police car that had appeared in her rear-view mirror. If she were pulled over, would the police officer notice she was wearing her pyjamas beneath her summer dress? Would they see the terror in her eyes and ask what she was doing? Would she tell them?

'Have you phoned anyone else?' Lucy asked as she took

the exit to the M56. The police car didn't follow and quickly disappeared from sight.

'Not yet,' Christine said, sounding scared but calmer.

'Then don't. Please, you have to let me deal with this,' Lucy said as she joined the motorway and caught her first glimpse of the sandstone ridge that cut a dark gash across the midnight-blue sky. Wisps of cloud swirled around the craggy tops like ghosts and she wondered if Adam were looking at the same view or if he had begun his ascent? It would be blustery up there and the babygro that Ava had been wearing would be too thin, even in August. Adam kept his three-wheeler pram in the boot but would he take time to clip on the apron? Would he bother to wrap up their daughter before subjecting her to the elements?

'Deal with what?' demanded Christine. 'You're scaring me, Lucy. Tell me what's happening.'

'Promise you won't try to stop me.'

'I can't—'

'What if Ava's life depends on it?' Lucy said abruptly. 'Adam's taken her and I'm on my way to get her back.'

'No. Oh, please, no,' Christine murmured with what little breath was left after the stomach punch she had received. 'You can't face him on your own, Lucy. You should have woken me. I want to be there with you. I can catch you up. Where are you heading? Home?'

'No, not home,' Lucy said. 'And I can't involve you. You have to let me do this my way.'

'And what is your way?'

'I don't know yet,' Lucy said. All she knew for certain was that she would return home with Ava or not at all. 'Mum, if I don't come back from this . . .'

'Don't talk like that!' Christine cried, her panic accelerating. 'You have to come back, Lucy. It would kill me if you didn't. *It will kill me.*'

Lucy flinched from the bite of her mum's words. 'If I don't,' she persisted, 'I want you to know that I couldn't have asked for a better mum.'

'But I failed you! Just like I did with your dad! Oh, Lucy, if I could go back, I'd do everything differently,' sobbed Christine, grabbing this last chance to confess her sins. 'I would have told you everything. I wouldn't have left you vulnerable to the likes of Adam.'

'I wasn't vulnerable,' Lucy countered. She gritted her teeth, giving herself time to form the words that might offer her mum some consolation in the dark days to come. 'I was a strong, confident, well-rounded young woman, which is how my mum brought me up to be. A bit immature perhaps, but any weaknesses I had were manufactured by Adam for his own amusement. You can't take responsibility for other people's actions, Mum. Not Adam's or Dad's, and certainly not mine.'

'Oh, Lucy, there must be another way,' wailed Christine. 'Scott will be landing in Manchester soon. Let me phone him. He understands Adam better than any of us. Let him go with you.'

'If you've taught me anything, it's that I don't need a man to come to my rescue. I can do this,' Lucy said as she slowed her breathing and prepared to say goodbye. 'I love you with all my heart and I'm so proud of you. You went through so much and still managed to give me a happy life. And I was happy.'

'Then don't give up on it. Not now. You have to fight,'

Christine said. She too had found the strength to hold back the tears so that every word between them would count. 'You fight for me and you fight for your daughter.'

'I'll text you my location when I get there so you know where to find us if something happens,' Lucy said.

'It won't come to that. It can't come to that.'

'Goodbye, Mum.'

'Lucy!' her mum cried out as she sensed Lucy leaning over to cut off the call. 'I love you, sweetheart. I love you so much, now you go and save your daughter from that man. Save us all.'

Lucy pulled up behind Adam's Lexus in a lay-by on an otherwise deserted road. Dawn was a long way off and, with very little light pollution, she was going to need the flashlight Adam had advised her to bring. He wanted to see her coming and she suspected he was watching as she got out of the car.

Slinging her handbag over her shoulder, Lucy set off to take back her daughter. The last time she had visited Heart's Leap had been when Adam had proposed and she wasn't sure she would find it again, but her mind was suddenly as sharp as the night. She recalled the handful of signposts and landmarks that would guide her to her husband and hoped that he would wait for her.

Skirting dangerously close to a farm, Lucy kept the beam of her flashlight low and picked up the path that rose steeply. She tripped a couple of times on tangled tree roots but it was the brambles tugging at her dress that thwarted her progress. She could feel trickles of blood cooling on her bare legs, but if there was pain, she didn't feel it.

Her breathing was laboured as she neared the top but her next breath caught in her throat and she came to a stumbling stop. Sweeping the flashlight from side to side, she picked out verdant undergrowth and a crowd of trees, but to her dismay, no path. She had taken a wrong turn, but there was no time to retrace her steps. If Adam could make the climb pushing Ava's three-wheeler pram, so could she, or so she believed until another thought struck her. What if Adam didn't have Ava with him? His car had appeared empty, but what if he had stowed away the baby in a footwell or the boot? Lucy could have been within feet of Ava and not known.

'Adam!' she screamed. 'Where are you?'

'Here!' came a distant voice above her head.

She cast her light around and eventually spotted the way up. Her legs ached as she continued her climb and her espadrilles slipped on damp mulch as she clawed her way through the bracken. The light breeze gathered momentum and as her view of the night sky broadened, she knew she was about to break cover, but before she did, she cowered behind a rock and took out her phone. The signal was weak but she managed to send her location to her mum. There were so many other things Lucy wanted to tell her, but Adam was monitoring her progress and would question the delay. Her final message would have to be delivered by her actions.

Stepping on to the exposed hilltop, Lucy made her way unsteadily towards the beam of Adam's flashlight. He swept it across her face, blinding her temporarily, but she pressed on. She was desperate to be reunited with her daughter but as her vision cleared, she saw only Adam's silhouette set against a landscape peppered with a thousand lights that stretched towards the horizon. He was twenty feet away, a bare few paces from the edge of the cliff.

With rising panic, Lucy scanned the narrow sandstone ledge. There was a scattering of low shrubs and a dead sapling that had been unable to root itself properly in the rock, but no pram. 'What have you done with her?'

'Me?' Adam asked with incredulity. 'You brought us up here. This is your doing.'

He turned slowly to the side so that Lucy could see what looked like a backpack strapped to his front. Adam had acquired a baby carrier, although at that precise moment, it looked more like a suicide vest.

'Is she all right?'

'She's sleeping. It must be all the fresh air,' he said as if they were simply out for a stroll.

'Don't do this, Adam. Please,' she said. 'Let's move away from the edge and talk.'

'I'll move when I'm ready.'

'It doesn't have to be like this. Remember how happy we were that day you proposed? It can be like that again,' Lucy tried as she edged closer.

'You want me to take you back?'

'If that's what it takes, yes.'

A gust of wind stole away Adam's laughter. 'You expect me to forgive you after what you've put us all through?' he said, his face ghoulish in the reflected light from the torch Lucy had trained on his chest. The baby carrier all but obscured Ava but Lucy could see an arm bobbing up and down as Adam spat out his words. 'Do you honestly think I brought you up here to bargain with me? You have *nothing* to offer, Lucy. There's only one thing I want now and that's to make you suffer.'

'Hurt me then,' she said. 'Hurt me all you like, but please leave Ava out of this.'

Adam glanced over his shoulder. 'You've left me with no other choice,' he said. 'I can't condemn her to a life with you as her mother, and what I'm offering should be mercifully quick.'

'You can't . . .' she said, training the beam of her flashlight on to his face. To her horror, he stumbled back half a step.

'Drop the torch!' he yelled at her.

The flashlight fell to the ground, the rubber casing bouncing off sandstone until the beam of light settled on a shining path that reached past Adam and over the precipice.

'Please, Adam. Why are you doing this?'

'Because I can,' he hissed. 'Did you seriously think I would slink away and let you all carry on with your miserable little lives? Give your mum a message from me: I *never* lose.'

With her knees about to buckle, Lucy stumbled towards him but Adam held out a hand to halt her before she came within touching distance.

'I'm going to make sure you think about me every day for the rest of your life. You're going to hate yourself and everyone around you who's interfered with our plans. I pity the wretched existence ahead of you, I really do,' he said, taking a step back without looking.

'No!' Lucy screamed. 'Please, oh God, please don't do this!'

'Pathetic little Lucy,' Adam said as he savoured her sobs. 'Say goodbye to your daughter.'

Lucy took gulps of air in an attempt to compose herself. She needed more time. 'Tell me why you hate me so much. You must have loved me once.'

Adam tutted. 'Don't be such an idiot. You annoyed me from the start.'

'No,' she said, thinking back to Ranjit's barbecue and how they had been drawn together like magnets. The attraction had been mutual. How could it not have been? 'You wanted me, and . . .' She held back from admitting she had felt sorry for him.

'And you were so full of yourself,' Adam continued for her. 'You paraded around that barbecue as if no one else could slap a bit of paint on to a stretched canvas. But it was all an act, wasn't it, Lucy? It didn't take me long to see through your winning smile to find that tortured soul.'

'I wasn't tortured. I was happy,' she said. 'And I was ready to share that happiness with you, but you had to take full possession. Having Ava was one more way of binding me closer to you. Isn't that why I'm here?'

'You tell me,' he said. 'What is it you came here to do?'

'You know I can't live without her,' she admitted. 'So don't imagine for a minute that my suffering will be for long.'

'At last, we get close to what Lucy really wants,' Adam replied, satisfaction pulling his lips into a smile. 'I don't think you are here to save Ava. I think you're here to put an end to a twenty-year fantasy about what it must have felt like for your dad to step off the edge of the world.'

'No,' she whispered.

'But you're not sure, are you?' he asked as he trained his flashlight on her face again.

Lucy closed her eyes and in the glare of the blinding light, she saw an upturned bicycle, except now she was the one turning the pedal and spinning the wheel.

'Maybe there is something you have to offer after all,' Adam said. 'How about another trade, Lucy?'

With her hand raised to shield her eyes, Lucy watched as Adam took another step, only this time it was to the side. He was giving her a clear path.

'Or have I got it wrong?' Adam continued. 'Don't you love Ava enough to give your life for her?'

'You'd walk away? With Ava?'

Adam tutted. 'Do you really think I'd want to hurt this tiny creature if I could avoid it?' he asked. 'Is it too much to believe that Ava is as important to me as she is to you?'

Yes, Lucy wanted to say. 'But what would you tell people?'

'Have you forgotten what happened tonight? Don't you remember waking up and being overcome with remorse for hurting me?' he asked. Pausing to kiss his daughter's head, he added, 'You realized you could never be the mother Ava deserved, not without me to support you, and so you scribbled a note to your mum and sneaked out of the house. Is it coming back to you now?'

Freed from any manufactured concern for Lucy's memory lapses, Adam didn't attempt to hide his amusement. His voice was almost lyrical. 'Oh, Lucy, I'm sorry to say I couldn't see a way back for us when you turned up on my doorstep. I was already at breaking point, just ask Ranjit. So when you realized it was truly over, you abandoned Ava and left. I realized too late what you were intending to do.

There might even be CCTV footage of me driving through the night looking for you, but it would be some lonely hiker who would eventually find you.'

'But the recording . . .'

'Proves nothing!' Adam snarled. 'And in honour of your memory, I hope no one else ever hears how crazy you really were. I'm sure your mum would be the first to agree, assuming she cares enough about her granddaughter. I expect we'll come to some understanding. Another trade perhaps.'

'So this was your real plan. You have it all worked out, don't you?'

'If there's anything I've missed, feel free to tell me,' he said confidently.

As Lucy's brain whirred with panic, she wasn't sure if she imagined the distant cry of a siren. 'There is one small issue,' she said.

Tilting his head to the side, Adam asked, 'Are you going to tell me?'

'I'll need to say goodbye to Ava before I do anything.'

Rolling his eyes, Adam said, 'Say it then.'

'No, not while she's strapped to you,' Lucy replied, and when Adam looked about to refuse her last request, she let out a wail. 'I can't do it unless I kiss her one last time!'

'For pity's sake,' Adam muttered. 'Fine, but don't move until I say so.'

Lucy waited and wept as Adam set down his torch to unfasten the straps that bound Ava to him. She doubted he noticed how the crossed beams of their abandoned flash-lights picked out carvings in the sandstone. Their names were being eroded slowly with time, too slowly in Lucy's opinion.

As the baby carrier came undone and Ava was deprived of her father's body heat, she began to cry in sympathy with her mother, which served to irritate Adam further. He offered no words of comfort as he placed her on the uneven ground between him and Lucy with only the padding of the carrier to cushion her head.

'Be quick and don't pick her up,' he told his wife, eyeing her with distrust. 'Don't think I've forgotten what you said about wanting both of you to die.'

Lucy hadn't forgotten either, and although there was more to her plan to separate the baby from Adam than a simple goodbye, it was the goodbye that consumed her thoughts. She dropped to her knees and stroked her daughter's cheek until they had both quietened. 'Please don't hate me for what I'm about to do,' she said. 'I love you, Ava. I'm doing this for you.'

As she planted a trembling kiss on her daughter's forehead one final time, the rending of Lucy's heart was sharp enough to make her gasp. 'Forgive me,' she whispered as she pulled away.

The wind whipped up and coils of Lucy's hair flew across her face as she stood. Her foot snagged on an unseen root but she wasn't ready to fall, certainly not on her own. She pulled her curls from her damp cheeks and looked past her husband to scan the vast landscape, her gaze settling on the twinkling lights of Liverpool. There would be another mother's heartbroken tonight.

You can do this, she told herself as the next gust of wind made her dress billow out like a parachute. A hundred feet below, she could hear heavy boughs trembling with anticipation.

'I want you to wear this,' Adam said, holding out the wedding ring she had never wanted to see again.

'Why?'

Adam gave her a scathing look. 'When I told you our marriage was over, you wrestled the ring off me. You said you would always be my wife, and it looks like you got your wish,' he said, his words choking him as if he were already standing at her graveside. 'Everyone will tell me not to blame myself and eventually I'll come to accept that it was your fixation on your dad that brought you out here. In some ways it was inevitable.'

Like so many of Adam's stories, there was some truth behind the tale he planned to tell the mourners at her funeral. Was she fixated? Was that why she had decided to take the fall the moment Adam had told her where to meet him?

She had assumed Ava would be in her pram and that she would be able to coax Adam away so that she could take him down with her. He had almost foiled her plans by using the baby carrier, but Ava was safe now and their orphaned daughter would be found.

Her mum would do a good job of bringing her up, Lucy reassured herself, but what if there was another way? Could she simply hold on to the baby until help arrived? Would Adam dare to drag her to the edge with Ava in her arms? And what if they all managed to walk away? Did she have the strength to face a courtroom battle? As her mind whirred with possibilities, she began to feel queasy.

'Lucy,' Adam said with the softest of warnings.

He was growing impatient and if she didn't act soon, her one chance to save Ava from her father's cruelty would be lost. Digging her heels into the ground, Lucy prepared to move, and move fast, but a sudden cry from Ava stopped her in her tracks. She couldn't soothe her daughter, there wasn't time, so Lucy pressed her fingers to her lips and recalled the touch of her baby's skin.

'Hush now,' she whispered under her breath. 'Mummy's here.'

'What?' asked Adam.

Lucy reached out for the gold band Adam insisted she take, and by doing so, positioned herself directly in front of him. 'I said, my mum's here. Or at least, she will be,' she told him as she let the ring fall to the ground. She savoured the look of confusion on his face and added, 'Did you seriously think I would let you walk away with my baby? I suppose it's lucky for me that you thought I really was that *pathetic*.'

Before Adam could react, the tension in Lucy's calf muscles travelled up through the rest of her body and she sprang forward.

'You crazy f—' he cried as she slammed into him.

Adam fell to the ground and Lucy went tumbling over him.

'No!' she screamed, realizing she was the only one sliding over the edge. Her legs kicked out into thin air but she managed to grab hold of Adam's jacket. Adam dug his fingers into the sandstone to save himself but loose rock came away in his hands and they both began to fall.

It was far from the clean jump Lucy had envisaged, and she released a painful grunt as her handbag caught on a jagged piece of rock to leave her dangling a few feet below the ledge. She grabbed hold of an old tree root as the leather strap of her bag cut into her neck. Somewhere below, she could hear Adam cursing. He had fallen further but not far enough and was using his rock-climbing skills to find purchase on the sheer cliff face.

The wind spiralled around them and grit blew into Lucy's mouth and eyes as she twisted and turned while Adam used her as leverage to climb back up. She felt his shoulder knock against her hip.

'You're going to pay for this,' he said through clenched teeth.

Lucy clung on desperately, surprised that Adam made no attempt to dislodge her. Realizing he was planning to leave her hanging, Lucy began writhing frantically. The bag strap creaked under the strain and her espadrilles slipped against smooth sandstone. Kicking off her shoes, she dug her toes into crevices in the rock, but Adam was gaining, climbing up her body, hand over hand. She could feel his breath on her neck.

'You could have saved her, you stupid bitch,' he said, spitting the words against her cheek. 'I hope you're ready to live with that.'

I hope I don't, Lucy thought as she prepared to let go of the tree root. The stitches holding her bag together would surely snap, and in a matter of seconds the strap would break, but seconds were all she needed. Bending her elbow into a sharp point, she released her handhold and rammed her elbow back into Adam's face. She heard the crunch of bone in his nose and they both teetered backwards as he reeled in pain, their dual anguished cries shattering the cool night air. Her fingernails scraped helplessly against sandstone, but a moment later his weight was gone. The snapping of branches smothered Adam's last words as he fell and the silence that followed was deafening.

No, she wasn't a bitch. She was a mother protecting her child and her job was done. As Lucy's fingers began to weaken and tremble, she thought how easy it would be to let go and escape the pain once and for all. Would that make her such a bad mother? It was certainly a tempting proposition, but Lucy knew in her heart she could do so much better.

Epilogue

Lucy stood in the middle of her darkened studio. The blinds were drawn so that she didn't have to look out at the grey autumn sky, although it was the twenty-foot drop she would rather not see. Heights still bothered her, but it wasn't only the memory of tumbling over the edge of a cliff that gave her nightmares. Sometimes she dreamt that Adam was still alive. Since that night, life had become impossibly frightening, which annoyed her. Hadn't she earned her happy ending?

It had been fortuitous that Lucy was scheduled to begin therapy a week after Adam's death, although the counsellor had been taken aback when her client presented as a victim of what Scott referred to as gas-lighting rather than post-natal depression. It was a term Lucy had never heard of but she recognized herself in the voices of other victims who had shared their stories online.

She wanted to believe that she would eventually recover, but if the first month was anything to go by, it would be a very long road. To some extent, Adam's prophecy had come true. She still thought about him every day and he continued to make her suffer.

Medication helped, but she had asked her doctor to prescribe different antidepressants from the ones Adam had encouraged her to take. Just looking at the sleeves of pills lined up on the kitchen counter where Adam had left them had sent her blood pressure soaring. There were so many triggers, and simply being in the house again could spark an anxiety attack, if not now, then later when she returned home to her mum's.

From behind her, Lucy heard a creak on the stairs and the sound of a man clearing his throat.

'How's it going?' Scott asked.

Lucy's broadening smile was directed at the baby in his arms. 'Hello, sweetheart,' she said, taking Ava without making eye contact with Scott.

Adam's brother moved slowly, as if he were afraid that any sudden movement might scare her off. In truth, it often did. The family resemblance was a constant assault on Lucy's senses and meeting him at the house magnified those traits that Adam had learnt to mimic.

'Feeling the urge to pick up a paintbrush?' he asked.

'Not here.'

'You know, my apartment doesn't have a particularly great view of New York, more an eclectic mix of air conditioning units, but the windows are huge and the light's perfect.'

Lucy sighed. 'You know I can't,' she said. It wasn't the first invitation he had extended and he already knew that she preferred to find her own escape route.

'But you will paint again, won't you?' he continued. 'I've had so many people comment on your seascapes. It wasn't all bluff. I do love them.'

'I know,' Lucy said, tensing at the nudge towards memories she would be happy to forget.

The past would be raked over soon enough at the inquest, although thankfully the police had completed their investigation. It had been no trick of the mind when Lucy had heard sirens and, as she dangled from the cliff edge, there had been shouts from the police officers that would come to her rescue if only she would hold on. She was still surprised that she had.

'What will I tell Ava?' she asked.

'You'll tell her that she's loved,' Scott said, but then corrected himself. 'No, you'll show her that she's loved, and when she's old enough, tell her how far you went to prove it.'

'And how will I know when the time's right?' Lucy persisted, wrestling with the question that bothered her most. In some ways, she faced a similar dilemma to her mum, and history had taught her that ignoring the past didn't work.

'Get professional advice where you can, and tell Ava as much as you think she can cope with as she grows up. Use your gut instinct.'

Lucy gave a soft laugh that blew against Ava's copper curls. 'Like I can trust that.'

Scott's expression remained serious. 'Are you saying that because your instincts have been off, or because Adam made you believe they were?'

Lucy stretched her neck to loosen the knots and avoid Scott's stare. Her brother-in-law had a head start when it came to recognizing the self-doubt Adam had nurtured in his victims. Her husband had left invasive weeds that would continue to seed themselves in Lucy's psyche for years to come.

'Another negative thought for my diary,' Lucy quipped. The diary in question was a gift from her therapist and part of her cognitive behavioural therapy.

'The CBT exercises might seem like a chore but it's worth persevering, I promise. It's working for me, and I hope it can work for you.'

'I'd prefer answers,' she said, finally looking Scott in the eye. 'Why did he do it?'

'I'm not sure we'll ever know,' Scott said with a sigh that churned up dust motes. 'Mum still blames herself, but coming from a broken home was always Adam's get-out clause to justify his behaviour. Personally, I think he was simply hard-wired that way.'

'He talked as if I were some creature he found to torture, as if he never loved me. But the man I fell in love with loved me back.'

'The man you fell in love with didn't exist,' Scott said bluntly. 'He had no concept of other people's feelings, but he knew how to emulate normal behaviours to control those around him. How many times have you heard someone express their shock and disbelief about what he did?'

Lucy thought back to Adam's funeral. She hadn't wanted to go but they had all made the effort for Viv's sake. The eulogies had been a challenge to write but Scott and Keith had stepped up to the task and concentrated on the man Adam might have been – if by some chance his feelings had been genuine. It had been a low-key affair, but there had been a few of Adam's colleagues in attendance, and they had looked upon Lucy with suspicion, including a red-eyed

Naomi who had no idea that she had been played too. Lucy was curious to know if her broken engagement had been caused by a developing relationship with Adam and how far that relationship had gone, but she wasn't curious enough to take on the task of dismantling someone else's false reality. Her own was enough.

'I wonder what the coroner will make of it all,' she asked.

'With any luck, the autopsy will prove that my dear brother didn't have a heart.'

'Or a conscience,' Lucy added, only to press her lips against Ava's scalp. She didn't want her daughter to grow up hearing nothing but bitterness and bile whenever her father's name was mentioned, but Lucy couldn't imagine talking about Adam in any other terms.

She was going to have to work on that, she told herself as she stared at the splashes of paint on the timbered floor. There were one or two colours she recognized from her paintings, triggering memories that for once didn't fill Lucy with anger or shame. There were times when she had held a paintbrush in her hand and had taken full control of that moment and place. She wanted that feeling back.

'I think I will have a go at painting soon,' she said, as her mind filled with abstract impressions of emotions she would like to capture on canvas. One image was the colour of sandstone and fear, while another was a spinning wheel of colour, but the one that focused her mind and stilled her thoughts was a bird rising up into the night sky. Her fingers tingled as she felt the urge to paint what would become a series of compositions that she could share with Ava until, eventually, her daughter was able to paint her own.

Acknowledgements

Although *The Bad Mother* is my eighth book, it's the first I've written since giving up my job of thirty years. I would therefore like to pass on my heartfelt thanks to all my readers who have made it possible for me to become a fulltime writer by buying, reviewing and recommending my novels. Writing books was an ambition I never thought I had until my three-year-old son taught me that life's too short not to have dreams, and my new career is part of Nathan's amazing legacy.

I would like to thank my wonderful agent, Luigi Bonomi, for seeing the potential in my writing, plucking my first novel from the slush pile and transforming me into a published author. Immense thanks also to the talented team at HarperCollins who have held my hand from the start and especially to Martha Ashby and Kim Young who set me some challenges with this book and deserve much of the credit.

Thank you to Kate Knowles for your insider knowledge of West Kirby, helping me extend the locations for my novels to the 'other side' of the Mersey. Thanks also to Jenna Rose, with help from babies Henry and Jessica, for giving me your invaluable experience of being a modern-day expectant mum – honestly, I didn't know the title of the book when I asked for your help, and for the record, you are an amazing mum!

This book explores a form of abuse described as gas-lighting, which would be a fascinating subject if it wasn't so appalling for the real-life victims. My heart goes out to anyone affected in this way and I wish you strength and happiness. A special thank you to my daughter Jessica for her assistance in researching the subject – it's always handy having a psychology student close to hand.

Thank you to Lynn Jones and Chris Valentine, my super talented siblings who inspired me to make my main character an artist. Having reacquainted myself with oil paints as part of my research for the book, I've discovered it's easier to describe a beautiful painting than it is to produce one, so I'll leave that to the two of you.

I would also like to offer apologies to any family or friends I might have unnerved by my questions about finding a location for 'Heart's Leap.' I have to admit that those conversations were decidedly strange, but I suppose that comes with the territory of keeping company with a writer.

As always, I couldn't do what I do without the amazing support of my family and friends, too many to name but I will mention my mum, Mary Hayes – I'd be in trouble if I didn't. A special note of thanks go to my ex-colleagues who have supported me and wished me well in my new career. I now work alongside my cat and dog, Spider and Mouse, neither of whom have ever made the coffee, organised baking competitions or tempted me to the pub, but their training continues!

"You might as well know from the start, I'm not going to tell on him and I don't care how much trouble I get in. It's not like it could get any worse than it already is.

I can't. Don't ask me why, I just can't."

When Nina finds out that her fifteen-year-old daughter, Scarlett, is pregnant, her world falls apart.

Because Scarlett won't tell anyone who the father is. And Nina is scared that the answer will destroy everything.

As the suspects mount – from Scarlett's teacher to Nina's new husband of less than a year – Nina searches for the truth: no matter what the cost.

OUT NOW

Everyone has secrets…

When eight-year-old Jasmine Peterson goes missing, the police want to know everything.

What is the local park ranger, Sam McIntyre, running away from and why did he go out of his way to befriend a young girl?

Why can't Jasmine's mother and father stand to be in the same room as each other?

With every passing minute, an unstoppable chain of events hurtles towards a tragic conclusion.

Everyone has secrets. The question is: who will pay the price?

OUT NOW

the
missing
HUSBAND
AMANDA
BROOKE